BREATH
of
WATER

Wings of Hope

BREATH
of
WATER

a novel by

CONNIE STEVENS

Published by Wings of Hope Publishing Group
Established 2013
www.wingsofhopepublishing.com
Find us on Facebook: Search "Wings of Hope"

Printed in the United States of America

Stevens, Connie
    Breath of Water / Connie Stevens
    Wings of Hope Publishing Group
    Print ISBN: 978-1-944309-40-4
    eBook ISBN: 978-1-944309-41-1

Cover artwork and typesetting by Vogel Design in Wichita, Kansas.

To Jonathan
You aren't just my son, you're my hero.

Come and see the works of God; He is awesome
in all His doing toward the sons of men. PSALM 66:5

Come and hear, all you who fear God, and I
will declare what He has done for my soul. PSALM 66:16

CHAPTER ONE

Dulcie Chappell bit back a grin. She'd predicted Grandma's reaction to changing the name of the town even before she told her the news. Virginia Chappell always studied a matter with the belief, *Don't mess with nothin' what don't need fixin'*. Grandma didn't like change.

"What fer do they wanna go and do a thing like that?" The syncopated rhythm of Grandma's uneven footsteps and the thump of her cane accompanied the clacking of the shuttle against the breast beam on Dulcie's loom. "Such nonsense. Town's been called Warm Springs as long as I've been putterin' 'round these parts."

"Grandma, you heard they uncovered another natural spring not far from here."

"I ain't deaf. I heard."

Dulcie glanced up. "Then you heard the water in the new spring is hotter. That's why they changed the name. The mayor and town council figured changing the name of the town from Warm Springs to Hot

Springs would make all those people who visited here in the past want to come back."

Judging by Grandma's scowl, Dulcie's explanation did little to convince her the change was a good idea.

Grandma snorted and rapped her cane on the floor, a sure sign of her agitation with something she couldn't control. "Plain silly. Iffen them folks that visited before be wantin' to come back, they will, an' it'll be for the same reason why they come in the first place. The mountains." She tipped her head toward the vista outside the open doorway. "Them hills sing to the soul. That's why folks wanna come here." She gave a tiny shrug of her bony shoulders. "S'pose the springs is nice, too."

Dulcie let Grandma fuss over the change she deemed unnecessary and kept weaving the fine purple woolen threads. Warp and weft fibers of silky soft lamb's wool caressed her fingers as they interlocked with each other into a herringbone texture on her loom.

Grandma sighed and flipped her hand in a dismissive gesture, but Dulcie would bet her best hair ribbon they hadn't heard the last of Grandma's opinion on the subject. For now at least, Grandma settled herself at the smaller of the two spinning wheels and began pumping her foot on the pedal in a measured rhythm. Her expert touch, twisting the fine fibers as they wound their way around the wheel, created a delicate strand of yarn.

Except for the comforting clacks of Dulcie's loom and muted thud of the spinning wheel's pedal against the worn floorboard of the small building Grandpa had dubbed the "wool shed," both women worked in silence for a few minutes. After a stretch of quiet, Dulcie steered her grandmother's attention to a more pressing topic: the dye baths she planned to prepare for the new wool they'd washed and carded last week. "If the weather holds, we can dye two more batches tomorrow."

"You find enough walnuts in the root cellar?"

Dulcie kept her attention focused on the intricate pattern taking shape on her loom. "I think so. I added some sweet gum seeds. I don't want a dark brown. This batch will be a nice tan."

Without looking up, she knew Grandma nodded in time with the turning of the wheel. "Grandpa said there are still two more ewes that haven't dropped their lambs yet." The four new lambs born last week already tagged after their mothers in the meadow, bringing the count to eleven. Delight tickled Dulcie's insides to watch the newest additions to the flock.

Grandma rattled off a list of ewes that had already given birth—she knew each one by name—and could remember how many lambs each one had borne over the past years.

Dulcie only half listened. She couldn't afford to lose her concentration. Each warp and weft fiber had to be shuttled firmly into place in such a consistent motion as to create a flawless length of yardage. The goods she sold to Eunice Mead, the dressmaker in town, had to be perfect. Those rich women who came to her from the resort accepted nothing less. The mauve color would make some wealthy tourist a lovely traveling ensemble.

Ensemble. Such a high falutin' word. Grandma would snort if Dulcie uttered such a word aloud, even though it was at her grandmother's insistence that she'd attended the school in Asheville. She had to admit, one of the benefits of extending her education beyond their little community school was the ability to converse with the well-bred visitors who patronized their area. Society's upper crust flocked to the warm springs resort to "take the waters."

A number of the wealthy visitors posed questions about the creative process of dying the wool and spinning it into yarn. Some of the tourists could get a bit tiresome, but they were willing to pay handsomely for Dulcie's fine fabrics and one-of-a-kind rugs.

Grandma finished loading the spindle and halted the wheel. A tiny *oof* puffed her lips as she rose and reached for her cane. She paused by the door of the wool shed, the sunlight turning her white hair to glowing silver. "I'm goin' to see if your grandpa needs any help with the shearin'."

Dulcie nodded, her fingers never wavering from their task. She still had several more hours of work before this piece would be ready to take to the dressmaker, but another errand called to her. No mention had been made of the significance of the day. Neither she nor Grandma voiced the words, but at some point today, each would make their way to the family cemetery where five generations of Chappells rested, including Dulcie's parents and baby brother. What a scourge the diphtheria epidemic had caused throughout their community.

On this very day, eleven years ago, the disease had robbed her of her family. She'd take time today to see to their graves, grateful that the disease didn't take her grandparents as well. What would she have done as a seven-year-old orphan had it not been for Grandma and Grandpa Chappell?

A half-hearted smile tugged the corners of her mouth as she threaded another length of yarn into the loom, scrutinizing the wool between her fingers. When it came to family, Grandpa didn't hesitate. After the Lord, nothing in the world was more important than family, except maybe the land.

Grandpa raised the sheep, she and Grandma washed and dyed the wool, Grandma spun it into yarn, and Dulcie turned it into something beautiful. The sale of the woolen fabrics and rugs put food on their table. But more importantly, the heritage they carried on—skills handed down from one generation to the next—perpetuated their family's history.

Dulcie glanced at the heddle to make sure the warp threads waited in a perfect line for their union with the fine weft. She slid the shuttle across the breast beam, interlacing the two threads with intricate precision, and nestling them together into a seamless river of pale purple.

"Dulcie!" Grandma's voice pulled her focus from the marriage of the threads. She leapt to her feet, and ran to the open door.

Grandma beckoned from the barn. "Need your help."

Dulcie hoisted her skirt and dashed across the smaller pasture, her bare feet pounding the cool spring grass. At the gaping door of the barn, she paused to allow her eyes to adjust to the darkness. The familiar musky scent of hay and sheep dung greeted her. A half-shorn sheep stood tethered to a post, where it contentedly munched alfalfa from a bucket.

"Grandma?"

"Back here. It's Dolly. She's birthin'."

Dulcie made her way to the far back corner of the barn. She slipped into the box they reserved for mama sheep about to deliver, and bent to take a closer look. A fat ewe struggled on a bed of hay while both her grandparents attended the animal. The ewes normally birthed their lambs on their own. Once in a while, a first-time mama needed help, but Dolly was one of their older ewes. She'd given birth before.

Dulcie bit her lip. "What do you need me to do?"

Grandma tilted her head toward the corner. "See what you can do for that one."

A minutes-old lamb lay motionless in the hay. Dulcie fell to her knees and began vigorously rubbing the wet newborn with handfuls of dry hay, and clearing sticky mucus from its nose and mouth. "Is the mother going to be all right?"

"Here it comes. She's havin' another one."

Twins? Grandpa called twins an extra measure of God's blessing.

A pitifully weak bleat mewed from the tiny animal in her hands. Dulcie rubbed the little one's neck and poked her pinkie finger into the lamb's mouth, encouraging the baby to suck. "This one's awful small."

Grandpa's gentle words of reassurance murmured behind her. "Come on, Miss Dolly." If anyone could successfully help a ewe deliver twins, it was Grandpa.

The ewe let out a sharp, guttural cry. The lamb Dulcie held called back with a stronger bleat.

"There now." Grandpa pulled the second lamb into the world. The exhausted mama lay in the hay, her sides heaving, while Grandpa handed the newest offspring to Grandma.

"This'n's a boy." Joy intoned Grandma's words. "How's that other little'un doin'?"

Dulcie nudged the lamb and was rewarded by watching it struggle to stand on spindly legs. "She had a bit of a rough start, but she'll be fine as soon as Mama's ready to feed her."

After a moment, Dulcie guided the newborn to its mother and slipped out of the box. Grandpa hummed as he performed the necessary tasks and got the ewe on her feet. His quiet, gentle ways coaxed Dolly into meeting her new babies.

As soon as the twins were introduced to their mother, Grandpa and Grandma joined Dulcie standing outside the enclosure. The emergence of new life never failed to leave her awestruck. "Let's leave them alone. I'm goin' to go get some taters from the cellar fer dinner." Grandma bustled back to the house as briskly as her cane would allow.

Grandpa wiped his hands on a rag and glanced at Dulcie. "Thanks. Wasn't sure that first little'un was gonna make it." He glanced over his shoulder for one last look at the new family. "God's sure blessed us with a fine crop o' lambs this year. This'n makes thirteen. Last couple o' years—"

He shook his head, and Dulcie didn't need him to finish his thought. Between coyotes and ewes delivering in the middle of a late season blizzard, they'd lost nearly half of their lambs. She'd never let Grandpa hear her thoughts, but she couldn't help wondering if God had forgotten the Chappell family.

Grandpa turned and looked her full in the eye. He placed his hands on her shoulders, and his blue eyes, warm and love-filled, arrested her attention. "It took all three of us. God made families to pull together, all in the same direction." He slipped his arm around her shoulders as they made their way back to the partially-shorn sheep. "God don't call us to go through this life alone. That's why He gave us families."

It wasn't anything Dulcie hadn't heard him say before, but every time he said it, she accused God again. She'd had a family and God took them away. Didn't He know she needed them? How could He take so much from a little girl? Had it not been for her grandparents, she'd have been sent to the orphaned children's asylum in Raleigh. She was thankful she at least got to grow up here on the mountain, on the land her parents had helped to work, but she'd never let Grandpa glimpse the concealed resentment in her heart.

"I love you, too, Grandpa."

She walked back toward the wool shed but paused at the fence. On the hillside of the meadow, the black and white dog, Malachi, lay in the grass, but he wasn't sleeping. His watchful eyes always held careful vigil over *his* sheep. The protective nature of the dog made her smile.

Beyond where the dog kept watch over the flock, in the far corner of the pasture almost completely concealed by scrub junipers, rhododendrons, and mountain laurel, the headstones of five generations lay tucked into the hillside. Knowing her loved ones rested nearby was a comfort indeed. She pulled back the curtain in her mind, and allowed the familiar images to form.

The childhood memory of the day all three of them died hadn't faded over the years. She remembered running, blinded by tears, climbing the rickety ladder in the barn, and collapsing in the hayloft, exhausted from crying. That was where Grandpa had found her. He'd wrapped his arms around her and held her tight as he told her that God had taken her mama, papa and baby brother to heaven. All she knew at the time was that she'd never see them again and God had taken them away.

Dulcie shook off the gloomy memory and hurried back to her loom with a lingering thought tiptoeing through her mind. Grandpa thought God was blessing them. Goodness knew they worked hard enough, from before dawn until the sun fell behind the mountain. Her heart chafed to watch her grandparents labor until their hands were calloused. Maybe this year, things would be better and they could afford to hire some help. A wry smile pulled at the corners of her mouth and she shook her head.

She'd never seen either of her grandparents take their ease and doubted they'd be in favor of the idea.

A sobering thought erased her smile. She was the sole heir. Until she married and had a family of her own—a sixth generation of Chappells—keeping this farm going fell squarely on her shoulders. She owed it to Grandma and Grandpa, to her parents, her baby brother, and to those generations who toiled and fought for the land, and now rested beneath it. One day she'd be responsible for not only this farm, but also for continuing the family legacy.

She ran her fingers over the finished portion of cloth on the loom. Fine Chappell wool produced from Chappell sheep on Chappell land. She drew in a deep breath. When she'd suggested perhaps they should raise their prices, since their wool and rugs were in such demand, Grandma chided her for entertaining pride. Even now, warmth filled her face as she recalled Grandma shaking her gnarled finger at Dulcie with the admonishment that it was God, and not anything they'd accomplished, who was responsible for their success.

Dulcie lowered herself to the chair and placed her fingers on the shuttle. Too many thoughts tumbled through her mind to concentrate on her weaving, however. Her heart burned with the desire to care for her grandparents, to make them proud of her. The mantle of responsibility weighed heavily.

The discovery of the new hot spring had done more than prompt the changing of the town's name. Many in their community believed it would bring in even more wealthy tourists. Without a doubt, her grandparents would credit God for the new hot spring. She shrugged her shoulders, unsure she'd call it a gift, but God didn't ask for her opinion.

~ CHAPTER TWO

The afternoon's shadows grew longer, and time to help Grandma put supper on the table wasn't far away. But an irresistible pull drew Dulcie to her family's graves. She closed up the wool shed and hurried across the meadow. The overgrown junipers almost tripped her, and she had to push back the rhododendron branches to make her way to the southeast corner of the little cemetery.

Two headstones—one larger and one smaller—positioned together in a silent and somber greeting. *Henry and Miriam Chappell.* Papa and Mama rested together in a single grave, and her brother's smaller headstone snuggled up next to his parent's. *Joseph Chappell ~ November 5, 1874-April 20, 1875.* Her sweet baby brother never even got a chance to celebrate a single birthday. Tracing her mother's name with her finger carved an ache in her soul.

The temptation to cut back the juniper and rhododendron to open up the entrance to the cemetery courted her notice, but she hesitated. Mama had always cut snips of juniper at Christmas to tuck around the candles in the middle of the table and line the fireplace mantel. Mama always said juniper smelled like Christmas. In the spring, Mama had gloried in the rhododendron, declaring them the prettiest flowers God ever created. She shook off the inclination and instead attacked the weeds around the graves. She didn't have the heart to remove the overgrown shrubs her mother had loved.

She stood gazing at all that remained of her family for a few minutes before turning back toward the house to help Grandma with supper. When she stepped through the door, her grandmother stood at the stove stirring a pot. The old woman didn't ask where Dulcie had been, but just hummed 'Jesus, Lover of My Soul,' the hymn Mama had sung as a lullaby after Joseph was born.

Dulcie fetched flatware and tin plates from the shelf, and arranged three places at the table. The aroma of savory cornbread coaxed her to peek into the oven. She slid out the heavy cast iron skillet with the golden-topped cornbread and set it on the table. "I'll go call Grandpa."

"Dulcie girl." Grandma's voice was tender and gentle. "Ain't nobody can tell ye how long ye should grieve, child. Fer some, it takes a lifetime. I be a-prayin' that you'll let God comfort ye."

Dulcie didn't reply, lest her resentment of God ring like a gong in her tone. Grief was some of the hardest work she'd ever done, and God had never helped her. She went to the front porch and clanged the bell, letting Grandpa know supper was ready. But even the pealing of the bell didn't drown out the quiet voice deep within her that tried to tell her it was time to put aside her resentment. She'd held on to it for so long, she wasn't sure how to let go.

After supper was over and the dishes cleared away, Grandpa opened the family Bible and read the account of God telling Moses to be strong and courageous. Dulcie gritted her teeth as she listened. Nothing wrong with being strong—she was strong. It was the part about God promising to never leave or forsake His people. Empty, hollow promises.

She closed her ears to the rest of the Bible reading, and silently accused God. *You turned Your back on me. I was just a little girl. I'll never understand why You took Mama and Papa and little Joseph. Why did You forsake me?* Her eyes burned and she blinked away the moisture before her grandparents saw it. She couldn't help the way she felt, but she loved Grandma and Grandpa too much to distress them by revealing the resentment she carried in her heart toward God.

Having faith like her grandparents must be a sweet, comforting thing. Grandma's faith made her who she was. Dulcie wished her faith was as strong as Grandma's. But Grandma didn't have to bury her parents when she was only seven.

James Chappell closed the worn family Bible and twined his fingers together atop the cover. He bowed his head and prayed, thankin' God for the blessin's of the day, all the while knowin' Dulcie still held a grudge against God. Even after so many years, the young'un hadn't let go of her bitter feelin's. God called a sour heart like hers 'wormwood,' but he reckoned his granddaughter wasn't much interested in God's opinion.

He finished his prayer and Virginia joined her 'amen' to his, but not Dulcie. She never did. Reckon she thought speakin' the word meant she agreed with what he'd prayed. In all the eleven years since her mama and papa and little brother went to be with Jesus, he'd never once heard her pray. Oh, she bowed her head and folded her hands respectful-like, like she'd been taught as a young'un. But she wasn't a young'un no more.

James's heart pinched to watch Dulcie's eyes go dark and shadowy when he and Virginia got to talkin' about how good God was. The chapter he'd read this evenin' from Deuteronomy told the story of how God promised He'd never leave His children, even when hard times hit and they was surrounded by trouble. As he'd read the words, he asked God to let them fall on Dulcie's ears like sweet honey, but she'd looked away and her mouth pressed tight like her jaw would break. She'd nary spoke a word to ever hint how she felt, but he knew. She didn't know it, but he knew. And it grieved him.

He set the Bible on the mantel and reached for Virginia's hand. "I'd sure like me a cup o' coffee while we's settin' on the porch."

Virginia gave him a gentle slap on his shoulder. "James Chappell, you say the same blessed thing ever' night, and ever' night I bring ye a cup. After fifty-six years, do you reckon I'd fergit?"

A chuckle worked its way up and tumbled out. "No, I reckon not."

Dulcie rose. "You two go on out to the porch. I'll bring the coffee." She flapped her hands and shooed them out the door.

The sun droppin' behind the mountain took the day's warmth with it and Virginia tugged her shawl more snug around her. "Y'think she listened when ye read how Moses told them folks about God goin' with 'em into the promised land?"

The worn, saggy oak splints of his favorite rocker sang out squeaks as he settled in to rock a spell. "She listened. Don't rightly know what was goin' through her mind, but she kept lookin' out the window like she was memorizin' the tree limbs yonder."

Virginia didn't answer, but James knew his wife's heart as well as he knew his own. It pained her to watch their granddaughter nurse her anger at God. Pained him deeper knowin' Dulcie tried to hide her feelin's from them.

Distant night birds called out their plaintive song, biddin' farewell to the sunset. The rockin' chair's creakin' added some disharmonizin' notes, but the music made James smile. Wispy clouds huggin' the mountaintops dipped feathery fingers into the gold and orange streaks that dangled in layers behind the pine trees atop the ridge. Sure was a peaceful way to end the day, except for frettin' over their granddaughter's spiteful heart.

The door hinges squawked and Dulcie stepped out carryin' two mugs. She handed one to each of them, and then leaned against the porch post. Her eyes closed and a furrow dug 'tween her brows like she was tryin' to recollect somethin', but it stung like an open wound.

After a time, the darkenin' sky chased the fadin' gold streaks behind the mountain. Dulcie pushed away from the post. "We have a lot to do tomorrow, running a couple of dye lots. I think I'll turn in." When she leaned to kiss his cheek, she smelled like sunshine and lye soap.

"G'night, Rosebud."

The pet name from her growin' up years lit a hint of a smile across her face, the way a lightnin' bug winked through the trees come twilight. "Rosebud. You haven't called me that since I was little."

A chuckle rumbled from deep in his middle. "You recollect why I give ye that name, don'tcha?"

She shook her head. "Not really. I remember you calling me that, even before—"

Before her mama and papa died. For sure, he remembered. "You was about five years old, and you wanted to s'prise yer mama with some wild roses. Ye picked some and got thorns in your little fingers, but you was so determined to give yer mama the purty flowers. They was about three or four full blossoms, and the rest was buds that hain't opened yet." He chuckled again. "Well, you thought them buds wasn't as purty as them roses that'd bloomed open, so you commenced to break off all the buds till I stopped ye. I told ye them buds was gonna open an' be just as purty as them other roses, but ye had to leave 'em be and let 'em bloom."

He snagged her pinkie finger and gave it a gentle shake. "You was like one o' them rosebuds. You was gonna bloom. We jus' had to give ye time."

Dulcie slipped her arms around his neck and gave him a squeeze. "Night, Grandpa." She turned and kissed her grandma. "Don't stay out here too long. It's a little chilly." She stepped back inside.

He met Virginia's downcast look. "Ain't nothin' better to do for her than pray, Love. We just pray."

James whistled for Malachi to bunch up the sheep to move them from the barn to the larger pasture. The dog could likely do the job by hisself. He nipped and barked at the woolies, and all James had to do was open the gate so Malachi could drive the critters through. Once them sheep got sight of the thick spring grass, they didn't need much proddin' to trot through the gate.

Malachi circled and pushed them further away from the fence while James closed the gate and dropped the hook through the latch.

"Good dog, Malachi." The black and white pup perked up his ears and waggled his tail.

They couldn't afford to pay a hired hand, but havin' the dog was next best. James smiled. Probably better, since Malachi ate table scraps and didn't draw a wage.

James double checked the gate latch and turned back toward the barn. Virginia waved to him from the side yard where she and Dulcie stirred the huge cauldron of steaming dye. James sniffed. Walnut husks, if his nose was workin' right. Made the wool a nice brown color. The purplish color she'd been workin' with was right pretty, too. He'd seen that color around the edges of a sunset over the mountains, and in the center of the nettle weed Virginia called Hen's Bit. Dulcie was mighty clever how she mixed a whole passel of bits and pieces of nature to make them colors. Flower petals, berries, vegetable peelings, leaves, roots, nut husks. Yep, she sure was clever. He cast a glance around him and mused. "Lord, You done made all these here colors by jus' speakin' the word. It's a might harder for Dulcie."

The few sheep he'd left in the barn needed tendin'. He still had one more ewe that was takin' her sweet time about droppin' her lamb. One of the mamas that had birthed last week was refusin' to feed her young'un, so James needed to bottle feed the lamb every couple of hours.

Another ewe, the one Virginia called Clara, had bled like a stuck pig after she gived birth, and James feared they'd lose her. For the time bein', she and her lamb stayed in the barn 'til she got her strength back.

Then there was the cantankerous ram. Critter managed to get his leg hung up in the fence and hurt hisself. James couldn't tell for sure, since the ram didn't exactly cooperate, but he hoped the fool sheep hadn't broke his leg. Took him and Virginia and Dulcie to wrangle the critter down so James could splint the leg. Meantime, the ram stayed penned up in the barn. Leastwise 'til he started walkin' normal again.

Truth be told, the aches and pains at the end of the day after workin' with the ailin' sheep reminded him of every one of his seventy-four years, but he'd never let on to Virginia or Dulcie. They'd tell him he was gettin' too old for such work. What was he supposed to do? Quit? Who'd take care of the sheep? These here critters—as ornery as they could be— were gived to him by God to care for, protect, to raise up. It humbled him to think God would set such a charge before him.

He made his way to the barn and poured some milk into a bottle. The little abandoned lamb bleated from his stall.

"I'm a-comin'." James took the tip he'd cut off one of his canvas gloves and tied it over the opening of the bottle. It wasn't his mama, but it got the job done, and the little'un didn't seem to mind. "Here now. Stop all thet belly-wallerin'." He held the bottle down and the little feller sucked so hard, James had to hold the glove tip in place. "I thought you was a lamb, not a piggy." In no time, the critter had slurped up his breakfast.

In the next stall, the pregnant ewe didn't give him so much as a passin' glance, more interested as she was in the feedin' trough. He patted the sheep's fuzzy head. "You'd sure make my life easier iffen you'd hurry up and birth that young'un." She ignored him and kept chewing her cud.

Across the way in another stall, the ewe that'd had such a hard time deliverin' lay in the hay instead of standin' up to let her baby nurse. He slipped in, and she barely turned her head. Usually the mamas were mighty protective of their babies, even around him. This one didn't seem to have the strength. He stooped beside her. "What'sa matter, Clara, old girl." He rubbed her neck. "Yer still awful weak, ain'tcha?" He tried to push her to stand, but she wouldn't. He wasn't in the habit of worryin'. He did what he could and let the Lord handle the rest. But this sweet, gentle ewe worried him.

He looked in on the ram and checked his leg. "Iffen you promise to behave yourself, I might be persuaded to let you go on out to the small pasture in another day 'r two."

James moved down the row of stalls, takin' note of things that needed fixin' or cleaned or changed. The work never ended, and sometimes put him to feelin' like he'd been wrung out and throwed over the clothesline. But he wasn't too old to do it. If he was, the Lord would have took him home by now.

‿✺‿ CHAPTER THREE

J ames tugged on the reins and pulled old Samson to a halt. He didn't bother to set the brake—the mule wouldn't take a single step if he didn't have to. Dulcie scrambled down from the wagon seat. He didn't like leavin' Virginia alone at the farm for too long, even if Malachi was there watchin' over things. "How long you reckon you'll be?"

Dulcie dug a scrap of paper from her pocket. "Shouldn't take me too long at the emporium, but I'd like to stop by and visit with Hester, if we have time."

James tried to frown but couldn't stop the smile from pullin' at his whiskers. "Mayhap I'll have time fer a game o' checkers over to the feed 'n' seed after all. When you two gals get to gossipin', a feller might as well set up camp."

"Grandpa!" Dulcie stuffed her list back in her pocket and plunked her hands on her hips. "Hester's my friend. We don't get to talk very often, only a few minutes at church, and she wasn't there yesterday. I want to see if she's sick."

He patted her shoulder and hooked the feed bag around Samson's head. "Tell her I said hey. When you 'n' Hester get finished a-jawin', you know where to find me." Dulcie had her own list of chores that needed doin' at home, so he knew she wouldn't be long.

He dropped off the barn door hinge fer the blacksmith to fix , and then he headed to the feed 'n' seed. Hollis Perdue called out 'hey' to him when he set foot inside.

Hollis stepped out from behind the counter and wiped his hands on his faded plaid shirt. The man were thin as a willow saplin', but stronger than he looked. "What you needin' today, James?"

James helped himself to a dipper of water from the barrel by the door and wiped his sleeve across his whiskers. "You got any o' them new oats I can mix with some 'lasses 'n' cracked corn? Got me a ewe that had a hard time birthin'. Lost a lot of blood, she did, and she's awful weak."

"Yup." Hollis bobbed his head. "How much ye want?"

"Fifty pound sack oughta do." James glanced about. "Y'reckon ye got time fer a game o' checkers? Dulcie's visitin' with Hester." He grinned. "Them womenfolk."

Hollis swung the bag of grain up to his shoulder like it were filled with feathers. James sucked on his teeth as a twinge of envy poked him. Let ole Hollis set himself down at the checkerboard and James would show him a thing or two. *Hmph.* Might not be able to toss a fifty pound sack around like it didn't weigh no more'n a toadstool, but he could play checkers.

After James beat Hollis two out of three games, there was still no sign of Dulcie. Just as he figured. Those two gals plumb forgot the time when it come to talkin'. He decided to wait out front on the boardwalk where he couldn't hear Hollis grumble about losin'.

A few feet away, a man with slicked-back salt and pepper hair and fancy duds that declared him a rich, city feller stood talkin' with a dozen other folks. His bright red vest was all shiny like the sun glinting off the surface of a lake. Only time James ever wore red was his red flannels. This man even had him a gold watch chain a-danglin' across his middle. What for did a man need to dress up like a dandy in the middle of the week. It weren't even Sunday.

A few of the folks hunkered around listenin' were locals, but most were them tourists Dulcie sold her wool goods to. The fancy man stood there like a preacher in a pulpit, proclaimin' all the benefits of the hot mineral springs.

"Spending a few days soaking in those magical waters has worked wonders. Why, I feel like a new man. I've not felt this good for years. After all the money I paid to my doctors up in Philadelphia, none of them did me as much good as coming to this place and taking the waters. Extraordinary, I tell you."

A few of the folks bobbed their heads, and others added their own two cents.

"I've had rheumatism for years, and nothing my doctor did brought relief."

Another man nodded. "I had pain in my legs and back, and no amount of medicine I took helped. The doctors in New York told me I'd probably be in a wheelchair in another year." He held his arms out. "Look at me. Walking with barely a limp."

A woman in a bright blue dress and twirlin' a lacy parasol piped up. "No doctor could even determine what was wrong with me. The swooning and fainting spells were happening almost daily." She looked around, appearin' like she wanted to make sure everyone was listenin'. "I finally told my husband I needed to get away and relax someplace where the air was pure and the water is medicinal." She heaved a sigh that would've made one of them stage actresses blush. "I plan to come here at least every few months. Maybe even more often than that."

Mr. Fancy Pants nodded. "I couldn't agree more, madam. These hot mineral springs are truly a marvel. They enhance the benefits of medicinal compounds, but I've heard folks discontinued using medicine after taking advantage of the mountain spring water." He pointed his cigar toward the new hotel—the tourists called the place a *resort*—and gave a sad shake of his head. "Too bad the Mountain Park Hotel doesn't offer all the latest amenities."

"Really? You don't think so?" The woman slapped one hand to her chest.

"No." He folded his arms across his red vest. "It's a shame they cut corners when they built the place."

Caleb Montgomery, a man James had knowed all his life, spoke up. "Well, mister, I was one of the men that helped build thet there place, and all us folks here in Hot Springs is mighty proud of the Mountain Park. They say it's ever' bit as nice as the hotels in the big cities."

"Let me introduce myself, sir." The man put his hand out to Caleb. "I'm Arnold DeWitt."

James bit his lip to hold back a snort when Caleb looked down at Arnold DeWitt's hand like it were covered in sheep dung. Caleb shook the man's hand and James was sure he was just being polite. "Caleb Montgomery."

James glanced down the boardwalk and caught sight of Dulcie hurryin' toward him. He moved a step or two closer to the group of people, interested in seein' how this DeWitt feller was gonna douse the fire he seen risin' in Caleb's eyes.

"I meant no offense, Mr. Montgomery." DeWitt's tone changed to pure syrup. "Only to point out that the establishment should have put a much greater emphasis on the health benefits and the healing properties of the hot springs."

Dulcie came up to stand next to him. "Sorry I'm late. Hester is sick. That's why she wasn't at church yesterday." She leaned close to his ear. "She's got the gripe."

"Did I hear you say an acquaintance is ill, miss?" DeWitt's question startled Dulcie and she turned to face him.

"Y-yes, sir. But she's already been to see Doc Pryor."

DeWitt held out both hands and turned toward the people in the group. "You see? Her friend ought to try soaking in the hot springs. Like I said, it'll cure just about anything."

James took Dulcie's arm. "C'mon. We gotta git on home."

"Why, sir. You appear as if you are a resident of this quaint little town, so you surely must know about the benefits of the hot springs."

James halted and looked over his shoulder. "You talkin' to me?"

DeWitt smiled, but it was one of them smiles like the snake oil drummers used to make folks think they was tellin' the truth. "Yes. Do you know how beneficial the hot springs are?"

"I know I got work waitin' fer me at home."

DeWitt stepped in front of him. "Sir, I would challenge you to take the waters yourself and see if it doesn't make you feel invigorated and revitalized."

James snorted. "I don't know what them fancy words mean, but I know all about the sweet mountain water that runs through my meadow."

"Is that right?" DeWitt rubbed his finger along his thick mustache. "Runs through your meadow, does it?"

Dulcie tugged on his arm. "Come on, Grandpa. We need to get home. Grandma will be worried."

"Wait a minute, if you please, sir. Let me introduce myself." DeWitt stuck his hand out to James like he'd done to Caleb. "I'm—"

"I know who you are, Mister DeWitt. I heard ye announce yer name to all these folks, and I still got work waitin' for me at home." James headed toward the wagon with Dulcie.

"Of course, of course. I don't want to keep a man from his work." DeWitt hoofed alongside him. "Would you mind if I accompanied you? I find the springs quite fascinating, you see, and I am especially curious about their origin. Perhaps you could answer some of my questions."

James stopped and studied the man's face. "You askin' to come to my place and see where the spring runs?"

"Yes, if you don't mind."

James scratched his head. This DeWitt feller sure was a caution, but he reckoned it wouldn't hurt to let him see where the spring bubbled up and how it run underground through the meadow. "S'pose it'd be all right."

"Splendid." DeWitt beamed. "Lead the way, sir. I'll follow you in my buggy."

Dulcie watched Grandpa and Mr. DeWitt walk the fence line while she unhitched Samson. Uneasiness seeped through her middle, but she couldn't say why. Their visitor had said nothing out of line—not really, although his speech and demeanor did mark him as an outsider. But then such was the case of many people who came through Hot Springs. While she found a few of them somewhat arrogant and irritating, none had ever made her feel unsettled, and most were friendly and likeable. What made Mr. DeWitt different? Grandpa didn't seem wary of him. Of course, Grandpa, being proud of the land as he was, would take pleasure in showing it to anyone.

She led the mule through the gate and closed him into the small pasture. While Grandpa was occupied, she heaved the fifty-pound sack of grain off the end of the tailgate and dragged it into the barn. Grandpa shouldn't be lifting heavy grain sacks, and catching a moment to do it for him while he wasn't looking gladdened her heart.

Dulcie carried the crate of supplies to the kitchen and then poked her head in the wool shed. "Grandma, I'm going to go help Grandpa for a minute."

Grandma paused pulling apart the strands of roving. "Help 'im do what?"

What indeed? Help him show a tourist around their farm?

"A man came back from town with us. He wanted to see where the spring is and how it flows." When Grandma's brow wrinkled with puzzlement, Dulcie shrugged. "I thought it was odd, too. That's why I want to go join them and hear what this man wants."

Grandma nodded silently and returned to her task.

Dulcie scanned the yard and saw the two men up the slope toward the west corner of their property. Grandpa was pointing and gesturing, and Mr. DeWitt appeared to be commenting. Or asking questions. What was so interesting about spring water?

She hiked up the slope and joined the pair in the middle of their conversation.

Mr. DeWitt bent to peer at the place between the rocks where the spring water emerged.

"So this is the origin?"

Grandpa squinted and tilted his head. "This here is where the spring comes outa the ground." He paced off the stretch of the stream that flowed from the rocks to the meadow and past the fence. "Over yonder where them rocks is piled in the middle of the meadow is where the water goes back under the ground an' down the mountain. But that's why our meadow is always green, even when it don't rain fer a time. The sheep always got good, thick grass."

"Huh?" Mr. DeWitt's brow dipped. "Sheep?"

Dulcie pointed across to the opposite end of the meadow where the sheep grazed in the shade of the oaks. "Sheep. We raise sheep for their wool. Finest wool goods to be found anywhere. Chappell wool."

The man returned his glance to the spring, and then across the meadow to the sheep.

"That's what you do with the spring water here?"

Dulcie didn't wait for Grandpa to reply. Her hackles were already on the rise. "The spring rises up from the mountain and flows underground into the fertile meadow, which feeds the meadow grass so the meadow grass can feed the sheep, yes. Any farmer will tell you it takes many things to have a successful harvest. The main necessity is water. Our harvest is the wool."

She watched his expression change ever so slightly from fascination to determination.

Her uneasiness heightened.

"Ah. I see." Mr. DeWitt stroked his chin.

But Dulcie suspected he didn't *see* at all. Why would a rich man from—where did he come from?—care about how the spring water flowed or what they did with it?

Connie Stevens

Grandpa laid his hand on Dulcie's shoulder, a sure sign he could hear the irritation in her voice. "It's been right nice havin' ye visit, Mr. DeWitt, but like I said in town, I got a passel of work waitin' on me in the barn. So iffen you'd 'scuse us, we'd best get to it."

Dulcie stiffened. The words hovered on the tip of her tongue. *Go away, Mr. DeWitt. I don't trust you. I don't know why, but there's something about you that stirs my suspicions.*

Before her lips could part to let the words escape, Grandpa's hand tightened on her shoulder and she dug deeper to find a more polite statement. Stiff, but polite.

"Yes, as my grandfather has explained, we're quite busy." She wasn't discourteous, but neither was she cordial.

DeWitt gave a slight bow. "Thank you both for letting me interrupt your day." He swept his hand from east to west. "You have a very. . .beautiful place here." He doffed his hat. "Good day." He strode to his buggy.

When she took a step toward the wool shed, Grandpa held on to her sleeve. "Dulcie Louise, I—"

"I know, Grandpa." She faced him and his blue eyes twinkled. He wasn't angry with her, not truly. "There was something about him—" She shook her head before finishing her statement. "—that made me distrust him."

⚘ CHAPTER FOUR

Gavin DeWitt sat back in the seat as the southbound train slowly pulled out of the Philadelphia station. Uncle Arnold's letter, brief though it was, described his newest venture in the mountains of North Carolina—a facility connected to the hot mineral springs in the area, intended to attract wealthy clientele from hundreds of miles around. Certainly different from Uncle Arnold's usual pursuits, but intriguing nevertheless. The letter hadn't outlined more, except to hint that this could be Gavin's opportunity to prove himself.

Prove himself. Isn't that what he'd been trying to do most of his life? He'd made a career out of disappointing his father, but that wasn't hard with an older brother like Harold. Harold had achieved everything he set his hand to—excellent grades, honor graduate from Harvard, an accomplished attorney by the time he was twenty-eight. While Harold gained much acclaim for some of the widely publicized trials he'd won, Gavin spent a total of eight years at Wesleyan University. Restlessness and dissatisfaction had driven him to change his course of study three times. Harold had laughed and teased, saying his little brother hadn't changed since they were in knee pants. Their father hadn't laughed, though.

Gavin squirmed in his seat even now. No, Father hadn't thought it funny that his younger son couldn't seem to find anything at which he excelled. Each time Harold pinned another feather in his cap, he drove another nail to secure his position as their father's favorite. Years of being compared to his older brother's achievements had left deep scars.

He closed his eyes against the image that rose in his memory, but there was no shutting out the accusation in his father's voice the night before he'd died. *"Why can't you be more like Harold?"* That was the night Gavin had determined to do whatever it took to succeed— to outshine and surpass Harold at something that would impress his father so much, Gavin would finally gain his acceptance. His recognition. His approval.

His love.

It didn't happen. It would never happen. His father had died the following day of a heart seizure. And Gavin wanted to hate his brother.

Wanted to, but couldn't.

He shifted his position again. Why was this seat so uncomfortable? Maybe because his thoughts were uncomfortable. He didn't like the way resentment made him feel, but he was caught in the trap of being helpless to change the past. His father would never know if he accomplished anything worthwhile now.

The echo of his father's voice reached beyond the grave when the will was read and Father had appointed Harold to run his import business. No mention was made of Gavin having a part in the business, but he'd expected as much.

Outside his window, the scenery changed from city streets and factories to countryside. A barn and farmhouse slid past. If only he could put his own insignificance behind him as easily. The train rumbled across a trestle bridge and settled into a rocking motion that nearly put Gavin to sleep. Instead, he opened the copy of the *Philadelphia Inquirer* he'd bought from a boy hawking newspapers at the train station. There must be something of interest within the pages to keep him awake.

There, in the center of the front page, was a headline proclaiming, *Harold DeWitt Wins Seat In State House of Representatives.* Bands constricted within his chest, nearly choking off his ability to take a breath. The train's motion had nothing to do with his stomach dropping.

A quick scan of the article confirmed Harold's victory in the hotly contested special election to fill the seat vacated by a representative who'd been convicted of fraud and corruption. Gavin closed his eyes and rubbed the middle of his forehead with two fingers, and tossed the newspaper on the seat beside him.

He should be happy for Harold. His brother's first time running for office and he'd won a congressional seat. The victory was predictable—of course he'd won. Being Harold, he couldn't do anything else. Gavin shook his head. Sour grapes tasted mighty bitter, and bitterness went down hard. He disliked his own company when he entertained such melancholy brooding.

At the onset of the campaign, Harold had taken on a partner to run their father's business without mentioning a word about it to Gavin. Now that Harold was elected to congress, he'd no doubt leave the running of the business to his partner.

Gavin forced his glum thoughts aside. He had a job. His uncle had been generous taking him on after Father died. Of course, Uncle Arnold and Father got along about as well as he and Harold did. Maybe it was hereditary for brothers in their family to be at odds. He shook his head. He and Harold didn't really dislike each other—not in the same way his father and uncle did. They simply traveled different life roads. At any rate, he didn't miss the gleam in his uncle's eye when he'd offered Gavin the position in his real estate development firm. Father would have been furious over his son going to work for his brother. Gavin couldn't help wondering if that was why Uncle Arnold had made the offer in the first place, but it was a job and his uncle paid him well.

The uncanny family resemblance between his father and uncle was so striking, he could almost imagine his father sitting at the desk in the plush Philadelphia office, especially since the two brothers shared more than a physical likeness. Listening to Uncle Arnold growl and bark orders and spew criticism was like listening to Father. Gaining his uncle's acceptance wouldn't be easy, but in his family, approval was gained through striving and meeting one's goals, and Gavin was determined to please his uncle. Would doing so make up for never having pleased his father?

Gavin straightened his shoulders and retrieved the newspaper from the seat. He folded back the front page and instead turned his attention to an article on page two about the laying of new trolley tracks in the city of Philadelphia.

Dulcie glanced over her shoulder where Grandma stood by the huge outdoor cauldron, washing the wool. The controlled fire beneath the vessel was kept small so the wash water stayed warm but not scalding. Since there was only the three of them, they did the shearing a little at a time over the course of a month. The practice stretched out the work into manageable chunks. It was still laborious, but doing the entire flock at the same time would require hiring help they couldn't afford.

Seeing her grandmother bent over with her hands down in the water both warmed and disheartened her at the same time. While she was grateful for the help and for the legacy of working together at their craft, she'd much rather see Grandma sitting at the spinning wheel. At least when she spun the wool rovings into yarn, she was off her feet and her back wasn't bent.

"Is that the last one?"

Grandma straightened and shook the soapy water from her hands. "Soon as I git it rinsed." She put her wet hand against her lower back and bent backward slightly. "Yer grandpa says we only got eleven more sheep to shear, an' he plans on doin' that next week."

Dulcie finished rearranging the cleaned, damp fleeces on the drying rack. This batch was the largest they'd done thus far—eighteen fleeces lay across the spindles, and she scooted them a little closer together to make room for the last one.

"The last eleven are the yearlings, so their fleece will be finer and easier to clean." She looked over the drying batch and tested them between her fingers. "Most of these will be for rugs, but there's five or six I'd like to use for fabric yardage."

Grandma dragged the back of her hand across her forehead and tugged her bonnet back into place. "Ye got colors in mind?"

"Some." She stepped over to the washing cauldron and took over the task. "First, I'd like to stop by Eunice Mead's shop to see if she will buy some yardage." The dressmaker in Hot Springs had kept a running order with Dulcie for fine woolens she crafted into cloaks, capes and jackets, skirts and winter bonnets, mostly for the wealthy women who came to visit the springs.

"Sometimes the tourist women will order something special."

"Ye ready fer the rinse yet?"

Dulcie lifted the heavy, sodden fleece and inspected it. "Yes, but don't you haul those water buckets. I'll do that."

"Pshaw! I been haulin' water longer than you been alive." Vexation threaded Grandma's voice. She didn't appreciate the implication that she was getting too old to do those tasks she'd always done.

The barrel that contained the soft rain water Dulcie preferred to use for rinsing the fleeces sat up against the house, at least fifty yards farther than hauling water from the pump at the far edge of the garden. Knowing the only way to dissuade her was distraction, Dulcie wiped sweat from her forehead.

"It's getting close to noon. Would you mind making dinner without me today?"

Her grandmother glanced at the sun overhead, and then leveled a squinty-eyed look at Dulcie. "Reckon I can manage."

She hadn't fooled Grandma for a second, but the older women snatched her cane from where it leaned against the drying rack and thumped her way to the house. A smile tweaked Dulcie's lips as she knocked the plug out of the bottom of the cauldron and let the wash water drain. The gushing, sudsy water doused the fire under the cauldron, but they rinsed the wool in cold water. In the meantime, she grabbed two buckets and crossed the yard to the rain barrel.

Before she could dip out the first bucketful, Grandpa emerged from the barn and walked toward her. She didn't like the way his shoulders slumped or the frown that pulled his eyebrows together. She set the bucket on the ground and walked out to meet him.

"What's wrong?"

He tilted his head back toward the barn. "Can ye help me a minute? Clara died."

Dulcie shot a glance past Grandpa, as if waiting to see if the ewe her grandma called Clara would come trotting out of the barn to prove him wrong. "Oh, Grandpa. Poor thing was so weak." She accompanied him back to the barn. This was the part of farm life she hated.

"Yeah, she was." Grandpa pulled off his hat and slapped his trouser leg with it. "She'd lost too much blood when she gived birth and couldn't git her strength back." He rubbed his hand over his beard. "Now we got two lambs t' feed. But first we gotta git thet little'un outa there and take the ewe out back behind the barn."

Dulcie knew Grandpa would butcher the dead sheep. As much as she would like to simply bury the poor mama and put flowers on her grave, the way she'd done as a child with baby birds that met their demise when they fell from the nest, they couldn't afford to waste anything. Farm life could be hard, but every year decisions had to be made regarding which animals to send to market, or which had outlived their usefulness. It was reality. Growing up on a farm, things of this nature happened, and they did what they had to do. She accepted that. But experience didn't make it any easier.

The first priority was separating the lamb from its dead mother. Grandpa paused outside the stall and waved Dulcie toward the rear of the barn. "Iffen you'll put some fresh straw in the lambing pen, I'll git the little'un. We'll put her back there fer now."

Dulcie hurried to do Grandpa's bidding and forked clean hay into the area they usually reserved for mothers giving birth. At least the little orphaned lamb would have a clean place that didn't bear the scent of her mother. She returned to the front stall and took the baby from Grandpa's arms. The lamb was small and thin, no doubt a result of her mother being unable to nurse her often enough. "Come on, little girl. I've got a nice clean, dry place for you." The lamb laid her head against Dulcie's chest and emitted a pitiful *baa*. "I know. You miss your mama. I know how you feel." She deposited the lamb in the clean straw and closed the stall door.

Grandpa had already removed the dead mother when Dulcie returned to the front of the barn. She grabbed the rake and began raking out the bedding hay. The stall would need to be completely cleared out, lime scattered on the dirt floor and fresh hay laid down. Dulcie gritted her teeth and wondered how she'd ever be able to eat the mutton of a sheep they'd named Clara.

From the rear of the barn, the newly-orphaned lamb let out a cry of protest at being alone. Grandpa had already been gone several minutes, and she didn't want to think about the sad chore he was performing. She turned all her attention to the task in front of her. By the time Grandpa returned, she had all the soiled bedding raked out and scooped into the cart. She let him wheel the cart out back to dump it. She didn't care to see the ewe hanging up ready for butchering.

When he returned, she leaned against the side of the stall. "What about one of the other ewes that are already nursing their lambs. Would any of them adopt Clara's baby?"

"I already tried that with the one lamb whose mama wouldn't feed him. None o' the others accepted him. But I reckon it won't hurt to try with Clara's lamb."

"What about the ewe who still hasn't had her lamb? What if we introduced Clara's lamb to her at the same time hers is born?"

Grandpa scooped up a shovelful of lime and scattered it over the dirt. "It's worth a try, iffen thet lady in th' other stall ever decides to give birth. What's yer grandma been callin' her?"

"That's the one Grandma named Gert. I sure wish Gert would get in a hurry."

Her grandfather smiled, but it was a sad smile. "There ain't no hurryin' things like a birthin'. Nature takes her time." He glanced over his shoulder toward the back of the barn where the orphan cried. "Reckon we oughta name that li'l girl?"

"Grandma usually does the naming, but I think I'd like to call her Lily."

Together they finished tossing clean hay into the stall just as Grandma rang the bell hanging on the porch post. Dulcie went to the open barn door and waved. "We'll be there directly." She headed to the pump to wash up, but wasn't in a hurry to sit down at the dinner table, despite the grumbling noises her stomach had been making. She didn't envy Grandpa. He had the unhappy chore of telling Grandma about Clara.

⤫ CHAPTER FIVE

The first rays of dawn were painting pink and gold streaks across the sky when Dulcie stepped out the door to tend to her chores. She didn't mind the morning chores. They gave her a chance to greet the day and the animals, and to get her thoughts together. Planning her schedule for cleaning and processing the wool, as well as the dyeing and weaving of the yarns, took patient consideration, something she could do best while feeding the chickens, gathering eggs, and milking the cow.

She scooped cracked corn into a basket and made her way through the semi-dark yard to the hen house. She lit the lantern hanging from a nail on the outside of the fence. The chickens roused when she unlatched the door of the coop, and welcomed her by pecking at her feet.

"Good morning, ladies. Are you ready for breakfast?"

Dulcie emptied the basket, scattering handfuls of corn across the ground on the side of the coop farthest away from the roosts. While the hens attacked the corn with greedy vengeance, Dulcie held the lantern aloft and deposited the eggs in her basket while the hens were occupied. They still were intent on gobbling up every speck when she whispered, "Thank you, ladies," and slipped out.

She forked hay to Samson and Honey, the cow, and pulled the stool over to Honey's side. While she washed the cow's udder for milking, a strained, harsh grunting sound reached her. Her hands halted. She held her breath and listened. A few moments later, she heard it again. She stood and patted Honey. "I'll be right back."

She snagged the lantern on the way out of Honey's stall and crept down the row of enclosures. The pitchfork hung from a nail on a post, and the idea of taking a weapon of some sort with her seemed prudent. With the lantern held high and the pitchfork in her grip, she inched back toward the sound.

As she approached the last stalls, the guttural bawl sounded a few feet away. Dulcie startled and swung the lantern to her left. *Gert!* The ewe lay in the hay, her sides heaving.

Dulcie set the pitchfork aside and hung the lantern on the door of the stall. She knelt beside the laboring ewe. Grandpa and Grandma were both probably up by now, but leaving the sheep to go fetch them didn't feel right. She ran her hands over the ewe's abdomen and found it convulsing. A cursory examination determined the sheep was going to deliver any minute. Gert groaned again, and a tiny foot emerged. Dulcie's pulse stepped up. She'd never done this by herself before. Whenever the ewes gave birth, Grandpa was usually the one to preside over the event.

Should she pray? Would God hear her? Would He listen?

Gert bawled again and a second foot peeked out. Dulcie leaned closer. Were they the front or back feet? Between the pale lantern light and the minuscule size of the feet, she couldn't tell. She wracked her brain to think what Grandpa would do. Didn't he usually let the ewe manage on her own? Unless she needed help. How did she know if—

The ewe rolled and heaved, the throes of labor seizing Gert in their grip. Dulcie crooned encouragement to the ewe and stroked her neck. "Come on, Gert. You can do this. Just a little more and you can meet your baby."

Her baby! The little orphan in the next stall bleated, no doubt awakened by the commotion. Grandpa had described what he planned to do—to rub the afterbirth from Gert on Lily's head and hindquarters in an effort to coax Gert into adopting the little one.

Gert pushed again, and what appeared to be a nose covered with a membrane pushed out. Dulcie scrambled forward on her hands and knees and pulled off her apron. She wadded up the cloth and wiped the emerging baby's face, clearing the lamb's nose and mouth. Then she leapt to her feet, dashed to the next stall and gathered Lily in her arms.

Please God, if You're listening, please let Gert accept Lily. When she re-entered the stall the new lamb's entire head showed. Dulcie set Lily in the hay beside her, and grasped the slippery, tiny hooves. "Push, Gert." *Please God. . .*

Had she just prayed? With no time to consider the answer, she snatched handfuls of hay and wrapped it around the lamb's forelegs to prevent them from slipping from her grip. She pulled gently but steadily. Gert convulsed and heaved again, and the new baby slid out onto the hay.

Dulcie went to work. She rubbed the rest of the membrane off the new lamb and massaged the little fellow's chest. He stuck out his tongue and wobbled his head, and pushed out a tiny squeak. Gert delivered the afterbirth with no help, and Dulcie swallowed hard, refusing to let herself gag. She picked up the afterbirth and rubbed it over Lily's head and neck, on her ears and down her spine, and finally around her hindquarters. It left a sticky mess on the lamb's fleece, but if things worked out the way Grandpa hoped, Gert would clean off her new adopted lamb.

She nestled Lily and the new lamb side by side in the hay, touching each other. Then she turned to Gert. A fleeting thought skittered through her mind. If God heard her prayer, now is when He would answer. *If* He would answer.

Gert lay, exhausted, in the hay. Dulcie held her hands that were still covered in sticky afterbirth where Gert could sniff. "You have two new babies waiting to meet their mama."

"I wondered what was takin' ye so long." Grandpa's soft voice pulled her attention from the new mother for a moment.

"I did what you said, Grandpa. The rest is up to Gert."

He stayed outside the stall, but leaned his forearms against the top rail. "Ye done good, Rosebud.Couldn't o' done no better myself."

Grandpa's praise gladdened her heart, but if Gert rejected Lily, it was for nothing. She moved around to nudge Gert, to encourage her to stand. The exhausted mama ignored Dulcie's prodding, but finally responded to the sound of the two lambs bleating nearly in unison. Gert lumbered to her feet and turned in the lambs' direction.

Dulcie backed away, ever so slowly. *Please God. . .* There it was again. The simple prayer issued from her heart, if not her lips, with no conscious thought. Maybe because it had been a very long time since she'd wanted anything as much as she wanted Gert to accept Lily as her own. Wanted it so much her subconscious petitioned God.

"Look there, Rosebud." Grandpa's whisper made her realize she'd closed her eyes.

The sight of Gert sniffing and licking and nuzzling both lambs nearly made her heart burst. Tears stung her eyes. *He heard.* A bubble of joy tickled, but she dare not release it and risk spooking Gert.

Dulcie inched backward and slipped out of the stall to stand beside Grandpa. "It worked, Grandpa, it worked. Lily's got a mama."

Her grandfather's arm tightened around her shoulders. They watched a few more minutes until Lily began to nurse. Gert nosed the newborn to its feet and the lamb tottered to its mother's side. Dulcie clasped her fingers together and tucked them under her chin, her heart exploding within her. Her cheeks hurt from smiling.

"C'mon. Let's go tell yer grandma."

"You go on and tell her. I still have to wash up and finish milking Honey." She hoped Honey wouldn't mind that her hands trembled with delight. "I'll be done in a few minutes. Here." She held out the basket of eggs. "Grandma will be looking for these."

Grandpa took the egg basket and winked at her before heading toward the house. Dulcie trotted to the pump out by the garden where she washed the afterbirth from her hands. She returned to the barn and settled back onto the stool, and apologized to Honey for making her wait to be milked. She leaned her head against the cow's warm side and began the rhythmic milking motion.

"God, did You really hear me? Did Gert accept Lily because I prayed?" She wanted to believe He'd answered her prayer, but she'd never know for sure.

Grandma hummed as she twisted the thin roving fibers between her fingers. The smile on her face when Dulcie had returned to the house with the milk was worth every bit of the messy task she'd had to perform in the first moments following the birth. Even now, hours later, her grandmother was still smiling. Knowing Lily would survive eased the pain of losing Clara. The relief Dulcie felt at knowing she'd had a hand in the successful adoption was exceeded only by the pure pleasure of seeing joy on Grandma's face.

The mauve woolen and a length of blue sat to one side, folded and ready for the trip into town. The tan wool fabric on her loom was nearly finished. As much as she enjoyed watching the precisely woven threads come together to create a length of quality cloth, her fingers itched to begin a new rug. Three rugs were completed. Smaller in size and simple in design, but often requested, so she continued to produce them. But the one she'd been designing in her head begged to be created. Wild mountain roses, wisteria, and forget-me-nots twined together with ivy would come together into the most beautiful rug she'd ever made.

Malachi began barking—not his usual yip he used when herding the sheep or the happy bark of greeting when they returned home from town. This bark was different—defensive and territorial—and combined with the frantic *baaing* of the sheep.

Dulcie dropped the spindle she held. "Something is after the flock." She jumped up so fast her chair tipped backward. She pushed past a crate holding the door of the wool shed open, and barely heard Grandma's shriek behind her.

"Take the gun. It could be a bear."

Her feet hesitated only a moment. Malachi's fierce barking and snarling had also brought Grandpa from the barn, and he carried a shotgun. Her younger and spryer legs ran to the meadow in time to see Malachi engaged in battle with a bobcat. Neither seemed inclined to give an inch. The way they tangled and went for each other's throats, Grandpa wouldn't be able to get a shot off without hitting the dog. She'd witnessed Malachi's protective behavior before, but she never knew he could be such a fierce fighter. The unearthly yowl of the cat made the hair on the back of her neck stand up. Shivers wrapped themselves around her spine. Malachi latched onto the cat's neck and shook. The bobcat screeched. The sound scraped Dulcie's nerves raw, but when Malachi dropped his foe, the cat ran off up into the hills above the meadow. Malachi continued his ferocious barking and gave chase until Grandpa whistled. The dog halted but stood at full alert, his hackles raised, his eyes watching the cat's retreat.

Grandpa whistled again, and Malachi reluctantly returned. Every few steps, the dog stopped and turned to make sure the bobcat wasn't returning. Finally satisfied he'd won the battle, the dog returned to the flock and began sniffing each sheep.

Grandpa tramped up the slope with his shotgun, but called over his shoulder. "Check the sheep."

Dulcie called back. "Be careful!" She approached the flock. Malachi had the sheep tightly knotted together with the lambs sheltered between the ewes. Since most of the sheep had been shorn, catching sight of a wound shouldn't be hard. She threaded her way into the flock, running her hands down each sheep, while Malachi limped around the perimeter, keeping them gathered together.

Grandma traipsed through the meadow grass and joined her, huffing from her haste. "Yer grandpa go after 'im?"

Dulcie glanced up the hill in the direction she'd seen Grandpa go, and nodded. "Mm-hm."

Grandma muttered something that sounded like *foolish ole man gonna git hisself tore up,* but she said nothing more. She bent over each animal, crooning reassurance and patting heads as if calming frightened children.

Having satisfied themselves that every last sheep was all right, they turned their attention to Malachi. The dog bore several bloodied scratches to his face, chest, and front legs, but Dulcie could find no puncture wounds through his thick fur. The difficulty was in trying to hold Malachi still to search for bites when the dog kept trying to pull away and return to *his* sheep.

"No sense in tryin' to take 'im to the barn. He'd never stay put. Go fetch my bag. I'll doctor 'im right here." Grandma's roots and herbs had seen a lot of use over the years, but Dulcie knew leaves and roots weren't the only thing in Grandma's bag. A small bottle of moonshine was tucked into the bag as well. She'd used it to disinfect cuts and scrapes for as long as Dulcie could remember, but Grandma thought nobody knew she kept the small amount of spirits in the house.

She brought the bag to Grandma, and then held the dog tight while Grandma cleaned and dressed the cuts. Malachi whimpered when the stinging ministrations were applied to the deep scratches, but the moment they turned him loose, he went straight back to the sheep. His sheep.

Grandpa returned, shotgun propped on his shoulder. "Followed a trail of blood fer a while. The rate thet cat's a-bleedin', he won't be back." He surveyed the flock. "'Pears the cat didn't get to any o' the sheep. Dog all right?"

At the moment, all Dulcie wanted to do was give Malachi a whole steak, but the bone Grandma had been saving for soup would have to do. "He'll be fine. Grandma fixed him up."

Grandpa finished reading the account in the Gospel of John of the good shepherd. Dulcie had heard it so many times, she could almost recite it for memory. But today the words seemed appropriate. Not only did Lily have a mama, but Malachi had protected the sheep.

After Grandpa prayed, he closed the Book and fixed his gaze on Dulcie, the lines around his eyes deepening. "What happened out there today is like what God's a-tellin' us in His word. The Father, He knows His sheep, His children. He don't lose track of 'em, an' He don't leave 'em when trouble comes. That ole dog was ready to fight to the death iffen he had to, all to protect his sheep. That's what Jesus did. Ain't nobody can take His sheep away from Him, an' He gived His life for the sheep." A softness gentled his expression, and he patted her hand.

For the first time in years, the illustration meant something to her. Of course, she was grateful the sheep were all right, grateful the dog had battled the predator, but she couldn't know with any certainty it was because God responded to her prayer. He *had* left her, after all, and she couldn't forget the feeling of abandonment. Maybe she didn't want to forget.

❦ CHAPTER SIX

G avin leaned forward and peered out the soot-darkened train window as the Hot Springs depot came into view. Not unlike the last dozen train depots over the past two days, this one was unremarkable. What he could see of the town of Hot Springs didn't impress him, either. The mountain vistas that embraced the town, however, were an artist's dream. The screech of the iron wheels against the rails and the hiss of steam punctuated the arrival at his final destination.

The train lurched and jolted to a halt. After days of the to and fro motion, and sitting trapped in a rail car with unwashed bodies and stale cigar smoke, bidding farewell to the great iron beast couldn't come soon enough. Gavin stood, stretched his cramped legs, and brushed his hands down his trousers in a vain attempt to erase some of the wrinkled evidence of traveling. He retrieved his satchel and made his way to the exit. The narrow steps to freedom were steep and the wooden step put in place by the conductor wobbly, but oh, how good it felt to finally stand on solid ground that didn't move.

Gavin sucked in a deep breath of mountain air. *Ahh. . .*

"Gavin!"

He scanned the platform. His uncle stood beside a carriage, his hand uplifted and beckoning.

"This way." Uncle Arnold didn't waste time on pleasantries or familial greetings.

"Hello, Uncle." Gavin jerked his thumb over his shoulder. "I need to get my trunk."

His uncle scowled and shook his head. "Have the porter deliver it to the Mountain Park Hotel."

Gavin hesitated and judged the storage space aboard the carriage. "It's not a large trunk. It won't take up much room."

Uncle Arnold's scowl deepened with impatience. "We don't have time to wait around while they unload baggage. Tell the porter to deliver it. We have important matters to discuss."

Ten minutes later, his uncle directed the carriage to the front door of the hotel. The ornate maroon and gold sign out front proclaimed it to be the Mountain Park Hotel. From the first glance, Gavin could tell this was no boardinghouse. Rising four stories over its elegant brick foundation, the place boasted stylish trims and moldings defining the Swiss style architecture, grand leaded glass windows, and stately turrets with spires pointing to the sky. The Mansard roof was the latest style among the resorts up and down the eastern seaboard.

He was ushered into a room bearing the number 148 engraved on a shiny brass plate on the door. The Mountain Park Hotel was certainly more than he expected for such a small town set out of the way in the mountains. Drapes of some kind of satiny-looking fabric hung at the windows, and matched the covering on the bed. Heavy oak and mahogany furniture anchored a rug that reminded him of some of the furnishings he'd seen in Italy the summer his parents took him and Harold to Europe. The bellman demonstrated how to operate the electric light and briefly outlined the availability of the bathhouse. Thoroughly impressed, Gavin dropped a coin into the bellman's outstretched hand and took the key the man handed to him. Placing his satchel on the bed, Gavin dug through the contents to find a fresh shirt.

"Do that later." Gavin had forgotten his uncle stood there in the open doorway. "Come to my room. Number 161. We need to talk." Uncle Arnold spun on his heel and strode down the hall, his footsteps muffled by a thick carpet runner.

Suppressing a tired sigh, Gavin exited his room, locked the door and dropped the key into his pocket. He took note of the paintings and other ornamental details on his way to Uncle Arnold's room. One painting especially caught his eye—a pool of water hugged by willow trees, and a hillside dotted with sheep in the distance. The picture lent a calming, pastoral air to the surrounding elegance, but he dared not take time to pause and study the scene. Uncle Arnold didn't like to be kept waiting.

He tapped on the door of room 161 and entered when he heard his uncle's response within. Uncle Arnold's room was larger and grander than his. The furnishings included an elegant desk with inlaid trim, overstuffed chairs, and a fancy tea table. A marble fireplace with a hearth covered in some type of tile with an intricate design occupied one wall.

"Come over here." Uncle Arnold strode to the desk and pushed a cut glass inkwell and a leather-bound journal to one side so he could roll out a large map.

The lines on the map weren't familiar. "What am I looking at?"

His uncle leaned over the desk and tapped a thick finger on the map. "This is Madison County." He pointed to the northwest corner. "This is Hot Springs. And right here—" He slid his finger to the right. " . . .is where I am going to build."

All his uncle had indicated in his letter was some kind of health spa, but he'd not included the details. "What exactly are you building, uncle?"

"You noticed, of course, the name of the town." Uncle Arnold straightened and pulled a cigar from his vest. He bit off the end and spit it in the direction of a brass spittoon.

"Hot Springs." Gavin looked from the map to his uncle and back to the map. "I read where they recently changed the name of the town. Something about the discovery of a new spring."

A tiny smile lifted the corners of Uncle Arnold's mustache. Was his uncle pleased that he knew a bit about the town? He waited while Uncle Arnold lit his cigar and puffed on it. The odorous smoke reminded him of the train car.

Finally, his uncle gestured with a sweep of his arm. "What do you think of this place?"

Gavin raised his brows and let his eyes travel around the luxurious accommodations.

"This room? Or the hotel?"

"The hotel. From what you've seen in the past thirty minutes."

What did the hotel have to do with his uncle wanting to build a health facility? "It's quite impressive."

Uncle Arnold puffed on his cigar, and pointed to the map. "These lines here..., here..., and here represent acreage that is occupied by area farmers. There is another tract along the river that a timber company is bidding for, but I know how to deal with those people."

His uncle wasn't making sense. Why didn't he spell out the details of his plan, plain and simple? "Uncle, what do the farms, and this hotel, and your plans have to do with each other?"

A chuckle from his uncle startled him. Gavin had rarely, if ever, heard his uncle laugh, especially when talking business.

"Boy, you might be impressed with this hotel, but the resort I plan to build—right here—" He stabbed his finger onto the map again, " . . .will outshine this one. Oh, I'm not saying the Mountain Park isn't plush. The quality is as fine as I've seen. But what I have in mind is bigger, better, with more luxury, more amenities to offer, a place that will out-class this hotel and any other. The entire estate will be over a hundred acres of rolling hills, mountain vistas, waterfalls, trout streams, shady woods, and magnificent gardens unparalleled by anything within a thousand mile radius. But more importantly, my facility will offer what the Mountain Park does not."

Gavin let his gaze drift around the finely-appointed room. He walked to the French doors and looked out over the balcony. "This place appears to be brand new. Electric lights? Up here in the mountains? From what the bellman said, they offer hot springs bathhouses as well as amusements of every variety. There was a sign in the lobby stating an orchestra plays nightly in the ballroom." He pointed across the stretch of meticulous landscape. "Is that a golf course?"

This time his uncle sneered. "It is. But what I have in mind will make all the amusements this place offers seem frivolous. I will put into place a full health resort with medical care second to none. I plan to take full advantage of the health benefits of the hot mineral springs to lure people with all types of maladies, both illnesses and injuries."

The idea of his uncle building a hospital facility took Gavin aback. Uncle Arnold? A humanitarian? Would wonders never cease? "A health resort."

His uncle pointed toward the open window. "The testimonies of healing attributed to the springs are widespread. In many cases, soaking in the waters brought about cures when medical science couldn't. Used in conjunction with medical treatment, the mineral springs will bring people who are ready and willing to pay whatever it takes to regain their health." He set his cigar on the edge of the ashtray. His voice lowered to a murmur, as if he spoke more to himself than to Gavin. "It's a goldmine."

He tapped his finger on the map. "The first step is to acquire the land. That's where you come in." He stared at the map for a long moment, his jaw set, fingers templed together, lips tight. When he finally spoke, he articulated his words with deliberation. "I've recently come into some information regarding the flow of an underground spring and how it feeds the hot springs."

His uncle twisted his mustache between his thumb and forefinger. "It is necessary to buy up partial segments of four farms. Not huge tracts, but enough to maintain clear rights to the water." He planted both palms on the desk and hovered over the map like a buzzard eyeing a dying rodent. "I will require somewhere between ten to fifteen acres of each of these four farms."

Gavin craned his neck to look over his uncle's shoulder at the map. There were names written on the plots of land he indicated. *Zeb Huxley. Reuben Ludlow. Simon Cutler. Dewey Tate.* These farmers were expected to sell his uncle part of their land? What if they didn't want to sell?

Uncle Arnold picked up a pencil from the desk and circled a fifth name. "This farm right here is approximately seventy acres, and I need this entire piece of land. All seventy acres." His uncle lifted his eyes to meet Gavin's, and the steel-eyed tenacity almost made Gavin flinch. Uneasiness spiraled through him, and he glanced back down at the map to read the name of the man whose farm his uncle wanted.

James Chappell.

His uncle spoke again and arrested Gavin's attention. "This is your task. You will use all your charm and powers of persuasion to pressure these landowners into selling. Remember, these mountain people are ignorant and backward. Most of them probably can't even read, so all you have to do is get them to agree to the terms and make their mark on the contract."

His tone sounded so like Father's, Gavin jerked his head up to see if his father had come back to haunt him.

James took the sack Virginia packed for him, and gave her a peck on the cheek. "Sure ye ain't needin' the mule today. I can walk to Dewey's place."

Virginia flapped her hands. "No, no, I ain't a-goin' nowhere. Got too much work to do to go traipsin' to town." She walked with him to the barn, like she figured he couldn't find his way. "I packed plenty o' biscuits an' fatback, enough for you an' Dewey. There's some boiled eggs, apples, and molasses cookies in there, too."

Old Samson turned woebegone eyes on him as he tied the sack to the saddle. "Don't reckon we'll starve. Y'all be careful an' keep the shotgun close. I 'spect that bobcat likely won't be back, but it don't hurt to be prepared."

He kissed her again, and hauled himself into the saddle. "Dewey said a couple other fellers was comin' by to help, so we oughta get that pig fence done before supper."

Virginia patted Samson's neck. "Dewey's a good friend. I worry about 'im, alone over there since his Martha died. You tell him to come to supper."

Sweet Virginia. She could be crusty as a hunk of week-old cornbread, but her heart were bigger than the mountains. "I doubt he'll come, but I'll give him the invite."

He nudged Samson with his heels and waved as he headed off to Dewey's place. It weren't a long ride, less than twenty minutes, he reckoned. But his old bones took to achin' iffen he had to hike too far.

He recognized Simon Cutler's swayback mare and Zeb Huxley's buckboard when he pulled the mule to stop in front of Dewey's place. "Dewey Tate!" James hollered loud enough to wake the lazy hound under the porch. "You around?"

Dewey hollered back from the barn and James joined him, Simon and Zeb. "You boys waitin' till I got here to start workin'?"

Simon grinned. "Wanted to save the best parts fer you, James."

Dewey sucked on his teeth. "Yup. We needed ye to start shovelin' out the muck 'fore we could pull out them old fence posts."

The other men cackled, and Zeb Huxley gave James's shoulder a shove. "Doncha know the last man t' arrive gits the best job." Loud guffaws followed.

James filled his pockets with nails and picked up his hammer. "In a pig's eye. The old men have the most experience, so we git to supervise."

Simon hooted at Zeb, the youngest of the bunch. "Reckon you got the muckin' job, Zeb." They picked up their tools and headed for the pigpen where the sow had busted through the rotted rails.

While James set to work knocking down what remained of the fence, Zeb leaned on his shovel, jawin'. "Y'all seen that fancy feller thet stepped off the train the other day?" Zeb scratched his head.

James snorted. "There's fancy fellers and their women steppin' off the train ever' week, what with the new hotel an' all."

Zeb's eyebrows shot up under the brim of his hat. "This feller were differn't. Didn't have no woman with 'im, but some feller what looked like he were dressed to meet th' king of England met 'im at the depot."

"Rich folks from all over been comin' to take the waters. They say the new hotel is pert nigh as good as them in New York City." James tossed a rotted board to one side. "Dewey, you wantin' to make the pen the same size it was, or you makin' room for more pigs?"

Dewey pulled off his hat and wiped his brow. "Don't have 'nough posts an' rails to make it no bigger, 'less I can talk Zeb into splittin' some rails from thet ole downed locust tree."

James smirked. "Best ye get busy, Zeb. Splittin' thet locust wood likely gonna take ye the better part of the day."

Zeb shouldered a load of the hickory rails Dewey had stacked next to the barn and carried them to one side of the pig pen where he dumped them in a pile. "I'll split that locust while y'all muck out the pen."

A wide grin pulled at Dewey's beard. "Reckon we'll jus' keep the pen the same size."

A chuckle rumbled up James's chest. These fellers were more like family than neighbors, and he always said there was nothin' more important than family, 'cept the Lord.

❦ CHAPTER SEVEN

Every time Gavin sat across the table from his uncle, his stomach knotted. Uncle Arnold stuffed a huge bite of sausage into his mouth, and then slathered a biscuit with jam. With his uncle's mouth occupied, Gavin didn't have to listen to the usual biting criticism—at least not until he swallowed. But it wasn't the man's lack of table manners that stirred discomfort in Gavin. For a fleeting moment four days ago, a pleasant surprise blinded him, thinking his uncle's plan was humanitarian and benevolent. For the space of a dozen heartbeats, Uncle Arnold had sounded as if he had compassion on those who suffered, and his grand agenda was to build a facility where all could come for healing.

Gavin should have known better. There was nothing humanitarian about his uncle or his purpose for building in these mountains. Like Gavin's father, everything Uncle Arnold did was for the purpose of making money. While the pages of testimonies his uncle had given him to read all attributed healing to the hot springs—at least in part—most also included medical treatment. His uncle's plan to advertise his health resort as an all-inclusive facility that offered the latest in medical treatments coupled with the therapeutic benefits of the mineral springs would bring in people from hundreds of miles around, willing to pay hefty sums.

It all began with the assignment Uncle Arnold had given him to procure the land. The elder DeWitt's scorn of the area residents rang in Gavin's memory, but his uncle wasn't finished.

Uncle Arnold sucked a noisy slurp of coffee. "As I was saying, these small communities are fraught with gossipers. Feed them the information you want them to spread, and they do the set-up for you. In a backward society like this, the people are distrustful of outsiders, but they're all chummy with each other. So you win over a few important citizens and they'll spread whatever you want the general population to know." He stabbed a forkful of eggs smothered in some kind of sauce and wrapped his mouth around it, then pointed his fork at Gavin. "Follow my lead, boy, and you'll learn how to deal with these yokels."

Gavin bit into a biscuit, but it lost its savor in the shadow of his uncle's admonition. Unless he misunderstood, his uncle expected him to intentionally mislead the citizens of Hot Springs in order to be considered a success.

Arnold wiped his mouth on his napkin. "Always look for the people of influence. They're the ones you can use to carry out your purpose."

Gavin set down his fork. "Influence. You mean like the mayor or town council or constable?"

The scowl on Uncle Arnold's face communicated his displeasure at Gavin's question.

"No! If this backwater has a mayor, he's likely an ignorant hillbilly like the rest of them. Whatever you do, don't alert the law. A lawman in a little hick town like this doesn't have any idea how the law reads or how to enforce it, but they act like they do."

Uneasiness squirmed through Gavin at his uncle's remark. Surely he didn't plan to do anything illegal, did he?

"Listen to me." Arnold swept a glance across the dining room and lowered his voice. "The people who make up the grapevine are usually the merchants—like that fool in the emporium. The postmaster. The barber. The liveryman. Spreading information—even if it's exaggerated—makes them look important. In their blissful ignorance, they work for me by piquing interest. The rumors get blown out of proportion, and people start getting worried. When the timing is right, I come forward, present the facts I want them to know, and look like a hero."

He sat back and took a sip of his coffee. "I'll draw up a basic contract for you to use for the land purchases. All you have to do is fill in the names and locations, the survey descriptions, and the offered price. It's simple enough for a hillbilly to understand at least in part, even if someone must read it to him. But it includes enough legal jargon to give us unrestricted access and camouflage the titles and easements."

Gavin had spent enough time at Wesleyan College to understand his uncle's meaning. He planned to use the land that belonged to someone else to access the land he actually wanted, even if he had to trick them into agreeing to it. Very neat and tidy, and the document would stand up in a court of law. The eye-opening realization shook him. He'd underestimated the level of ruthlessness it would take to gain his uncle's regard. Nevertheless, if that's what it took, he'd give it everything he had.

Gavin tapped his finger on the rim of his coffee cup. "How do you know when the time is right to come forward with your facts?"

Arnold stirred sugar into his coffee. "The time is right when enough interest is aroused and people are asking questions."

Gavin supposed a certain amount of experience was necessary to possess such instincts, but another question continued to nag him. "What if the landowners don't agree to the price or what if they simply don't want to sell?"

His uncle leveled a glare at him reminiscent of his father's. He set his coffee cup down with a *clunk* against the saucer and leaned forward. "It's your job to make sure they *do* agree. That's what you're getting paid to do."

Gavin nodded. If that's what his uncle required, then that was his goal. He'd listen and learn. He'd watch his uncle, pick up the tricks and skills that made him the successful businessman he was, and he'd emulate his elder. "Yes, sir."

"Now, to map out our next strategy." Arnold pulled a leather-bound notebook from his inside coat pocket. "You must remember that even though there are only five landowners we are targeting, we can use the people of the community to pressure them into agreeing to the plan. When people think there is something in it for them, they can be very persuasive."

That made sense—get the entire town behind them. Gavin wrote the note in his mind. Perhaps if he could think of ways to achieve such community support for their plan, he'd gain a level of respect in his uncle's eyes.

Arnold tapped the page in his open notebook. "We'll give the rumor mill a couple of weeks to get going. Then we'll come forward with our first announcement. Let's see, tomorrow is Sunday, so two weeks from tomorrow. These backwoods people are a bunch of Biblepounders, so they'll all be in church. It'll be a good time to disclose enough to pacify them, while they're all together."

The picture his uncle's statement painted didn't feel right. Did he intend to go into the church and talk about land deals and business propositions? Gavin wasn't a religious man, but even he knew interrupting a church service to talk about business was inappropriate.

"Uncle, I don't think these people, even if they are as backward as you say, would look kindly on us using their worship service to present our offer to buy their land, especially since they are all religious people. They might view that as offensive. Since we are trying to gain their trust, it might be better if we actually attend the service. If they see us sitting in church, they'll be more likely to accept us."

His uncle stroked his mustache and appeared to be weighing Gavin's suggestion. "Not a bad idea. Appearances are important and can be a valuable tool." He picked up his cup and held it aloft in a mock toast.

"You go tomorrow. Shake some hands. Smile and be friendly. Act like you're a friend of the preacher's. The people will see that."

Uncle Arnold's affirmation of his recommendation bolstered Gavin's confidence. "Another thing we might wish to consider: Might it be better if we approach each farmer individually instead of as a group?"

"Why?" His uncle barked out the challenge. "It's more efficient to make the presentation to all of them at the same time."

Gavin didn't want his uncle to think he couldn't handle speaking to a group or address questions that came more than one at a time. He swallowed back the intimidation that threatened to strangle him and forced a cool smile. "Well, for one thing, it might be to our advantage to negotiate with each one privately. It will take more time, of course, but if each man believes he is being offered the best price, he will be more inclined to go along with the deal, and less inclined to talk with his neighbors about it."

His uncle's eyebrows furrowed in a scowl, and Gavin hurried to continue before the man could shoot down his suggestion. "We *want* the town people to talk about it and spread the information. That will build support for us. But it might be better if the five landowners didn't discuss the terms of the contract amongst themselves, so each man wouldn't know how much the other men are being offered."

His uncle studied him with such scrutiny, sweat popped out on his upper lip and his collar felt uncomfortably tight. Finally, the man gave a slight nod. "We'll try it, but I don't want the process dragged out. You'll have a deadline to get all five tracts of land contracted."

James closed his eyes and listened as the notes Otis Hogan plucked on his dulcimer soaked into his soul. His favorite hymn, "Guide Me O Thou Great Jehovah." The words spoke worship to him. "'Songs of praises, I will ever give to Thee.'" He lifted his heart's praise to Almighty God.

When the final notes of the hymn faded, he tucked Virginia's arm through the crook of his elbow and followed Dulcie toward the door. Daniel Montgomery stopped her to talk, and Dulcie smiled. Could somethin' be a-brewing there? Daniel was a nice young feller, worked as a harness maker with his pa. Caleb Montgomery and James had been friends since before the War Between the States. James couldn't find fault with Caleb's boy, but Daniel's heart weren't in the soil or raising sheep. Dulcie needed a man with a love for the land.

Up ahead, a stranger stood talking with the preacher. James had never seen him before. Looked like a fancy pants—like one of them tourists that come to take the waters. He and Virginia wove their way past folks to shake the preacher's hand. James stopped to have a word with Reverend Bradbury while Virginia and Dulcie went ahead to chat with friends.

James poked the air with his thumb. "Who's that young feller that visited this mornin'?"

The preacher glanced in the direction James's thumb pointed. "He's new in town. Name's DeWitt. Seems like a friendly sort."

"DeWitt? There's another feller in town by the name o' DeWitt. Was awful interested in seein' how the water flowed through my meadow. Reckon they're kin?"

"Could be, but this one came to church alone." The preacher tilted his head toward the church yard where folks congregated to chew the fat. The visitor stood amongst them appearin' as if he'd knowed them all his life. A few of them smiled and nodded, like they agreed with whatever he was sayin'.

This DeWitt was younger than the one askin' questions about the water, but like the preacher said, he was real friendly-like. DeWitt raised his hand in farewell and strolled down the street. Curiosity nudged James forward to join the men.

Hollis slapped James on the back. "How ye been keepin', James?"

"Right fine."

"You meet that new feller? DeWitt's his name." Hollis tilted his head in the direction young DeWitt had headed. "Seems him and his uncle is plannin' on settlin' in to these parts. Ain't that a caution? A coupla Yankees wantin' to settle down in Hot Springs."

James went still and cut his eyes to DeWitt's retreating form in time to see him round the corner at the emporium. "Ye don't say."

Hollis rubbed his chin. "That's what he said, ain't it, boys. Dewey Tate said he thinks they got plans for startin' some kind o' business. Reckon that means they gonna be our neighbors."

Thatch Davis shook his head. "Ain't never a met a yankee I wanted to trust. Don't know that I want him or his uncle movin' in part an' parcel, like he's one o' us."

James folded his arms across his chest. The memory of Arnold DeWitt askin' questions about the spring stirred concern in his gut. "This DeWitt feller say what kind o' business?"

James's friend, Reuben, scuffed his shoe in the dirt. "Didn't say, but he was smilin' an' shakin' hands like he was runnin' for office."

James's belly flipped like a possum tryin' to escape a snare. He'd admonished Dulcie for the way she spoke to Arnold DeWitt the day he'd come out to the farm. Maybe she was right not to trust him.

He crossed the church yard to their wagon and climbed into the seat. He itched to get on home, but Virginia and Dulcie were still talkin' with the other ladies. He unwrapped the reins from the brake lever. He didn't plan on leavin' without them, he just needed somethin' in his hands to grip.

DeWitt's interest in the way the spring bubbled up and ran across his land suddenly made his skin crawl—like their land was bein' threatened the same way the bobcat had threatened the sheep. What kind of plans did these men have and what was the rumor? 'Cause that's all it was-a rumor, as empty as a rain barrel with a hole in the bottom.

Their home, their heritage, Dulcie's legacy. They weren't wealthy, not by a long stitch, but there was always food on the table and God met their needs. Every mornin' when he rolled out of bed, his old bones complained. He weren't gettin' no younger, but he still had work to do. He had to make the farm and the flock the best it could be. For Dulcie. It was all he had to give her, and right now, a strange urge to protect Dulcie's legacy stirred deep down in his soul.

CHAPTER EIGHT

The dressmaker counted out the money for two dress lengths of woolen yard goods into Dulcie's hand. "I jus' love that plum color one, an' I know one o' the ladies from the Mountain Park will like the tan. I hope you can make me more o' both o' these."

Dulcie tucked the money into her pocket. "I can. When would you need them?"

"Let me think." Eunice tapped her chin with one finger. "A couple o' months, I reckon. That way I'll have 'em on hand when the ladies get ready to plan their fall wardrobes."

After a quick calculation, Dulcie nodded. "We finished the shearing and we'll get the last of the fleeces washed and carded in another week or two. I'll have several fleeces I expect will make very fine material. I'll put them aside and mark them for you."

"Thank you, Dulcie. Now don't you go sellin' your woolens to any other dressmakers."

Eunice patted Dulcie's back as she walked her to the door. "With all these rich folks comin' into Hot Springs, I want my shop to be the only place they can get such fine fabrics."

Dulcie stifled a chuckle. There weren't any other dressmakers in town. "I won't, but I do sell my yard goods to Luther Dempsey at the emporium."

"Oh, yes, I know." Eunice held the door open. "But those rich ladies that come to visit the hot springs, they don't do their own sewin'." A wide grin punctuated her statement.

Dulcie hopped up onto the wagon seat and snapped the reins. She had a lengthy shopping list for Mr. Dempsey at the emporium. She hoped the merchant had sold a rug or two for her. With Grandma's birthday coming up in a few weeks, Dulcie hoped to surprise her with a new bonnet and a birthday cake.

She halted Samson outside the emporium and set the brake. The cool mountain breeze stirred the tendrils of her hair that had escaped the single braid, and she tucked them behind her ear. The little bell over the door sang a welcome as she entered the store.

"Morning, Mr. Dempsey."

"Mornin', Miss Dulcie." Mr. Dempsey wiped his hands on his apron. "That rose-colored rug got sold to one o' them rich folks. Lady said how the color reminded her o' the roses growin' wild all through the mountains." He pulled a small tin box out from under the counter. "Ever' time I sell your goods, I put your money in this here little box to keep it separate."

Pleased for at least one sale, she pulled out her list. "We need quite a few things." She handed him the scrap of paper. With the sale of the rug, and the yard goods to Eunice, she'd have more than enough for Grandma's birthday. "I'm going to look at your calico."

Mr. Dempsey picked up the list and adjusted his spectacles. "Mm hm. Flour, cornmeal, ya want twenty pounds of each?"

"Yes, please." She mentally listed the ingredients for Grandma's cake. "I'd best get a couple pounds of sugar, too."

"I s'pose you heard all the goin's on." Mr. Dempsey measured out the sugar, and Dulcie forgot about the calico for a moment.

"What's going on?"

Mr. Dempsey looked over top of his spectacles at her. "You ain't heard all the talk?"

Dulcie pursed her lips. The shopkeeper was worse than a woman when it came to gossip.

"I don't pay attention to what doesn't concern me."

The merchant chuckled. "Ye sound jus' like yer grandpa." He checked the list again, pulling items off the shelves as he went. "Molasses. Rolled oats. How much coffee ya wantin'?"

"Two pounds, please." She returned her attention to the calico. Grandpa always said he liked Grandma to wear blue because of her blue eyes. She half listened to Mr. Dempsey yammer while she compared three different bolts of blue calico.

"Them fellers from up north, they gonna put Hot Springs on the map. They're fixin' to buy up land for some kind o' business."

His mention of the visitors intending to buy land caught her attention and she glanced up at him. Discerning fact from speculation was a challenge when Mr. Dempsey did the talking.

He peered at the list. "Salt, cloves, cinnamon. Lemme see iffen we got sorghum syrup. It's a mite early in the year for that." He added the items to the stack on the counter, and kept up a nonstop chatter about how prosperous the town was going to become, and how all the businesses were going to grow. "Thet young feller was in here yesterday and said they was gonna bring— What did he call it?"

Mr. Dempsy knocked his spectacles askew when he scratched his head. "Commerce. Said it meant good payin' jobs." He straightened his spectacles and checked the list. "Slab o' side pork, bakin' soda, bottle o' blue ink. How many cakes o' castile soap?"

Dulcie selected her calico and set the other bolts back on the shelf. "A dozen will do. I also need ten yards of plain muslin."

"Ten yards o' muslin. Ya makin' a quilt, are ya?"

"No. It's for wrapping the cleaned fleeces." She laid out the calico. "A yard of this, as well."

He measured the yard goods and continued talking about what he called the 'excitin' goin's on.' He barely stopped for a breath while he cut the muslin and calico. "'Course, none o' that can happen till them fellers get the land they need." He tapped his stubby pencil on Dulcie's shopping list.

By the time he got all her purchases added up, her ears rang with the man's blather. She couldn't help but wonder if Mr. Dempsey had been employed by the two men "from up north" to advertise for them.

The storekeeper wrapped her yard goods. "Folks're sayin' them fellers want to buy up land 'round the springs."

Dulcie's hands froze counting out the money she owed the man. The uneasy picture in her memory of that man, Mr. DeWitt, studying their meadow and asking nosy questions sent a chill down her spine.

It's gossip. Nothing but rumors.

She held her tongue while Mr. Dempsey continued to prattle on about the benefit to the entire community. As he carried the sacks of flour and cornmeal out to her wagon, he repeated his earlier declarations of prosperity as if he wished to put an exclamation point to his words.

Finally, she could be silent no longer.

She looked him squarely in the eye. "Mr. Dempsey, I'm in favor of friends and neighbors benefiting from some kind of new business coming to the area, but you should know that *our* land is not for sale and never will be, no matter what everyone is saying." She held her unblinking stare for an extra moment before hoisting one crate on top of the other.

"Good day, Mr. Dempsey."

Carrying both crates impeded her line of sight, but she was peeved enough to resist asking for help. Two steps from the entrance, the door swung open and knocked against the load she carried, causing the crate on top to crash to the floor and nearly knocking her off her feet.

"*Oopff!*" She tightened her grip on the crate still in her possession, but the other one spilled its contents across the floor.

"Pardon me!" A masculine voice rang so close to her ear, she startled. "I'm so sorry."

"Miss Dulcie, you all right?" Mr. Dempsey called from behind the counter.

"I'm fine." Dulcie set down the crate in her hands and straightened to meet a pair of warm brown eyes. "Excuse me. I wasn't watching where I was going."

"Oh no, it was entirely my fault." His eyes swept over her. "Are you quite sure you're uninjured?"

"Quite sure." She began picking up her purchases to return them to their crate, but the young man stopped her.

"Please, let me help you. It's the least I can do." He bent and began scooping up each item, brushing it off before placing it in the crate.

"That's not necessary. I can—"

"I insist." A smile tugged at his tawny brown mustache. "A lady shouldn't carry so heavy a load."

A lady? Dulcie didn't consider herself a lady—not like the ladies who bought her yard goods. But she had, after all, attended the school in Asheville to learn to become a lady.

The man finished re-packing the crate and then hoisted both of them. "If you will lead the way, I'll take these to your wagon for you."

She showed him where Samson waited and he proceeded to secure the crates in the back.

"Dulcie. That's a very pretty name. Reminds me of the dulcimer the man played in church Sunday."

Warmth crept up into her face. "Thank you, Mister . . ."

"Gavin."

"Mr. Gavin."

His smile unsettled her. "Just Gavin."

Had her tongue not been tied, she might've explained that her mother played the dulcimer and that's why her parents named her Dulcie, but divulging something of such a personal nature to a perfect stranger didn't feel right.

She couldn't deny *Just Gavin* was handsome—she noticed that much. She drew in a steadying breath. "Thank you for your help . . . Gavin, but I need to be on my way. I don't like to leave my grandparents with all the work." She gestured toward the crates. "Thank you again for carrying my packages."

"It was my pleasure, Miss Dulcie." He gave a slight bow. "I hope we run into each other again. Next time, I promise not to knock you over." His eyes smiled and her breath caught.

He gave her a hand climbing into the wagon. She hoped he didn't notice the tremble in her fingers. Gavin tipped his hat. She gathered the reins and released the brake. "Goodbye." A strange tug of reluctance poked her, but she ignored it and slapped the reins on the mule's rump.

The toe of her shoe bumped the two jars of blackberries at her feet, yanking her attention from the distraction of brown eyes. Why had she brought the berries to town with her? Oh, yes. Hollis Perdue at the Feed and Seed mentioned he'd take them in exchange for a quart jar of honey. If Mr. Dempsey had already spread the rumor about the northerners wanting to buy land, Hollis would likely quiz her as well. She scurried into the Feed and Seed and made the swap with Hollis before he could ask a lot of questions. Not only did she not have the answers, nobody else seemed to be in possession of the facts, so even the questions were vague. Whatever land those men wished to buy, it wasn't Chappell land. She steered Samson toward home.

Accompanied by the crunching of the wheels over dirt and gravel, the *clip clop* of the mule's feet, and the song of mockingbirds, *Just Gavin* eased into her mind. He seemed a nice enough gentleman, but she had no time or inclination for romance—not when she was needed to take care of her grandparents. Besides, one of the things she'd learned at the "high-falutin'" school in Asheville was making proper introductions. The way she'd met Gavin could hardly be deemed proper.

The lines on the map spread across the small desk began to blur. Gavin leaned back and closed his eyes for a few minutes. He'd been studying the five pieces of property his uncle intended to acquire in the hopes of adjusting the lines in such a way the landowners, all of whom were farmers, would be minimally impacted. Uncle Arnold would call him a fool for wasting so much time—the people who currently occupied these plots of land were nothing more than inconvenient pests to be shooed away like gnats.

He squinted at the map again. Arranging the lines to include the source of the spring and the entire underground flow limited him to few options, because the underground spring flowed diagonally from northwest to southeast across the middle of the Chappell property. There was simply no other way to maneuver the lines to avoid encompassing nearly the total of the Chappell farm. His uncle required a buffer on either side of the flow, as well as a wide radius around the source of the spring. All the erasures on the map testified to the fact of Gavin's multiple attempts to find the best possible solution.

The Tate farm and the Huxley place would each be reduced by around ten acres. Uncle Arnold's plan only cut into the Cutler homestead and the Ludlow place six or seven acres. Once the Chappell land was incorporated and all the contracts were signed, his uncle's holdings would total one hundred eight acres for the therapeutic clinic and surrounding grounds. Gavin could only hope all five farmers were agreeable to the proposal. Uncle Arnold's architect back in Philadelphia was waiting for the final survey before he could begin working on the plans.

Even though his uncle expected his report first thing in the morning, a distraction kept pulling his attention away from the map. A lovely distraction, to be sure, but all he had was her first name—Dulcie. That and the memory of her walnut brown eyes and a wayward lock of mahogany hair that had escaped its braid. She'd blushed when he said her name was pretty. He'd been tempted to ask the man at the emporium about her—Who is she? Where does she live? Is she single? But he'd hesitated. She might not appreciate being the topic of conversation or the target of his inquiries.

Try as he might, he couldn't remember if he'd seen her in church two days earlier. His main reason for attending was to be seen and be friendly. He'd shaken a lot of hands, but didn't recall hers being one of them. Dulcie wasn't anything like the young women on the Philadelphia social registers. She didn't flirt, nor did she snub him. Despite her simple, modest attire and primitive wagon drawn by a single, swayback mule, he'd found the lady fascinating, even in the span of the few minutes they'd spoken. Most of the locals he'd met used crude grammar and spoke with a regional twang. Dulcie's speech, while definitely seasoned with a charming accent, didn't reflect what his uncle called ignorant and backward. He wanted to learn more about her.

He could only hope he would, indeed, run into her again.

CHAPTER NINE

Dulcie leaned against the fence and watched Grandpa shoo Gert and her two babies—the one she'd birthed, whom Grandma had named Petey, and Lily, the one they'd persuaded Gert to adopt—through the gate to the larger meadow with the rest of the flock. After spending a few days in the barn getting acquainted, and a few more days in the smaller enclosure, Grandpa was satisfied the trio had bonded and Gert had accepted Lily as her own, but Dulcie wasn't so sure.

Perhaps it was only her imagination, but Gert seemed to be nursing Petey more than Lily. Likewise, Petey stuck closer to his mama than did Lily. But as Grandpa pointed out, Lily was almost two weeks older than her adopted brother and was more independent.

Still, a worried sigh escaped. If Dulcie had her way, she'd keep them in the barn where they were safe. Even though they'd not seen any evidence of the bobcat returning, she kept casting her gaze across the meadow and along the fence line in search of the predator.

Grandpa fastened the gate behind the trio and joined Dulcie at the fence. Gert halted, as if she didn't know where she was. Lily and Petey bumped up against her, and Lily leaned into her, searching out more breakfast. The lambs didn't appear concerned over the larger meadow, but Gert visibly stiffened and sniffed. She let out a panicky *baa*.

The other ewes lifted their heads briefly to observe the new family and returned their attention to the lush grass. Their lambs approached, eyeing the newcomers, no doubt investigating Petey and Lily as potential playmates. Grandpa gave a short nod. "See there? They gonna be jus' fine."

Dulcie pursed her lips. "I'm afraid the rest of the flock will reject Lily. What if they try to hurt her? What if Lily tries to play with the other lambs and their mamas go after her?"

Grandpa shook his head. "Neither Gert 'r Malachi'll let that happen. 'Sides, with you and yer grandma in the wool shed over yonder, and me in the barn, we'll hear if a ruckus starts. Stop worryin'. God answered our prayer and gived Lily a mama." He tipped her chin up with two calloused fingers. "Dulcie girl, He don't answer a prayer and then yank it away."

Grandpa's faith never seemed to waver. How could he be so sure the little adopted lamb would be safe in the big meadow? Surely God had more important things to look after. But here was Grandpa, bowing his head and speaking to the Lord as he would a most trusted Friend.

"Lord, Ye know how thet little'un lost her real mama, and how we prayed thet ole Gert would take 'er to suckle. Ye heard our prayer, God, and we're mighty grateful Ye gived thet sweet lamb a new mama." A tiny groan rumbled in Grandpa's throat. "God, Yer a good Shepherd. Yer love is so great, there ain't beginnin' nor end to it. Now God, Dulcie here is frettin' 'bout thet little lamb. I'm askin' Ye to shepherd her heart jus' like Ye shepherd them sheep. Thank Ye, God for hearin' us an' lovin' us, an' for carin' for us like Ye do the sheep."

Grandpa leaned close and pecked a kiss on Dulcie's cheek. "Reckon they'll be fine." Contented pleasure threaded his tone. He thumbed the bib of his overalls and bestowed a look of adoration on her. "Mm hmm, God's lambs'll be just fine."

Between his prayer and words of reassurance, Dulcie wasn't certain if he referred to the four-legged sheep in the meadow or the two-legged one worrying. She pressed her lips together, unwilling to allow her doubts and resentments to spill out and hurt Grandpa's feelings.

Grandpa winked at her. "Got work to do." He returned to the barn, leaving Dulcie to watch Gert's lambs inspect their new surroundings.

Malachi trotted over to say hello to the new arrivals, his neck extended and his nose twitching, but halted when Gert grunted and planted herself between the dog and her babies. The ewe stamped her foot and lowered her head, ready to butt the dog if he came too close.

Malachi let out a soft *woof*, his version of *Howdy, Gert. Welcome back,* but Gert shook her head and stamped her foot again. The *baa* she bleated out this time bore no tone of panic, but rather sounded as if she was telling Malachi who was boss. Malachi gave a low whine and perked up his ears.

Dulcie watched the encounter, drawn more to the dog's watchfulness than Gert's defensive stand. Malachi intended no harm to Gert's babies, and the ewe likely knew that. She was simply insisting the dog keep his distance.

Malachi dropped to a prone position in the grass, his head on his paws, and Gert nudged her lambs past him. He followed them with his eyes, watchful without intruding. Protective, but not bossy. Dulcie grinned. The dog knew his job and how to handle the sheep as well as Grandpa did. Maybe better since Grandpa wasn't inclined to lie in the grass to watch.

She had to admit, Malachi had more patience than she did.

A thought unfolded in her mind. Is that what God had been doing with her all these years? Watching over her, but not pushing His way into her life? She squirmed inwardly, but couldn't take her eyes off the dog. Even from afar, he kept his attention on Gert and her babies, as if wanting to make sure they were safe and comfortable despite Gert's less than welcoming attitude.

Dulcie forced her gaze to the right and studied the ewe. Wary, standoffish, not allowing her protector to come near. Dulcie's own attitude, for more than a decade, mirrored that of the mama sheep—stamping her foot and lowering her head to butt God out of her life. Heat rose up from her belly and flooded her face. Comparing herself to a sheep wasn't exactly flattering, but then comparing God to a dog was neither gracious nor respectful. She'd pushed Him away for so many years, the separation had become comfortable. Perhaps too comfortable. Was it time to reconsider her grudge against God?

She couldn't deny God had answered the prayer for Gert to accept Lily. Of course, it might have been Grandpa's prayer rather than hers. Grandpa was one of those people the Bible described as godly and righteous. Grandma, too. No doubt the Lord listened to their prayers. But Dulcie hadn't given Him any reason to listen to hers. Quite the contrary, she'd given Him every reason not to.

But what if He *was* like Malachi—watching, protecting, listening, in spite of her rebellious heart? Maybe it was time to approach the Almighty and see if He was willing to hear her. Was she ready to drop her guard and let God in?

James clucked his tongue and urged Samson forward a few more steps where the mule could wait in the shade of the churchyard's wide sycamore while the family worshiped with their friends and neighbors. Dulcie hopped down from the tailgate to greet her friend, Hester. James set the brake and climbed down over the wheel hub, and then lifted his hands to help his Virginia down. Nearly as spry as she was fifty years ago and ever' bit as pretty.

As soon as she was safely on the ground, he leaned close to her ear. "That there new blue bonnet makes ye look like a bride, even purtier than ye was when we was courtin'."

Virginia clutched the Bible with one arm and swatted at him with her free hand. "You still know how t' make me blush, y'old rascal."

He grinned at her and looped her arm through his. Before they could take more than three steps toward the front door of the church, James's friend, Caleb Montgomery, hurried over to say howdy.

"James. I been waitin' on ye to git here."

By the look on Caleb's face, ye'd think his harness shop'd burned down. "Caleb? Somethin' troublin' ye?"

Caleb looked at him like he was trying to decide if James was a friend or an enemy. "Reckon that depends on wuther 'r not yer fixin' to sell."

Suspicion stirred a whirlwind in his belly. "Don't know what yer talkin' about, Caleb. What is it ye think I'm sellin'?"

Before Caleb could answer, Otis Hogan and Reuben Ludlow joined them. Otis nudged Caleb with his elbow. "You ask 'im? We all's wonderin' about what ever'one's been sayin' about them fellers—how they're wantin' to buy up half the mountain. They gonna buy your land?"

Reuben shook a fat finger, first at Otis and then at Caleb. "Y'all give James a chance to catch his breath." He shot a narrow-eyed look at James. "Is ye, James? Is ye gonna sell? Ye know how talk is goin' around about how them Yankee fellers wants to move in hereabouts an' buy up all the land for miles around. Luther Dempsey said so. Luther says them fellers is gonna bring pros— prosp— They gonna bring more business into our community, and more money. Luther says—"

James held his hand up and silenced Reuben with a scowl. The storm brewin' in his innards was about to bust wide open. He sucked in a breath and turned his scowl on Otis and Caleb. "What're you fellers gettin' so het up about? Y'all sound like a bunch o' cacklin' hens, spooked by a shadow. Ain't nothin' but a rumor, boys."

"But, James." Caleb's voice rose a titch. "They's lookin' to buy up all the land around the springs. I think they wanna control the water rights, that's what I think. You ain't gonna let 'em do that, is ye, James?"

Reuben piped in before James could take a breath. "They's wantin' to buy up half the countryside—all the farms hereabouts—"

They were joined by a few more neighbors, all pressin' in to listen and addin' their opinions. Eunice Mead waved her hand for attention. "What Reuben says is so. Luther Dempsey tol' Hollis Perdue that those men wanna build a new business in Hot Springs. You know what that means for all of us. It means our businesses will grow, too. More tourists comin' in. Rich tourists with money to spend in our shops."

Waldo Granger, the banker, puffed out his chest and hooked his thumbs in his vest. "New business means more capital. Ye need capital—money—for a town to grow an' prosper. I say if these men bring more money into town, then they're as welcome as a warm spring day after a hard winter."

A dozen people now crowded around, some bobbin' their heads like they was agreein' to turn over the deed to every parcel of land in the county to those two strangers. Others looked doubtful, studyin' on it. James could only hope folks would use the sense the good Lord gave 'em. Rumors were spreadin' faster than a forest fire, and by the sound of all the yammerin' goin' on, some was already formin' opinions.

"Well, James?" Waldo Granger arched his eyebrows to a chorus of voices. The doubts and questions fillin' the air in front of the church steps clattered like empty buckets at feedin' time. 'Peared like folks was split down the middle—some willin' to trust the outsiders to bring money into their town and fill the pockets of every neighbor, and them what wasn't so sure.

James released Virginia's arm and held up both hands. Folks was gettin' all het up and they didn't have all the facts yet. "Y'all, simmer down. All I've heard is a lot o' grapevine talk. Anybody here talk direc'ly with them fellers? We don't know fer sure what they're wantin' to do or what land they're wantin'—"

People James counted as friends interrupted and shouted him down, and he petitioned heaven for the words to calm their riled up tempers.

Virginia thumped her cane against the side the of the wagon, and the loud bangin' brought instant silence. She pointed the stick at Waldo, Reuben, and the others. "Y'all oughta be 'shamed o' yoreselves. Here we are, ready to step into th' Lord's house and worship together, and all y'all is screechin' and bawlin' like a bunch o' moon calves. Like my James says, ain't nobody got the facts. All yer hollerin' about is a rumor. Gossip." She clucked her tongue. "Y'all do remember the Lord's opinion o' gossip, don't ye?"

James bit his lip to keep from grinnin'. The way Virginia was wavin' her walkin' stick around, he wouldn't be surprised if she delivered a lick or two to some of the folks.

She shook a bony finger at the group. "Who is it spreadin' such nonsense? 'Fore ye start squawkin', ye best make sure yer speakin' truth."

Reverend Bradbury stepped out onto the front step and pulled on the rope, ringin' the bell to call the faithful to worship. James blew out a relieved sigh. One by one, the group broke up and headed toward the front door, a few mutterin' as they went.

James reclaimed Virginia's arm and patted her hand. Caleb Montgomery lingered on the church steps, pulled off his hat and held it against his chest. "I 'pologize, Miz Virginia, iffen I got folks to fussin'." He turned to James. "But what if they's some truth to what folks is sayin'? If one o' them Yankee fellers comes an' wants to give you a bushel full o' money for your land, wouldja sell?"

For as long as it took to suck in a breath, he pondered the question—a question he'd never spent a single heartbeat thinkin' about before. Virginia stared at him, waitin' for his answer. The betrayal in her wide eyes and lift to her eyebrows shook him all the way to his innards.

◖◗ CHAPTER TEN

A s Gavin passed the ramshackle post office with its front door propped open with a rock, the man behind the counter called out and waved an envelope. "Mister DeWitt. Ye gotcha a letter."
Gavin halted and retraced his steps. He had to duck his head to enter, the overhead part of the doorframe hanging askew. He accepted the fine linen envelope and thanked the clerk, waiting until he returned to the street to read the return address. Two forwarding addresses were scribbled beside the original ornate lettering, but the scrawls did not dim the grandeur of the missive. There was no questioning who'd sent it.

He tucked the envelope into his pocket. It weighed like a rock in its hiding place. He lengthened his stride to cover the distance back to his room. Ten minutes later, behind the closed door of his room at the Mountain Park Hotel, he retrieved the piece of unexpected mail. The gold-stamped address on the flap with its purple wax seal declared the envelope had followed him all the way to North Carolina from his brother's new congressional office in Harrisburg. Pennsylvania. He should feel honored.

Instead, the sting of jealousy once again burned his throat. He broke the wax seal and pushed back the flap. The filigree trim on the edge of the paper inside matched that of the return address. He slid the single sheet out and read:

The Honorable Harold William DeWitt
requests the honor of your presence at a Reception
May 28th, 1886 at 4:00 PM
to celebrate his official swearing in as Congressman for the Coventry District.
Reception will be held at The Abbey Gardens Ballroom
207 Laurel Boulevard
Harrisburg, Pennsylvania RSVP by May 17th, 1886

Echoes of Harold's accolades taunted him from the page, accomplishments Gavin would never achieve. Between each line, the disapproving frown of his father glared. His stomach tightened.

The invitation was forwarded first from his former residence in Philadelphia, then to Uncle Arnold's office, and finally to the Hot Springs post office. Judging by the post mark, the missive had followed him around for nearly a month. The requested date to respond was almost two weeks past, with the event taking place three days hence. Even if Uncle Arnold agreed to let him go, the train wouldn't get him there in time.

Not that he really wanted to go. He'd spent a lifetime in his brother's shadow. Why inflict more humiliation on himself? Nobody from his brother's social circles knew him, so he'd either end up sitting in the corner behind a potted palm or enduring the embarrassment of having to introduce himself as Harold's little brother who never did anything of importance.

Bitterness soured his stomach. He disliked admitting his resentment, even to himself, but there it was. He tossed the invitation on the desk and loosened his tie. Even if he couldn't attend, ignoring the invitation wasn't an option. He doubted the Hot Springs emporium stocked fine stationery, but the hotel might have something suitable.

He hurried to the front desk. The desk clerk flicked his gaze to Gavin's loosened tie and collar, and greeted him with a disingenuous smile. "Yes, sir. How may I help you?"

Gavin ignored the man's perusal. "I need to write a letter and have neglected to pack suitable stationery. Might the hotel supply me with a couple of sheets and an envelope?"

The clerk cleared his throat. "Of course." He returned a moment later with the requested articles.

Gavin gave him a nod. "Thank you."

"I'll make a notation on your bill, sir."

Lips pressed together, Gavin held back the reply that sought escape. Arguing with a desk clerk over a miserly charge for two sheets of paper and an envelope wasn't worth the effort. Instead, he forced a smile. "Very well."

Back in his room, he settled himself at the desk and stared at the blank paper in front of him. After "congratulations," what did he have to say?

Thank you for the invitation. . . Sorry I can't be there. . .

A cacophony of memories collided in his head, each one filled with plaudits and acclaim Harold had received over the years—praise Gavin had listened to from his youth with equal measure of awe and envy— envy that evolved into jealousy the older he got. How long would he feel small in comparison to his brother? He dipped the pen nib into the inkwell and took a deep breath.

> *Dear Harold,*
>
> *Congratulations on your well-deserved win to the state general assembly. I wish I were able to attend the reception to congratulate you in person. However, as you know, I am working with our uncle's real estate development firm, and have been quite busy traveling and assessing potential building sites. I apologize for taking so long to re-*

spond to your invitation, but it has taken nearly a month for it to catch up with me.

Because I am responsible for a great many contracts and settlements, the details for which can be rather complicated, I regret I am unable to get away at this time. It is imperative that I oversee the operations of our newest venture here in North Carolina to ensure the success of our investment. I'm sure you understand.

Perhaps I will have a few days later in the year to travel to Philadelphia, and we can enjoy a brotherly reunion at that time.

Yours,

Gavin

He signed his name and laid the pen aside. Unable to remain in the chair without squirming in discomfort over his exaggerations, he rose and paced back and forth, clenching and unclenching his fingers. At some point, the success he'd implied to Harold might become fact if he lived up to Uncle Arnold's expectations. *If* he accomplished the assignment his uncle had given him. *If* he proved himself worthy. *If—*

The letter called to him from the desk. He reluctantly returned and folded it to put into the envelope. But the inked words stared back at him. They painted a glowing picture indeed, a picture of a successful, enterprising, ambitious . . . liar.

Instead of stuffing the letter into the envelope, he wadded it into a ball and threw it across the room. He was tired of being a failure, but regardless of how much he wished to garner the acceptance of his uncle and the admiration of his brother, lying wasn't the way to achieve either.

He returned to the desk and took the second sheet of paper. After composing a short note of apology for the lateness of his reply, he added his congratulations to his brother, and sealed it in the envelope with the intention of taking it to the post office in the morning.

The folder containing the tentative land contracts lay open on the corner of the desk. He'd laid them side by side along with the map he'd been studying until his eyes crossed. There must be a better solution, something he hadn't yet thought of to ensure signatures on all five contracts.

He rolled up his shirt sleeves and loosened another collar button. "I'll make them proud-Uncle Arnold, Harold . . . Father." He swallowed past the tightness in his throat. "I'll make them all proud."

Dulcie slid a sideways look to Grandpa on the wagon seat beside her. The tiny scowl between his brows reflected his opinion of her insistence upon accompanying him into town. It was easier to keep her balance on a fallen tree across a gorge than to know when to let her grandparents do the work they'd done all their lives, and when to step in to help. She often had to bite her lip and look the other way when either of them performed tasks she wished they'd leave for her, but not today.

Grandpa was irritated that the grindstone he'd used to sharpen his tools and knives had fallen and broken into three pieces. He didn't admit to it, but Dulcie suspected he'd tried to lift it and the weight was too much for him. There was no point in telling him he should have asked her to help him. Rather than demand to go with him to town to get a new stone, she'd simply climbed up to the wagon seat and took her place beside him before he could gather the reins and release the brake. He'd said nothing, and she hoped he wasn't shamed by her actions.

Replacing a piece of their family history rankled Grandpa— she knew that. Perhaps if she could get him to reminisce about it, he'd be less disgruntled by her presence.

"Grandpa, tell me again—how old was the old grindstone?"

His bushy gray eyebrows arched and his expression clearly indicated he wasn't fooled by her attempt at conversation. "Yer great grandpa carved thet grindstone 'afore I was borned. Mayhap around 1795." He gave the reins a gentle slap on Samson's rump to hurry the mule along.

"I never learned the craft o' stone cuttin'. Wishin' now I'd paid closer attention. Iffen the old skills ain't handed down, they'll disappear." He tipped his head toward her. "Reckon there's a lot o' things your grandma an' me taught you. Sure hope you can pass 'em on one day."

A smile eased into her face. "But not stone cutting."

Grandpa's chuckle brightened his countenance and his dark mood dissipated. He leaned back in the seat. "I seen Daniel Montgomery moseyin' 'round you last Sunday. He ain't come to tell me his intentions yet. Is he fixin' to?"

Dulcie's face heated. "No, Grandpa. Daniel and I are friends. Nothing more."

A soft snort from Grandpa told her he doubted the validity of her statement. He nudged her with his shoulder. "Me an' yer grandma'd kinda like to meet our great-grand-young'uns 'afore we die."

The heat climbing up her neck intensified and she was grateful to see the town and emporium up ahead. Grandpa halted Samson in front of the emporium, and Dulcie scrambled down over the wheel. She followed Grandpa inside and listened while he told Luther Dempsey what he needed. As she feared, Mr. Dempsey wanted to know how the old grindstone met its demise.

The storekeeper scratched his head. "How'd thet happen, James? Grindstones don't jus' break by themselves."

Dulcie threw a glare at the merchant, but he ignored her.

"Whadja do? Try to bounce it?"

Grandpa's deep sigh reached her ears. "The wood frame had some dry rot an' the spindle gived way." He lifted his shoulders. "When I tried to lift the stone back into the frame, I dropped it."

Mr. Dempsey *tsked*. "James, y'oughta know you're gettin' too old for such things. Shoulda asked for help."

Dulcie gritted her teeth. Didn't Mr. Dempsey know when to keep his mouth shut?

Grandpa drummed his fingers on the counter. "Ye got one in stock?"

Instead of answering Grandpa's inquiry, the storekeeper brought up the topic that had tongues wagging all over town. "Glad ye stopped by, James, 'cause me an' a lot of other folks is wantin' to know if you're planning on sellin' out? Think about what that'll mean for our community. Like Waldo Granger down at the bank said, it's prosper-terity knockin' at our door. Oughta be a heap o' money for you, too. Means you can retire."

Dulcie sucked in a breath to fire a retort at Mr. Dempsey, but Grandpa's firm, quiet reply beat her to it.

"Don't got no plans to retire or to sell."

Mr. Dempsey hiked up one suspender. "Why not? You might get enough money as to get outa the sheep business an' take your ease."

Grandpa smiled, but it wasn't one of his usual soft, tender smiles that made his eyes twinkle. This smile looked carved into his face. "Why would I want to do that?"

The merchant narrowed his eyes. "Even iffen ye don't want to do it for yerself, think o' the folks you'd be helpin'." He gestured toward the open door. "Don'tcha know when that DeWitt feller builds his business, he's said it'll mean more visitors comin' in, and more jobs for folks, an' that means more money for ever'one. Iffen you don't go along with De-Witt, you'll hurt a lot o' people. Why, it's plumb selfish to keep that to yerself and not sell."

Dulcie seethed at the man's accusatory tone. How dare he insinuate such a thing? It was none of his business. She took three strides toward the two men, but Grandpa shot her a sharp look that halted her steps. She swallowed back the words she wanted to sling at Mr. Dempsey.

God, why can't You stop these people from spreading these rumors? How can You let people say things like this about Grandpa?

Grandpa stacked his forearms on the counter and leaned forward. "First of all, Luther, DeWitt, nor nobody else, has said nothin' to me about wantin' to buy my land. An' second, it's *my* land, Luther. It belonged to my pa before me and his pa before him. One day it'll be Dulcie's. Ain't nothin' selfish about handin' down family heritage."

Mr. Dempsey's face reddened. "Well, iffen DeWitt can't buy the land he wants, he's liable to take his business an' his money somewheres else."

Dulcie curled her fingers into fists. She wanted to grab Mr. Dempsey's apron and stuff it into his mouth, but that would hardly be ladylike, much less neighborly. Not that Mr. Dempsey was being very neighborly right now. She stepped up to stand next to her grandfather.

Grandpa cupped one elbow and pulled his fingers through his beard. "DeWitt tell you this hisself, did he?"

"W-well, no, not exactly." The color in Mr. Dempsey's face deepened, and he looked from Grandpa to her and back to Grandpa again. "DeWitt didn't tell me d'rectly, but ever'one's sayin'—"

Grandpa's tone changed to one she'd dreaded as a child. "You don't know nothin' for certain, do ye, Luther? You don't even know what kind o' business this DeWitt feller wants to start."

Mr. Dempsey took a step backward and licked his lips, one hand splayed across his chest. "But that don't mean—"

Unable to hear one more slanderous word against her grandfather, Dulcie could hold her tongue no longer. "What it means, Mr. Dempsey, is that you are spreading nothing but gossip, and in doing so, you are turning my grandfather's friends and neighbors against him without even knowing any of the facts."

The storekeeper planted his hands on his hips. He looked her up and down with a frown. "What it means, young lady, is it sounds like yer grandpa here don't have no intention o' cooperatin' for the good o' the community."

Every muscle in her body tensed and the back of her neck began to throb. Grandpa laid his hand on Dulcie's arm, and she knew he'd scold her all the way home for being disrespectful, but she was loathed to let this man utter one more word to damage her grandfather's good name.

Grandpa patted her arm. "Dulcie, go on out and wait by the wagon."

She hesitated, then spun on her heel and headed toward the door, where she paused.

Grandpa cleared his throat. "Luther, ye didn't answer my question. Does ye 'r don't ye have a grindstone in stock?"

CHAPTER ELEVEN

James pressed a hand to his sore ribs where that ornery ram butted him. Pullin' in a deep breath made him wince as pain seized him around the middle. Fool sheep. Tryin' to examine the ram's injured leg to see if he was ready to go back out to the meadow had earned James a glimpse of the ram's cantankerous side.

Ire stirred him and he grabbed hold of the ram's horn. "Now looky here, ye mean ole cuss. Yer a-gonna stand here whilst I look at that there leg." He slid a rope around the ram's horns and tied him to the gate post of the stall. The ram bawled like he was bein' slit up the middle.

"I oughta let ya run back out there and get hung up in the fence again, that's what." James leaned into the animal and pressed him up against the wall. "Now hold still 'r I'll turn ye into mutton stew." He ran his fingers down the ram's leg, lookin' to see if there was any more swelling or bone out of place. The leg felt straight and sturdy.

"No wonder yer so stir crazy. Yer jest fine an' dandy, and wantin' free o' this barn, I reckon." James straightened slowly, snaggin' a breath when his ribs barked at him. He dusted his hands on his britches. "Ya stay put for a minute whilst I get the back door open."

He headed toward the rear of the barn to the door that led to the smaller meadow. Every step sent a jolt of pain through his mid-section. He pushed the door open and propped a rock against it. Headin' back to the ram, James loosened the rope around the animal's horns, and stepped aside.

The ram stood statue-still, like he weren't sure what to do next. "Confound sheep. Whatcha waitin' fer? Git." James nudged the ram's backside with his foot.

The ram bleated and looked at James like a stray puppy.

James plunked his hands on his hips. "Iffen yer lady friends was in that small meadow, you'd be a-bouncin' out thet door." He limped toward the door, hopin' the ram would follow. "C'mon, you ornery critter. There's alfalfa an' sweet clover out there."

The ram peered at him from the stall.

James's belly rumbled with a chuckle, but he immediately grimaced. It hurt to laugh. "All right. I know whatcha want." He went to the open barn door and whistled. A minute later, Malachi came running. James rubbed the dog's head.

"Good boy. Now see what you can do with that stubborn ole cuss in yonder."

Malachi tilted his head and trotted into the barn, stoppin' to look back at James like he was askin' for directions.

"Bring him out."

Malachi darted into the stall and a moment later, the ram leaped out with the dog nippin' at his heels. He skedaddled out the door and into the small meadow as nice as you please for Malachi.

James patted the dog and told him he was the best dog in the world. Malachi licked his hand, barked at the ram like he was telling him to stay put, and headed back to the larger meadow with the ewes and lambs. James shook his head and pulled the barn door closed. There was some days he didn't know how he'd manage without that dog.

He latched the back door and began cleaning out the stall where the ram had stayed for the past three weeks. Naggin' thoughts pestered him while he raked out the stall. Askin' Dulcie to take over more of the chores weren't right. She already did the work of two people, what with all her mornin' chores, workin' with the wool all day, and then helpin' her grandma with supper, and cleanin', and laundry and such.

They wasn't poor and needy like some others, but they didn't have much extra, neither. He could thin out the flock, sell off a few more sheep this fall. Then they might be able to afford a hireling. But if he was to sell more sheep, Dulcie wouldn't have as much wool. Mayhap he should wait till next spring, after shearin'. But facin' another winter carin' for the sheep without help made his innards cringe.

He leaned on the rake handle and cradled his sore ribs with the other hand.

"Mr. Chappell? You in here?"

James propped the rake against the wall. "Back here. Who's there?"

A young feller with a thatch of yellow hair stood in the front doorway of the barn. James recognized him as one o' Hollis Perdue's strappin' boys. The youngster sure had filled out from the scrawny kid he used to be. He was near as tall as his pa. "Whatcha need, boy?"

The young man remembered his manners and stuck out his hand. "Mornin', Mr. Chappell."

James nodded and shook the kid's hand while he sized him up. He looked to be a right strong and able feller. Might even be useful around a farm. "Yer Hollis's boy, ain'tcha?"

"Yessir. I'm Tad. I'm the oldest."

Polite, too. Wonder, had he come lookin' for a job?

Tad pulled an envelope from the bib of his overalls and held it out. "Man in town paid me t' come and give this to ye."

A sliver of disappointment poked James. Appeared the kid already had him a job. Ah well, he couldn't afford to pay the boy right now, anyway. James took the envelope. "Obliged, son. Go on over yonder to the well an' get ye a dipper o' water afore ye head back."

The boy doffed his hat. "Thank ye, Mr. Chappell."

Tad got his water and headed on back down the road and James stepped back into the barn. What was so important that a feller had to pay someone to carry a message two miles out of town? James opened the envelope and unfolded the single sheet of paper.

Let this notice, dated the twenty-eighth day of May, Eighteen Eighty Six, serve as an official offer to purchase the seventy acres in Madison County, North Carolina, located approximately two miles northeast of the town of Hot Springs, and two and a half miles southeast of the state line bordering Tennessee. Said property is currently deeded to James Chappell.

Negotiations for the potential purchase will take place one week hence.

Signed, Arnold T. DeWitt

James scowled at the paper. There was some words there he didn't know, but he understood enough to know Dulcie'd been right about that DeWitt feller. He was curious about more than the way the water flowed. His interest went a lot deeper.

James lowered himself down onto the bench he'd used the past few years for sittin' while he sheared the sheep. Even now, the weight of that letter felt every bit as heavy as one of the sheep. After grousin' about that fool ram bustin' up his ribs, and needin' help to keep the place goin', was God givin' him a sign right here in his hands? Was this the direction he was supposed to go?

An ache that started in his toes pounded its way up to his heart. Sell the farm? The very thought plowin' through his mind hurt. How could he even ponder such a thing? From the time he was old enough to tag after his pappy, he'd listened to the man teach him about the legacy of the land, and the importance of passin' on that teachin' to his own children. He'd preached it to Dulcie, and to ponder otherwise was nothin' more than a betrayal. Sellin' the farm was contrary to everything he'd held dear all his life. But there it was, scribed on the paper in black ink. He read it over again, thinkin' mayhap he'd mistook its meanin'.

James bowed his head. "Lord, You gonna hafta show me clear what to do 'bout this. Ten years ago, I wouldn't hadta even think for a minute. But I'm gettin' old, Lord. Ye seen what that fool sheep done to me this mornin'. You seen the way I've had t' slow down, how wranglin' them sheep is gettin' harder ever' year, not to mention all the things what need fixin' and lookin' after. I don't know how much longer I'll be able to manage."

His thoughts traveled out to the wool shed where Dulcie and Virginia worked together. Burdensome cares where Dulcie was concerned had troubled him for years, but even more so now. The farm was her inheritance, but whenever God took him on home to his reward, she couldn't work this place alone. Trouble was, she didn't seem a bit interested in bein' courted. There was a few fellers around who'd asked her for a waltz a time or two when there'd been a barn dance, and two fellers had tried to outbid each other last year at the church box social when Dulcie's basket came up for auction. She was polite, friendly-like. But that was all. Seemed like she weren't even aware there might be life beyond the farm. If she didn't marry, not only would the farm be too much for her to handle by herself, the Chappell lineage would end with her.

The ache in his heart twisted, but the most worrisome thing lay in his hands—the letter. What to do with the letter? He'd surely spend some time prayin' on it, but the one thing he wouldn't do was show it to Virginia or Dulcie. Neither one o' them needed to be worryin' over this. Besides, he already knew what they'd both say. No, he needed time to ponder God's direction before he shared this with Virginia.

He rubbed his hand over his eyes. "Lord, tell me what to do." Listenin' for God's voice took patience. And time. And faith. And...

His eyes popped open. *The cemetery.* Generations of Chappells rested beneath the grass in the far corner of the meadow. Sellin' a piece of land with a house and barn on it was one thing, but a feller didn't go sellin' the ground where his kinfolk rested.

Dulcie lingered by the open door of the wool shed and looked at the road where young Tad Purdue had disappeared minutes before. She'd watched as Tad handed Grandpa some kind of letter. The very sight unnerved her.

She cast a glance over her shoulder. Grandma sat with her back to the door, leaning over the small spinning wheel. Was it Dulcie's imagination, or was she noticing signs of weariness and discomfort in her grandmother? Little things—Grandma's step was slower, her shoulders and back a little more stooped and bent, and the lines between her brows furrowed into a wince every now and then—a sure sign something hurt, but Grandma never complained.

One more look toward the barn showed Grandpa had already gone back to work. Curiosity over the paper Tad Purdue delivered grabbed her and didn't let go. But if she went to speak to Grandpa about it now, Grandma would want to know where she was going. She gazed for a moment at the hunch in Grandma's back, and a sense of protectiveness rose up in her, a desire to shield her grandmother from anything that might upset her.

"Grandma, why don't you take a break?" The words slipped past her lips before she could pull them back.

The spinning wheel halted and Grandma turned stiffly and fixed her eyes on Dulcie. The usual blue of those eyes that Grandpa said reminded him of the summer sky now darkened into storm cloud gray.

"What fer do ye think I need a break?" Grandma's eyes narrowed. "Is the work all done?"

She'd done it now. Grandma would be peeved for sure. Dulcie jerked a hand up and brushed hair off her forehead and tried to maintain an even tone. "No, it's not. But we've worked hard all morning. I think we deserve a break. Can I bring you a dipper of water?"

Suspicion pulled Grandma's expression into a scowl. "Reckon I can fetch my own water iffen I need it." She turned sideways on her stool. "What's this about?"

Dulcie sighed and gave Grandma a tiny, apologetic smile. "I'm worried about you. I can tell you don't feel well, and I wish you'd take it easier."

Her grandmother huffed. "Ye hear me grousin' 'bout anything?"

Dulcie shook her head. "No, but—"

"But, nothin'. Long as I can do the work God gived me to do, I'm gonna do it." She pointed an arthritic finger at Dulcie. "An' don't ye be tellin' me I'm gittin' too old. I'll have time to rest when I'm dead."

The words sent a chill through Dulcie, and she suppressed a shudder. She lifted her chin. "Well, I'm going to make a pitcher of lemonade, and take some to Grandpa." She turned toward the door, but before she could take three steps, Grandma stopped her.

"Wait a cotton pickin' minute." Grandma reached for her cane and struggled to her feet. "Iffen yer so all-fired set on lemonade in the middle o' of the day, I'll make it. Don't reckon you know how yer Grandpa likes his lemonade tart, since you al'ays put too much sweetenin' in it."

She thumped her cane harder than needed, no doubt to punctuate her annoyance. She started down the hard-packed path to the house, but paused. "Reckon I'll start dinner whilst I'm in there." She pointed her cane at Dulcie. "But don'tcha go gettin' no more ideas about me takin' it easy. I'm as fit as I ever was."

She made her way to the house and Dulcie watched her progress, certain she detected a more pronounced hunch in her grandmother's shoulders and a shorter stride. No, Grandma wasn't going to take it easy, at least not willingly. Dulcie would need to think of creative ways to distract her away from working so hard. Of course, that meant Dulcie herself would have to take on the spinning as well as the weaving. Perhaps if she talked to Grandpa about it, she'd gain him as an ally. Grandma always listened to Grandpa.

She returned to the loom and resumed marrying the warp and weft.

After a few minutes, however, she stopped and stared at Grandma's empty stool. "God, if You're listening, please help Grandma get over her stubborn pride and take it easy. I'm so afraid of—"

She couldn't finish the thought, as least not out loud. If God *was* listening, He knew what she was about to say. Instead, she directed her thoughts back to Grandpa and the letter that was delivered this morning. It couldn't have been a normal letter sent through the mail. They'd pick that up at the post office when they went to town. This one was carried to the farm and placed in Grandpa's hand. The same unsettled nerves that attacked as she watched Tad Purdue ride off returned.

Thankfully, Grandma hadn't seen the boy. If that paper had anything to do with the rumors going around town, she'd rather Grandma didn't know about it yet—at least not until she had a chance to discuss it with Grandpa.

CHAPTER TWELVE

The plush grandeur of his uncle's hotel suite reminded Gavin of his father's elegant study—a room Gavin had always avoided when he could. Then, as now, he only entered when bidden. He rolled out the map on Uncle Arnold's desk and traced his finger along the line that joined the Tate property to Chappell's. "This line could be moved another two hundred yards or so to the east if Mr. Tate desires, but here it includes a rocky ridge unusable for farming, but offers an incredible view to the west. I can only imagine the sunsets from that vantage point. Clients of your therapeutic clinic would marvel at such a view."

Uncle Arnold flicked his cigar ashes on the floor as he leaned over the desk and scrutinized the map that reflected hours of work. After a dozen grunts and *hmms*, his uncle leaned back in the desk chair and puffed on his cigar. His gaze still on the map, he gave slow, deliberate nod. It wasn't the praise Gavin hoped for, but at least his uncle didn't criticize his work.

Very aware of the fact his uncle always had a carefully calculated plan with every business deal, Gavin posed a question. "What is the next step?"

Uncle Arnold speared him with a steel-like focus. "The letters of introduction, stating the offer to purchase, were delivered yesterday. If these farmers can't read, and they likely can't, they'll probably have to go halfway to Asheville to find someone to read the letters to them."

The disdain in his uncle's voice rang reminiscent of his father's. Such a broad statement describing the entire population of Hot Springs seemed condescending, but Gavin chose not to voice his opinion. Instead, he jerked his thumb toward the window where a view of the quaint, mountain community spread past the trees. "There's a schoolhouse on the edge of town so there must be some literate people in town."

Uncle Arnold ignored him. "We'll wait a week." The elder DeWitt laid his cigar in the leaf-shaped bronze ash tray on the corner of the desk. "Then we'll begin with Chappell. From what I've been able to learn, Chappell is a well-respected man around here." He snorted. "As much as one can respect an ignorant hillbilly. He's the key to making this deal work. If Chappell will sign the contract, getting the others to go along with it won't be hard." His uncle pointed at him. "I want you to be prepared to talk to Chappell. Learn all you can about him. How long he's been farming that land and how much money he makes. The day I went out there and looked over his land, his granddaughter told me they raised sheep." He smirked when he spoke the word, as if the occupation were aligned with the dregs of society.

His uncle retrieved his cigar from the ashtray. He drew in a puff and leaned back, blowing smoke rings. "I never heard of anyone getting rich by being a farmer. Seventy acres at four dollars an acre comes to two hundred eighty dollars. That old man's never seen that kind of money in his whole life. You make him believe this is the best thing he can do." He pulled his ornate silver watch from his brocade vest pocket and opened the cover, scowling at the face before snapping it shut.

Gavin swallowed. Ever since he'd arrived in Hot Springs, he'd tried his best to accomplish the tasks his uncle assigned to him. If he pleased Uncle Arnold and somehow gained his regard, then perhaps such an achievement might make up for never having known a single day when his father was proud of him. He studied the tips of his shoes. Father was dead. It shouldn't matter anymore, but it did. What kind of a son didn't live up to his father's expectations?

On the other hand, every time he thought of the farmers his gut tightened. What if they didn't want to sell? What if they simply wanted to be left alone? He'd read over the basic contract his uncle had drawn up, and the terms were pretty one-sided. His uncle got all the mineral and water rights, timber rights, and right of way through the portions of land he didn't buy. The farmers got four dollars per acre. After traipsing through the countryside for the past two weeks, filling his lungs with clean, mountain air, quenching his thirst from a mountain stream, basking in the last rays of spectacular sunsets, gazing upon fields of crops grown in fertile soil, and soaking in the hot springs, he knew beyond any doubt the land was worth far more than four dollars per acre.

"Uncle, I noticed you already have the contracts printed up." Gavin cleared his throat. "How can you be sure the land owners will agree to the offered price?"

The elder DeWitt, who so closely resembled his father, waved a dismissive hand. "You have to remember who you're dealing with, boy. These mountain people are so backward, they'll think a few measly dollars amounts to a fortune."

Pleasing his uncle was one thing, but deliberately taking advantage of people was another. He did have a conscience, after all. Maybe that's why he never gained his father's approval. "But the land is worth more than four dollars an acre."

His uncle's face reddened and his eyes became slits. "I told you before, your job is to convince them to accept the contracts. Your job is *not* to tell me what to do."

"I'm not trying to tell you what to do, Uncle. But—"

His uncle leaned forward, neck veins throbbing, his hands gripping the armrests of his chair. "No buts! I don't care what you *think* the land is worth." The words spat out like arrows seeking a target. "These ignorant hillbillies won't know the difference, and four dollars is my offer."

"Yes, sir." Gavin despised his own cowardice. Acquiescence might appease his uncle, but it turned his stomach.

James drained his coffee cup and gave Virginia a peck on the cheek. "Good breakfast."

Virginia took his empty plate. "What you got waitin' on you out there in the barn?"

Her question stopped him in his tracks. How could she know about the paper that had been delivered yesterday—the one he'd hidden under his tools in the barn? Guilt sent skewers through him. In fifty-six years, they'd never had secrets from one another. Not a single one. He swallowed and tried to find his voice, but before he could form words, Virginia pulled a folded scrap of paper from her apron pocket.

"Iffen ye got time, here's a list of things I'm needin' from town." She held it out to him, and relief rained down all the way to his toes. His breath *whooshed* out and the lump in his throat went down hard.

Virginia cocked her head and studied him like she could see clean through him. "You got the mully-grubs?"

He took her list and waved it like he was shooin' off a fly. "Feelin' just fine."

Virginia clearly wasn't convinced. She jutted her chin and tapped the bib of his overalls with her boney finger. "Then what fer ye actin' like ye swallered backerds?"

He tweaked her nose and headed out the door. The creaky hinge on barn door squawked a welcome and he slinked back into the shadows where his workbench sat. He rummaged through the rough wooden box that held his shearin' tools. Down at the bottom, underneath the tools, his fingers found the paper Tad Purdue handed him yesterday.

The inked words hadn't changed overnight, nor had they taken on new meanin'. That DeWitt feller sure enough fooled him the day he asked all those questions about the spring and the way the water flowed. Mayhap he was losin' his ability to judge a man's character.

He tapped the paper on the work bench. His first inclination yesterday was to toss the thing in the cook stove. Why didn't he? How could sellin' the farm be an option? A naggin' deep inside wouldn't leave him be, poked at him all night every time he closed his eyes. Like a tug-o-war, two thoughts battled. All his life, he'd believed the only things more important than the land were the Lord and family. Family meant Dulcie. This farm was hers when he died. He didn't have the right to yank it out from under her.

What would happen when he couldn't do the shearin' anymore, or separate the lambs from the ewes? In his younger days, that cantankerous ram never would've got the best of him.

But sellin'? How could he consider it?

"Grandpa?"

He gave a start and shoved the paper back into the tool box. So deep in thought, he hadn't even heard Dulcie come in.

"Grandpa, I need to talk with you." She came up beside him and put her hand on his sleeve. "I saw Tad Purdue stop by yesterday, and I saw you hide the paper in the tool box just now. What is it? It's about the farm, isn't it?"

His own thoughts stated her right to know. *This farm was hers when he died. He didn't have the right to yank it out from under her.* He reached into the tool box and pulled out the letter. Before handin' it to her, he glanced past her to the barn door. "Where's your grandma? Do she know young Tad come out here yesterday?"

Dulcie shook her head. "No, she didn't see him. She's in the wool shed changing out the spindle on the big wheel." She leaned on one elbow against the work bench. "I don't want to upset her any more than you do. I suppose that's why you didn't mention Tad's visit last night at supper."

That thread of guilt tightened around his chest again, and he nodded. "I ain't never keeped nothin' from yer grandma before, but this . . ." He held the paper out to Dulcie. "This is gonna upset her."

Dulcie read the paper over, raised up her eyes to him lookin' like she'd swallered a toad, and read it over again. "Grandpa, why were you hiding this? You aren't actually thinking about selling, are you? You can't! How could you even consider such a thing—selling our home, our land, the sheep? All these years you've preached to me about the land and the sheep being my heritage, the legacy I will someday hand down to the next generation." Tears formed in her eyes and she swung her arms wide to gesture to the barn, the sheep, and the meadows. "Grandpa, we don't know any other way to live. This is who we are."

Pride swelled through him as he witnessed the passion he'd instilled in her. He beckoned to her to follow him out the rear door, where he could see the door of the wool shed and be assured Virginia couldn't hear him.

He nodded toward the fence, and she perched on the top rail. Where did he begin? Could he even speak the words?

"Rosebud, I'm tryin' to look at this from both sides. Ain't nobody knows better'n me how I've raised ye to love the land and love our fam'ly hist'ry." He stared at the worn toes of his boots for a minute. "I can't make a decision without thinkin' it through. An' talkin' to you and yer grandma."

She opened her mouth to speak, but James held up one hand. "Hear me out." He turned from her. Speakin' the words while lookin' into her eyes was too hard. "Dulcie girl, this farm, this land—" He pointed to the big meadow where Malachi kept watch over the flock. "Them sheep, the wool, the craft o' turnin' the wool into somethin' beautiful—this is *your* legacy. Sixty years ago, it were mine. Now it be yourn."

He forced himself to face her again. "You have as much say in this decision as I do, but ye gotta look at all sides of it. I ain't gettin' no younger, an' as much as it pains me to say so, the chores around the farm are gettin' harder an' harder for me. This ole body jus' don't have the strength it used to."

"But, Grandpa, I can—"

He hushed her again. Why did womenfolk always bust in before a man could speak his mind? "I know what yer thinkin', but you cain't run this farm by yerself, not lessen you sold off half the sheep. Then you wouldn't have 'nough wool to work."

He couldn't tell her how his bones ached before the day was half over, or how the ram had near busted his ribs. Tellin' her she couldn't manage the farm by herself was one thing, but pointin' out that she didn't have a suitor so there was no husband for her in the near future was downright hurtful. No, he couldn't say those things to his granddaughter.

"Ten years ago, it'd be a mite easier to decide. But now—" He shook his head. "I know yer heart, Dulcie girl. I know how you feel about the land and the sheep, and I ain't brushin' that aside. But we gotta be practicable, reason it out." He reached out and cupped her chin. "We need to pray, Rosebud. We need God's wisdom to make the right decision."

To his surprise, she nodded. Didn't know if that meant she'd pray, but at least she didn't turn away from him. "In the meantime, let's keep this 'tween us. I don't like keepin' things from yer grandma, but she'll learn about it soon enough. No sense in upsettin' her, yet. Let's me an' you think on it and pray on it before we talk to your grandma."

Dulcie reached out and snagged his fingers. "You already know how I feel, and I think I know what Grandma will say, too." Her fingers tightened around his. "But, Grandpa, what if she finds out before we tell her? What if someone from town says something to her?"

James frowned. "How's anyone else gonna know that we got this here letter?"

Dulcie pressed her lips together and dropped her gaze, as if there was somethin' she didn't want to say. "Grandpa, so many people in town are talking about this. We don't know if any part of these rumors are true, and neither do they. But if any part of it is true, then there's a possibility you aren't the only one who got one of those letters."

Her reasonin' made sense, and with it, another layer of concern threatened to smother him.

✒ THIRTEEN

Dulcie took the extended hank of cleaned and dyed fleece Grandma handed to her and drew it across the thin wire tines of the card she held between her knees. Twice, three times. The fourth draw produced a sufficient quantity of fiber collected on the wire teeth. Using a second card, she caught and extended the fibers until they were parallel and even. With practiced skill, her fingertips coaxed the wool from the card until it was rolled into fleecy balls, ready for spinning.

"This yearling fleece is especially fine." Dulcie fingered the plump roll of soft wool roving before adding it to her grandmother's basket on the floor. "Let's put this aside for the yard goods I'm going to weave for Eunice Mead." She tilted her head toward the larger basket against the wall that overflowed with thicker, coarser fleece. "Tag that basket for rugs."

Grandma nodded her approval. "The way folks is talkin', there'll be tourists a-plenty comin' with pockets full of money and nary an ounce of good sense. Ya oughta be able to sell all the rugs you can make."

"Grandma!" Dulcie put on a tone of mock indignation. "Are you saying people who buy my rugs have no sense?"

The lines in Grandma's forehead deepened as she flapped her fingers. "No such thing. You know what I mean. Easy to sell to them folks 'cause they got more money than they know what to do with. It ain't fittin' for a body to have more'n what they need."

For a fleeting moment, Dulcie wished she had that kind of money. First thing she'd do is hire someone to help Grandpa so he wouldn't have to work so hard, and buy one of those chairs stuffed with soft padding so Grandma could relax and put her feet up. A silent chuckle shook her middle at the very thought of Grandma taking her ease. Her grand-mother would call such inactivity nonsense and a waste of time.

Dulcie shrugged away the idea. A few of the young women she'd at-tended school with had daydreamed about marrying a rich man who could give them everything their heart desired. She'd always refrained from joining the conversations. Her heart was bound to the land, her family, and the sheep. She didn't need a rich man.

The troubling thought that rose to nag her from time to time in-truded again—she did need a husband to produce a new generation of Chappells. But how was she to find a suitable husband? With all her time taken up between farm chores, working with the wool, and caring for her grandparents, her list of prospects was short. Zero wasn't even a list.

She finished carding another fat roll of wool and turned her eyes to watch Grandma pick through the cleaned and dried fleeces with an ex-perienced touch. The woman could pick out the best fleece blindfolded.

"Ye wantin' to finish up the yearling fleeces before we start cardin' the others?"

Dulcie sent a searching eye over the basketful of carded wool, es-timating how much spun yarn it would produce. "Two more yearling fleeces. Eunice said she doesn't need the yardage until August, and I have enough spindles of rug wool set aside to get started on a new rug while you spin the yearling wool. Mr. Dempsey wants three different colors of woolens for the emporium."

Grandma pulled another fleece from the pile. "At the rate you're goin', your grandpa is gonna hafta whittle a dozen more spindles in his spare time."

"What spare time?" The laugh in Dulcie's throat tightened. "Both you and Grandpa go from before dawn to after sundown now."

A grunted *oof* slipped from Grandma's lips as she rose from her stool and fetched an empty basket. "Muddles my mind tryin' to keep all the orders and projects straight. You got yardage fer Eunice Mead on the loom, and here y'are talkin' about yard goods fer Dempsy's Emporium, an' all the while yer puttin' new rugs together in yer mind." She shook her head. "Don't know how you do it."

The compliment should have made her smile, but instead, a frown tugged at her lips. Organizing upcoming projects in her mind and preparing the yarns so they'd be ready kept the work moving forward. A pause in production delayed everything—delivering the goods as well as the payment received. They couldn't afford to not have money coming in. She had to show Grandpa she could keep things running.

Grandma returned to her stool and put her gnarled fingers to work. The silence in the wool shed was broken only by Grandma's humming as she worked the spinning wheel, and the clacking of Dulcie's shuttle on the loom. The rhythm of the two sounds wove under and over, intertwining the threads of each into comforting music that soothed her soul. Even though raising the sheep and processing the wool was hard work with many steps in between, holding a length of fine woolen fabric in her hands settled her. But the words of the letter Grandpa had received two days earlier threatened to unsettle her, and she directed herself to keep her mind on her work.

After a time, Grandma spoke without lifting her head from her task. "You hear any more talk 'bout someone wantin' to buy land?"

The question punched Dulcie in the stomach. She couldn't lie to Grandma. "Nothing that can be substantiated."

The wheel halted. "Sub— what's that ye say?"

Dulcie rolled her lips. It was at her grandmother's insistence she furthered her education and learned to converse with what the sweet woman called "high falutin' book learnin'," but she sent narrow-eyed glares at

Dulcie when she used those high falutin' words at home.

"It's only gossip." Grandma hated gossip.

"*Hmph.*" The wheel started up again with a rhythmic *whir*. "What's folks sayin'? An' before you go accusin' me o' gossipin', don't fergit I don't get to town as often as you, 'ceptin' for church. Makes a body restless knowin' someone's goin' around talkin' about buyin' up land hereabouts."

Grandma's word, *restless*, perfectly described Dulcie's heart as the contents of the letter echoed in her head, but the will to protect her grandmother mushroomed within her. "As far as I know, nothing is for certain. After all, nobody can be forced to sell their land if they don't want to." She stated truth, but Grandpa hadn't yet agreed with her.

Grandma's attention was riveted on the spider web-like threads twisting between her fingers. When she had something to say, she generally didn't hold back. If Dulcie waited long enough, Grandma would confide what was on her mind.

Grandma's tone turned pensive, as if talking more to herself than to Dulcie. "In fifty-six years, James ain't never kept nothin' from me, at least nothin' important. Don't reckon he'll start now."

Dulcie arrowed a glance at her grandmother. "Grandpa loves this land."

Grandma halted the wheel again and her rickety stool squeaked a protest as she turned. Her clear blue eyes, embraced by lines and wrinkles that mapped out years of sorrow and laughter, held Dulcie captive. "Child, this land is part of our family. Them hills and trees, rocks and meadows, the water that gurgles up from the ground to refresh body and soul, an' the dirt that's known the footsteps of five generations o' Chappells—the heart an' breath o' this here land is in yer blood as much as it's in mine and your grandpa's." Her eyes glistened with emotion. "The blood an' sweat o' those who've gone on t' glory a'fore us is soaked into the soil. The bones o' them loved ones that rest up yonder in the meadow are the boundary monument of this farm. This is yer heritage,

Dulcie. Yer the next caretaker o' this place God gave us."

Dulcie tried to swallow back the lump that formed in her throat, but it stuck and held fast. It didn't matter how many times she'd heard her grandparents talk about the land, or how many stories she heard about how her great grandparents and great-great grandparents cleared the land and raised a line of sheep that produced the finest wool this side of heaven, the words never failed to stir her own soul. She had a rich heritage, indeed.

Grandma reached over and squeezed her hand. "Don't reckon we've gived ye nothin' but a lot o' hard work. But it's hard work that raised strong families, an' we learned to love each other and love the Lord." Dulcie tried to pull her hand away, but Grandma tightened her grip and gave her hand a little shake.

"Grandma—"

"Yes, lovin' the Lord, child. Me'n yer grandpa, we know you an' the Lord ain't good friends." Blue sparks of determination filled her eyes. "But the Almighty loves you with a fierce love, girl. Ye can argue with that all ye want. Don't change nothin'."

Grandma released Dulcie's hand and the disconnection sent a strange chill through her. For the first time, the realization struck— holding God at arm's length also meant putting distance between her and everyone who loved God, including her grandparents. She reclaimed Grandma's hand.

"Grandma, I don't want to hurt you and Grandpa. I love you both with all my heart." Her breath caught. "But—"

"I know, child. Ye ain't forgived God yet for takin' yer mama an' papa an' baby brother." Grandma pulled Dulcie's fingers up and placed a gentle kiss on them. "Holdin' a grudge against God don't hurt Him, girl. It hurts you."

Dulcie pressed her lips tightly against the retort that swelled in her chest. She didn't like being at odds with God, but she couldn't forget all He'd taken from her. If only she knew how to set aside her resentment.

Threads of envy tied knots in her stomach every time Grandpa read from the Bible, or Grandma hummed a hymn while she worked. Faded memories of her mama singing "Amazing Grace" as she taught Dulcie how to knead bread, eased into her mind. Mama had loved God, and she'd taught Dulcie to do the same. Would Mama be disappointed in her—the same disappointment she saw in Grandma's face now? Yes, she'd uttered a few short prayers recently, but she suspected it was Grandpa's prayers God responded to, not hers. Perhaps the Lord would listen and answer Grandma's prayers for a husband for her granddaughter.

Grandma patted her hand and returned to her task at the wheel. The friendly *whirring* of the spinning wheel accompanied Grandma's humming, but she knew Grandma's words would return to visit her in the night hours when sleep was elusive.

"There were a young feller visitin' in church the past couple o' Sundays." Grandma slowed the wheel to twist the beginning of a new roll of carded wool roving into the one she'd been working to produce a continuous length of yarn. "Mattie Walton an' Ruby Keegan was yammerin' about him after service. O' course they was all a-flutter about him 'cause he's comely and they have daughters o' marriageable age. They was talkin' 'bout holdin' a church picnic, so's they can introduce their daughters to this here feller. Ain't fittin' to do it at church, but perfectly fine to do their courtin' at a social."

Dulcie had briefly noticed the young stranger from a distance—the same handsome man who'd collided with her at the emporium. She shrugged. Strangers came and went all the time, now that the Mountain Park Hotel was open. Of course, they didn't usually attend church. A thought fluttered through her head. What if the comely visitor was one of the men seeking to buy up land. She dismissed the thought. No, the signature on the letter Grandpa received was Arnold DeWitt, and she was fairly certain he'd not been to church.

She shook herself out of her musings. Grandma was speaking, talking about the women at church pushing their daughters forward to capture the favor of the handsome young man. Dulcie had only heard half of what she'd said. Just as she directed her attentiveness to her grandmother, however, Grandma steered a change in topic as deftly as Grandpa steered old Samson down the mountain road.

"Hear tell there's gonna be a barn dance over to the Montgomery place next week. Ye reckon on goin'?"

Dulcie fed a fresh weft yarn into the yardage growing on her loom. "I don't know. There is so much to do here, and now with the new hotel bringing in more tourists, I probably shouldn't take the time. I need to finish this length of fabric, and I want to get a new rug started on the other loom."

Grandma *tsked*. "Daniel Montgomery asked iffen ye was comin', so I reckon he's sweet on ye." She glanced over her shoulder at Dulcie. "'Sides, I'd kinda like to see my great grandchildren a'fore the Lord calls me home."

Dulcie grimaced. "I know you and Grandpa are anxious for me to find a husband, but it has to be a man who loves the land and the sheep as much as I do. It's the only way I can hand down the craft." She sent Grandma an indulgent smile. "Daniel and I have known each other all our lives. We're friends, but that's all. Daniel has always said he wants to head out west some day, and I will never leave here. This is my home." Dulcie paused the motion of her fingers and shrugged. "What if God doesn't have plans for me to marry?" God would do as He pleased regardless of what she wanted.

Despite Grandma's back to her, she knew her grandmother was smiling. "Ye prayed on it?"

Dulcie pushed out a sigh. "No." She had no plans to do so, either. As perceptive as her grandmother was, she likely suspected that to be the case, and Dulcie didn't relish seeing that look of disappointment on Grandma's face again, knowing she'd put it there. She'd swallowed all she cared to today about her estrangement from God. Dulcie redirected the conversation.

"Remember how you and Grandpa saved and scrimped so you could send me to school in Asheville? All three of us worked hard for that education so I could present our craft to wealthy clients. Now it's time to make that education pay off. I can converse with those people and present myself and our craft in such a way they think I'm as *high falutin'* as they are."

The quip, using Grandma's own words, brought a smile to the old woman's face, as Dulcie hoped it would. It wasn't as if she didn't like the barn dances. She hadn't attended one in quite a while and missed the fun. But truth be told, attending a barn dance simply didn't rank very high in importance. Not like the daily chores, helping Grandpa look after the sheep, and weaving fine woolens. Her most important job was taking care of her grandparents. A dance? Who had time? She had about as much time to attend a barn dance as she did to pray to a God who didn't listen to her.

 FOURTEEN

Dulcie caught Grandma's hand and looped it through her arm as they ascended the church steps. A few neighbors called greetings to each other, and Grandma returned their smiles and *good mornin'*s as they worked their way toward their usual pew. Grandpa tapped Dewey Tate on the shoulder and challenged him to a game of checkers whenever both of them could find a free hour.

Mr. Tate gave a slight nod and leaned close to Grandpa. "Need t' talk to ye 'bout somethin'." When Grandpa's friend saw Dulcie listening, he said no more, but she'd bet Grandma's best laying hen Mr. Tate had received one of those letters.

Mattie Walton scurried as fast as her rotund figure could move and planted herself in front of Grandma. "Virginia. . ." The woman's bodice rose and fell as she heaved her breath in and out. "Me an' Ruby talked to the preacher an' he said we should plan the church picnic for the first Sunday in August. I think it should be a box social an' give all the young men a chance to bid on the picnic basket of their choice." Her wide lips stretched in a smug smile, as if her idea was the cleverest and most original plan since the beginning of time. Then her tone took on a thread of disdain. "Ruby thinks we should have a pie bakin' contest an' have some of the men be the judges, but I disagree. Lettin' the men judge wouldn't be fair. Why, all them men would vote for their own wife's pie, don'tcha know." Since everybody was aware the men who bid on picnic baskets already knew which basket they were to bid on based on identifying ribbons, Dulcie suspected Mattie's opinion grew from her inability to produce a decent pie crust.

Mattie sent her glance skittering sideways and Dulcie turned to see what had pulled the woman's attention from her mission of seeking Grandma's endorsement of her plan. Coming in the front door was the handsome young man who had collided with her in the emporium. *Just Gavin*—she didn't know if Gavin was his first name or last name—graced several folks near the door with a polite smile.

While Mattie nudged Grandma and made a surreptitious gesture toward him, Dulcie watched as he spoke and nodded to folks on his right and left. Was she hoping he'd look up and see her? Warmth filled her face. What a foolish thought. Hadn't she only a few days ago concluded she had no time for attracting the attention of a man? Judging by the way a few of the young, single women smiled back at him, he could take his pick of any of them.

Otis Hogan began to pluck the strings of his dulcimer, and Ada Frobush followed with squeaky notes from the small pump organ. Reverend Bradbury squeezed between folks with an "Excuse me" and made his way to the dais.

Grandpa herded Dulcie and Grandma to their pew before Mattie could coax a response.

Dulcie slid one last look over her shoulder and caught sight of Gavin near the back of the church. Mattie Walton's daughter, Cora, sat beside him and smiled adoringly at him, but his gaze connected with Dulcie's. He gave her a tiny smile and nod.

A muscle tightened in her stomach and she averted her eyes, returning her attention to the front. She certainly hoped he didn't think she was looking at him. But wasn't she? Didn't a thin thread of envy spiral through her at the sight of Cora sitting next to him? She used one of her school chum's favorite words.

Preposterous!

Reverend Bradbury raised both his hands. "Y'all give me your attention, please." He motioned for Otis Hogan and Ada Frobush to cease the music, and beckoned to Doc Pryor. "Folks, the doc here has somethin' he wants to say." The preacher stepped aside as the doctor stepped up to the pulpit. He waited until everyone was seated and looking his way.

"Y'all know Duffy and Sarah Marlow." Folks glanced at each other, apprehension etched across their faces. "Their boy, Lester, fell from the loft window of the barn last evening. He's got a broken arm and collarbone." He rubbed his hand over his chin. "Most worrisome thing is he can't walk. Can't move his legs. I've examined his legs, his back and hips. Can't feel anything wrong other than some bruising, so I don't know why his legs aren't working."

A murmur rumbled through the congregation. Some shook their heads in sympathy, and Dulcie slipped her hand up to cover her mouth. Doc Pryor glanced to the preacher. "Reverend Bradbury is going to lead us all in prayer for Lester and the Marlow family. Duffy and Sarah are going to take him down to Asheville in the morning to the hospital there."

The preacher stepped up to the dais. "Let's pray together, folks." He bowed his head and began pleading with God for the healing of the Marlow boy.

Dulcie bowed her head but didn't close her eyes. She gritted her teeth. Young Lester was the same age she'd been when her family died. While she wished she had the faith to believe God heard the preacher's petition for the injured child, the memory of standing beside her family's graves as a seven-year-old girl wondering why God didn't answer her prayer loomed in her mind and crowded out hope for the prayers being voiced.

But what if God *was* listening? Grandma and Grandpa both believed God heard every prayer. Maybe now was the time to set aside her resentment toward God. She closed her eyes and joined her heart to the preacher's prayer.

God, I know it's been a very long time since I prayed, really prayed. I asked You to help Gert adopt Lily, and You did. She lifted her shoulders in a small shrug. *Maybe You answered Grandpa's prayer, not mine. But please, if You hear me, please help Lester Marlow. Grandpa says You are all-knowing, so even if the doctor says he doesn't know what's wrong with Lester, You do. He's just a little boy, God. Please heal him.*

Her plea to God all those years ago echoed in her soul. *Please, God, make them well . . . make them well . . . make them well . . .*

Reverend Bradbury and everyone in the congregation joined their voices in a resounding 'amen.' Dulcie startled and raised her head. The preacher shook the doctor's hand and turned to the congregation.

"Our prayers don't have to stop here. Y'all keep on prayin' tomorrow as Duffy and Sarah and young Lester travel to Asheville, and in the following days. Our God is mighty. We can trust Lester Marlow to His care."

Doc turned a grateful smile to those sitting in the pews. "Thank you, folks. I'm sure Duffy and Sarah thank you, too. I'm going to head back to my office to be with them now, but I'll be going to Asheville with them. We'll leave at first light."

Several folks called out their good wishes as Doc strode back up the aisle toward the door. Dulcie watched until he reached the back of the church, and she caught sight of Gavin rising when the doctor left. He paused only a moment, and then Gavin exited the church after Doc.

Uncertainty tugged at Gavin. According to the written testimonies his uncle had given him to read, the hot mineral springs were documented to have health benefits. If Uncle Arnold's plan didn't include spreading the word about the facility he intended to build yet, Gavin might be committing a grave error. Hearing the report of a youngster unable to walk or move his legs, however, changed his perspective. The child deserved every chance at recovery.

"Doctor, wait." Gavin hurried down the church steps after the man who'd just finished telling the congregation about the injured boy.

The fiftyish man with a receding crop of salt and pepper hair and a slight paunch halted and turned. He frowned, as if trying to remember if he'd met Gavin before. "Yes?"

Any reservations he might have had regarding his uncle's reaction vanished. "Sir, I heard you speak about the boy Lester, and his parents."

The doctor nodded. "I don't believe we've met."

Chagrin poked Gavin. "I'm sorry." He extended his hand. "I'm Gavin DeWitt. I think I might be able to help."

"Doctor Stuart Pryor." Doctor Pryor shook Gavin's hand. "Are you a doctor?"

"No, sir."

"How do you intend to help? If you're thinking of giving the Marlow family money to help pay the medical bills, I can tell you, they are proud people, and likely wouldn't accept it."

As much as he would like to help financially, the suggestion of using the hot springs seemed much more practical. He gave a dismissive wave with his hand. "Doctor, I don't presume to know how to treat the boy's injuries, but I do know the hot mineral springs have great beneficial qualities. I'm suggesting you might try letting the lad soak in the springs."

Doctor Pryor pressed his lips into a thin line and raised his eyebrows. "I appreciate you wanting to help, but giving the boy a bath isn't going to—"

"No, sir. Not a bath." A hint of urgency pushed Gavin to continue. "The heat and mineral content of the water have health benefits."

The man pulled his pocket watch out and glanced at it. "Look, you said you aren't a doctor, and I really need to get back to my office. I promised Duffy and Sarah Marlow I'd only be gone a few minutes. So if you'll excuse me—"

"Please, doctor." He didn't wish to be overbearing, but a child's health hung in the balance. How much should he push? "I'm not saying to use the springs *in place of* medical treatment. Certainly, the boy should receive everything you and the doctors in Asheville can give him. What I am suggesting is that the hot mineral springs, used in conjunction with medical treatment, might be able to enhance his chances for recovery."

Doctor Pryor cocked his head to one side and scrutinized Gavin. "What kind of scientific proof do you have that a soak in the springs could be beneficial. Don't get me wrong, sitting in that hot water is mighty relaxing. That's why so many of you rich folks come to '*take the waters.*' But before I can prescribe water therapy for a patient, I need documentation that sitting in a pool of hot water is going to accomplish more than getting the patient wet."

"What can it hurt?" Gavin knew his plea sounded like he was begging, but an unfamiliar desire to help this child, whom he had never met, urged him to continue. "If the boy can be safely moved from your office to the springs, and carefully positioned in the pool, what harm could it do?"

The doctor took a half step backward and rested one elbow on his palm, rubbing his hand over his chin. "Why are you so interested in the boy, and what is it about the springs that has you so sure the water can help him?"

Gavin held out both hands. "I've never met the boy or his family. But my uncle and I are here to establish a health facility that would combine medical treatment with the therapeutic benefits of the hot mineral springs."

Pryor crossed his arms and narrowed his eyes. "So this is about drumming up business for your enterprise?"

"No, sir." Conviction filled him and he shook his head. "We haven't even acquired the land to build yet. I have a stack of papers in my hotel room written by people who have used the hot springs for a variety of ills, and all received a positive result to one degree or another." He gestured toward Pryor. "You are the doctor. You prescribe medicine and other scientific treatment. I'm only suggesting you give the child every opportunity. If a soak in the springs can help, then why not try it? Can you honestly give any reason why the boy shouldn't take the waters?"

This time the doctor appeared to turn Gavin's argument over in his mind. Gavin took advantage of the silence.

"You said the family was leaving in the morning. Speak to the boy's parents. If they would be willing to let the child soak in the springs today, I'll be happy to personally help move him over there, and I'll pay whatever fee Mountain Park Hotel charges."

A myriad of emotions ran through Gavin while he waited for Pryor's response. A quick introspection attested to a genuine desire to see the child recover. But along with his good intentions, he couldn't deny a sliver of hope that his uncle would look upon his efforts with favor, and guilt assaulted him for his less-than-benevolent motivation, however small a part it played.

After a long minute, Doctor Pryor gave a slow nod. "All right. I'm not so narrow-minded that I will completely dismiss the possible benefits of water therapy. Be at my office in an hour. I'll speak with Duffy and Sarah, and if they agree, we will move the boy as soon as arrangements can be made." He pointed his finger at Gavin. "But I must warn you. Since we don't know yet why Lester can't move his legs, we can't rule out spinal damage. So it is imperative that he is moved with utmost caution."

Perspiration broke out on Gavin's upper lip. What had he done, volunteering to help transport the fragile young patient? What if he dropped the kid? He gulped. "You show me what to do and I'll follow your instructions."

The doctor gave a single nod, gratification carving a grim smile onto his face. "Glad to hear you're willing to follow directions." He turned to walk away. "One hour."

One hour. He lengthened his stride and headed to the hotel to make the arrangements, encouragement thrumming through him.

✧ FIFTEEN

Morning sun glistened off the dew-kissed meadow as Dulcie made her way to the wool shed. She slowed her steps and lifted her eyes to the mountain ridge fringed with pines and oaks, sweet gums and sycamores against the sky of robin-egg blue. Sliding her eyes closed, she filled her lungs with cool air. A chorus of birds greeted the new dawn, a soft breeze stirred the trees, and damp grass caressed her toes. The soothing *baas* of the sheep beyond the fence accompanied her grandmother's voice coming from the wool shed's open door as she hummed along with the spinning wheel. The music of the mountains.

She propped one foot on the bottom rail of the fence. A half dozen tasks called to her, each one waiting impatiently for her hands and energy. The new rug taking shape on the rug loom—this one with an intricate design and five different colors—promised to be her best one yet. Grandma had already exclaimed over it, insisting it was pretty enough to grace the governor's mansion in Raleigh. Even Grandpa stated the rug needed to fetch a higher price because it was taking longer to complete and the design was unlike anything else she'd ever made. Several baskets of cleaned fleeces still waited to be carded. This morning at breakfast, Grandpa had asked for her help with separating a few of the older lambs from their mothers for weaning. Laundry, cleaning, and garden chores never ended.

But for now, this moment, she let the morning breeze lift the tendrils of hair framing her face as she savored these brief, lazy few minutes before sitting down at the loom. She might have no time for socializing, and most nights she fell into her bed, weary. But this was her life and she'd not trade it for anything city folks enjoyed. Her heart belonged in the mountains.

She crossed the remainder of the still-damp grass to the wool shed, and paused at the open door. The elderly woman already sat at the spinning wheel, feeding woolen fibers between her skilled fingers as the wheel formed them into yarn. She glanced up as Dulcie entered.

"Wonder how little Lester Marlow is doin'. Been prayin' for the young'un since Sunday."

Dulcie shifted two baskets of carded wool rovings closer to the rug loom. She, too, had lifted a tentative prayer for the boy, but she didn't have the faith Grandma did. If God hadn't listened to her prayer, she'd not be surprised. But Grandma's prayer—that was another story. Grandma was as close to God as one could get to the Almighty this side of heaven.

Dulcie seated herself at the loom and picked up a fat skein of rose-colored yarn. "When I was at the post office yesterday, I heard Mrs. Montgomery and Mrs. Huxley talking. They said Duffy and Sarah Marlow took Lester over to the Mountain Park Hotel and let him soak in the hot springs."

Grandma looked up from the basket in her lap. "That so? They reckon it'll help him?"

Uncertainty lifted Dulcie's shoulders. "I think they were willing to try anything. I heard it was that young man I met—" She bit off the rest of her thought. No point in stirring Grandma's imagination. "A visitor staying at the hotel suggested they try the springs."

A frown carved furrows in Grandma's brow. "I thought they was gonna leave to take the boy down the mountain to them big city doctors in Asheville first thing Monday mornin'."

"I believe they did, but Mrs. Montgomery said they spent Sunday afternoon at the springs. Afterward, Lester said his legs felt like bumblebees buzzing. Doc said it was a good sign." Dulcie didn't look over at Grandma, but she could feel her grandmother's eyes on her.

"We need to keep prayin' for Lester. God hears."

Dulcie could have disagreed, but then she'd be contradicting herself. After all, she *had* offered a prayer for the boy, but it was a 'just in case God happens to be listening' prayer. Guilt gnawed at her. If she were God, would she listen to that kind of prayer? Regardless, she didn't wish to engage in a discussion about prayer with her grandmother. She already knew what Grandma would say.

She set aside the skein of yarn and rose from the loom. "Before I start working on this rug, I'm going to go check with Grandpa and see when he wants to separate those lambs from their mamas."

She hadn't yet taken a step toward the door when Grandma spoke. "Dulcie girl, how long you gonna stay mad at God?"

Dulcie sank back down on her bench in front of the loom and stared at the partial design winding its way across the breast beam. Before her, the warp and weft yarns in blue, green, rose, and butter yellow in a field of ivory wove a graceful pattern with curves and loops, like the music of the mountains. She'd never included talking to God as part of that music. The bitterness that tainted her heart had been part of her life for so long, she hardly knew anything different.

No, that wasn't so. She did have dim childhood memories of kneeling beside her bed with her mother and talking to Jesus. Distant, faded music. The sweet melody of that remembrance was elbowed aside by her recollection of weeping in the hayloft, begging God to make her parents and baby brother well again. That was the day prayer had become dissonant and strained, like banging on an empty tin bucket. Over the years, she'd fed and nurtured her resentfulness, and tried to justify it by blaming God for her loss. She wanted to let go of it, truly she did. How did one turn loose of a habit, an emotion that had her in its grip?

Out of respect for Grandma, she softened the tone of her voice. "I did pray for Lester along with everyone else at church last Sunday." She believed God heard the corporate prayers of the congregation, the preacher, Doc Pryor, her grandparents. But after she'd resisted God for so long, how could He listen to her now? She leaned in and kissed Grandma's wrinkled cheek, then hurried out the door before her grandmother could press her further.

Dulcie took her time. After checking with Grandpa, she returned to the spot by the fence where she'd lingered earlier and watched the lambs playing tag with butterflies and grasshoppers. Malachi raised his head and trotted over to her, as if he expected a handout from the breakfast table. She scratched his ears and fended off his sloppy dog kisses. The breeze dancing through the trees and the sun on her shoulders tempted her to take the rest of the day off and listen to the music. But part of that music—the *whir* of Grandma's spinning wheel and the slide and clack of the loom's shuttle awaited her hands in the wool shed.

She gave Malachi one last pat. "Go take care of your sheep now. Good dog." She headed back to the shed, determined to make up the time she'd spent being lazy.

When she reentered the wool shed, Grandma's hum didn't greet her. Instead, Grandma sat at the still spinning wheel with her head in her hands. Dulcie's heart squeezed and she was at her grandmother's side in three strides.

"Grandma? Are you all right? What's wrong?"

Grandma rubbed her temple. "Just a pain in my head. I shoulda knowed it were comin' on when I bent over this mornin' to pull my shoes on."

Dulcie brushed back a lock of silver hair and tucked it behind Grandma's ear. She swallowed and cleared her throat before attempting to speak. "You had a headache last week."

Grandma flapped her hands. "That were the day we was dyin' fleeces and the sun were hot enough to fry an egg on a fence post." She straightened and picked up the basket of wool she'd been sorting through earlier. "Got work to do. Best get to it."

She chose one of the blue-dyed fleeces and began picking apart the fibers, twisting them between her fingers. "Thought you had a rug to make."

Her grandmother could try to throw her off the trail all she wanted, but Dulcie wouldn't back down. "Grandma, maybe you should go see Doc Pryor."

An unladylike snort in response to Dulcie's suggestion bounced off the walls of the wool shed. "Foolishness. I ain't never been sick a day in my life. Besides, Doc Pryor went with the Marlows to Asheville." She straightened her back and set the spinning wheel in motion. Stubborn old woman.

Dulcie tapped her finger on her chin. Primrose tea was good for headaches. "It's a little early in the year for primrose, but I'll go through the meadow and see if I can find any."

A forced smile pulled on the corners of Grandma's lips, but the crease between her brows spoke greater volume. "I'll be right as rain iffen I can rub some mint leaves on my temples. Should be some in the garden."

Dulcie bit her lip, but tramped across the yard to the garden to do her grandmother's bidding. She climbed over the rickety picket fence meant to keep out foraging animals, and ran her fingers through the tendrils of pea vines climbing the trellises made of tree branches—thin, delicate as lace but strong as a spider's web threads spiraled out to grab hold and twine around the rough bark of the branch. Such a mystery how something so fragile could support the growing vine as it leafed out and filled the pods with peas.

Prayer seemed that way. Words whispered to God by a heart filled with hope and expectation of changing one's circumstances. Who was to say how prayers were answered?

Maybe all the prayers lifted together for Lester Marlow *would* change his circumstances. How, then, did she explain her solitary prayer when the ewe, Gert, was giving birth? Gert had taken to Lily as quickly as she had her own lamb. An answer to prayer?

Was that the key? As long as she wasn't praying for herself, but rather for someone, or something else, God listened. Prayers for Lester, even prayers for a sheep opened God's ears. If that's what it took for God to pay attention, she could be persuaded to pray for Grandma.

She moved down the row of peas to the corner of the garden where a patch of mint grew. "God, if You're listening, please make Grandma's headaches go away and help her to feel better. I'm not asking for myself. I'm asking for Grandma. She works too hard. Maybe You can convince her to take it a little easier. Please, God, for Grandma." She added a hesitant amen, and hoped with everything in her that God had taken note of her prayer.

She picked a half dozen leaves and held them to her nose. The vibrant fragrance of the mint did invigorate her. Perhaps they, along with her prayer, would do the same for Grandma. But wasn't praying for Grandma to feel better the same as praying for her parents to get well? That prayer hadn't been for herself either, it was for her parents. Or was it? Perhaps it was a selfish prayer. She didn't want her parents to die from the diphtheria, because she wanted them with her. Was praying for Grandma just as selfish?

A cold chill shook her.

James spoke a quiet and heartfelt, "Amen," and laid the Bible on the hearth. The words he'd read in Deuteronomy weighed heavy in his mind as he'd led Virginia and Dulcie in prayer, knowin' what he had to tell his wife. Virginia reached for her cane and started to push up from her chair, but James caught her arm.

She sent him a perplexed look. "I'm goin' to fetch yer coffee."

He tried to smile at her, but his face were froze as harness leather in January. "Sit. I got somethin' I need to tell ye."

She reclaimed her chair, glanced at Dulcie and back at him. Instead o' twinklin' like her eyes usually done, they snapped like she knowed all along what he'd been hidin' from her. "Go on, then."

He pulled the letter from his pocket and handed it to her. "This come a couple o' days ago, and I been ruminatin' over it."

She didn't blink as she took the paper. "Couple o' days ago, ye say?"

His conscience pinched, but he kept quiet and watched her squint and turn the paper to catch the light from the window. While she read, he looked over at Dulcie who watched Virginia with her lips pressed together.

Virginia lowered the paper to her lap. Those pretty blue eyes of hers goin' all dark reminded him of the way the storm clouds built over the mountain. "So them rumors goin' 'round town is true? That DeWitt feller thinks he's goin' to take our land?" She snatched her cane and thumped it on the floor, rattling the dishes in the cabinet. "Well, he can jus' go on back to wherever he come from, 'cause Chappell land ain't for sale—not now, not ever. Leastwise not while there's still breath in this here ole body."

She stood and shook her finger at him. "Mark my words, James Chappell. Anyone comes 'round here thinkin' on buyin' our land, I'll whack 'em over the head with my cane!" She thumped her way to the kitchen.

James looked over at Dulcie. "Reckon that settles that. We cain't have yer grandma in jail fer whackin' anyone over the head."

ॐ SIXTEEN

Gavin took a sip of his coffee to occupy his mouth while he digested Uncle Arnold's statement. His mind scrambled to form an acceptable response. After his uncle had gotten the reverend's permission to stand up at the end of the service yesterday and announce his intention to build a new health clinic that would provide a complete range of care for a variety of ills, Gavin had assumed their plan was ready to launch. But he didn't expect to launch it alone.

He set his cup on the table. "How long do you plan to be gone, Uncle?"

Uncle Arnold took a noisy slurp from his cup. "Two weeks. Three at the most. The Philadelphia office has some important clients who demand that I handle their closings personally. Then I'm going to look at some properties in Baltimore that could mean a very lucrative turn around if they are handled right. I don't trust anyone else to do it."

Gavin nodded. To protest his uncle's absence would imply he couldn't do the job. He gulped back his apprehension. "I'll take care of things here, the way you told me."

His uncle harrumphed. "You have all the necessary papers. The contracts include clauses that give us all the water and mineral rights as well as easements through adjoining land. They won't understand what they are signing, but that works in our favor." He pointed his cigar at Gavin. "You remember what I've told you. These people are backward and ignorant. That means you will have the upper hand. If they start asking questions about those clauses, you smile and assure them everything is fine. What they don't know won't hurt them—at least not until all the documents are signed and filed."

Doubt accused Gavin. His uncle's remarks implied that he planned on swindling these people, or at the very least, fooling them into signing a contract they didn't understand. Doing so might please Uncle Arnold, but using devious tactics pointed a finger of indictment at Gavin. Did he possess that kind of ruthlessness to achieve his goals, even if it meant using unscrupulous practices?

The elder DeWitt narrowed his eyes. "You've been attending their church for a few weeks, they've seen you there, smiling and shaking hands. People like this have to think you're one of them before they'll trust you." A sneer pulled his mustache up at one corner. "Use that leverage."

Gavin drained his coffee cup. "You said the contracts are already—"

"They're printed up with the names, legal description of the land, and the price per acre."

His uncle's interruption didn't answer the questions on the tip of his tongue. "The landowners may want to negotiate both the amount of acreage and the price."

Uncle Arnold lit a cigar. "They'll agree to what's printed on the contract because you will convince them to agree. You're their friend, remember?"

Was he? Did a friend finagle a signed contract from someone who didn't understand what he was signing? "I'm not really their friend. I'm only pretending to be."

A harrumph shook his uncle's belly. "You're catching on. You do whatever is necessary to get what you want in this world. If you want to be successful and wealthy, you can't let anyone or anything stand in your way."

Gavin blew out a breath he hadn't realized he was holding. How far was he willing to go to achieve his goals?

Gavin watched the train disappear through the cloud of black smoke. The elder DeWitt's words still echoed in his ears. *Take control of the conversation. Make them understand how this will benefit them. Use the threat that their refusal to sell will hurt everyone else.*

But his uncle's last statement speared him. *Don't let me down.*

Gavin rented a horse and buggy at the livery. He planned to target James Chappell first. He could use the Chappell contract to influence the others. He'd keep it simple—for a simple man, like dangling a carrot in front of a mule. The prospect tugged his lips into a tentative smile, but unease knotted his stomach. He urged the horse up the rutted mountain road.

Up ahead, the roof line of a barn appeared beyond the trees. As the buggy drew closer, the Chappell homestead came into view. A quick perusal revealed a simple, but well-kept place. Laundry flapped on a clothesline. Humble structures—a modest farmhouse and barn, both in need of paint. Beyond the split rail fence, sheep dotted a hillside meadow. A small outbuilding was tucked into the trees.

No immediate signs of life indicated anyone was home, but then the muted sound of hammering came from the direction of the barn. Gavin set the brake and climbed out of the buggy, brushing dust off his coat and trousers.

He straightened his shoulders and walked to the barn, pausing to peer inside. The hammering was louder, coming from the rear of the building. Gavin hesitated, allowing his eyesight to adjust to the dark interior. "Hello?"

The hammering halted. Gavin made out the silhouette of a man walking toward him.

"Help ye?" An elderly man with thin gray hair and a bushy white beard stepped into the section of light cast by the open doorway.

Gavin stepped toward him and extended his hand. "Mr. Chappell?"

"Yessir. What can I do for ya, young feller?"

Friendly sort. Hope he was still friendly when Gavin presented Uncle Arnold's contract. "Good morning, sir." He shook Mr. Chappell's hand. Rough calluses bespoke years of hard work. "I'm Gavin DeWitt." *Keep it simple.* Gavin pasted on a patronizing smile. "This place is very nice. My uncle visited here a few weeks ago. He liked it. He liked it so much that he wants to buy it."

Mr. Chappell didn't respond, but raised his caterpillar-like eyebrows and stared at him. Maybe he didn't understand what Gavin meant, but he wasn't sure how to put it in any simpler terms. Was the man dull-witted? Uncle Arnold had warned him these mountain people were ignorant.

Gavin moderated his tone, as one might do to soothe a distressed child. "My uncle wants to give you money and buy your farm." He gestured around them. "He wants to buy the barn, and the fence, and the shed, and the house. He wants to buy all the fields."

Mr. Chappell still did not answer. His eyes narrowed and his brow scrunched up, like he struggled to comprehend Gavin's words.

"Do you understand what I'm saying?" He spoke slowly and over-enunciated.

"He understands just fine."

Gavin whirled around. A woman stood in the doorway. The bright sunlight behind her framed her outline, but Gavin couldn't see her face.

She took three strides into the barn and he came face to face with the lovely young woman he'd met at the emporium in town. Dulcie. The girl with the charming laugh and enchanting eyes. His thoughts had returned to the memory again and again, and he'd hoped to run into her and perhaps take her to dinner, but—

Dulcie planted her hands on her hips. She circled around Gavin with indignation darkening her eyes. "Up until yesterday when you and your uncle made your announcement in church, I didn't understand why you wouldn't give me your full name the day we met. Well, Mr. *Just Gavin* DeWitt, my grandfather is not a simpleton."

Mr. Chappell laid his hand on her shoulder and gave Gavin a hard stare. "Now, Dulcie girl. This here young feller ain't from around here. He don't know us."

Gavin flicked a quick glance past her shoulder at Mr. Chappell. Did she call him her grandfather? Thoughts raced through Gavin's mind. The day he'd met her, he'd declined to ask the man at the emporium her last name.

"How dare you speak to my grandfather like that." Fiery darts shot from her eyes, and he resisted the urge to duck.

"I-I'm sorry, I—" Whatever apology he might sputter out was too late. She was already loading up for bear, and he envisioned his hide stretched out across the side of the barn.

"Who do you think you are, speakin' to my grandfather like he doesn't have a brain in his head? You ever learn common courtesy or how to respect your elders?" She took a step toward him. Her scathing tone raked his ears. "You don't speak to *nobody* that way, 'specially a man who's worked hard all his life, and probably has more wisdom in his pinkie finger than you have in your entire bein'."

She advanced another step, and had the circumstances been different, he would have welcomed her closeness. Her lapse in proper speech hinted at her ire. As it was, he gave backing up some serious consideration.

"Dulc— I mean, Miss Chappell, I didn't—"

"Let me tell you somethin', Mr. DeWitt. A man who's disrespectful to his elders is a despicable man. The book of Proverbs says white hair on an aged man is a crown o' glory to him if he's a righteous man, and my grandfather is as righteous a man as you'll ever find."

In the space of time she took to gulp a breath, Gavin saw her fervent zeal. Was it her faith? Her loyalty to her grandfather? Or was she simply defending her territory? His jaw dropped open in awe, but she clearly wasn't finished yet. He braced himself.

Dulcie pointed to her grandfather. "You know how old this man is? He's seventy-four years old. He's worked this land for sixty-eight of those years. He's bent his back and dirtied his hands—somethin' I suspect you know nothin' about—and has carried on the legacy handed down from his father. He's a man of honor and integrity, and might I add, intelligence. He does not deserve to be treated the way you treated him." A vein at her temple twitched and she fisted her fingers. "The book of Hebrews says we're to give reverence to our fathers and our fathers' fathers. Reverence is deep respect. Do *you* understand what *I'm* sayin'?"

Her jaw line stiffened and the eyes he'd not been able to forget made themselves even more unforgettable as they carved him with searing heat. "You an' your uncle think you're so high an' mighty." She shook her finger at him as one might admonish a rebellious child. "'Pride goeth before destruction, and an haughty spirit before a fall. Better it is to be of an humble spirit with the lowly, than to divide the spoil with the proud.'"

Gavin suspected her last recitation also came from scripture, and he was standing on unfamiliar ground. He'd attended church the past few Sundays, but it was all for show. Shame crept up and warmed his face.

Mr. Chappell slipped a gentle arm around her and spoke quietly, but firmly. "That's enough, Dulcie girl. I reckon this young feller's had all the preachin' he can stand. Y'all go on back an' see to yer grandma, now. Me an' Mr. DeWitt will have a little talk 'fore he heads on back to town."

She hugged her grandfather, sent Gavin a scathing glare that no doubt was a warning to remember his manners, and huffed as she brushed past him and out the door.

Gavin pulled in an uncertain breath. "Mr. Chappell, I apologize. I certainly didn't mean to offend you."

James Chappell folded his arms over the bib of his faded overalls.

"Young feller, what my granddaughter was tryin' to tell you is this here land's been in our family for five generations. We done worked it, sweated over it, bled over it, an' cared for it 'cause God gived it to us. It's our legacy." One corner of his mouth pulled at his white whiskers, and Gavin wasn't sure, but he thought he saw Chappell wink. "I know that's a high-falutin' word, but I b'lieve I used it right."

The heat in Gavin's face intensified, but Chappell simply tilted his head toward the door, indicating he wanted Gavin to follow him. He stopped in the yard beside the well and faced the hillside dotted with sheep. "See that? This be the land God gived us." Chappell hooked his thumbs in his pockets. "'And thou shalt do that which is right and good in the sight of the Lord; that it may be well with thee, and that thou mayest go in and possess the good land which the Lord sware unto thy fathers.' That's in the Good Book, too. Deuteronomy, chapter six."

He hoisted the bucket up from the depths of the well and handed Gavin the dipper. "Have yourself a cold drink o' water 'fore ye head back." He patted Gavin's shoulder. "An' ye can tell yer uncle I don't never plan on sellin' our land." He walked away without another word.

Gavin watched the shadows of the barn's interior swallow the old man. He felt like he'd just been to school, and the education he'd received humbled him. Not only was his uncle wrong about these people—they weren't ignorant—his plan for procuring the land was flawed. He'd not considered the connection these mountain people had with the land. They viewed their land like their life blood.

The newly acquired knowledge that still had his head spinning, however, was learning Dulcie was James Chappell's granddaughter. He scooped up a dipperful of water and let the cold refreshment slide down his throat and cool his embarrassment. Dulcie's fervent protection of her grandfather and her readiness to go to battle over their land startled him. It was a quality he'd never seen before in a woman. He'd noticed she was well-spoken and educated the day they'd met in the emporium, but her anger caused her Appalachian heritage to spill over.

He dropped the dipper back into the bucket and walked to his buggy. With one last look over the hillside these people cherished, he climbed in and set the horse in motion. He had a lot to think about.

James smiled to himself. Of all things, he'd pert near had a spell when Dulcie'd spit out the scripture verses without so much as a blink. Reckon he shouldn't be surprised. God's word didn't return void, and Dulcie grew up listenin' to him and Virginia quote scripture. Them verses was rooted in her mind, and no amount of turning away from God would erase them, no matter how hard she tried to ignore them. A battle raged in her soul that had nothin' to do with that DeWitt feller wantin' to buy their farm.

He set back to work repairing one of the feed bins and rolled over in his mind the events of the past fifteen minutes. Once again he realized Dulcie's distrust of DeWitt the day he'd come askin' questions about the spring had been right.

His earlier thoughts about sellin' the farm came back to nag him, but he figured whether or not to sell was up to Dulcie. He still fretted over her not havin' a husband to help her work the land. Taking on the farm and sheep, as well as washin', dyin', spinnin', and weavin' the wool would be a load of work when he and Virginia passed on. Not that Dulcie wasn't strong and able. He'd put her skills up against any man's. But there were some things a body ought not to try to do alone.

SEVENTEEN

Dulcie pulled her brow into a frown. Grandma had always told her that God's word would find its way into her heart one way or another. Spouting those scriptures may well have produced the desired effect on Gavin DeWitt, but hearing them spilling so effortlessly from her own lips took her aback. She suspected her grandparents' prayers had something to do with anchoring those words in her subconscious.

Dulcie stepped into the wool shed and reclaimed her seat at the loom. Grandma's spinning wheel still maintained an easy rhythm. Hopefully, she wouldn't have to relate the exchange that had taken place in the barn. No point in upsetting Grandma.

"Who was that feller that was here?"

So much for hoping. "Nobody important."

Grandma threaded another section of roving into the fibers she was twisting and feeding onto the wheel. "You tellin' me he lost his way and needed pointin' back toward town?"

Dulcie grimaced. She couldn't tell Grandma a falsehood. "You remember the two men who made the announcement in church yesterday?"

The spinning wheel slowed. "Two fellers named DeWitt."

Vexation tightened Dulcie's gut. "The man who stopped by is Arnold DeWitt's nephew. He came to tell Grandpa his uncle wants to buy our land."

The wheel halted, but before her grandmother could utter a syllable of indignation, Dulcie held up her hand. "You know Grandpa will never sell. Gav—that is, Mr. DeWitt doesn't understand our ways. At least he didn't. I think he does now."

Grandma's sharp blue eyes sparked. "I hope your grandpa gave him what for."

Dulcie bit her lip. Grandpa didn't, but she had, and she wasn't terribly polite about it. But then neither was Gavin. Gavin *DeWitt!*

Up until yesterday, she hadn't realized who he was. She should have known an outlander wouldn't come to the mountains with any other goals but self-indulgence. Had she been so bewitched by his handsome face that she'd allowed foolish notions to blind her? Good thing Grandma couldn't read her thoughts.

She'd fantasized about seeing him again, and welcomed him into her dreams. Her foolish imaginations crumbled when he'd spoken so condescendingly to her grandfather. She'd always been wary of outsiders. Other than selling her woolen goods to them, she'd never had much use for anyone she didn't know and therefore couldn't trust. She hazarded a glance at her grandmother and found her waiting for an answer.

"You know Grandpa. He never speaks ill of anyone."

Grandma grunted and set the wheel in motion again. "Sometimes I wished he'd get his dander up. There be things in this life worth a man's ire." She mumbled something under her breath Dulcie couldn't hear. Maybe that was a good thing, too.

"Mr. DeWitt isn't from around here. He doesn't understand our ways or what the land means to us." Dulcie shook her head as she echoed Grandpa's observation. How could she have ever indulged in fancy dreams over the man?

She set to work, but her thoughts kept returning to Gavin DeWitt. She hoped he didn't realize the blow her pride had taken. Regardless of how appealing she found him, he had no conception of what their heritage meant to them. She'd tried to tell him in the barn, but judging by the deep creases between his brows, either anger or confusion prevented him from truly hearing what she said. She wished she'd hidden behind the barn door and listened to what Grandpa said to him. Given how he'd talked to Grandpa, however, she doubted Gavin had listened to him, either.

Dulcie rolled her head from side to side to release the tension in her shoulders. If circumstances were different, she might enjoy sharing with him the ways of the mountain folk and the weight of importance they put on their land and family history. But as long as the man talked down to Grandpa and treated him like an imbecile, she'd not waste her time—either trying to educate him or dreaming about him. She only hoped he didn't notice her attraction.

The sun grazed the treetops along the ridge to the west by the time Gavin halted the buggy horse outside the livery in Hot Springs. His shoulders drooped with the thought of having to tell Uncle Arnold he'd been unsuccessful. Four of the five farmers whose land his uncle wanted to buy had told him no.

That wasn't entirely true. Three of them had scratched their head or stroked their beard and asked what James Chappell had told him. Tiptoeing around the answer hadn't worked. Narrow-eyed frowns had met his attempts to be elusive. These people whom his uncle declared ignorant were mighty wary of anyone who wasn't one of them. James Chappell apparently was held in high esteem by his neighbors, because there was only one man—Dewey Tate—who had been ready to sign. Even he wanted to know if the others were going to sell before he'd agree. Once

Gavin admitted his uncle required all five contracts for the deal to proceed, Tate refused to sign.

Clearly his target had to be James Chappell, but Uncle Arnold's tactics weren't effective. Gavin drew in a deep breath. With his uncle gone for a couple of weeks, he had a respite—enough time to come up with a different way to approach Chappell. His uncle might not approve of Gavin deviating from the plan, but there was no choice. If he could hand his uncle five signed contracts upon his return to Hot Springs, Gavin doubted Uncle Arnold would care how he managed it.

The livery man—Otis something or other—stepped out and took hold of the reins. His shaggy beard brushed the top button of his faded denim shirt, and he wiped perspiration from his forehead on his dirty sleeve. "Howdy, Mr. *DeeWatt*."

Gavin cringed, imagining his uncle's indignant response to the mispronunciation. He climbed from the buggy and retrieved his portfolio of papers from the seat. "Good evening, Mr. . . . ."

The man let loose a stream of tobacco juice that landed a few inches from Gavin's shoe. "Hogan." He pointed to the lopsided sign that hung above the double doors proclaiming *Hogan's Livery* in faded and chipped green paint. "Otis Hogan." Hogan patted the horse's neck. "Heard you an' yer uncle tell the congregation y'all're fixin' to build another hotel, or somethin' or other. We already got one. What for we need another 'un?"

Gavin wasn't in the mood to try to explain all their plan entailed. He'd had a long and disappointing day, and all he wanted was a hot meal and a comfortable bed. Chatting with the locals wasn't in his plans for the evening. He turned around and met Hogan's raised eyebrows and puzzled expression. The liveryman pulled off his hat and scratched his head.

"I'm jes' wonderin' 'cause iffen the town's gonna grow, mayhap I oughta build on." He gestured toward the side of the livery where a half dozen horses meandered around in a fenced enclosure. Hogan straightened his shoulders and thumbed his suspenders. "I run the town's only livery, y'know. Wouldn't be right for them tourist folks to not be able to rent 'em a horse or rig."

Pride colored the man's tone and he leaned forward toward Gavin, as if sharing a confidence. "Iffen there's gonna be another . . . what is it they're callin' it? A reesort. Well then, Hogan's Livery's gotta be able to meet all the needs, y'know."

"Y-yes." A light crept into Gavin's conscious thought, as the pieces of Mr. Hogan's reasoning fit together. "Yes, I understand, and you're right about wanting to be prepared. The new resort will be bigger, and will serve a wide variety of health needs in addition to offering some of the same benefits and amenities as the existing resort."

A tiny furrow creased Mr. Hogan's brow, signaling a less than complete understanding.

Gavin attempted to slow his mounting eagerness to redirect his uncle's plan, based on the livery man's comments. "You're right, Mr. Hogan. When the new resort is built, it will mean more business for the town. Not only for Hogan's Livery, but Mr. Dempsey's Emporium, the bank, the cafe, the ladies' dress shop, the hardware store, the harness maker, the wheelwright—everyone in town will see their businesses grow."

As Gavin spoke, Otis Hogan's eyes widened. "Jes' like a boom town, huh?"

Gavin grinned. "We have to get the resort built first." He stroked his chin and then pointed to Hogan. "You might be able to help get things going, Mr. Hogan."

"Me?" The man's thick gray eyebrows shot upward.

"Yes, sir." Gavin clapped him on the shoulder. "If you will talk to some of the other merchants and business owners, and help them understand what the new resort will mean to them, the whole town will support the project."

A smug grin pulled at Hogan's beard. "Y'know, the mayor is my brother-in-law. I could talk to him. Lots o' folks here 'bouts listen to him. An' I could talk to ole Waldo Granger, too." Hogan stroked his tangled beard and twisted his lips as if he was planning on letting another spit of tobacco juice fly.

Gavin stepped sideways to avoid being in the line of fire. "And who is Mr. Granger?"

Hogan looked at him like he didn't have a bit of common sense. "Waal, he's the banker, o' course. An' he's on the town council."

"Of course. By all means, talk to Mr. Granger. And your brother-in-law, the mayor, too." Gavin hiked up his portfolio to his shoulder. "I'll speak with Luther Dempsey first thing in the morning. We'll let everyone know how good the new resort will be for the entire community. Thank you, Mr. Hogan." He turned in the direction of the hotel, but halted and turned back to the livery man. "If it's all right with you, could I reserve that horse and rig? I'll be needing it regularly."

Hogan spat and bobbed his head. "Yessir, Mr. *DeeWatt*."

Gavin strode toward the hotel. He cared little if the man could pronounce his name correctly if he'd help gather community support for the project. If James Chappell and the others knew that building the resort would help the town and bring prosperity to their friends and neighbors, that might be the motivation for them to sell. The question was how much latitude could he employ to close the deals without riling his uncle's anger?

James barely had to tug on the reins for Old Samson to halt in front of the Feed and Seed. The mule knew where he was going as well as James did. He set the brake and wound the reins around the lever before climbin' down from the wagon. His old bones protested even the memory of the way he used to jump down from the wagon seat.

Hollis Perdue met him at the door. "Hey there, James."

"Mornin', Hollis." James pulled his hat off and mopped his brow with his faded bandana.

"You here for a game o' checkers?"

James slapped his hat back on his head and stuffed the bandana into his pocket. "Nope. Got me too much work to do. Need me some cracked field corn and buckwheat. Sorghum heads, too, iffen ye got 'em. Virginia's got her a couple o' dozen chicks and bantams she wants to fatten up, and she ain't got enough tater peelin's and kitchen scratch to go around."

Hollis pulled a burlap sack from the stack and shook it open. Dust and grain particles flew in every direction. "How much ye needin'?"

James ran his sleeve across his nose to block the dust. "Reckon twenty pounds oughta be enough. Them chicks are growin' fast. Be ready to eat grasshoppers an' forage 'longside their mamas 'fore too long."

Hollis gave a single nod and began dumpin' scoops of cracked corn and buckwheat into the scale hopper. "Ye can have them sorghum heads piled up out back. No charge."

James raised one eyebrow. Hollis was his friend, but he'd never known the man to give anything away for free. "Mighty generous of ye. It ain't my birthday, y' know."

The needle on the scale wobbled over the twenty pound mark, and Hollis dumped the grain into the burlap sack. He gathered the open side of the burlap together and wound a length of twine around it, cinchin' it tight before tyin' it off.

"I reckon one good turn deserves another." Hollis scribbled the transaction in his ledger.

James puzzled over Hollis's response, tryin' to recollect if his friend owed him a favor. He dug into his pocket and pulled out some coins. "Whatcha talkin' about?"

"The talk's all over town." He tapped his stubby pencil on the ledger. "That'll be a dollar and twelve cents."

James counted out the money and dropped it into Hollis's outstretched hand. "Maybe you oughta tell me . . . 'zactly what talk is all over town?"

Hollis's brows arched in surprise. "Y'know, 'bout you and them other fellas sellin' yer land so's that DeWitt feller can build that there place he were talkin' about last Sunday at church. Gonna put Hot Springs on the map. The whole town's gonna benefit. It'll mean more business fer ever'one. Good jobs, too." Hollis cackled. "Ain't that somethin', Hot Springs havin' a hospital *ree*sort place fer treatin' all sorts o' miseries?"

Anger smoldered in James's gut. Didn't that young feller understand that he wasn't gonna sell? He thought back over the conversation that took place a few days ago in his barn. James's body might not be able to do as much as it used to, but his mind worked fine, and he could still recall every word he'd spoke. His words were pretty clear when he'd told that young DeWitt feller he wasn't gonna sell their land.

James sucked on his teeth. "Ye must o' heard wrong, Hollis. I ain't sellin' our farm. That young feller come out and done talked to me about it, but I told him no."

Hollis jerked his head up. "Ye ain't sellin'? But that DeWitt feller said—"

"I ain't sellin', Hollis."

"Why not?" Hollis plopped his hands on his hips. "I knowed you and yer pa was brought up there, an' his pa settled there a long time ago. Don't rightly know why DeWitt's got such a hankerin' fer your place. Seems to me he could build anywheres." He held his hands out, palms up so James could count every one of his calluses. "But, James, iffen he's a-willin' to pay you good money fer your meadow, why not sell? Ye'd be doin' the town a lot o' good."

James narrowed his eyes. "You tryin' to tell me the town's makin' up my mind fer me? You sayin' folks is gonna get fractious iffen I don't sell?"

Hollis reared his head back a mite. "Ain't no need gittin' yer tail feathers in a fluff. I'm only tellin' ye what folks is sayin'."

James studied his friend for a long moment and then dug in his pocket. He withdrew several more coins, grabbed Hollis's hand, and plunked the money into it. "For them sorghum heads out back."

$\backsim$ EIGHTEEN

G avin leaned against the counter at Dempsey's Emporium. His glance swept around the store, compact as it was. For a town as small as Hot Springs, the size of the place was sufficient to meet the needs of the citizens. However, that was exactly what he hoped to focus on when speaking with the town folk.

Mr. Dempsey removed the lid from the jar of gumdrops, helped himself to a handful, and then pushed the open jar closer to Gavin. "Never thought I'd see the day our little town would grow like you're sayin'. You reckon I oughta draw up plans to expand? Most o' the business owners are thinkin' the same." He popped a couple of gumdrops into his mouth.

Gavin smiled. If everyone else in town was anticipating prosperity based on Uncle Arnold's health resort, all he'd have to do would be sit back and watch the locals persuade James Chappell to sell. "Never hurts to plan."

The merchant's salt and pepper mustache wiggled like a puppy with a new bone. Perhaps Gavin had found the ally he needed. "Of course, the resort will bring in good paying jobs to the community. Initially, there will be construction jobs, of course, but also after the place is open." He gestured around the emporium. "When the town grows and people earn a good wage, they'll have more money to spend. More visitors to the area will also mean more sales."

Dempsey made a slow turn, his chin wedged between his finger and thumb, as if imagining the possibilities for expansion. He walked to the rear of the store. "Mayhap I could knock out this wall and add onto the back. Seein' as how the post office is right next door, can't push out that wall." He turned to face Gavin. "Wonder if I should ask the town council to move the post office."

Gavin helped himself to a gumdrop. "Don't go making too many plans yet. Chappell and the others still haven't signed the contracts." He picked up a pair of boots and examined them. "Your store here is the social center of town." And Luther Dempsey was more than willing to spread information. "If you have any influence around here, especially with James Chappell, I encourage you to do all you can to convince him that selling his farm is the best thing he could do for this town, for his friends and neighbors. The other farmers won't sell unless Chappell does."

Dempsey harrumphed. "James Chappell can be mighty mule-headed, 'specially when it comes to his farm. Reckon them dumb sheep are more important to him than his friends."

Gavin bit his lip. If this was true, he'd have a harder time than he figured dealing with the man. "It's not like anyone is asking him to give up his sheep. He can take the money and move his sheep to another piece of land. Sheep can graze anywhere, can't they?"

"Not Chappell sheep."

Gavin spun around. Dulcie Chappell, her arms full of folded rugs, stood by the door. He nearly choked on his gumdrop.

She skewered him with an unblinking scowl. "I can't speak for the other men, but I can assure you my grandfather knows his own mind and needs nobody to help him make decisions."

Gavin cringed. This was the second time in less than a week she had walked in while he was speaking about trying to buy James Chappell's farm. No doubt she had a higher opinion of her sheep than she did of him. After the tongue-lashing she spewed at him the other day over what she perceived as disrespect of her grandfather, he braced himself for a second helping of the same dish.

Dulcie shifted her focus from Mr. DeWitt and nailed Luther Dempsey with an accusing stare. It had only taken standing in the doorway a few moments to realize the storekeeper was on DeWitt's side in this matter. Some might call it petty, viewing a long time friend with reproach for taking sides, but as far as Dulcie was concerned, DeWitt was the one who'd declared this war, not her. Anyone who took up his cause was no friend to her family.

Mr. Dempsey sputtered, obviously embarrassed at being caught gossiping about her grandfather. "M-Miss Dulcie. I-I'm surprised to see you."

"Why is that, Mr. Dempsey?" She lifted her chin. "My family and I have traded here for many years." Her underlying message was as clear as the water from the spring. "Why would you be surprised to see me here?"

The man's face flooded red. Good! He *should* be embarrassed.

His mouth opened and closed with a puppet-like motion. The wooden lid in his hands flipped from his grasp and clattered to the floor. He snatched it and plunked it down on the open candy jar.

"It-it's only Th-Thursday, Miss Dulcie. You usually come on Saturdays."

Did that make it all right to call Grandpa "mule-headed" and accuse him of caring more about the sheep than he did his friends—because he assumed she wouldn't come to the store today? Anger boiled through her veins and she ground her teeth.

Gavin DeWitt stepped forward. "Those rugs look heavy. May I carry them for you?"

She shot a 45-caliber glare in his direction, and he halted in his tracks. She shouldered past him and spread her craft out on the counter, transferring her disapproving frown to Mr. Dempsey. "I wanted to get these rugs in here before Saturday, since I know it's your busiest day." Behind her, Mr. DeWitt's footsteps retreated toward the door. She wouldn't give him the satisfaction of looking at him. She only hoped he didn't notice her trembling fingers. After all, she'd made a fool of herself when she'd ranted at him several days ago, even if he did deserve it.

She anchored her focus on the rugs. "All three of these are special orders. The green and yellow one is for Mrs. Sanderson, and the blue one is Mrs. Drummond's. Both ladies paid a deposit, but the balance is owing."

She pulled out the third one, done in brown, tan, and ivory, from the bottom of the stack and draped it over the cracker barrel. "This one is for the manager at the hotel." She punched out the word, reminding Mr. Dempsey that Hot Springs already had a resort, implying they had no need of another. "I believe you told me he'd already paid in full." She tipped her head toward the door. "I have three more rugs for display." She turned to retrieve them from the wagon, but came face to face with Mr. DeWitt who already had the rugs in his arms.

"These are beautifully done." His appraisal of her work meant nothing to her. What did he know of creating hand-made rugs on a loom? She ignored his compliment and took the rugs from him.

She spread them out on the counter and hefted the corner of the top one. "This one is two dollars more than the usual price. It's larger and the pattern is more intricate, five colors instead of two. It required more steps to produce the dyes and extra wool fibers to create the design."

Having regained his composure, Mr. Dempsey nodded. "Sure is purty. Ye sure two dollars more is enough? Seems like a lot o' extry work."

Both men were full of compliments when she stood in their midst, but they didn't mind saying uncomplimentary things behind her back. "I'm sure. I'll take special orders or you can sell them outright."

Mr. Dempsey's head bobbed. "I'll put 'em right there yonder by the front door, so's folks can see 'em when they first walk in."

"Make sure they aren't where the sunlight can fade them." She stacked them again with the special one on top. "Tell customers I can produce almost any color from flowers, bark, nuts, roots, and leaves, and if they have a certain design in mind, have them sketch it out."

He fumbled with the apron strings that tied in the front at his waist. "There was a lady in here coupla days ago. I recollect she's from up around Washington way. Her husband is some kind o' big fish in the capitol. She was askin' for fine wool yard goods to take back to her dressmaker. Said she needed a dark green, the color o' the pine trees."

Dulcie finished arranging the rugs on a stand near the door. "How much does she need?"

"A full dress length plus an extry yard."

Dulcie nodded, glad she had curbed her anger when she'd walked in. She did, after all, depend on Luther Dempsey to sell her goods for her. "I have some fine lambs' wool fleece that I can have ready for her in about three weeks."

Something akin to relief washed over Mr. Dempsey's face. "I'll tell her next time she comes in."

She couldn't explain why she also felt relieved. Hadn't she every right to be indignant—angry, even—that these men were discussing her grandfather in such a flippant way? The choice lay before her. She could berate them for their remarks, or she could let it go. Grandpa would let it go.

But she couldn't.

"Gentlemen." She divided her gaze between Mr. Dempsey and Gavin DeWitt, and kept her tone even and coolly polite. "Please do not mistake my calm demeanor for lack of caring. Your insulting comments about my grandfather and our land have tarnished whatever friendship we've had in the past." She shifted slightly, and Mr. DeWitt's contrite expression was almost her undoing. She steeled her spine. "Or any friendship we might have had in the future."

Without giving either man the opportunity to respond, she walked to the door the way she'd been taught at that fancy school in Asheville like a lady.

Gavin's gaze followed Dulcie out the door. Mingled emotions spun and twisted, churning through his spirit and anchoring his feet to the floor. His tongue struck momentarily dumb, he could only wish to turn back the clock a half hour and rewrite the inconsiderate words that fell from his mouth. Why had he not been more discreet? Dulcie and her grandfather had certainly given him an earful the day he'd visited their farm. Their admonition had rolled through his head for days.

Additional pieces of the puzzle sat before him on the counter and display rack. The rugs Dulcie made were of the highest quality. She possessed an incredible talent. Her assurance that she could fill the request for fine woolen yard goods in any color further defined her skill. A light dawned within him—the Chappells viewed him as a threat to their very way of life. That wasn't his intention at all. All he wanted to do was purchase their land at a fair price.

As if prodded by a pitchfork, he broke free of his frozen state and hastened after her. "Miss Chappell. Miss Chappell, please wait." He barged out the door, grateful he didn't plow over any customers on their way in.

She halted with one foot on the wheel hub in preparation to climb into the wagon. When she turned, her dark brown eyes no longer held acrimony, but rather hints of sorrow. Within a heartbeat, however, her brows dipped and lips pursed in suspicion.

"Mr. DeWitt, I can't imagine you having anything further to add to what you've already said."

Regret crashed over him, and for the first time, he wished he could distance himself from his uncle's plan. "Miss Chappell, please forgive me. I apologize for what you must have heard. I never intended to hurt you or your family."

She stepped back down and dusted her hands. "Then why did you say those things?"

Gavin ducked his head, his chin dropping to his chest. "I wish now that I hadn't." He hazarded an upward glance.

Her expression reminded him of a stern schoolmaster he'd once had. She clasped her hands in front of her homespun skirt. "Once words are spoken, they can't be retrieved, be they kind words or hurtful ones."

One more thing about her to admire. "A wise saying for one so young."

She lifted her shoulders. "My grandfather has told me that on more than one occasion."

A fleeting thought tagged his mind. If he'd been raised by someone like James Chappell, would he be a different man than what he was? "I wanted to tell you how impressed I am." He gestured back toward the emporium. "Your craft is extraordinary. The art you've created rivals some of the finest rugs I've seen." Not only was she an artist, she also possessed a fine business astuteness. He could no longer question whether his uncle's assessment of these people being ignorant was accurate. Uncle Arnold was wrong.

"Thank you. It's a skill that's been handed down over several generations of Chappells."

Interesting. Her craft had been in her family for decades, but she was different. "At the risk of making you angry again, I noticed you don't speak like most of the people around here."

A tiny lift of her chin warned he'd best tread carefully. "I attended Maple Hill Academy for Young Ladies in Asheville for three years. My grandparents felt it beneficial to be able to converse in an educated manner with our customers." She leveled an unblinking stare at him. "That doesn't mean I am in any way ashamed by my grandparents or their manner of speaking, or by the way I was raised."

He understood, all right. He'd gotten an education in the past week himself. What was he to do? Could he change his uncle's thinking? He still shouldered a responsibility to carry out Uncle Arnold's orders.

He took a deep breath. "Miss Chappell, please understand. I'm only trying to do my job-the job my uncle expects of me."

She gave a single nod. "I will ask the same of you. I, too, have a job to do. My job is to care for the sheep, be a caretaker of the land, create woolen goods, and move heaven and earth to protect my grandparents."

Gavin witnessed a momentary gentling of her features, quickly replaced by the stubborn independence he'd grown accustomed to seeing in her. "Miss Dulcie, would you have time to accompany me to the hotel dining room for tea?"

She blinked and arched her eyebrows. "Thank you, but I must get back." She hesitated, her gaze lingering on his for a moment longer than necessary. Then she gathered her skirt to climb up to the wagon seat. She slapped the reins on mule's rump. "Hup, Samson."

Gavin tugged on the brim of his hat. "Good day, Miss Chappell." He regretted her decline of his invitation, but got the distinct impression she'd wanted to accept.

↜ NINETEEN

There was nothing like a sleepless night to make a man rethink his position. The pre-dawn darkness enveloped Gavin in a cocoon where he felt utterly alone. Not necessarily a bad thing, since the need to find answers to some unspoken questions made him glad his uncle was in Philadelphia instead of Hot Springs, pointing a dictatorial finger at him.

Such a nagging conundrum. Opposing emotions engaged in battle for his peace. How was he to ask a question if he didn't know what or how to ask? And to whom would he pose the questions? He needed someone with wisdom, discernment, someone who could reason things out and clear his muddied thoughts. Someone like. . .

Gavin sat up and turned up the wick on the oil lamp beside his bed. The Mountain Park Hotel boasted electric lights, but Gavin preferred the softer glow of the lamp. He swung his feet over the edge of the bed and curled his toes into the plush bedside rug. Scrubbing his hands over his face, he weighed his options. He could send a telegram or letter to his brother. No, Harold would berate him for not being decisive. The local reverend seemed a nice enough fellow, but Gavin didn't know him well enough to bare his conscience. One of his college professors? No, they'd all thought him foolish and flighty for not being able to settle on a major course of study.

What would it be like to be able to pray? He'd gone through the catechism classes as a boy, but everything he'd memorized was long forgotten. He leaned forward and propped his elbows on his knees, his head in his hands, eyes closed.

My grandfather has more wisdom in his pinkie finger than you have in your entire being.

The book of Proverbs says that white hair on an aged man is a crown of glory to him if he is a righteous man, and my grandfather is as righteous a man as you will ever find.

He is a man of honor and integrity, and might I add, intelligence.

Someone like. . .

"James Chappell." The whisper startled Gavin until he realized it had come from his own lips.

How could he talk to Chappell about Uncle Arnold's business plan when his uncle's goal was to push Chappell off his farm so he could take over that piece of property? Interesting that his thoughts painted such a picture. They were, after all, offering to purchase the land.

"Hmph." Gavin glanced over at the cherry desk in the corner, atop which was a neat stack of land purchase contracts, all still unsigned. He padded across the room and leafed through the pages. An unexpected ripple of comfort stirred him that all five were still without signatures. Wasn't the whole point to have all the contracts signed before his uncle returned?

Why then would the empty lines waiting for signatures be a comfort to him? His gaze traveled up the pages to the terms of the offer. "Four dollars per acre." From the beginning, he'd questioned Uncle Arnold. *"What if they don't agree to the purchase price?"*

His uncle's blustering retort had been enough to silence him at the time, but now in the silent semi-darkness, he revisited the question. He hadn't truly been asking, *What if they don't agree?* Deep within his conscience he was asking, *Is this really a fair price?* He'd hoped his uncle would have given him more leeway to negotiate the price, but he'd remained tenaciously firm.

Gavin already knew the answer. No doubt it was why he couldn't sleep. He still wished he had someone like Dulcie's grandfather in whom he could confide, but at least he could define one question. The answer wasn't hard.

He didn't have the authority to change the price. Uncle Arnold would fire him, and he needed this job, if for no other reason to prove his worth. It was too late to prove anything to his father, but maybe he needed to prove something to himself. What exactly did he want to prove? That he could be as shrewd a businessman as his uncle? That he could meet his uncle's expectations?

What about his own expectations?

Gavin pulled out the desk chair and lowered himself to the striped, cushioned seat. He spread all five contracts out on the desk. If he was able to hand five signed contracts to Uncle Arnold upon his return, would that justify overstepping his bounds? Acting as his uncle's representative meant performing the required tasks exactly the way the elder DeWitt had dictated—no more, no less. The longer he spent in his uncle's employ, the tighter the stranglehold of uneasiness gripped him. Perhaps being a ruthless businessman wasn't the path to contentment he sought.

He'd believed for so many years, the only ladder to self-worth was gaining his father's favor. Since his father's passing, transferring that belief to his uncle had seemed the logical thing to do. But why?

Why couldn't he find satisfaction in pursuing his own goals? Did he even have goals of his own? A man who had no goals except to do the bidding of others wasn't much of a man. He stared at the row of papers spread across the desk. If this was where he sought satisfaction, he must be going about it wrong. Achieving his uncle's goals wasn't what he wanted. Figuring out his own goals, however, would take some thought.

He stacked the contracts, tapping the edges on the desk, and left them for later. He'd pinpointed the reason he couldn't sleep. He still wasn't sure what to do about it, but he was certain of one thing: even if it cost him his job, he could not be as cutthroat as his uncle. The first step to defining his goals must be deciding what he *didn't* want.

Chasing after acceptance and approval for half his life hadn't result-ed in contentment. Why in the name of everything that was good did he ever believe he should be like his father and uncle?

Gavin stacked his arms on the desk and laid his head atop them. He could groan because he'd wasted half his life doing something he was never meant to do, or he could refocus his attention on discovering his own goals. His true goals.

No streaks of dawn lightened the sky to the east yet. Perhaps he could capture an hour or two of sleep. Returning to the bed, he extin-guished the lamp and fell back against the pillows.

Two hours of sleep was better than nothing, but not by much. Grit burned and itched his eyes, but hope seeped through him. The brief slumber had afforded him an unusual dream in which he'd seen a hillside meadow surrounded by a split rail fence. He remembered hearing the music of sheep *baaing* in the distance and the breeze stirring the pines—a com-forting, pastoral scene, but there was a person he couldn't distinguish. He'd wanted to go to the person, talk to them, but some unseen force prevented him. If only he could have seen the person's face.

Deciding to forgo the suit and tie, he dressed in casual trousers with a striped shirt, sleeves rolled up to the elbows. One more choice he'd made to distance himself from the image of his uncle.

He stifled a yawn as he made his way to the dining room, and gave the waiter a grateful smile when the man filled his coffee cup. After scarfing down his breakfast and a second cup of coffee, Gavin walked out to the long porch at the rear of the hotel and looked out across the staggered mountain ranges, one behind the other, each one draped with a haze of blue.

He hiked down the fieldstone walkway to the wide gravel drive, and walked toward town. Along the way, he bid a good morning to those he met, paused to admire some clumps of daisies and buttercups waving in the breeze, and chuckled at two giggling little boys chasing each other in circles around an enormous hemlock tree. Had he ever taken the time to enjoy his surroundings when he was in Philadelphia?

Hogan's Livery loomed ahead. Otis Hogan smirked at him when he asked the liveryman to hitch the buggy. "Looks like ye had a rough night."

Apparently the second cup of coffee wasn't sufficient to erase the dark circles under his eyes. "I was working late." It wasn't a lie. Hour after hour he'd lain awake trying to think of every scenario he could to get the contracts finalized. His conscience and Uncle Arnold's schemes kept colliding with each other. Lying in bed hadn't made the process restful. Once again, the desire for a trusted confidante carved a hollow place in his chest. He paid Hogan the rental fee for the whole day and climbed into the buggy seat.

The mountain air blew a breath of encouragement as the horse navigated the mountain road. The first farm closest to town was Zeb Huxley's. The farmer sat on an overturned bucket on the porch, working on what appeared to be a piece of harness. He eyed Gavin with suspicion when the buggy came to a stop.

Three dogs scrambled out from under the porch, baying at the tops of their lungs. Mr. Huxley didn't call them back. They circled him, growling. He halted, letting them sniff him. Apparently satisfied he wasn't a threat, they slumped down in the shade of a massive pine tree.

Gavin moved a few steps closer, taking note of the shotgun leaning against the house. "Morning, Mr. Huxley."

Huxley nodded. "Mornin'."

Gavin stopped at the porch steps. "Sure is a pretty day."

"Yep."

He tipped his head toward the dogs. "Some nice hounds you have there. Do you use them for hunting?"

"Yep."

"I suppose they're good watch dogs, too."

"Yep."

He shoved one hand in his pocket and leaned on the porch post with the other, looking out across the field where Huxley's corn was knee-high. "Crop looks good."

"Yep."

Gavin sighed. How did one start a conversation if they couldn't get past *yep*? "Uh, Mr. Huxley, is it all right if I sit down?"

"Yep."

Progress. At least the farmer didn't run him off or send the dogs after him.

Gavin lowered himself to the top step and propped one leg over the other. "What a beautiful day."

"Y'already said that."

The man wasn't making this easy. Gavin uncrossed his legs and leaned forward. "Have you made a decision yet about our offer to purchase your land?"

Huxley nudged his hat toward the back of his head. "I ain't sure." He rubbed his hand over his stubbled chin. "I know James Chappell ain't gonna sell. What happens iffen I sign that there paper o' yours? You git my land, but you don't got Chappell's. What good'll that do ye?"

It was a fair question. "To begin with, all my uncle wants to buy from you is ten acres, not your whole farm. He needs small sections of three other farms as well to give him what's called an 'easement.'" Gavin paused, waiting to see if Huxley had any questions.

The farmer scrunched up his brow. "Easement. Reckon that means a stretch o' land on both sides o' the Chappell place."

Gavin nodded. "That's right."

Before he could elaborate, a *halloo!* echoed through the trees. Huxley craned his neck and shaded his eyes. "Dewey? That you?"

"'Course it's me, ye ole buzzard." Dewey Tate came tramping up the path to the porch, eyeing Gavin's buggy as he hiked past it.

Gavin stood when Tate approached the porch. "Good morning, Mr. Tate."

Tate arched one eyebrow, took a long, pensive look at Gavin, and then nodded. "DeWitt." The bow-legged farmer spat a stream of tobacco juice before straddling a short bench in the yard and turning his attention to Huxley. "Wondered iffen I could borrow yer mule for a day 'r two. Mine's got a stone bruise, and I gotta finish plowin' the last few acres to plant a crop o' late corn." He looked at Gavin. "But I reckon I'm kinda curious to hear what DeWitt here has t' say, first."

Wrestling with the issue all night hadn't brought any new revelations of his own goals. He might not yet know what they were, but he knew what they weren't, and he was determined to not let Uncle Arnold's frowning bluster sway him from his decision. "I'm glad you're here, Mr. Tate. What I was about to discuss with Mr. Huxley concerns you, too."

Tate cocked an eyebrow, his gaze fixed on Gavin.

Gavin divided his focus between the two men and pulled in a deep breath, ready to plunge into deep water. "After thinking about these contracts for a while, I've decided the offered price isn't right."

Huxley and Tate exchanged glances, and Dewey Tate's brow dipped. "Ain't right? Mayhap ye oughta make clear yer meanin'."

The image of Uncle Arnold's face loomed in his mind's eye. He stiffened his spine and pushed past it. "I don't believe the offered price on the contracts I showed you last week was fair. Your land is worth more than four dollars an acre."

The two farmers traded looks again, but didn't interrupt.

"I have changed the price to eight dollars per acre."

Huxley's mouth fell open and Tate scrunched his eyes in skepticism. Neither man responded for a full minute, but they communicated plenty between staring at him and then shooting warning looks of suspicion at each other.

"I can see you are both troubled by what I've said." Gavin clasped his fingers together and leaned back against the porch post. "What questions do you have?"

Tate thumbed his suspenders. "Well, I reckon my first question is iffen ye knowed four dollars weren't a fair price, why was that whatcha said to begin with?"

How did he respond without making his uncle sound dishonest? If he still aimed to collect all five signatures, these men were going to have to trust not only him, but also his uncle. At the moment, he wasn't sure his uncle was worthy of their trust. Tiptoeing around the issue seemed the best way to answer.

"My uncle hasn't had the time to visit each farm or to explore the countryside as I have. When the time came to draw up the contracts, he felt four dollars was fair." He was stretching the truth. Did the two men sitting before him realize it? "Now that I've had the chance to walk this land and see for myself how rich it is, I realized we weren't offering a fair price."

Huxley spat to one side again. "Ye said ye didn't wanna buy my whole farm. Jus' part of it."

Gavin nodded. "That's right." He shifted his glance between both men. "My uncle only needs a small section of both your farms, so you can continue to stay in your homes."

Tate jerked his thumb toward the northeast. "What about James Chappell? He git to stay on his land?"

Gavin couldn't keep the grimace from his lips, in the same way he couldn't bring himself to cheat these men. Lying to them wasn't the way to gain their trust.

✍∽ TWENTY

Realization dawned. He'd identified one of his goals. More than pleasing his uncle or achieving success as a businessman, or even competing with his brother, Gavin gained a sense of how he wanted others to perceive him. In the pre-dawn hours as he'd searched his own heart, he knew aligning himself with his uncle, so people believed they were of the same ilk, wasn't what he wanted.

Now he had an opportunity to move forward and let people see him in a different light—as an honest and trustworthy man. A sense of affirmation spoke calmness to his spirit. This was the right step.

He held out his hands, palms up, looking Zeb Huxley and Dewey Tate in the eye. "My uncle needs to acquire Mr. Chappell's entire farm. However, I am prepared to help Mr. Chappell search for a suitable piece of good grazing land with a water source for his sheep. I'll even help him relocate his sheep if need be. It's not my aim for anyone to be without a home or livelihood, and I do want everyone involved to be treated fairly." He searched the faces of the two men for some kind of reaction and found none. Perhaps redirecting the topic might bring a positive response.

Gavin cleared his throat and hooked his clasped hands around his upraised knee. "I was telling Luther Dempsey the other day that this health resort my uncle wants to build will be the first of its kind in the country. The plan is to bring the best in medical care and join it with the therapeutic benefits of the hot mineral springs." He brought his hands together and interlocked his fingers, creating a picture of how the two aspects of the health resort would come together. "The folks who come seeking treatment will find the best care in the country."

Both men fixed courteous, if wary, attention on him, but neither made a comment. He supposed they wanted a broader explanation regarding how they and their neighbors might be affected.

He cleared his throat. "There will be construction jobs initially. We will want to employ as many local folks as we can. People who are building part of their own community will do a better job. We will also use as many local materials as we can. Lumber and stone from right here on the mountain. Of course, we will pay any landowner for timber or quarried rock." Both men sat in silence, watching him with such intensity, he was tempted to check behind him to see if some animal was stalking him.

He swallowed back the foolish thought and continued. "Then, when the resort opens, we will want to hire people who have a knowledge of the hot springs and can answer the visitors' questions." A growing discomfort accompanied their silent scrutiny. He tamped down his nervousness, but his hands seemed unable to find a purpose. Certainly Harold never failed to appear composed and dignified. He shoved the accusation aside. Comparing himself to Harold or anyone else must stop. He tucked his hands under his arms and clamped them down.

"Since our aim is to combine the best medical treatments with the therapeutic advantages of soaking in the hot mineral springs, we will need to bring in medical staff, of course, but we hope to employ all local folks for the resort. There will be many good-paying jobs to fill, and we want the people of this community to join us and be part of this wonderful opportunity. So, you see, folks for miles around will benefit, even the farmers."

Zeb Huxley narrowed his eyes. "How ye figure that?"

The farmer's simple question stirred a wave of relief that almost made Gavin's shoulders sag. He grabbed onto the query like a lifeline and gestured toward Huxley's fields. "The resort will purchase local farm produce so you won't have to carry your harvested crops down the mountain. You'll be paid top dollar."

Huxley simply grunted, but finally Dewey Tate took the twig he'd been chewing out of his mouth and tossed it aside. "Got three things to say. First off, I don't aim to sell nothin' till I see that eight dollars an acre in writin' and your uncle signs it." He took off his battered hat and scratched his head. "No offense, young feller, but we don't know you or yer uncle."

Chagrin poked him. More confirmation that his uncle's assessment of these "mountain people" was inaccurate. Like James Chappell, these men were neither ignorant, nor backward. Tate's request proved it. Of course, getting his uncle to agree and sign off on the higher price would require a miracle. He'd hoped to get the men to sign the contracts before his uncle returned. No doubt his uncle would grumble and bellow about the change, but Gavin hoped he'd be satisfied to have the signed contracts in hand. Tate's demand for Uncle Arnold to sign the change first didn't change Gavin's resolve. If a confrontation resulted, then so be it. Gavin gave both men a nod.

Tate scrunched his eyes and drew up his mouth like he was tasting something for the first time. "Might you an' yer uncle be interested in buyin' my whole farm? I know y'all are hankerin' to buy the Chappell place, but mine's right next to his."

The unexpected question took Gavin aback. He forced his thoughts in line. Gavin had no real answer. He'd already crossed the line offering the men a higher price. "I'd have to speak with my uncle about that, and he's not in Hot Springs right now. He was called back to Philadelphia on business. But I expect him to return in a couple of weeks, and of course, I'll be in contact with him by letter."

The first two statements on Tate's list already had Gavin backped-
aling. He sucked in a breath, almost afraid to ask. "What was the third
thing you wanted to say?"

Tate rose from the bench he'd been straddling and adjusted his
britches. "Jus' this: iffen you think ye can talk James Chappell into sellin'
ye his farm, yer dumber'n a coal bucket."

James patted Malachi's head and told him to be a good watchdog. Early
mornin' fog hung low on the mountain, blottin' out the sun. Not a single
breath of air sighed through the trees. Even the sheep were quiet. No
lambs frolicked in the meadow, nor did the mamas *baa*, callin' to them.

He didn't know what it was puttin' him on edge. Was that bobcat
back? Could be a bear in the alder patch up on the hillside, pickin' out a
lamb. James glanced down at Malachi, but the dog thumped his tail and
showed no sign of wariness. If a predator was close by, the hackles on
Malachi's back would raise and the dog would growl like he were plannin' on attackin' anything that moved. Still, uneasiness twisted through
James. He'd left Virginia and Dulcie alone plenty of times when he went
to town, or to help out a neighbor. Today shouldn't be any different.

He snorted. "Y' old fool. Jus' yer imagination a-skedaddlin' like a
squirrel what cain't make up its mind which tree he wants to climb."

Malachi whined and licked his hand, as if he could read James's
thoughts. "Y' tryin' to tell me ain't nothin' gonna happen as long as yer
on watch?" James ruffled the dog's ears. "I know, yer a good dog."

The thud of the treadles and clackin' of the shuttle of Dulcie's loom
carried over the stillness. She'd looked at him like she reckoned he'd
taken leave o' his senses this morning when he suggested she take the
shotgun to the wool shed, but in Virginia's presence she'd made no comment. Last Sunday's announcement from the DeWitt men triggered a
rise in his defenses, and he'd learned to trust his instincts. The thought

of takin' on another bobcat seemed less of a threat than a two-legged predator.

Samson stamped his foot when James cinched up the saddle. No point in takin' the wagon. He could get to town and back faster ridin'. "C'mon, mule. Iffen ye don't give me no trouble, I might be persuaded to slip ye a carrot from the garden onest we git home."

He hauled himself into the saddle. Whether or not Samson understood the bribe, he swung his head toward the road and broke into a bone-jarring trot. The eerie silence shadowed him down the mountain road. No birds sang, no hawks screeched, no squirrels chattered—like they was all in hidin'.

Never one to waste a good opportunity to talk with his Heavenly Father, James cast a glance to the dreary, gray sky. "God, I sure wish Ye'd give me the wisdom I need in these troublin' times. Virginia and Dulcie, they neither one'll hear a word about sellin' the farm, but I need to hear from You. Show me, God. Show me. And iffen it ain't too much trouble, could Ye be showin' me Yer plans fer Dulcie? I'm afeared for her, Lord. Won't be long 'fore Ye be callin' me an' Virginia home. Don't know what Dulcie'll do all by herself. Sure wish she'd soften up her heart toward Ye."

The remainder of the ride into town James spent listenin'. Mayhap it were a good thing there weren't no birds singin'. Made hearin' God's voice a mite easier.

James walked out of the Feed and Seed and slipped the bottle of liniment into his pocket. As he unwrapped Samson's reins from the hitching post, he heard a familiar, "Halloo." Dewey ambled toward him from across the street.

"Hey there, Dewey." James lifted his hand. "Whatcha doin' in town in the middle o' the week?"

Dewey gave a sheepish shrug and held up his hand wrapped with a bandage. "Hadda come and see Doc Pryor. Was sharpenin' my plow blade and near cut my finger clean off. Doc stitched it up, but he told me I need a keeper. He might be right."

James shook his head. Ever since Dewey's wife died, he'd gotten careless, like he couldn't keep his mind on what he was doin'. "Ye need t' be more careful, Dewey."

His friend nodded. "I know, I know." He flapped his good hand. "Had me a visit with that there young DeWitt feller."

"Oh?" The hair on the back of James's neck stood up. "What'd he have to say?"

Dewey slouched to one side and leaned his hip against the hitchin' post. "Well now, thet there is the surprisin' thing. I went by Zeb's place to borrow his mule, and the young DeWitt feller were there talkin' to Zeb." He rubbed his hand over his chin whiskers and waggled his head like he were tryin' to shake a doodlebug out of his ear. "Ye ain't gonna believe this. He said he wanted to raise the price he's offerin' for our land. Said he don't think the first offer were a fair price. Don't that tear ye fer a duster?"

James blinked. "Ye don't say." Suspicion waved red flags in his mind. He never heard of nobody ever wantin' to pay *more*. Didn't make sense. "He say why?"

Dewey glanced to and fro, and lowered his voice. "That's the part I don't reckon I understand 'ceptin' God works in mysterious ways." He looked over his shoulder and up and down the street. "Said he thought the land was worth more than his uncle offered. Said he's changin' the price to eight dollars an acre. Ain't that a caution?"

Caution was the word, all right. "Well, I declare." James tapped his finger on Dewey's chest. "Ye sure he ain't had a touch o' the 'shine?"

"Don't think so." Dewey's brow furrowed. "Leastwise he didn't sound like he were likkered up. Said the first offer weren't a fair price." He hooked this thumb on his suspenders. "Y'know, I'm of a mind to take him up on it. Asked him iffen him and his uncle could buy my whole place outright."

James widened his eyes. "Why you askin' him that?"

Dewey shrugged again and held up his bandaged hand. "I don't get on so good anymore, what with Martha gone on to Glory. My daughter an' her family want me to come live with them down the mountain. I'm thinkin' on it."

The news caught James flat-footed. Dewey was a good friend, and he'd surely hate to see him go. "Did DeWitt say they'd buy your whole place at the eight dollar price?"

A soft huff blew a few of Dewey's whiskers askew. "Didn't say. Said he'd hafta talk to his uncle, and 'pears like his uncle ain't in town. Gone back north fer a spell."

"Hmm." James studied on Dewey's reply. "Make sure ye get it in writin', and have someone look it over b'fore ye sign anything. Mayhap Waldo Granger or Preacher Bradbury." The distrustful feelings Dulcie'd had the day they met the older DeWitt hunkered down to stay a spell in his own spirit. "Jus' be careful. Make sure ye understand and agree with ever'thing he writes down."

"Y'know," Dewey said, twiddlin' his beard between his thumb and pointer finger, "thet there young DeWitt feller ain't a bad sort." He caught the sleeve of James's faded flannel shirt in his fingers. "Now I heared ye good, and I'm thinkin' it's good advice to make sure ever'thing's writ down proper-like, an' havin' someone like Waldo Granger look it over is smart. But sometimes ye jus' hafta go on faith an' what yer gut tells ye."

Right now, skepticism stirred James's gut. "What ye meanin'?"

Dewey patted ole Samson who didn't appear in any hurry to start back up the mountain.

"I mean thet younger DeWitt didn't hafta come and tell us the first price weren't fair. Me an' Zeb, we ain't said nothin' one way or 'tuther about agreein' to sell. DeWitt come and told us he were offerin' a higher price 'cause he says it were the right thing to do. Now iffen his uncle ain't in town, thet means he decided thet on his own." His bushy eyebrows raised like he were askin' a question. "Don't thet tell ye somethin' 'bout the young feller?"

Dewey had a point, but James wasn't willin' to let down his guard where either DeWitt was concerned. "I reckon. But ye gotta remember the nephew is actin' under orders from his uncle, and the uncle is the one I don't trust."

✌️ TWENTY-ONE

Gavin climbed the plush carpeted stairs at the Mountain Park Hotel with leaded feet. The sour taste in his mouth sent his appetite into hiding, so supper held no appeal. He couldn't put off writing to his uncle. The man expected to hear from him with a report of how well their plan was going. Recording the events of the past couple of days in a letter rather than informing his uncle face to face might be temporarily easier, but it only delayed the inevitable. Once again, the wish to have a wise and trusted advisor in whom he could confide arose in Gavin's chest, but the truth was he didn't have a single person he could call a friend or confidante.

Discovering his own goals didn't come without convictions. He questioned his own fortitude for the space of time it took to walk to his room, but the very act of turning the key in the door lock underscored his need to be completely open and forthright with his uncle. He dismissed the idea of waiting until they could speak face to face. If he couldn't describe his goals and why he was determined to achieve them in a letter, how did he hope to stand firm once his uncle returned to Hot Springs?

Gavin closed the door and tossed the key on the dresser. A nagging thought pestered him. What if he could persuade Uncle Arnold to see things his way? He tried to visualize the coming confrontation and see his uncle acquiescing to the changes he'd made in the contracts, and why he'd made them, but the picture struggled to manifest in his mind. Doubt smothered the fantasy of believing Uncle Arnold might listen and agree with him.

He wasn't even sure where to begin his report and accompanying explanation. Until he could sort out his thoughts and form a better picture of exactly what his hopes and aspirations were, how could he write to his uncle? Updating Uncle Arnold on the status of the contracts and the conversations he'd had with some of the landowners couldn't be disconnected from distinguishing his own goals.

He sat at the desk and pulled out a sheet of paper. The pristine, blank paper invited a world of possibilities. For the first time in his life, the desire to explore his own destiny and shape his own objectives overpowered the feeling of obligation to achieve the goals someone else designed. He closed his eyes.

Think, man. Dig deep. What is it you truly want to do above all else? Not what Uncle Arnold wants, not to compete with Harold, not Father's demands. What do you want to do? Who do you want to be?

Realization startled him. He couldn't remember ever allowing himself to think this way. The empty sheet of paper beckoned and an eagerness he'd not known before threaded through him. He removed the lid from the inkwell and dipped his pen. Hesitating only a minute, he began to write.

The man I wish to be:
Honest, trustworthy, reputation for treating people fairly

He paused and stared at the words. Treating people fairly was one thing. Refusing to take advantage of people took fairness to another level. He dipped the nib of his pen again and added those words to his list. Even as he did so, he could hear his uncle scoffing.

How many times over the course of the past week had he wondered what it might be like to know how to pray? Did God really hear? Did the Almighty give advice? He set the thought aside, intending to investigate the possibility of prayer later.

Gavin rubbed his chin. Of course, he wanted to be successful, but what defined success? He turned and gazed at the fading light through the window. Purple and dark blue swathes gathered and closed in on the glimmers of the gold sunset over the mountain. An unfamiliar tug pulled an emotion he'd not entertained in a very long time to the front of his thoughts. The feeling of belonging somewhere, the comfort of knowing one was *home*.

"Home?" Where did that thought come from? This place wasn't his home. His home was in Philadelphia, cold and austere as it was.

He couldn't tear his gaze from the ever-changing colors beyond the confines of his room. He rose from the desk and walked to the window to watch the last streaks of light fall beneath the veil of the mountain. This place—not necessarily the Mountain Park Hotel, but these mountains and hillsides, the breath-robbing sunsets, pure air and sweet water, the music of wind in the trees, the down-to-earth folks, and the simple, unhurried life they led—this drew him in a way Philadelphia never did. For so many years, he measured success by achieving the marks set for him by others. What equated to achievement in a place like this?

He returned to the desk and took up the list he'd begun. He had one more thing to add to his list of goals, but how did one describe an encounter with something he'd never before experienced?

Gavin worked his head from side to side to ease the tension in his neck. The dozen or so pieces of crumpled paper scattered on the desk and floor around his chair testified to the numerous attempts he'd made composing the letter to Uncle Arnold. He pulled his watch from his pocket. The numbers on the face swam as he tried to focus.

After midnight. No wonder his muscles were so stiff. The letter lay before him on the desk, complete except for his signature. He picked it up and began to read for the hundredth time. The update wasn't what his uncle was expecting, for sure. Stating that he'd increased the price to eight dollars per acre, because the land was worth twice what they'd offered, would likely send his uncle into a rage. The farmers' request that the new offer be signed by Arnold DeWitt very well might result in the loss of his job. His weary eyes focused on the carefully penned words:

> *I know your instructions were to not go over four dollars per acre. However, we both know the land is worth well over that amount, and to offer less than the land is worth amounts to duplicity.*
> *I have not yet been able to convince James Chappell to sell, but I hope to meet with him later this week, as I have been studying the possibility of helping him relocate his sheep to alternate grazing land. Perhaps such an offer will prove to him our good will and intentions.*

Even as he'd scribed the words, his uncle's voice boomed in his subconscious. Nobody ever crossed Arnold DeWitt without expecting to suffer the consequences. It was altogether possible he'd penned his own dismissal, but the prospect didn't rattle him as it once did.

Gavin sucked in a fortifying breath and affixed his signature to the letter. Fatigue blurred the words of the missive. He blew on his inked name to hasten the drying before folding the stationery and sealing it with blue wax. Once he handed the letter to the postmaster, the fuse would be lit and the resulting explosion was a certainty.

Grandpa closed the Bible, and the old rocking chair creaked against his weight as he leaned back. The scripture he'd read wasn't new to Dulcie. She'd heard it before—the story of Joshua sending men to spy out the

land around Jericho. The repeated directives to be strong and courageous echoed through her, reminders of the challenges that lay before
her.

The farm, the sheep, her work at the loom—all were part of who she
was as a Chappell. Every aspect of her life bore its own special challenges, but none compared with the responsibility she held in the highest
priority. She recalled the words she'd spoken to Gavin DeWitt several
days ago.

*I, too, have a job to do. My job is to care for the sheep, be a caretaker of the
land, create woolen goods, and move heaven and earth to protect my grandparents.*

Had he listened? She certainly hoped so. She cast a quick glance at
Grandma and found her with an adoring gaze fixed on Grandpa as he
spoke of Joshua and the courage he learned from trusting God. Once
again, a hesitant, tentative prayer slipped from her spirit heavenward.

*God, please hear me. Help me take care of Grandpa and Grandma. I know
You love them—they've always stayed faithful to You, even if I haven't.*

Grandpa carefully pointed out the strength and courage weren't
Joshua's, and repeated God's promise that He'd be with His people wherever they went. "Them fellers didn't have no strength their own selves.
It were God thet give 'em His strength, so they could do the job God sent
'em to do."

Dulcie fixed her gaze on her shoe tops. Like she'd so pointedly told
Gavin DeWitt, she had a job to do, and she feared she wasn't strong
enough to do it on her own. She needed help-God's help.

The wagon rattled down the rutted road toward town. Grandma sat
straight as a wheel spoke on the seat beside Grandpa, while Dulcie sat
cross-legged in the bed of the wagon. One good thing about the rickety
wagon's noisy trek was that it prevented normal conversation. She loved
talking with her grandparents, but she'd lain awake most of the night,

rolling over in her mind the scripture Grandpa had read last night. Even now, as they made their way to Sunday services, sorting out her priorities to her grandparents and all her other duties shed fresh light on her need to discover—or rediscover—the faith she'd once had to trust God.

No doubt her grandparents would be overjoyed if they could read her thoughts. For the first time in many years, she looked forward to the prospect of having a long talk with them about the Lord. Perhaps later today after—

"Whoa, mule." Grandpa pulled Samson to a halt in the church yard. She'd been so lost in her thoughts, she hadn't realized they'd arrived. She scrambled over the tailgate and hurried to catch Grandma's hand to help her down from the wagon. Church was the only place Grandma went anymore. She said it was because she was too busy, but Dulcie suspected climbing in and out of the wagon was growing more difficult on her grandmother. Dulcie paused once Grandma was safely on the ground, using the excuse that she'd left her shawl in the back of the wagon. In reality, the short delay was to let Grandma catch her breath, but saying so would stir the older woman's indignation.

Grandpa hung a feedbag over Samson's head and came around to hold out his arm for Grandma to grasp. She smiled up at him and slipped her arm through his. Dulcie fell into step behind them, her heart warming at the sight.

Preacher Bradbury was already ringing the church bell when they stepped inside. They greeted friends and neighbors. Dulcie's friend, Hester, occupied her usual spot and Dulcie stepped over to say hello. Before she could tap her friend's shoulder, she collided with an elbow to her ribs.

"Oh, pardon me. I'm so—" Gavin DeWitt's mouth hung open like hooked trout when their eyes locked for a brief moment. "Dul— Miss Chappell." He backed up a step. "Please excuse me. It seems we're making a habit of bumping into each other."

Dulcie pressed her lips tightly together to prevent the retort she wanted to fire at him from escaping. She was in church, after all, and her grandparents were within earshot. She couldn't say she was surprised to see him. He'd attended their church regularly for over a month, even if his motives for attending were deceptive. "Still trying to make business deals, I see."

"No, . . . I mean yes, but no, that's not why I'm here." A flush crept into his cheeks and highlighted the gold honeycomb strands of his hair.

"Really? Why *are* you here, Mr. DeWitt?"

He stammered for the space of a couple of heartbeats, but before he could reply, Reverend Bradbury called everyone to take their seats. She slipped into the pew next to Grandma, but focusing her attention straight ahead became a challenge when Mr. DeWitt took a seat two rows ahead and across the aisle where he occupied her peripheral vision.

He sang along with three hymns, even though he obviously wasn't familiar with all the words. When Reverend Bradbury opened his Bible and began to read the account of the Samaritan woman coming to the well to draw water, Mr. DeWitt appeared to focus on the preacher's words.

"If thou knewest the gift of God, and who it is that saith to thee, 'Give me to drink; thou wouldest have asked of *him*, and he would have given thee living water.'"

Her gaze crept over to where Mr. DeWitt sat, leaning slightly forward and paying rapt attention—what she should have been doing. Instead, she took the opportunity to study his profile. His furrowed brow suggested he was weighing the preacher's words and rolling them over in his mind. Was he? He looked different somehow. The shadow of hardness she'd seen in his features a few weeks ago was missing. She didn't know why she found him so intriguing. After all, he and his uncle were trying to take their farm.

A sliver of guilt pricked her. To be fair, they were trying to buy the land, not take it. But he was still the enemy, and sizing up one's enemies was a prudent thing to do. Grandma nudged her and Dulcie jerked her attention away from Gavin DeWitt. Her grandmother frowned and tipped her head toward the pulpit. Dulcie complied, but over the course of the next half hour, she stole a few more glances across the aisle at Arnold DeWitt's nephew. Was he really paying attention to the preacher's sermon, or was it an act to fool the town folk?

After the final *Amen* was spoken, Mr. DeWitt made his way over, gave Dulcie and her grandma a polite nod, and shook hands with Grandpa. "Mr. Chappell, I'd like to talk with you again, but church isn't the place to discuss business."

Grandpa lifted his chin and sent a steely gaze toward the young man. "Ain't that what you an' yer uncle did a couple o' weeks back?"

Mr. DeWitt's face reddened. "You're right, and I apologize for that. It wasn't the right thing to do."

Grandpa folded his arms across his chest. "I been hearin' 'bout you doin' what you think is the right thing."

Dulcie wondered at the statement, but remained silent and watched Grandpa take stock of Gavin DeWitt—not unlike she'd been doing during the church service.

"If yer of a mind to come out to the farm fer a neighborly visit, yer welcome to share a cup o' cold water with us." Grandpa clapped Mr. DeWitt's shoulder. "Jus' so ye know, I ain't changin' my mind 'bout sellin', but ye can drop by iffen it pleases ye."

Dulcie's face heated and she bent down, pretending to fuss with her shoe. What was Grandpa thinking, inviting the enemy into their midst? Maybe she could arrange to be occupied at the loom, or taking wool goods into town when Gavin came to visit.

Gavin? She hadn't thought of him by his given name since she'd learned his last name was DeWitt.

&ℯ TWENTY-TWO

Gavin paused on the boardwalk as two women carried bundles from Luther Dempsey's store. He held the door for them and tipped his hat. He'd seen both of them in church, and if he wasn't mistaken, the younger of the two was Dulcie Chappell's friend.

He bid the women good morning, and continued on toward the livery. He hoped Otis Hogan had a rig available today, but even if he didn't, Gavin might decide to walk the two miles to James Chappell's farm. He'd found two possible tracts of land within ten miles of Hot Springs that appeared suitable for grazing animals. One of them even had a small stream bordering it.

Anticipation had made him wakeful and restless most of the night, and not only because he was anxious to share his idea of relocating Mr. Chappell's sheep. The prospect of spending time with James Chappell stirred a hunger within him that he couldn't explain. Perhaps it was the still incomplete list of goals lying on the desk in his room that urged him to glean nuggets of wisdom from the elderly gentleman.

Maybe catching a glimpse of Dulcie and getting to know her a little better wasn't such a bad prospect either.

"Mr. DeWitt. Hey there, Mr. DeWitt!"

Gavin turned. A skinny young fellow with yellow hair sticking out in a dozen directions slapped bare feet across the dirt street, raising dust with every step. Gavin recognized him as the boy his uncle had hired to deliver copies of the letters of intent to purchase to each of the land-owners a while back. The lad waved a piece of paper in his hand as he approached.

"Mr. DeWitt." The young fellow panted and wiped sweat from his brow as he held out an envelope. "This here telly-gram come fer ye."

Gavin reached into his pocket for some coins. "Thank you. Tad, isn't it?"

The boy nodded. "Yessir."

Gavin took the envelope and deposited the coins in Tad's out-stretched hand. "Thank you, Tad."

Tad glanced at the coins in his hand. "Thank *you*, Mr. DeWitt." He raced off back toward the telegraph office.

Gavin smiled and shook his head at the boy's energy. He slid his finger under the envelope flap to loosen the seal, and unfolded the piece of yellow paper.

Received letter. Cease all activity regarding land deals. Wait for my return. Arnold DeWitt.

Gavin's breath escaped in a *whoosh*. He knew his uncle wouldn't be happy with the news Gavin had shared in the letter, but he didn't anticipate being told to cease and desist. His shoulders slumped along with his spirits. He had no regrets over the letter. Every word came from his heart and his newly-emerged resolution to be an honest and forthright man. He'd not back down.

He looked at the telegram again. Did this mean he couldn't go visit James Chappell today? If he did, what could he tell the man was his reason for coming? Mr. Chappell had told him he was welcome to drop by for neighborly visit, but Uncle Arnold wouldn't see it that way.

He crumpled the telegram and shoved it into the pocket of his trousers.

Gavin stood on the platform of the train depot as the iron monster hissed and screeched to a halt, steam spewing. Porters pushed past him with luggage carts, lining up beside the baggage car. Gavin waited, hands twitching in his pockets. The confrontation he'd anticipated was about to explode. His conviction that the money his uncle had offered the farmers wasn't a fair price had not changed, and he was prepared to stand by what he'd said.

He squared his shoulders and straightened his tie. More than the terms of the contracts, he was determined to defend his own goals and principles. He might be out of a job within the hour, but this time he would not be bullied.

Arnold DeWitt stepped down from the first class car, paused a brief moment when he caught sight of Gavin waiting for him, and then shoved his luggage ticket at a porter. "Bring my bags to the Mountain Park." With a withering glare at Gavin and an almost imperceptible jerk of his chin, he stomped toward the waiting buggy. Gavin followed without comment. Apparently he wasn't worthy of a greeting.

Gavin climbed into the buggy and reined the horse around in the direction of the Mountain Park. He drew in a breath to speak, but his uncle beat him to it.

"Who do you think you are, going against my directives?"

"Uncle, I wanted to talk—"

"No, you're going to listen." The harshness of his uncle's tone echoed with a familiar intimidation. "I'm going to talk and when I get through, we're going to go pay a few visits to these farmers who have manipulated you into thinking you could cross me."

Gavin tightened his grip on the reins, but he refused to cower in the face of his uncle's threats. He'd remain silent—for now.

The hotel came into view. As they reached the entrance of the drive, the elder DeWitt turned to point his finger at Gavin. "If you think going behind my back and altering the terms of the contracts was acceptable, then you've forgotten who and what you are. You work for me. You are my employee. You do as I say. You are nothing!"

Nothing? Gavin drew in a breath and held it, waiting for the same knife of pain he'd experienced standing in front of his father. His father might be gone, but nothing had changed. "I am your nephew, your blood kin, your brother's son. Family."

His uncle's face mottled and a strangulated snort blew from his nose. A growl rose up and rumbled from his lips "You think that matters to me? I only took you into my employ as a favor to your brother. Harold was embarrassed by you, and asked me to try to make something of you since your father never could."

Gavin pulled on the reins and halted the horse. There was a time hearing such demeaning and hateful words would have caused him to be physically sick to his stomach. Now, they simply blew through the hollowness that was his soul. He stared at his uncle as the man lumbered from the buggy and strode toward the front door of the hotel without even looking back to see if Gavin followed.

His uncle directed Gavin to wait in the lobby while he went and freshened up. "Be ready to leave in ten minutes." He aimed a thick finger in Gavin's face. "And don't keep me waiting."

Less than ten minutes later, Uncle Arnold emerged from his room and headed toward the door and the waiting buggy. Gavin climbed in and gathered the reins. They were barely past the lamp posts that marked the hotel drive entrance when Uncle Arnold resumed his rant.

"You keep your mouth shut and pay attention. I'm going to show you how to steer a business deal with authority." His lips flapped with contempt. "I'm beginning to think you are as ignorant as these backward mountain people. If you'll listen and use your head, you might learn something—how to persuade people to make decisions. If force is needed, then so be it." He stuck a cigar in mouth and mumbled around it. "Watch and learn."

Did his uncle have nothing to say about Dewey Tate's inquiry about purchasing his entire farm? Uncle Arnold likely cared as much about that as he did Gavin's declaration of having goals of his own. Nothing mattered to Arnold DeWitt except the land deal going as planned, and making money.

Arnold directed Gavin past the turn off for Zeb Huxley's place and instead pointed up the rise to the Chappell farm. "I told you early on that getting James Chappell's mark on a contract was the key to making this entire project work, that he's the one we'd have to go after."

Gavin's chest tightened and a notion stirred within him—an inclination of protectiveness. Within minutes they rolled into the yard at the Chappell farm. The aroma of stewing chicken greeted them. Gavin set the brake and glanced up as James Chappell stepped out the door of the modest house with a toothpick in his mouth. Dulcie was on his heels, untying her apron. She sent a pointed look first to Arnold, and then to Gavin, the question in her eyes clear: *What are you doing here?* She tossed the apron on the porch step.

Gavin stopped a few feet short of his uncle, choosing instead to stand behind him and off to one side. He was unwilling to present a unified picture of himself and his uncle to Mr. Chappell. Besides, he got a better view of Dulcie from where he stood. Uncle Arnold straightened his lapels as he approached the man and his granddaughter standing on the front porch. "Chappell? We need to talk. You should know why I'm here."

Gavin cringed inwardly. What a rude way to greet the elderly man. Dulcie must have agreed as the scowl on her face deepened and she tried to step past her grandfather.

Mr. Chappell took her elbow and pulled her back, gently patting her shoulder. "I believe I know why yer here, Mr. DeWitt. I already told yer nephew here I ain't changin' my mind. Don't reckon there's anything else you can say what'll turn my thinkin' around."

Uncle Arnold stepped up onto the porch without waiting for an invitation. "Now see here, Chappell. You're not getting any younger, and I would imagine this place takes a lot of work. Who's going to do it after you die?" He jerked his thumb at Dulcie. "That girl?"

Anger coiled in Gavin's gut. A tremor—not of trepidation, but of outrage—swept through him. Keeping his mouth shut as his uncle had instructed became more difficult by the minute. His teeth hurt from clamping them so tightly.

Arnold shook his head. "You and I both know that selling is the best option for you. Besides, you're doing your neighbors a great disservice by refusing to sell. They are all going to miss out on the prosperity that could come to this backwoods, all because of your selfishness."

Dulcie's face blanched and then reddened. Her shoulders hiked up and stiffened, and her jaw twitched. She wasn't going to be able to control her temper much longer. What did she tell him not long ago? Her job was protecting her grandparents. Uncle Arnold had no inkling the fury that was about to unleash in the form of *that girl*.

Mr. Chappell stroked his beard. "This land and those sheep are my granddaughter's inheritance."

"Bah!" Uncle Arnold scoffed at the old gentleman. "Listen. Women don't want to inherit a farm. They want to inherit money. If you will comply—"

Dulcie pushed past her grandfather. *Here it comes.* Gavin had seen locomotives barreling down the track with less tenacity.

Dulcie shook her finger in Arnold's face. "You listen to me, Mr. De-Witt."

Mr. Chappell tugged on her arm. "Dulcie girl, go on back inside."

"Mr. DeWitt, you are a rude and despicable man, and you got the manners of a polecat. How dare you—"

"Dulcie girl, go inside."

"No, Grandpa. This man is trespassin', and if he doesn't leave right now, I'm goin' to go speak with Sheriff Harper and swear out a complaint."

Mr. Chappell grasped both Dulcie's arms and made her look at him. "Go inside, child." While spoken quietly, the firmness of his voice left no room for misunderstanding.

A chuckle rumbled from Uncle Arnold's chest. "That's right, little lady. You go on in there and leave the business to the men."

His uncle's condescending tone grated on Gavin's ears. A tremble visibly shuddered through Dulcie, and Gavin waited for her response to his uncle's disparaging statement. Her eyes fired daggers at his uncle for the space of several heartbeats, but then she returned her focus to her grandfather.

"Out o' respect to you, Grandpa, I will. But I'll be right inside the door, and if these men try to bully you, they'll have t' deal with me."

These men? Of course, she would include him in her statement. Like everyone else in town, she connected him with his uncle. Why wouldn't she? Everything he'd attempted to do since arriving in Hot Springs, he'd done in his uncle's name. Regret knotted his belly.

Mr. Chappell turned his attention back to Uncle Arnold. "'Thou shalt not remove thy neighbor's landmark, which they of old time have set in thine inheritance, which thou shalt inherit in the land that the Lord thy God giveth thee to possess it.' The Lord God has given us this land to possess, Mr. DeWitt." He gestured toward the hillside. "This is our inheritance."

Mr. Chappell's words were, no doubt, found somewhere in the Bible, and unlike his uncle, Gavin had nothing but respect for the old man.

Uncle Arnold sputtered and snorted in derision. He pointed a finger and leaned forward to poke Mr. Chappell's shoulder. "Let me spell it out for you real clear, Chappell. I am offering you good money to buy your land. The longer you refuse, the harder you're making it on your family and your neighbors. For now, my offer stands, but it won't stand forever. You wait too long, and I might be tempted to offer someone else a lot more money."

Even to Gavin's ears the "offer" sounded more like a demand. Every minute that ticked by made Gavin wish he'd never gotten involved in this venture. For a fleeting moment, he recalled the list he'd written down—the kind of man he wanted to be—and the memory of it slapped him into awareness. Could he do nothing to stop this harassment of an elderly man and his family who simply wanted to be left in peace?

His uncle took another step closer to Mr. Chappell, almost stepping on his toes, but Mr. Chappell didn't back away or flinch. Arnold bent his head until he was almost nose to nose with the older man. "You know, I'd sure hate to see anything bad happen to your sheep."

Mr. Chappell didn't blink, obviously not taking the veiled threat seriously. But the little old woman Gavin had seen in church sitting beside Dulcie came bursting out the door wielding a broom. Mr. Chappell made a grab for the broom, but missed, and she aimed every bit of her spit and vinegar at Uncle Arnold.

She shook the broom at him. "Y'all git on off o' this porch and off this property. My husband done tol' you he ain't sellin' you our land. You cain't come 'round here with yer bullyin' and threats." She whacked Uncle Arnold on the shoulder with the broom. "Go on, git on outa here. Git!" She whacked him again, and swung the broom back like she was aiming for his uncle's head. Uncle Arnold beat a hasty retreat toward the buggy.

"You'll be sorry. When all your friends and neighbors turn against you because you stood in the way of prosperity, you'll wish you had—"

"I said, *git!*" Mrs. Chappell took out after his uncle like she was chasing a fox out of her hen house. She flailed the broom in his direction, nearly spooking the buggy horse.

Gavin almost couldn't hold back a grin, but he managed to do so. He held up both hands. "We're leaving, ma'am." He glanced over his shoulder at his red-faced uncle who scrambled into the buggy wiping spit from his lips.

Before Gavin turned to get into the buggy, he met the resolute gaze of all three Chappells and mouthed, 'I'm sorry.' He climbed aboard and sent the horse toward town in a hurry. He'd learned something, all right.

He learned that when Dulcie Chappell said she'd move heaven and earth to protect her grandparents, she likely inherited her determination from her grandmother.

❧ TWENTY-THREE

Dulcie clenched her fists. "Argh! The nerve of that man, talkin' to you like that." The buggy had disappeared past the hill and around the bend, but she stood there looking down the road like she expected the two men to double back.

Grandpa slipped his arm around Grandma and took the broom from her. He leaned close and gave her a peck on the cheek. "Go on in and make yerself a cup o' tea. Set in the rockin' chair and spend some time with the Lord." She grasped the broom handle and tugged, but Grandpa held it fast. "Now, Virginia, ye already done enough sweepin' fer one day. Where's yer walkin' stick?"

Dulcie stepped over and looped her arm through Grandma's. Her grandmother's hand trembled. "Let's go finish cleaning up the dinner dishes. I'll help you."

Grandma stiffened and shook her head. With a deep scowl between her narrowed eyes, she pulled her arm away. "Reckon I better do them dishes myself. As peeved as I am right now, I might throw a dish or two across the room and enjoy doin' it." She hiked up the hem of her dress and marched up the porch steps, her tiny feet stomping out a staccato beat.

Dulcie's insides trembled with fury as she watched Grandma until the door closed behind her. The very idea of her grandparents being subjected to such intimidation sent waves of wrath through her. She turned to Grandpa. "Why didn't you let me run that awful man off?"

He huffed, the noise coming out as a muffled growl. "Yer Grandma done a pretty good job o' that."

"But she shouldn't have to." Agitation curled her toes. "And neither should you. That's my job. I'm supposed to take care of you both, I'm supposed to make sure nothing and nobody ever—"

"Now hold on there, Rosebud. Don't fret yerself." Grandpa reached out and gathered her into his arms. "First of all, it ain't yer job, it's God's job, an' He does it purty well."

Tears burned and she sniffled against his shirt. "But it's up to me to protect you."

A gentle chuckle shook his chest. "Where'd ye git an idea like that?"

She pulled back and looked at his dear face, lined with wisdom and softened by compassion. "From the Bible, Grandpa."

Moisture glinted from his eyes, and calluses scratched her cheek when he cupped her face in his work-roughened hands. "Tell me."

"It says in Exodus we are to honor our father and mother so that our days will be long upon the land that God has given us." She swallowed hard and battled for control. "You and Grandma are the only parents I have. I believe God wants me to honor you the same as I would Papa and Mama, and He will give us long days on this land."

"I'm right happy to hear ye care what God thinks, Rosebud." He snugged his arms around her again.

"I do, Grandpa." She gently pulled out of the embrace. "I know I've held a grudge against God for a long time. I believed He didn't care about me. But I've watched you and Grandma over the years. Your faith has never faltered. I tried to stay angry at Him, but . . ." She tilted her head. "It was time for me to put away my resentment."

Grandpa pulled his sleeve across his eyes. "Yer Grandma'll be right pleased that her prayers been answered."

She took another look over her shoulder toward the road, and was relieved to see no evidence of the DeWitts returning. "Grandpa, I don't understand something. Doesn't that man know our family, generations of Chappells, are buried in the cemetery over the rise, behind the junipers?" She tried to recall if the topic had ever been discussed with DeWitt.

Grandpa shrugged. "Reckon not, but it don't make no difference."

She squinted against the confusion Grandpa's statement stirred. "Why didn't you tell them there is a cemetery located on the property. Surely he wouldn't want to buy land with a cemetery on it."

She looked past the meadow dotted with sheep, and let her gaze travel to the far corner. From her vantage point in front of the house, one would never know the cemetery existed for all the junipers and rhododendrons. She looked back at Grandpa. He, too, gazed out across the meadow toward the resting place of their family members. "Why didn't you tell him, Grandpa?"

Wisdom deepened the lines around his eyes. "When ye was a young'un, an' me or yer grandma told ye not to do somethin', did we list all the whys and how comes and what fors?"

Dulcie shook her head. "No."

Her grandfather leveled a look at her that she remembered from when she was a little girl. "It were enough that we said no. It'll hafta be enough for them city fellers that I said no."

His response made perfect sense. It should be enough that the land owner's final word on the subject was no, he didn't want to sell. Grandpa had turned the matter over in his mind, but once they'd discussed it, his answer was steadfast.

The image of Grandpa standing there, quietly telling DeWitt he'd not changed his mind drew a corresponding picture of God never moving, never changing. Her stilted, tentative prayers over the past few weeks eased into her thoughts. She'd not had to search for God to ask His forgiveness. He didn't change. None of the promises in the scriptures she'd heard all her life ever changed. She was the one who'd stepped away and argued with God. She'd stubbornly dug in her heels and refused to trust Him. But after all these years, God had remained the same. His love was the same, His power, His comfort, and His plan—all were unchanged from her earliest recollection.

Grandpa pulled out his faded bandana and mopped his face. "I got work waitin' fer me in the barn. Why don't ye go in an' see iffen ye can help yer grandma, an' git her settled down. I hate seein' her so riled. Try 'n' git her to rest a spell." He stuffed his bandana back into his pocket. "That won't be easy. She ain't happy 'less she's got somethin' to keep her hands busy."

A tiny smile tugged at the corner of Dulcie's mouth. Grandpa's statement was certainly true. Even when Grandma sat, she never wasted a moment. The only time her grandmother was still was when the woman prayed. Except recently. The memory of Grandma sitting beside her spinning wheel, holding her head in her hands, rushed back to remind Dulcie that perhaps her grandmother was a bit more frail than she'd like to let on.

The image pulled Dulcie's smile from her face. "I'll see if I can convince her to rest a while."

Streaks of gray lined the eastern horizon, promising a rainy, dismal day when Dulcie peeked through the muslin curtain in her loft bedroom. It appeared the sun had decided to sleep in and had no intention of showing its face. She pulled on her work skirt and shirt as quietly as possible, hoping her grandparents would sleep a little longer.

Grandma wasn't herself last night. During supper she barely spoke, and didn't argue when Dulcie'd said she'd clean up. She hadn't even wanted her usual cup of coffee with Grandpa after they'd had their scripture reading, instead opting to turn in early. Perhaps a little extra rest was all she needed.

Irritation stirred Dulcie's middle as she climbed down the loft ladder. That awful Mr. DeWitt got Grandma so agitated yesterday. Dulcie wanted to give him a piece of her mind. Gavin had stood there, silent, but his eyes had reflected his disagreement with his uncle's behavior. The next time she saw him, she'd have to ask him about that.

She crossed to the kitchen, and checked to see if there were any embers still glowing in the stove. After adding a few sticks of kindling and some fatwood, a tiny flame sprang to life. She placed a few more pieces of stove wood atop the kindling, and left it to grow into a hot fire. The empty graniteware coffeepot sat by the sink. She ladled water from the bucket into it, but as she moved to set it on the stove, a blood-chilling sound like she'd never heard before rent the air.

"Aghhhh!" A pain-laced cry carved a gash through Dulcie's being. "Nooooo, Virginiaaaa . . . Oh, nooo . . ." The strangled, groaning sob from her grandparents' bedroom stole her breath and cramped every muscle in her body, paralyzing her in place.

The coffeepot fell from her hands, the water splattering down her skirt and across the floor. Sickening dread crashed over her. "Oh, God, no." The excruciating whisper raked past her throat. She clapped both trembling hands over her mouth. *God, please . . .*

She pushed her feet toward the bedroom. Where did the strength to do so come from? At her grandparents' bedroom door, she halted as if slapped in the face by the scene before her.

There, sitting on the bed, Grandpa held Grandma in his arms, weeping and rocking back and forth. His eyes squeezed shut and deep furrows of agony between his brows gave her the answer she wanted to deny.

No, God, You can't do this to me—to us—again.

The floor beneath her moved, as her world tilted. An unseen force carried her to the side of the bed where she lowered herself to the edge. Grandpa's guttural moan sent shards of ice down her spine. She wrapped her arms around Grandpa, with Grandma between them, lying limp against Grandpa's chest. Grief drops coursed down his face and dampened his beard, mingling with her own hot tears.

After an undefined stretch of time—a few minutes? An eternity? Grandpa stirred. Dulcie eased herself from the edge of the bed and helped him lay Grandma down against the pillows, but she couldn't bear to pull the sheet over her grandmother's face. Instead, she stared at Grandma, marveling how the lines of age around her eyes, forehead, and mouth had smoothed out, as if every hardship and worry she'd ever known no longer weighed on her.

Grandpa's nightshirt tucked around his knees when he knelt by the bed, still clinging to Grandma's hand. His bowed head rested against the bedding, as if he had no strength to hold his head in a prayerful position.

"Almighty God, Yer the Giver an' Taker o' life. We don't understand Yer ways, but we trust Ye. O God, give us Yer mercy an' grace jus' now. We're needin' Yer peace and comfort, 'cause our hearts is painin' somethin' fierce. Receive Yer daughter into her heavenly home. She loved Ye real good, Father."

A long, grief-saturated silence followed Grandpa's whispered 'amen.' How many years ago had Dulcie tried to hide from death's sorrow in the barn hayloft? She longed to do the same now.

"Buttercups. Queen Anne's Lace. Black-eyed Susans."

Dulcie blinked. "Grandpa?" Had grief robbed him of his senses?

Grandpa rose to his feet and smoothed Grandma's hair away from her face. "Them's her favorite wildflowers." He straightened, but didn't take his eyes from his beloved. "You pick some on yer way into town to fetch the preacher."

Dulcie's throat tightened, barely allowing enough life-sustaining air through. She swallowed past the lump. "Grandpa, why don't you go and pick—"

"No." He picked up Grandma's hand and bent to place a kiss on her fingertips. "You go. I must get yer grandma ready."

"Grandpa, let me—"

Grandpa turned, arresting whatever she'd started to say. The tiniest smile pulled at his white whiskers, and his eyes softened. "Child, I need to do this, to spend this time with her. Go on, now. Do as I ask. Go fetch the preacher and bring your grandma back some wildflowers. Ye might stop by Dewey's place an' let him know. His Martha were yer grandma's best friend."

She gave him a gentle hug and brushed a kiss on his damp face. "Yes, Grandpa."

Two hours later, Dulcie returned with Reverend and Mrs. Bradbury, and Grandma's favorite wildflowers. Grandpa had dressed Grandma in her blue calico dress—the one she wore to church—and had her laying like she was sleeping.

Dulcie stood by Grandpa and looked down at Grandma's face—so serene. "Dewey Tate is gathering folks. They'll all be here this afternoon."

Mrs. Bradbury enveloped Dulcie in a tight hug, and the reverend laid his hand on Grandpa's shoulder, speaking in solemn tones. "Virginia is home, James."

Grandpa gave a mute nod.

Within a few hours, friends and neighbors began to arrive—women bearing baskets of food and men armed with picks and shovels. Dulcie stood beside Grandpa, her chest numb. Words mumbled from her lips, but she couldn't recall what she'd said to any of the visitors. The preacher's wife took charge of the women, and Grandpa accompanied the men to the family cemetery.

Dulcie sat close to Grandma, swallowing back sobs to remain strong, and watched as the women of the community performed the traditional duties of preparing for a funeral. Vaguely aware of the house being cleaned and prepared for tomorrow, and mountains of food being set out on a makeshift table that stretched the length of the room, she never thought she'd be so grateful for so many people in their house. They didn't let her do a thing, but assured her they'd do everything necessary.

Dewey and Zeb brought the coffin. Dewey crushed the brim of his hat in his hands and mumbled something about being 'so sorry.' Together, the women placed Grandma gently and lovingly into the pine box with her favorite quilt tucked around her.

The men returned, presumably finished preparing the grave site. They ate a bite, paid their respects to Dulcie, and filed past the coffin. Their quiet exit left her and Grandpa alone with Grandma to perform the age-old mountain custom of sitting up all night with the dead.

The following morning, the gray clouds still obscured the sun, but people began to arrive for the funeral shortly after daylight. Dulcie watched Preacher Bradbury, Dewey Tate, Zeb Huxley, Caleb Montgomery, and Otis Hogan help Grandpa carry Grandma's coffin to the wagon. They led old Samson through the foggy mist, across the meadow, while Dulcie and the rest of the mourners followed up the rise to the far corner among the junipers and rhododendrons. There they laid Grandma to rest beside Dulcie's parents and baby brother.

Reverend Bradbury read Grandma's favorite scripture, Psalm 139, and lifted a heartfelt prayer to heaven for the comfort of those left behind. Then Otis Hogan played his dulcimer while the gathering sang *Amazing Grace*. Grandpa stepped forward with the wildflowers Dulcie picked and laid them on the fresh mound of dirt. He kissed his fingers and pressed them to the flowers.

"I ain't never loved another. Ye wait fer me, my love. I'll be there soon."

༄ TWENTY-FOUR

ulcie stood with Grandpa by the fireplace, their arms entwined, as their friends filed past and expressed their condolences. When they'd all left, the preacher stepped over and placed his hand on Grandpa's shoulder.

"Dewey and Zeb wanted me to tell you they took care of all the chores. The cow is fed and milked, chickens are fed, eggs gathered, stove wood split."

The chores hadn't even occurred to Dulcie. "Please thank them for us." She glanced at Grandpa. "I'm not sure we'll be at services this Sunday."

The preacher nodded. "I understand."

"We'll be there." Grandpa turned, and for the first time spoke in his usual steady voice. The lines between his pained eyes deepened. "We'll be in church."

The preacher smiled and shook Grandpa's hand. "See you Sunday, James."

After Reverend Bradbury took his leave, Grandpa fetched his hat. "I promise I won't be long. I just want to go sit with yer grandma fer a while." He reached out his hand and touched Grandma's shawl hanging on a peg by the door. "Need some alone time to have me a talk with the Lord. He's takin' care o' her now."

Dulcie steeled her spine. She couldn't allow Grandpa to see her cry. She must stay strong, like the mountains of her birth. Dependable, like the waters of the spring that never went dry. Supportive, like every breath God gave her. More than ever now, Grandpa needed her.

The door thudded closed behind Grandpa. Finally alone, she allowed the grief to course down her cheeks and flood her soul. She sank to her knees by the hearth. "God, I don't know why You took Grandma. I don't know why You took Mama and Papa. I don't understand—after so many years I finally turned my heart and came back to You—why did You take Grandma now?" She dragged the palm of her hand over her face, but the tears kept coming. "Why now, God?"

Sorrow and confusion wrestled in her heart. Did she have to understand why? Grandma always said God's ways were higher than anything she could understand. What would Grandma tell her now?

Trust, child. Just trust.

She rose and stood at the window. Wisps of fog hung low through the hills and trees, as if heaven was weeping with her. She couldn't see the cemetery from the house, but she could picture Grandpa there. Was he trusting God, even though Grandma was taken from them? Dulcie couldn't picture Grandpa doubting God, but her newly-restored relationship with God was still fragile, tentative. Uncertainty shadowed her like a predator.

The door to her grandparents' bedroom stood open when Dulcie descended the loft ladder the next morning. Frail light filtered through the flour sack curtains at the kitchen window, barely enough light to see the fog that lingered from yesterday's rain. She lit the lamp on the table and carried it to the bedroom door. The bed was neatly made and Grandpa was not there.

Dulcie stuffed a few sticks of kindling into the stove and blew on the tiny red embers that remained from last night. They glowed and danced, eagerly reaching out to join with the dry wood and leap into a friendly flame. She placed the freshly filled coffeepot on the stove, but where was Grandpa?

She opened the door and peered through the pre-dawn gloaming. Lantern light flickered from the window of the barn. What could he possibly be doing out there? She checked the coffeepot again, certain it wouldn't boil for a while, and ran barefoot across the yard. The barn door stood ajar, and she peered inside. The door hinge gave a slight protest when she pushed it open enough to slide inside.

There, with his back to her, was Grandpa, bent over his workbench. The lantern hung from a nearby hook, illuminating whatever occupied him. His quiet voice and a *scritch-scratching* noise captured her attention.

"She's took my heart with her, Lord. Reckon Ye know that."

Scritch-scratch.

"Cain't rightly understand why heaven needs her more'n I do, but I reckon Ye know that, too."

Scritch scratch. Scritch scratch.

"Ain't nothin' Ye don't know. Yer God, an' Yer good, an' I trust Ye. I know You'll take good care o' my Virginia."

Scritch-scritch, scritch-scratch.

"Ye can come on in, Rosebud. I know ye're there."

Dulcie took hesitant steps toward the workbench. "I didn't want to interrupt. What are you—"

The rest of the question strangled in her throat. Laying on the workbench was a wooden cross where Grandpa had carved, *Virginia Lucille Chappell, 1814~1886.*

The sight of the cross with Grandma's name crudely etched across it seared Dulcie's heart with the finality. Never again would she share the space of the wool shed with Grandma as they plied their craft together. Never again would Grandma fuss at them for not wiping their feet.

Grandma's rocking chair wouldn't sing with squeaks while she sat and snapped beans from the garden. Who would name next year's new lambs?

Dulcie's stomach cramped and her breath came in quiet, shallow gulps. The cross lying on the workbench was her new reality.

Grandpa turned, his motion slow and stiff, as if he'd not slept. The ghostly lantern light cast eerie shadows across his face, making him appear older, more fragile. He caressed the cross with his fingertips. "It's only till I can talk to Del Bohanan over in Spring Creek and have him carve a proper headstone, but that'll take some time. I want yer grandma to have a marker, showin' the world she's loved and missed."

Dulcie bit her lip and held her breath, tamping her emotions down. How she wished she could step out of this nightmare and everything would be the way it was again. But no amount of wishing would change the way things were now. The cow bawled in her stall, waiting to be milked.

Grandpa rubbed his whiskers. "Reckon we need to start doin' things a little different. I'll tend to the cow and mule iffen you'll feed the chickens and gather the eggs."

Dulcie nodded. "I'll take care of break—" *The coffeepot!* Her eyes widened and she ran back to the house. The smell of burned coffee and a sizzling puddle on the stove greeted her when she stepped through the door. She grabbed a towel and moved the coffeepot. "I reckon we'll need to start doin' things more than a *little* different," she muttered, as she mopped up the mess.

After promising Grandpa she'd figure out a way to prepare breakfast and clean up afterward, as well as doing her barn chores, Dulcie trudged out to the wool shed almost two whole hours later than usual. Despite Grandpa assuring her that he'd help by doing some of the morning chores—chores that had always been her responsibility—she was determined to carry her own load and take on Grandma's household duties as well. But as she entered the wool shed, she stopped. Across the small space stood Grandma's two spinning wheels. Without her grandmother to spin the wool for her to weave, her production would slow down, and so would their income.

The fine, dark green woolen cloth stretched across the loom. She only needed to complete another half yard before taking it to Mr. Dempsey's store. She ran her fingers along the edge of the yard goods. Grandma had loved the color and Dulcie had hoped to have enough of the fine lamb's wool left to make Grandma a winter shawl for Christmas.

Christmas.

It was months away, but the thought ushered in an ache in her throat. She tried to swallow, but the dread stuck hard. How could they have Christmas without Grandma? She glanced out the small window and spotted Grandpa squatted down in the meadow grass, running his hands over one of the smaller lambs. With him safely out of hearing range, Dulcie sank down onto Grandma's stool and reached her arms to embrace the idle spinning wheel. Her sorrow demanded freedom and tears dripped down her face, unchecked. How she longed to hear Grandma humming along with the spinning wheel, or watch her grandmother's work-worn hands with their gnarled fingers expertly twist the spider web-like fibers together into fine wool yarn.

"Oh, Grandma, what am I going to do without you?"

The question she'd asked God yesterday after the funeral still lingered in the back of her mind. How could God be loving and caring, and take someone so dear to her? She could hear Grandma admonishing her to trust God, even when hard things happened, even when prayers weren't answered the way she wanted, even when she couldn't understand why.

Tears dripped onto her lap and created dark spots on her tan skirt. "I know You want me to trust You, God, but I needed Grandma. I needed her and You took her." A whisper echoed through her soul. *Lean on Me, child. You need Me.*

Maybe she didn't have to understand in order to trust.

James tucked his Sunday go to meetin' shirt into his britches and hiked his suspenders up to his shoulders. He blew out a shaky breath and glanced to the corner of the bedroom where Virginia's blue calico dress usually hung from the peg. The sight of the empty peg begat a hard longin' in his chest when he remembered dressin' Virginia in her Sunday best for her burial. An ache he could barely contain filled his whole bein'.

He cleared the thickness from his throat and stepped out of the bedroom to see if Dulcie was ready to leave for church. Judgin' from the thumps that came from the loft overhead, she was still dressin'. He called up to her. "Dulcie girl, we better git on. Ye know how yer grand—" The recollection of the wooden cross he'd tapped into the ground at Virginia's grave yanked the rest of his words back afore they spilled out. "Gonna go hitch up the mule."

The ride to town passed by with nary more'n a few words 'tween him and Dulcie. Her heart was painin', and he weren't sure how to comfort her when his own heart was splintered like an old fencepost. He halted Samson, and they barely had time to climb down from the wagon and folks lined up, sayin' how sorry they was over Virginia's passin'.

One glance at Dulcie and he knew she were about to bust into tears. Her face were like carved stone, but her hands shook. The ladies hugged her and wagged their heads, each one tellin' her that her grandma was in a better place and time passin' would ease her hurt.

Long-faced men shook James's hand and clapped him on the shoulder, speakin' in somber quietness with downcast eyes. They meant well, but if one more person told either of them they knew how they felt, he feared Dulcie mightn't be able to hold herself together.

He sure was glad when the preacher come out to the front steps and rung the church bell, callin' the faithful to worship. Instead of their usual spot on the fourth row, James steered Dulcie to the last row along the back wall so they could slip out whilst the preacher was offerin' up the last prayer. No point in repeatin' all the sad-faced words of sympathy.

When the congregation sang Virginia's favorite hymn, *Fairest Lord Jesus*, tears burned his eyes. The broken pieces of his heart all cried together to hear Virginia's voice singin' beside him. God's whisper rained sweet mercy-drops of peace over him.

She's singing, son. She's singing.

With a tremulous smile, he lifted up his voice, 'cause that's what his Virginia would've done. Still, he were right glad when the preacher began to pray the closin' prayer. He tugged Dulcie's arm and she readily followed, the two of them tiptoein' out the door while everyone still had their heads bowed.

They were near a half mile up the road before Dulcie spoke. "Thank you, Grandpa. I don't think I could've lasted another minute in there." She rubbed her belly like it pained her. "I'm trying to be strong, really I am, but it's the other way around. You're the strong one instead of me." She sniffed hard. "Look where I'm sitting—here on the seat beside you instead of in the back. This is where Grandma always sat. I don't belong here."

James gripped both reins in one hand and reached over and patted her knee. "You belong beside me, Dulcie girl, fer as long as God leaves me here. Even when ye hitch yerself to a husband, you'll always be my Rosebud." He clucked to Samson. "B'sides, how'd ye git the idea ye hafta be the strong one? You an' me, we'll be strong fer each other. Ain't that what yer grandma woulda said?"

"That's another thing." Dulcie palmed the tears from her face. "How do those people know what I'm supposed to feel?"

He rested his elbows on his knees. "Aw, Rosebud, they're jus' tryin' to be nice. I know, it ain't comfortin' when folks tell ye they know how ye feel, 'cause they don't know, not really."

He flipped the reins when Samson slowed down to take a mouthful of grass at the side of the road. "Let me ask ye a question. Do ye really want them folks to know how ye feel? 'Cause fer them to really under-stand, they'd hafta lose someone they love. Is that what ye want?"

A regretful look filled her eyes. "No, Grandpa."

His throat tightened. "I reckon folks get a mite uncomfortable when they're around other folk what're grievin', so they just say things they hope'll sound nice an' purty. But it don't always come out soundin' that way to the one doin' the grievin'." He slipped his arm around her shoulders.

She gave a little nod, almost too small to notice, and wiped her eyes on her sleeve.

They rolled along the rutted road in silence for a stretch, the birds fillin' the quiet with song. Seemed God's critters rejoiced when one of His saints came Home. Even in his sorrowin', he couldn't resent their music.

He cleared his throat. "You needin' Samson tomorrow?"

Dulcie shook her head. "I have plenty of work to catch up on. You planning to go by Dewey Tate's place to help him with something?"

He pulled in a slow, deep breath. "I was aimin' to go on down to Spring Creek and see Del Bohanan. Been rollin' around in my mind what to have him carve on your grandma's headstone. Ye got any thoughts?"

Her shoulders shook and she sucked in a sharp breath.

He waited, but she didn't answer. Mayhap she couldn't make the words come. He sure understood that. They rolled into the yard and he halted the wagon. "Thought mayhap you'd want to go with me. We could pick out the headstone together."

She were as froze as a statue. Her lips trembled like leaves in a spring storm. "I . . . I'm sorry. I have . . . work . . ."

He made his voice as gentle as he could. "It's all right, Rosebud." He squeezed her hand. "Just thought I'd ask."

She grabbed a handful of her skirt and scrambled down from the wagon, and scurried in the door. He wished he hadn't asked her to do such a hard thing.

TWENTY-FIVE

Three days after Grandpa returned from Spring Creek, they still hadn't spoken of Grandma's headstone, and Dulcie didn't ask. It wasn't that she didn't care. She simply couldn't trust herself not to cry, and Grandpa didn't need to see her tears. From before dawn to long after sunset, she pushed herself to do more—the household chores, the morning barn chores, the cooking and laundry, and processing the wool—alone. At night she sat up late in the wool shed, spinning the cleaned and carded wool so she'd have something to work on the loom the following day.

She didn't resent the extra work, but only wished she could fall into bed at night so exhausted that sleep would come immediately. Instead, she lay awake, her back and fingers aching. But the physical pain was nothing compared to her aching heart. She longed to comfort Grandpa, but how did one give comfort when they needed it themselves?

The fine, dark green woolen cloth was finished. Dulcie removed it from the loom and folded it carefully, wrapping it in muslin sheeting to keep it clean on the way into town. Grandpa said he'd accompany her. He needed to pick up some feed at Hollis Purdue's place and drop off his adz at Otis Hogan's livery to be repaired.

"I'm thinkin' on buildin' a smokehouse." Grandpa urged the reluctant mule down the road. "Mayhap this fall, I'll get us some venison or a turkey."

Dulcie nodded. "That'll be nice, Grandpa. Maybe I can help you."

He looked sideways at her from under the brim of his battered hat. "Don'tcha think ye got enough to do? Reckon iffen I need any help, I'll get Dewey to come an' give me a hand."

Dulcie lifted her shoulders. She likely wouldn't be much help to him anyway, never having gotten the knack of hammering a nail. Maybe having Dewey to talk to would be a comfort, both of them being widowers now.

Grandpa pulled Samson to a halt in front of Luther Dempsey's Emporium and waited for Dulcie to climb down before he handed her the muslin-wrapped bundle. "Will a half hour be long enough fer ye to git done with yer business?"

She gathered the bundle and held it to her chest. "More than enough time. Do you want me to meet you at the Feed and Seed?"

Grandpa gave a short nod and released the brake. "That'd be jus' fine." He flipped the reins against Samson's back. "Hup, mule."

Dulcie turned toward the door of the Emporium, but before she reached the door, a voice stopped in her tracks. "Let me get that door for you." Gavin DeWitt opened the entry door and held out his hands. "May I carry that for you?" He reached for the bundle, but Dulcie shook her head.

"No, thank you, *Mister* DeWitt." Did her reply sound as cold to him as she'd tried to make it? She brushed past him, marched to the counter, and deposited the bundle.

"Miss Dulcie, good to see ye." Luther Dempsey hurried over, wiping his hands on his apron. "Whatcha got there?"

She unwrapped the muslin. "This is the woolen cloth the lady from Washington wants. I believe you told me her name was Mrs. Farling. Can you send word to her that it's ready to be picked up?"

"I can do that." Mr. Dempsey bobbed his head. "Sure was sorry to hear about your grandma. She was a fine Christian lady. 'Course now she's in a better—"

"Yes, thank you, Mr. Dempsey." She straightened her shoulders. "There is a balance owing on the green wool. Mrs. Farling paid three dollars down. She needed a full dress length plus an extra yard, so the balance is two more dollars. Will you please collect that when she comes in?"

Her instructions weren't necessary. Mr. Dempsey had been selling her goods on consignment for a long time. But for some reason she felt the need the fill the space with words. Perhaps part of that need had to do with the fact that Gavin DeWitt had followed her into the Emporium and stood a few feet away to her right, as if he were waiting for her.

The last person she wished to speak with was anyone named De-Witt.

Mr. Dempsey lifted the folds of the cloth. "This is right nice goods, Miss Dulcie. I'll wrap it in paper for Miz Farling. She usually comes in a couple o' times a week. I'll collect the balance for you. I'll go get some paper to wrap it." He started toward the stockroom, but paused at the doorway. "Again, Miss Dulcie, I'm sure sorry about your grandma." He disappeared through the door.

"As am I, Miss Chappell." Gavin DeWitt, apparently assuming her business with Mr. Dempsey was concluded, stepped forward. "Please accept my sincere condolences."

She drew in a slow, deliberate breath and turned to face him with narrowed eyes, resentment eating at her. "Mr. DeWitt, forgive me if I doubt your . . ." She threw him a hostile glare. " . . . your *sincerity*. You and your uncle are nothing but carpetbaggers, and I'm sure my grand-mother's death is of no concern to either one of you." A knot formed in her throat and an ominous burning behind her eyes warned she was about to lose control. She wanted to tell Gavin DeWitt to stay away from her and her grandfather, and let them grieve in peace, but something more than her tight throat stopped her.

After all, it wasn't Gavin, but his uncle, who tried to bully them. She recalled Gavin stood there silent. She'd intended to ask him about that, before—

Before Grandma died.

Maybe someday she'd be curious enough to ask him why he'd said nothing, why his eyes contended with his uncle's words, why she got the distinct impression Gavin disagreed with his uncle. But none of that was important now. Still, she couldn't ignore the prodding she felt in her spirit. It wasn't Gavin's fault.

He dipped his head and shuffled his feet, his hands shoved into his pockets and his head down as if he was studying the floor boards. She'd embarrassed him. Grandma would scold her for the way she'd spoken to him. *Ain't never no excuse fer bad manners.*

She released the breath she'd been holding and ran her hand over her face. The tightness in her throat eased. "I apologize, Mr. DeWitt. My grandmother's death wasn't your fault. It was—"

His quiet voice, so unlike his uncle's, disarmed her. "No apology necessary. I understand." He raised his head. "Really, I do."

The warm sympathy she saw in his expression nearly unraveled her. Dulcie wasn't sure why, but she believed him.

Gavin tipped his head toward the counter where the green woolen cloth still lay. "You do beautiful work. That green is the same shade as the pine trees on the mountain."

She acknowledged his compliment with a brief nod and a mumbled thank-you. "I used pine needles and nettle weed to make the dye bath."

His brow rose in surprise. "You make your own dyes, too? That's fascinating."

A tiny tremor swirled in her middle. This man was nothing to her. Less than nothing since he and his uncle were trying to coerce them to sell their land. His opinion shouldn't matter. What did she care what he thought? Why did his interest affect her?

A weak, forced smile was all she could manage before hurrying out the door toward the Feed and Seed.

Gavin watched Dulcie's retreating back from the wide storefront window. Why did this beautiful young woman affect him so? He'd socialized with beautiful young women before back in Philadelphia, but none turned his head.

He knew what she'd been about to say—that her grandmother's death was his uncle's fault. He was no doctor, but the inclination to agree with her unspoken accusation bit him. Uncle Arnold's aggressive and arrogant manner had certainly gotten the elderly woman upset and agitated that day. Word around town was that she'd succumbed to an attack of apoplexy. Needles of guilt pierced Gavin as the scene rolled through his mind. He turned from the window, but the impulse to do something for Dulcie Chappell and her grandfather remained. Especially since he knew his uncle wouldn't back off.

Mr. Dempsey returned to the front of the store with a length of paper and began wrapping the green wool. "Somethin' I can do for ye, Mr. DeWitt?"

Gavin's gaze fell on the table near the door where Dulcie's handmade rugs caught the eye of everyone who entered the store. *Anything I can do for you, Miss Dulcie Chappell?* All the rugs were lovely, but one stood out from the rest. He traced his finger over the rug's pattern of roses and ivy twining around the border. If his memory served, this was the one Dulcie said should be two dollars more than the others because of the extra colors and work that went into it.

"Yes, Mr. Dempsey, I think I'd like to purchase this rug. I've never seen anything quite like it."

The merchant moved to the display table and hoisted the rug into his arms. "This here's one of Miss Dulcie's purtiest ones, but I hafta charge you extry because it's got more—"

Gavin waved away the man's apologetic tone. "Perfectly all right. It's worth the price." The workmanship and quality, along with the higher price, gave him an idea. What if he could contract with the Chappells to create unique rugs for his uncle's new resort? Perhaps that would be incentive for them to agree to his uncle's purchase of the land. He'd already found a couple of tracts of land to show Mr. Chappell. Certainly their sheep would be happy anywhere they had grass. He hoped Uncle Arnold would be amenable to the offer and his idea would show Dulcie and her grandfather that he cared.

Gavin laid the money down on the counter, and Mr. Dempsey assured him the rug would be delivered to his room at the Mountain Park Hotel. He exited the Emporium and strode down the street toward the hotel. Uncle Arnold liked to relax in the hot springs before lunch. Gavin hoped taking the waters would improve his uncle's disposition and make him receptive to the idea of contracting with Dulcie to weave one-of-a-kind rugs. More importantly, he hoped he could talk his uncle into leaving the Chappells alone for a while.

When the hotel came into view, Gavin rubbed his palms against his trouser legs and pressed his lips together, trying to think of how to bring up the subject. It would all depend on his uncle's mood.

Instead of heading inside to his uncle's room, Gavin opted to check the men's bathhouse first. Sure enough, Arnold DeWitt leaned back against a tub railing, soaking in the hot springs, with his ever-present cigar stuck in his mouth. Gavin halted and rolled his shoulders and neck before proceeding into Uncle Arnold's line of vision.

The elder DeWitt scowled when he caught sight of his nephew. "Where've you been?"

Gavin refused to let his uncle's bluster stop him from advocating on the Chappells' behalf. "I stopped by the Emporium, and while I was there, I had an idea that will help James Chappell and his granddaughter decide to sell."

Uncle Arnold harrumphed and climbed out of the hot water. A steward stepped forward with a towel and robe, and then left to attend another client. Arnold tied the sash on the robe, sat on a bench, and reached for his slippers.

"Well? Let's hear it. What's your brilliant idea?"

Ignoring the sarcastic tone in his uncle's voice, Gavin sat on an adjacent bench and propped his elbows on his knees. "If they were assured of a source of income, maybe they'd be more inclined to accept your offer."

His uncle puffed on his cigar. "Maybe the girl can get a chambermaid job at the resort once it's built, and the old man can work as a gardener or something."

The image of Dulcie mopping floors and cleaning spittoons induced a growl deep in Gavin's gut, but he bit back the retort that formed on his tongue. He'd let go of the desire to strive for his uncle's approval, but the hope that the man would listen to his idea compelled him to speak.

He swallowed his indignation. "You know the Chappells raise sheep. But did you know that the granddaughter creates some beautiful rugs with the wool? They are especially unique and reflect the colors of the scenery around here. Those rugs would be a wonderful addition to your resort, and no doubt you'd need quite a number of them."

Uncle Arnold stared at him, silent, so Gavin rubbed his chin and did a quick calculation in his head. "Between the main lobby, the hotel rooms, and all of the common area rooms, I'd estimate—"

"Have you lost your mind?" Uncle Arnold tossed his cigar aside and stood. "You think I should tell these backward idiots that I'll buy a pile of homemade rugs if they'll sell me their land? Bah!"

"But Uncle, if it's a way to finalize the sale—"

"You listen to me, boy." Uncle Arnold pointed his pudgy finger at Gavin's nose. "The only way to bring these yokels in line is to put pressure on them. Now, you're going back out to the Chappell place this afternoon, and use whatever means necessary to bring back a signed contract."

"No!"

Uncle Arnold's thick eyebrows shot up toward his hairline and his face mottled red. He gripped the front edge of his robe and yanked on it. "What!"

"Uncle Arnold, they've had a death in their family. Mrs. Chappell passed away suddenly last week."

"The old lady with the broom? *Pfft*." He dismissed Gavin's concern with a flip of his hand.

Gavin gritted his teeth and gripped his temper before it erupted. "Uncle, they're grieving." Conviction threaded the urgency in his tone. "Common decency requires they be left alone, at least for a while."

His uncle snorted. "All right! A few days, but no more." He straightened his robe and took a menacing step toward Gavin, pulling his eyebrows together into a single, woolly whorl and hissed out a threat. "But this is your last chance, boy. I'm tired of your incompetence and your milksop demeanor. I'm giving you an ultimatum. You find a backbone and present me with a signed contract by the end of this week or look for other employment."

His uncle pushed past the louvered door and exited the bathhouse, leaving Gavin staring, slack-jawed at the door swinging in his wake. How were Dulcie and her grandfather to get over the loss of their loved one in a couple of days?

Try as he might, he couldn't identify with the aching of Dulcie's heart. She and her grandmother clearly shared a deep devotion for each other. That wasn't something he'd ever known. His own grief over the loss of his father was different. How did one grieve lost opportunities to earn a father's love?

& e TWENTY-SIX

Gavin waited until Friday. His uncle hadn't stipulated a day, simply "by the end of the week." Glad the Chappells had a few days without the interference of a DeWitt, he wasn't sure if the extra time helped him prepare what he was going to say, or if the waiting period only made him more nervous. Was it presenting his ideas to Mr. Chappell or meeting his uncle's expectations that produced the jitters? Maybe it was neither. The thought of seeing Dulcie again—what would she say if she knew he called her Dulcie instead of Miss Chappell in his private thoughts?—stirred feelings within him that he dared not explore. At least, not yet.

The livery horse likely knew the way to the Chappell farm by now, and it was a good thing. So engrossed in practicing his speech in his head, Gavin almost missed the turn. He slowed the horse as the rig drew within sight of the house and barn. A sweeping glance across the yard didn't reveal anyone around, but the barn door stood open.

He pulled the mare to a stop and set the brake. He climbed from the buggy. "Hello? Anybody home?"

The bark of a dog answered, and moments later, Mr. Chappell emerged from the barn. He stopped and pulled his bandana from his back pocket and mopped his forehead before approaching.

"Afternoon, Mr. DeWitt." Mr. Chappell's eyes skittered around the parked rig. "See ye didn't bring yer uncle with ye."

"Good afternoon, Mr. Chappell." Gavin hesitantly extended his hand. He wouldn't blame the man for refusing to shake his hand, but James Chappell gave him a cordial nod. His grip surprised Gavin with its strength—like that of a man who'd worked hard all his life.

"Mr. Chappell, I want you to know how very sorry I am for your loss." The words sounded lame and placating, but it was all he could think of to say.

The older man stuffed his bandana back into his pocket without taking his eyes off Gavin. "Right nice of ye to say so, young feller."

Gavin sucked in a deep breath. "Mr. Chappell, I know you've already said you don't want to sell your farm, but I've come hoping you will listen to a couple of ideas I've had."

Mr. Chappell gestured toward the well. "Listenin' don't cost nothin'. Let's go have us a drink o' cold water whilst you unload what's on yer mind."

"Thank you, sir." Gavin followed the man to the well, noticing as they went that Mr. Chappell's steps seemed a bit slower and more labored than he remembered. He accepted the dipper of water Chappell offered and the cold liquid washed some of the nervousness away—until he saw Dulcie approaching from a small outbuilding that sat back under the trees. He waited until she reached them, since his plan involved her as much as her grandfather. Judging by her scowl and determined stride, Gavin wagered she didn't plan on being amiable.

"Miss Chappell."

She folded her arms and her chin lifted a bit as she tossed a look at him that resembled a slammed door. Before she could tell him to get back in his buggy and leave, her grandfather placed his hand on her shoulder.

"A'fore ye get yer feathers ruffled, let's hear him out."

She slid her gaze sideways to her grandfather, and a momentary softening fell across her features. But when she returned her gaze to Gavin, her eyes darkened and her lips hardened with a distinct warning that he didn't miss. She gave him a clipped nod, but given Uncle Arnold's tactics of the past couple of weeks, her defensive posture and suspicious demeanor were predictable. At least she agreed to let him speak. If nothing else, he hoped to show both of them not everyone named DeWitt was aggressive and cold-hearted.

"Miss Chappell, Mr. Chappell, I've had a couple of ideas I hope you'll consider." He interlaced his fingers. "I know raising your sheep is very important to you. Your family has done this for a long time, so I think I understand why you're hesitant to relocate. But if you'll allow me . . ." he pulled his notebook from his coat pocket, "I think I may have a solution."

He flipped a few pages in the notebook. "I found a couple of tracts of land, both with plenty of good grazing, not too far from here. There is a small stream on one piece of land, and the man at the land office assured me water could be found without too much trouble on the second tract."

Dulcie drew her shoulders up and opened her mouth, but her grandfather's fingers tightened on her shoulder. Not knowing how much longer Mr. Chappell could keep her reined in, Gavin hurried to continue.

"In addition, I had the opportunity to examine some of your beautiful rugs at the Emporium a few days ago. They truly are quite unique. I'm sure once my uncle sees them, he could be convinced to contract with you to purchase rugs for his new resort, which would guarantee you an income for some time." He sent his gaze to Mr. Chappell to gauge his reaction.

"I'd like to show you these tracts of land. Perhaps we could—"

Dulcie stepped toward Gavin and out of her grandfather's reach. "Mr. DeWitt, are you forgetting my grandfather was born right here on the side of this mountain and is well acquainted with every rock and blade of grass for miles around? He is aware there is a lot of farming acreage in these parts, but this . . ." She swung her arm in a wide arc.

"This is our home. Or, perhaps you have forgotten, he already explained that this land is our heritage. If that is the case, then let me refresh your memory."

"Dulcie . . ." The gentleness in Mr. Chappell's tone didn't disguise the admonition in his eyes, but she didn't acknowledge it.

She held both arms out, palms up. "Everything you see all around you is fought for land. Generations of Chappells have worked and sweated over this land, but there is much more than sweat and labor spent here. This land represents not only our heritage and the family values we cherish, but also our faith. You see, Mr. DeWitt, we believe God gave us this land and expects us to be the caretakers of it."

The glint in her eyes as she gestured to the house, the barn, and the meadow reflected a passion Gavin could not identify. He wanted to reassure her that he understood, but he couldn't because he didn't.

He cast a glance at Mr. Chappell, expecting to see the elderly man's disapproval of his granddaughter's diatribe. Instead, misty eyes accompanied a hint of pride on the farmer's face.

Dulcie pointed. "You see that barn? My father and my grandfather built it. A couple of neighbors helped, but they did it mostly themselves. My grandmother and I planted that garden behind you, like we did last year and the year before and the year before. This house is the second one on this land. The first cabin burned when raiders came through here in 1863. We never did determine if they were Union or Confederate. A dozen other neighbors lost their homes during that raid, and they all helped each other rebuild."

She picked up the dipper and held it out to Gavin. "My great-grandfather dug this well. He did it so my great-grandmother wouldn't have to tote water from the spring. He told her when it was finished that he dug it deep so her grandchildren and great-grandchildren would always have sweet, fresh water."

She turned and pointed through the towering oaks to the little outbuilding. "I helped my father and grandfather build that shed. It houses the spinning wheels, looms, and other tools and supplies we use to process the wool. Of course, I was only six at the time, but I toted boards and handed my pa nails, and he told me I was the best helper." Her voice broke, but she cleared her throat. Gavin was too mesmerized by the passion of her description of her home to interrupt.

She continued. "Do you see that fence around the sheep meadow? That's made from split black locust wood—the hardest wood God ever created. It will last for a hundred years. Grandpa had to resharpen his axe and saw blade two or three times a day while he was cutting locust wood for that fence.

"And up there on the rise . . ." Emotion clogged her voice, and he assumed she was going to tell him about the sheep. "Up there past the junipers and rhododendron in the far corner of the meadow . . ."

Mr. Chappell came alongside Dulcie and slipped his arm around her. "All right, Dulcie girl. You've said enough." He touched her cheek with his fingertips.

Gavin released a breath. Conflicted feelings sparred within him. While his original goal was to persuade the Chappells to consider relocating and presenting his uncle with the demanded contract, a sliver of disappointment arrowed through him when Dulcie heeded her grandfather and stopped describing the history of their homestead. He'd never heard anyone speak of their heritage and God the way these people did.

Mr. Chappell clapped him on the shoulder. "Don't reckon I can add anythin' to what my granddaughter told ye. The good Lord put us here. Reckon we'll jus' stay here till He takes us home. I hope yer uncle ain't too riled, but we ain't gonna sell, son."

Gavin bit his lip. His uncle would fire him, of course, but somehow it didn't seem so important anymore. After striving to please his uncle for so many months, and struggling to identify his own goals, the tiniest beam of light seem to break through the fog of turmoil in his soul. He gave Mr. Chappell a nod and locked his gaze on Dulcie for the space of several heartbeats. "I'll bid you good day, then, and I'm sorry to have troubled you." He climbed into the buggy and released the brake, but before he directed the mare back to town, he paused long enough to tug on the brim of his hat. Dulcie didn't respond, but she didn't look away.

Grandpa finished reading in chapter four of the Gospel of John and closed the old family Bible. Dulcie had seen him earlier, touching Grandma's freshly inked name and date on the page where the family deaths were recorded. He didn't grieve openly, but then, neither did she. Seeking solitude to release her tears and acknowledge the aching in her heart kept Grandpa from witnessing her pain. Did he do the same?

Grandpa placed the Bible in its usual place beside the hearth, and rested his gnarled hands on the arms of the old chair. She felt his look on her before she raised her eyes to meet his gaze.

He studied her as if he tried to read her thoughts.

"Ye been mighty quiet, Rosebud. Reckon yer missin' yer grandma." His eyes misted and his voice became tender. "It ain't good, keepin' yer feelin's all closed up."

Dulcie swallowed hard. "I miss her so much my heart is bleeding, but I don't want to hurt you, Grandpa."

His faded blue eyes softened. "Ye think not talkin' about her will make me forget?" He shook his head. "No, we gotta talk about her. We gotta share what's on our hearts with each other." He reached over and gently cuffed her chin. "I were kinda proud o' you today. Listenin' to you point out all them things about our home an' what they mean to you. Made me feel real warm-like." He patted the bib of his overalls. "Right here."

She allowed herself a smile, even if she hadn't much felt like smiling in almost two weeks. "It's not only the house and barn and wool shed. When I think of all the things Grandma taught me over the years . . ." She sent her gaze out the front window and swallowed hard. "Everything I know about cleaning and dying and carding and spinning wool, everything I know about the looms and how to weave, Grandma taught me. She guided my fingers when I was a little girl, and as I got older and more skilled, she's the one who encouraged me to take my craft beyond what she taught me. That's Grandma's legacy to me."

Dulcie stood and moved to the kitchen. She checked the coffeepot and took two mugs from the shelf. There were so many things Grandma did, so many roles she played, so many habits and chores she performed on a daily basis that Dulcie found herself doing in Grandma's place. Of all the acts of love and servitude Grandma did, bringing Grandpa his evening coffee was the one that triggered the sharpest ache in Dulcie's chest.

She handed Grandpa his cup and paused, unsure if she should speak what was on her heart. Grandpa'd said they needed to share their feelings with each other. "I wish I understood why God took Grandma."

Grandpa's eyes brimmed and he wrapped both hands around his cup. "I know. Ye hanged on to yer grudge against God fer a long time. Then, soon as ye made peace with Him, He decided to call yer Grandma home. I don't understand it neither. But just 'cause we don't understand don't mean He ain't wise an' good an' holy." He rose from his chair, his knees crackling as he did so, and carried his coffee to the door. "Reckon I'll sit out on the porch and rock a spell."

She watched him move stiffly out the door. She had a rich legacy, that was for sure, but who would she hand it down to when she died? What if she couldn't find a man who loved the land and the sheep the way she did, the way her grandparents did? If there was no man who would give his heart and life and sweat to caring for the land and producing the wool, the legacy would die with her.

The weight of responsibility hung heavily on her shoulders, but her first responsibility was to care for Grandpa. In the last few weeks, the rhythm of his steps had slowed, his shoulders were a little more stooped, the lines furrowed across his brow and around his eyes deepened. She'd already failed to take care of Grandma. How could she seek a man to court when the man whose roof she lived under needed her more than ever?

❧ TWENTY-SEVEN

Gavin leaned back in the chair in his hotel room, his hands tucked behind his head. This place had changed him. After striving for so long to please first his father, and then his uncle, achieving what they wanted had always taken priority. Now, a curious calm pervaded his spirit, despite not meeting his uncle's ultimatum. The fear of failing to gain acceptance faded. Even knowing he'd probably lose his job no longer disturbed him. A few months ago, success was all he thought about. After listening to Mr. Chappell and Dulcie talk about their home and the way they and their family members had built it, the way they cared for it, the stories behind every part of it, he saw the success he'd been trying to achieve for what it was—hollow, temporal, and lacking foundation.

He rummaged through the drawers of the desk, looking for the list he'd written more than three weeks ago. Finally, he knew what else he wanted to add.

Roots
Building relationships with people
Doing something I love
Knowing I can be proud of my work

He needed more than ambition and drive to attain these goals, he needed a heart for the place and people around him. But where was he meant to put down roots? How did he go about finding the passion he saw in Dulcie? For that matter, what kind of work did he want to do?

His uncle would scoff at every one of these goals, but he'd come to realize Arnold DeWitt wasn't the man he was supposed to impress. Neither did he have any further desire to follow in his uncle's footsteps. Having been blinded by ambition for so long, these pinpoints of light shining on areas of his life he'd never before examined surprised him and scared him at the same time.

He needed time and some soul-searching, but the concept was foreign to him. Once again, the desire to know how to pray arose in his conscious thought. Perhaps he'd pay another visit to James Chappell, not for the purpose of trying to coerce him into signing Uncle Arnold's contract, but rather to ask the man if he could explain what it meant to talk to God.

Gavin rose and moved to the window overlooking the immaculate hotel grounds. Below his window, a man worked in the garden. When a woman wearing an apron and maid's cap walked by, the man straightened and gave her a broad smile and pointed to some of the flowers. The expression on his face reflected pure pleasure and pride. He held up one finger, indicating he wanted the woman to wait. As Gavin watched, the gardener retrieved a pair of clippers from his back pocket, snipped a beautiful red rose, and then handed it to the woman. She accepted it and held it to her nose, smiling before hurrying on her way. The gardener doffed his hat, and returned to his task with a smile on his face.

The story that unfolded before Gavin's eyes painted a picture of a man who enjoyed his work so much, he wanted to share the fruit of his labors with someone else. How did one become so contented with his work, regardless of how menial someone else may view it, he smiled and enjoyed whatever task lay before him?

Gavin stared out across the well-kept grounds without focusing on anything except the inward truth he couldn't ignore. "I've never felt that way about the work I did for Father or anything I've done for Uncle Arnold. In fact . . ." In fact, he didn't like his job. He found no pleasure in the kind of success his uncle spouted.

Once again, the images of James and Dulcie Chappell came to mind. They, like the gardener beneath his window, loved what they did so much they were willing to fight for it. They had something he didn't. Their devotion to family and sense of belonging to the land they demonstrated sharpened his awareness of the void within him. But Dulcie and her grandfather claimed more than just land and family ties. They had faith—a connection to God.

James Chappell called God a loving, heavenly Father, but the only father Gavin had ever known always told him he wasn't good enough. How did one believe in a God they couldn't see? Did God allow people to hold grudges in heaven? He supposed there were rules of some sort.

Strange how he'd never considered before what happened to a person when they died. He'd simply never given it any thought, not even when Father's casket was lowered into the ground and the church official spoke solemn, morose words as he tossed a handful of dirt into the hole. Something about ashes and dust. Why did it make a difference now?

The door opened and Uncle Arnold strode in without knocking. "Hmph. Figured I'd find you hiding in here."

His uncle's pompous disdain no longer intimidated him. Gavin turned away from the window and crossed to the desk. "I'm not hiding, Uncle. In fact, I was about to seek you out to inform you of the results of my visits earlier today." He sat at the desk and motioned to the adjacent upholstered chair.

"Well? Get on with it." Arnold waved his fingers in an impatient flip. "Where are the contracts?"

Gavin tipped back in the chair and folded his hands over his middle. "Tate and Huxley are both in possession of their contracts because, as

Dewey Tate said, they want to go by the bank and have Waldo Granger look over the contracts before they sign anything." Gavin tipped his head and scratched his chin. "Rather astute, if you ask me."

Arnold sat forward and flicked the ashes from his cigar onto the floor. "I didn't ask you. I told you I wanted the signed contracts in my hand by the end of the day."

"Mm-hmm." Gavin gave a brief nod and put all four legs of the chair on the floor again.

He picked up a pen and twiddled it between his fingers. "Of the two smaller contracts, Reuben Ludlow signed his. Of course, you are only purchasing six acres of his land. Simon Cutler is still thinking about it."

His uncle's face reddened and his mustache skewed around his scowl. His brocade vest rose and fell as Gavin watched imperious anger unfurl over the elder DeWitt. Might as well spill the rest of the bad news.

Gavin tugged at his collar and loosened a button. "After Tate and Huxley get approval from the banker, they say they will only sign if James Chappell signs. And I can tell you with confidence, James Chappell is *never* going to agree to sell his land."

Arnold leapt to his feet.

Gavin remained seated and unruffled. "You might try convincing Tate and Huxley to sign. Maybe if Chappell sees his neighbors signing their contracts, he might relent and sign his, although I doubt it."

"How dare you attempt to direct me." He pointed a thick finger at Gavin. "Your time is up. I don't see why I ever thought I could turn you into a businessman."

Gavin withdrew a sheet of blank paper from the desk. "I assume you want my letter of resignation?"

Purple veins on both sides of Arnold's neck bulged and he bellowed. "I don't need your stinking letter. You're fired! You are as worthless as your father said you were."

Normally, such an indictment would have generated an inward cringe, but not anymore. He tucked the paper back into the desk drawer and rose. "Then I suppose we have nothing left to discuss."

"Only this." His uncle practically spat the words. "The reason I took you on was to prove I could do something my brother couldn't. Your father raised two sons—one a successful attorney and statesman, and the other a worthless excuse for a son. Your father always thought he was better than me, and never missed an opportunity to show me up." Arnold took another step forward until he loomed over Gavin with the posture of a threatening grizzly bear. "He went to his grave laughing at me, and I hated him."

Bitterness dripped from his uncle's words unlike anything Gavin had ever heard. The elder DeWitt spewed every ounce of animosity within him. His diatribe drew a dark and repulsive picture of the same feelings of resentment Gavin had in his heart toward his own brother. No, he didn't hate Harold, but Gavin couldn't deny the rancor between them. He wished it wasn't so, but it stared him in the face in the form of the hostility that, at this very moment, poured from his uncle's mouth.

"That hate has driven me to succeed, to be better than my brother, to show the world I came out on top. That's why I wanted to take you and mold you into a businessman—to show him I could succeed at something he never could do. And now, because of your ineptitude, you are causing me to fail once again in my brother's eyes." Uncle Arnold wiped spit from his chin.

Gavin walked to the door and placed his hand on the doorknob. "Then I suppose we are done here."

Arnold stomped across the room and raised his hand in Gavin's direction. Gavin almost ducked, half expecting his uncle's hatred to turn to violence. But Uncle Arnold only stabbed his finger against Gavin's chest, hard enough to cause Gavin to teeter backwards momentarily. "Don't think I'm done here. I'm not done by a long shot. Not with Chappell or these other ignorant simpletons, and not with you." He shoved Gavin aside and yanked the door open, then barged into the hallway and nearly collided with a maid carrying a stack of linens.

Gavin silently bade his uncle goodbye, and nodded an apology to the maid. A season of his life had ended, and he quietly closed the door. He crossed to the desk and retrieved the paper he'd deposited into the drawer. After being shown such an accusing picture of himself, Gavin resolved to end the same hardness that turned his father and uncle against each other. Dipping the pen in the inkwell, he tapped the nib gently before writing at the top of the sheet.

Dear Harold . . .

James pulled Old Samson to a stop in front of the blacksmith shop. Next door at the livery, Otis Hogan barely lifted his hand in greetin' as James passed. Asa Cooper looked up from his work, and his hand halted pumpin' the bellows.

"Mornin', Asa."

"James." Asa's mouth pinched like he'd sucked on an unripe scuppernong.

James poked his thumb over his shoulder toward the wagon. "Got me a busted bracket an' shaft from my hay tedder. Gonna be needin' it pert soon, puttin' up hay fer the winter."

Asa cast a glance at James's wagon, and then returned his hard gaze to James. "Heard some talk 'round town about you, James. Folks is sayin' you're bein' pig-headed about sellin' your land to them Yankee fellers. Now, I don't cotton to outsiders neither, 'specially Yankees. But them fellers're sayin' they gonna bring p'ospaterity to our town. More business means more money in my pocket, and I don't take kindly to anyone who stands in the way o' that happenin'. Cain't understand why'd you be all uppity and refuse to sell land that ain't nothin' but sheep grazin' pasture. Don' you know yer the one stoppin' our town from growin' and bringin' in more trade?"

Asa's accusin' words didn't surprise James, but they stung for certain. He'd heard the talk, too, some of it from the same folks who'd stood around Virginia's grave with their hats in their hands. Right peculiar how some folks could twist their opinions overnight.

He pushed his hat further back on his head and stuffed his hands in his pockets. "Well, ye heard right. I ain't aimin' to sell my land. It's my home and it's Dulcie's heritage. Ain't sellin' that jus' so them fellers can take over the spring." He replaced his hat. "Now, can ye fix my busted shaft, or do I hafta take it down the mountain?"

Asa's eyes narrowed into slits. "Reckon I need the business, 'specially if we ain't gonna be able to look forward to all that new p'ospaterity." He shuffled out to the wagon and picked up the broken shaft hanging from the bracket. "Might be a week afore I can get to it."

James nodded. He knew Asa weren't that busy, just draggin' his feet. "Don't reckon I'll start hayin' fer another couple o' weeks." He reached into his pocket. "Ye want I should pay ye now?"

Asa's face reddened, and a tad of satisfaction twirled through James's belly at the man's embarrassment. Reckon he oughta be rightly ashamed. The blacksmith carried the bracket and shaft into the smithy. "Ye know I run my business cash on the barrel when the goods is done."

James tugged on the battered brim of his hat. "See ye in about a week, then." He walked out and closed the tailgate, pokin' the steel pins down through the holes that held the tailgate firm.

"Hey, James."

He turned to see Otis Hogan standing at the door of the livery next door. He stepped over and stuck his hand out to shake the liveryman's. "Otis. Ye keepin' well these days?"

Otis shook his hand, but it were a mite feeble grip. "Not so's you'd notice. Had me some big plans to knock out a wall 'r two and add more stalls an' a bigger corral. Buy me a few more saddle horses, carriage horses, and couple o' them fancy rigs like the rich folks drive." Otis thumped the palm of his hand on the open livery door. "But it don't look like thet's gonna happen iffen you don't sell yer land to them city fellers." He looked around the place, a frown pulled his eyebrows into a fat caterpillar. "Folks is sayin'—"

"I know what folks is sayin'." James set his hands on his hips. "Otis, you an' ever'one else around here needs to r'member that land's been in my family fer five generations, and it ain't nobody else's business what I decide. I ain't sellin' that land out from under my granddaughter."

Otis stepped closer and lowered his voice, as if he were sharin' a secret. "Even the mayor an' the town council're in favor o' new business and the town growin'. They say it's plumb crazy you holdin' out like y'are. A lot o' the others who got businesses in town, they's sayin' the same thing. I know it be yer land, James, an' Miss Dulcie's, too, but the whole town is hopin' thet DeWitt feller'll bring in . . . what'd he call it?"

"Prosperity."

Otis bobbed his head. "Thet's it. Means more business an' more money."

James wrinkled his nose like there were a skunk in the neighborhood. "I know what it means. Since when did you start trustin' big city fellers who come in an' start makin' a lot of windy promises?"

He didn't wait for Otis's reply, but stomped to the wagon and hoisted himself up to the seat. Samson jerked his head up when James snapped the reins. "Hup, mule." He felt like spittin' in the eye o' the next man who tried to tell him what he needed to do. Mayhap the ride back home would cool his temper.

TWENTY-EIGHT

James wiped sweat from his forehead and turned his attention to the thick clouds rollin' in. He'd welcome some rain, sure enough. It were so hot and stuffy in the barn, he opted to sit on the porch and whittle some pegs for the latches on the holdin' pens. Ornery ram done busted out one latch, and a couple of others was about worn through. He set his knife to the peg in his grip and pulled another curl of wood off, narrowin' down the piece at one end.

A slight breeze picked up and the clouds hid the lowerin' sun. Sure made it a mite cooler. He slid his knife down the peg again, rememberin' how Virginia used to fuss at him for leavin' a mess she'd have to sweep off the porch. His knife paused. Heart-sore, he raised his eyes toward the gray sky, longin' to sit and rock on the porch with her again, to hold her hand and talk about their day. This mornin', he'd glanced toward the kitchen expectin' to see her standin' at the stove in her faded apron with the yellow flowers on it. If only he could see her smile once more, that special smile she saved only for him for fifty-seven years.

"Lord, I jus' wish I could go to where she is, an' be with her an' Jesus." He shook his head. "I know that be selfish, Lord. I cain't leave Dulcie here alone—not yet. She ain't got a man to join up with her and help her run this place and care fer the sheep. She ain't got nobody but me. So I reckon, iffen it's all right with You, I'll stay here a while longer. I sure do miss Virginia, though."

Thunder growled over the mountain. He rose from his rocker, peerin' out from under the saggin' porch roof. Sure enough looked like they was in for a storm. Dusk would settle in soon, but the dark clouds churnin' in made it seem later. In another few minutes it'd be hard to see what he was doing without a lantern. Lightnin' flashed, followed seconds later by another roll of thunder, this one a mite louder. Sometimes summer storms came across the mountains like a young'un throwin' a temper tantrum. "Lord, I reckon we oughta bring the sheep in so they don't get spooked."

He crossed the yard and headed for the meadow, callin' for Dulcie. James whistled for Malachi. The sheep, already restless, milled around and *baaed* in a nervous chorus. Lambs that had already been weaned hung close to their mothers. Malachi came toward the fence, but refused to get too far from the sheep.

Dulcie joined him, castin' wary eyes to the sky. "Storm coming, Grandpa. Sure is getting dark."

"Let's get 'em in the barn. Storm might spook 'em and they'll scatter an' try to jump the fence." He whistled again for Malachi and the dog perked up his ears.

"Bring 'em in, Malachi." He and Dulcie split up, her headin' to one side of the flock with arms outstretched, encouragin' the animals to bunch together. James shadowed her on the other side. He gave the dog a few more whistles, and Malachi knew what to do. The three o' them together pulled the flock tight and headed them toward the barn.

Lightnin' streaked across the darkenin' sky, splittin' a black cloud. Thunder boomed on its heels, and Malachi raced back and forth, barkin' and pushin' the sheep. No rain yet, but James knew it weren't far away.

"Dulcie, go open the gate and the barn door!" He had to shout for her to hear him above the wind. With her runnin' to secure the large gate to the open doors of the barn, it was all he and Malachi could do to keep the sheep from runnin' scared.

Another loud clap of thunder pealed across the mountain. James caught one ewe by the ears and turned her back into the flock. Malachi barked and nipped at the sheep, forcin' 'em forward toward the now-open gate. Dulcie worked to get the wide fence gate connected to the barn door that made a funnel fer the woolies to go from the meadow to the barn.

With the barn doors open, James reckoned they'd head straight for the shelter. They did, and Malachi chased them, pushin' them into the barn ahead of the storm. James waded through the *baaing* sheep toward the front of the barn. The critters complained about the storm, but would have scattered to wherever they could find a low spot in the fence if Malachi hadn't kept 'em all tightened up.

Dulcie took care of pullin' the rear doors of the barn shut, closin' the flock safely inside, while Malachi threaded his way through the crowd, pokin' his nose at each of the sheep. Flashes of lightnin' and booms of thunder urged James to hurry. He and Dulcie together pushed the front doors closed against the wind, and James slid the thick wood bar into the brackets with a thud.

"C'mon! Let's get to the house before the rain starts!" James tugged her arm.

She shouted back above the risin' wind and thunder. "I'll be there in a minute. I need to close up the wool shed."

She'd not taken more than two steps toward the wool shed when a blue white bolt of lightnin' slammed into the barn along with an explosion of thunder that shook the ground. James staggered and ducked. Stunned, he looked for Dulcie. She stood a few feet from him, wide-eyed and white-faced, pointin'.

"Grandpa, the barn! The barn's afire!"

"Oh, help us, Lord!" With all the speed his old bones could muster, he ran toward the barn door he'd barred only a few moments ago. Frantic *baas* and barkin' from behind the doors begged him to hurry.

He reached out to grab the heavy wooden beam that held the doors securely closed, a large tree branch from a nearby oak crashed to the ground in his path. He tried to jump over it, but he weren't as nimble as he used to be. His foot got tangled in the branch and he stumbled and fell hard. White hot pain shot from below his hip all the way down past his knee.

Thank the good Lord for the boomin' thunder so Dulcie didn't hear him cry out. But tryin' to get to his feet only brought on another wave of pain that made him sick at his stomach.

"Grandpa!" Dulcie's hands grabbed his arm. She pulled, but there weren't no way he could stand.

"The sheep! Git the sheep!"

She ignored his command, and instead kept tryin' to pull at him.

"Open the barn door and git the sheep out, girl!"

She grabbed both his wrists and pulled his arms over his head, draggin' him away from the burnin' barn. He never knowed she had such a grip.

"Dulcie girl, leave me! Git the sheep!"

He might as well have been givin' orders to an ole stump for all she heeded him. A little at a time, she dragged him further, a safer distance from the barn. She finally fell to her knees and wrapped her arms around his neck, buryin' her face in his shoulder.

"Grandpa, are you all right?" Her words muffled against his shirt, but the fear in her voice sounded loud and clear.

"The sheep, Dulcie." But even as he raised up and tried to prop himself on one elbow, the flames were eating the barn. Billows of black smoke pushed across the yard by the wind. The sheep and dog were doomed. He wrapped his fingers around her arm to prevent her now from doing what only a minute ago he'd told her to do.

"Grandpa, are you all right?" Terror seized Dulcie's heart. In the space of time it took for another flash of lightning to illuminate the roiling smoke, she imagined a second fresh grave, positioned beside Grandma's, and a shard of grief stabbed her.

"I'm all right, Rosebud, but I think my leg's broke." He struggled to raise his head. "And the sheep—"

The sudden realization that the sheep, along with Malachi, were trapped in the burning barn yanked her into awareness. Grandpa was a safe distance away, but the sheep, *her* sheep. . .

Grandpa dug the fingers of both his hands into her arm, clamping onto her for all he was worth. "No, Dulcie. It's too late."

Through the smoke, the form of a man ran. In her panic, was she imagining things? The roar of the flames grew louder and competed with the wind and thunder as the man pushed the bar away from the cleats and kicked open the door. The cries of the sheep and Malachi's barking added to the cacophony. Shouts of, "Go on, get out of here!" filtered through the smoke. Malachi snarled and bit at the sheep, driving them out of the barn along with the stranger who waved his arms, and shoved the sheep away from the barn.

Dulcie sat on the ground beside Grandpa, paralyzed. When the last sheep leapt past them, and the man stumbled out and collapsed in the dirt a few feet away from them, she recognized Gavin DeWitt.

Where had he come from? How did he. . . Did God send him? But how? When? Her heart constricted and she shook her head trying to comprehend what had transpired in front of her, but clarity of thought eluded her. The only thing she knew for certain was that Grandpa was hurt. He was away from the fire, but injured.

A new sensation penetrated her conscious thoughts. *Wet.* Heavy drops of rain pelted her, running down her face, washing the burning smoke from her eyes, soaking her clothing and hair. She raised her face heavenward and let God bathe her in comfort. After a moment of refreshing, she directed her focus to the sizzling barn roof where the pouring rain battled the flames. Finally, the rain had come.

Gavin crawled over to her and Grandpa. "Mr. Chappell, are you all right?"

"His leg is broken."

The deepening dusk together with the deluge of rain made it difficult to see, but Gavin glanced around. What was he looking for? "Where is your wagon. It wasn't in the barn, was it?"

Dulcie gasped. "No! And neither was Samson or the milk cow. They always stay in the meadow during the day, and they didn't go into the barn with the sheep. The wagon, it's—" She spun back to nail Gavin with her eyes. "Where did you come from? How did you get here?"

Gavin waved her questions away and stood. "Where is the wagon? And the mule?"

She pointed. The wagon sat beside the garden. She glanced down at Grandpa who was now grimacing in pain. "Can you help me get him to town to the doctor?"

"That's the plan." The cloudburst was beginning to slow to a steady shower. "Go get the mule and hitch him up. I'll take care of your grandfather."

"But—"

"Do it."

As she'd done all her life, she looked to Grandpa for direction.

He nodded to her. "Go do as he says."

Without further hesitation, she ran to comply. On her way to the meadow to fetch Samson, Malachi ran to and fro, herding the sheep, rounding them up and pushing them back toward the safety of the fenced meadow. Bless that dog!

By the time she was able to catch Samson and lead him back to the yard, the fire was mostly out and only small pockets of flames flickered here and there. The rain slowed to a soft shower.

Gavin had found the lantern they kept on the porch, lit it, and hung it on the corner of the wagon. Grandpa still lay on the ground, but two sticks that appeared similar to the ones she used in the garden to prop up the pea vines, were snugged on either side of his leg and tied with rags. She didn't ask where Gavin had gotten the rags.

He was on his knees, giving Grandpa sips of water, but he told Dulcie to hitch the mule. "You need help?" He shrugged as if he knew it was a foolish question. As she backed the mule into the traces, she wondered if Gavin DeWitt had ever hitched an animal to a wagon.

In minutes, Samson was ready to go. He snorted in protest, probably still nervous from the storm and fire. She led him forward and drew the wagon up beside Grandpa. When she started to take Grandpa's arm, Gavin stopped her.

"Do you have a quilt or a blanket we can roll him onto? That will make lifting him a lot easier and we won't hurt him so much."

Not hurting Grandpa appealed to her senses, and she raced into the house, returning a minute later with an old quilt.

Gavin knelt beside Grandpa and carefully rolled him onto his side, directing Dulcie to spread the quilt on the wet ground behind Grandpa. Then he gently rolled him back onto the quilt. Rising, he showed Dulcie how to pick up the quilt with Grandpa in the middle. "I'll get his head and shoulders. The splint will hold his leg in place. You take that end and let me pull him into the wagon bed."

They managed the task together, not without a few groans of pain from Grandpa that tore Dulcie's heart. Full darkness had fallen by the time they got him in the wagon and made him as comfortable as possible. The soft rain had come to an end, and they'd have to wait until daylight to assess the damage to the barn. For now, the damp, blackened beams smoldered, but there was no sign of flames or glowing coals.

Gavin jumped down from the tailgate. "You drive. The mule doesn't know me and I'm not as familiar with the road. I'll ride in the back with your grandfather. Let me tie my livery horse to the wagon."

As soon as he'd secured his horse, he scrambled back into the wagon. "Hang on, now, Mr. Chappell. We're going to get you to the doctor as quick as possible in the dark."

Dulcie steered Samson toward town. The sure-footed mule knew the road better than she did, but with her precious cargo in the wagon bed, she took the steep road slow and easy. Every few minutes she glanced over her shoulder to where Gavin cared for Grandpa.

"You never answered my questions. Where did you come from and how did you know we needed help?"

A low chuckle rumbled from behind her. "Well, I came up to tell you I was leaving Hot Springs, and I wanted to say goodbye, and I hoped you'd forgive me for any trouble my uncle or I may have caused. Secondly, I didn't know you needed help until I arrived. That storm was really something."

"I'll need to account for all the sheep, but the dog was herding them back into in the meadow. They all would have died in that barn if it hadn't been for you. That was a very brave thing you did."

Gavin's chuckle deepened. "I don't know about brave. Foolhardy, maybe. Those sheep didn't want to leave the barn. I had to push them out. They were stubborn—like their owner."

⤜✦ TWENTY-NINE

Gavin marveled at Dulcie's skill in guiding the mule down the rain-soaked, rutted mountain road in the dark. Even the lantern hanging on the front of the wagon shed little light up ahead. The bumping and swaying of the wagon brought occasional groans from Mr. Chappell, but Gavin tried his best to hold the old man steady.

He didn't tell Dulcie, but when he'd splinted Mr. Chappell's leg while she fetched the mule, he'd run his hands over the swollen leg and encountered at least two places where the bone bulged, creating a grotesquely-shaped protrusion. It wasn't a simple break, but it'd be better if she heard that from the doctor.

Mr. Chappell hiked his arm up and held his ribs.

"Does it hurt there, Mr. Chappell?" Gavin traced the path of the old man's hand with his own fingers. "Here?"

"Mmmph." The old gentleman muttered under his breath. "Confounded ram butted me a few weeks back. Like to busted my ribs. Reckon fallin' like I done musta hurt 'em again."

Dulcie slowed the mule and turned in the seat. "Grandpa, you never told me the ram hurt you. When did this happen? Why didn't you say something? You should have gone to see Doc Pryor."

"Don't harp at me, girl. Don't need my ears hurtin', too."

Gavin pressed his lips together. Dulcie didn't need to hear him laugh, but he supposed even a sweet-natured man like Mr. Chappell could get grouchy if he was in pain.

Dulcie called, "Hup, Samson!" to get the mule to pick up his feet again. A few minutes later, she pulled the animal to halt in front of the white clapboard house with black shutters that Gavin remembered from the day he helped the doctor with young Lester Marlowe. Brightly burning lanterns hung from the porch posts like a warm welcome. Dulcie set the brake and scrambled down from the wagon seat before Gavin could aid her. She dashed up the porch steps and knocked on the door.

"Doc? Doc Pryor?"

The door opened, pouring lamplight from the house onto the porch. The doctor wiped his mouth with a napkin. They'd apparently interrupted his supper. "Well, Miss Dulcie, what brings you out at this time of night?" He peered past her. "Who is that in the back of the wagon? Your grandpa?"

Dulcie nodded. "His leg is broken, and maybe his ribs, too."

The doctor *tsked*. "I won't ask you how that happened—at least not right now."

Gavin jumped down from the wagon bed and nodded curtly at the doctor. He kept his voice quiet, his words intended only for the doctor's ears. "Sir, you give Mr. Chappell your very best care, and make sure I get the bill."

Dr. Pryor frowned. "All my patients get my very best care, young man. And why do you want the bill? You didn't do this, did you?"

"No, sir, and I didn't mean to imply— That is, I know you always— What I'm trying to say is, Mr. Chappell is a very special man."

The doctor's expression softened, and he glanced at Dulcie who remained on the top step while the men slid her grandfather back to the open tailgate. "All the Chappells are special folks. I promise you, I'll do my best, young fella. As far as the bill goes, we'll talk about that later."

Gavin and the doctor together transferred Mr. Chappell to a stretcher, sturdier than the quilt they'd used to get him onto the wagon. They carried him up the four porch steps and across the threshold.

Dulcie started to follow, but the doctor stopped her. "You wait right here in the front room, Miss Dulcie. This young fella will help me get your grandpa situated, and then I'll send him out, too. Let me take care of your grandpa, and then I'll come out and tell you how he's doing."

Dulcie wrung her hands, but gave a single nod. They carried Mr. Chappell past the curtained doorway and into the same room where Lester Marlowe had been. A table held a variety of instruments, all shiny clean and laying in perfect order on an immaculate white towel. One wall held a wide cabinet with glass doors, the shelves inside stocked with medicine bottles, boxes, folded cloths, and rolls of bandages. The opposite wall appeared to be the place where the doctor mixed medical preparations, like an apothecary. The doctor's wife, a tiny little woman in a blue dress and white apron, bustled around, efficiently readying everything for her husband.

They placed Mr. Chappell on a table covered with a white sheet, and the doctor began removing the makeshift splints and cutting off the man's overalls. The elderly farmer stiffened and clamped his lips down to stifle the moan that tried to escape. As soon as the doctor uncovered the leg, he winced. "I best give him something for pain before I do anything else."

He mixed some white powder into a tin cup of water, and held it to Mr. Chappell's lips. "I know it's bitter, but drink all of it. It will help you relax and relieve the pain."

Mr. Chappell's face was already pulled into a contorted mask from the pain, and the bitterness of the morphine caused him to respond as expected. But in a few minutes, he slipped into a sleep.

Gavin heaved a sigh of relief. "Unless you need me, doctor, I'm going to go sit with Miss Dulcie."

The doctor waved him away as he concentrated on doing what he had to do to repair the broken bones. "My wife is a trained nurse. She'll assist me. Tell Dulcie this is going to take a while."

When Gavin returned to the front room, he found Dulcie pacing, twisting her fingers, and biting her lip. Gavin took her hand. "Come and sit. The doctor said it's going to take a while, so you might as well get comfortable." She blinked and stared at his fingers wrapped around hers. He pulled his hand away, but regretted the disconnection.

They sat opposite each other on chairs that bore as many scars and scratches as the patients that had come through the doctor's office over the years. Not unlike some of the emotional and relational scars Gavin had encountered over his lifetime. But while a doctor could fix broken bones and bodies, how did one seek restoration of a broken spirit?

Dulcie cleared her throat. "Thank you for your help. I don't know if I could have gotten Grandpa here by myself."

Gavin shrugged. "I'm glad I was there."

She cocked her head and studied him for a long moment. Her scrutiny made him squirm. "You said something about coming to say goodbye and leaving Hot Springs. Does that mean your uncle has given up trying to force people to sell him their land?"

Her pointed question pierced like a thorn. He only wished the answer was yes. "I'm afraid not."

"But you're leaving?"

"Yes." An abundance of uncertainty filled that single-word response. He had money saved, but where did he go from here, and what should he pursue? The unanswered questions that had plagued him over the past few weeks still swarmed around his head, and a tug to find answers to some of his deeper questions overrode where he would go and what he would do. A space of uncomfortable silence stretched between them. "I wanted to apologize for the distress my uncle and I caused your family."

She still maintained a steady focus on his face, as if she was trying to determine if he was sincere or not. "You already said that. I'm trying to figure out exactly what you mean. You're leaving, but your uncle isn't?"

"That's one way of putting it." He leaned forward and propped his elbows on his knees. He dropped his gaze to his loosely-clasped fingers. "My uncle and I don't exactly see eye to eye on some things—many things. I—I have decided. . ." How to find the right words of explanation? "I have come to the conclusion I cannot do what he wants me to do, or be what he wants me to be."

She sat in silence and didn't pry, but when he raised his eyes to meet hers, he found something he didn't anticipate in her expression. Respect. She gave a slow, almost imperceptible nod.

Parting ways with his uncle was the right thing, he had no doubt. But regret still hounded him. "I wish I could tell you my uncle will stop harassing you to sell, but I'm sorry to say he adamantly told me that you haven't heard the last of him."

"I see."

Tiny worry lines between her brows made him wish he could smooth them away. She leaned back against the worn cushion and closed her eyes. Was she praying? Was she attempting to sleep? Her hair hung in damp, stringy tendrils that had escaped the single braid she wore, and her clothing bore mud stains. Dirt smeared across her cheek and her fingernails were caked with mud. But she was still the loveliest woman Gavin had ever laid eyes on.

Gradually, she appeared to relax, and Gavin whispered silently to a God he hoped could hear him. *God, I don't know if this is the right way to pray. If I'm doing this wrong, I apologize. But could You please help Mr. Chappell be all right, and can You help Dulcie feel at ease?* Gavin hoped he didn't offend God with his crude prayer. Should he have used Thee and Thou? Should he have added something else to make his prayer acceptable? The man he'd gone up the mountain to see, to ask for help in knowing how to pray, lay beyond the curtain and behind a door where a country doctor worked on him. Perhaps he was under more than the doctor's care.

Maybe God cared for a man like James Chappell.

After an indeterminate length of time, the doctor emerged from the inner room, wiping his hands on a towel. Dulcie's eyes flew open and she leapt to her feet, hunger for good news filling her expression. Gavin rose and stood by her, ready to support her in case the news wasn't what she hoped.

Dr. Pryor patted her shoulder. "He's resting easy. I set the leg—it's broken in two places— and wrapped his broken ribs. He's going to need a lot of rest, and his old bones aren't going to mend as quickly as they did thirty years ago. I'm afraid you're going to have your hands full, Miss Dulcie. James Chappell is a hard man to keep down." He tossed the towel over his shoulder. "I want to keep him here for a few days to watch for infection."

The doctor shifted his attention to Gavin. "Young man, you did a good job with those splints. If you hadn't, the damage would have been a lot worse."

Mrs. Pryor parted the curtain and peered out. "Dulcie, I expect you want to stay tonight with your grandpa. I've fixed up a cot for you in the corner so you can be close by if he awakens."

"Thank you." She turned to Gavin. "And thank you. I'd like to talk more, but—" She glanced toward the curtain where her grandfather lay on the other side.

Gavin sent her a weak smile. "You go on and be with him." He gestured toward the door. "I'll make sure your wagon and mule are cared for over at the livery."

A softness he hadn't seen before glimmered in her eyes. "Thanks."

Dulcie slipped through the curtain with the doctor and his wife, leaving Gavin alone in the front room. An odd feeling came over him—a desire to stay close by, to wait to hear what the doctor would say tomorrow and the next day. An unfamiliar longing filled him, wanting to do those things a family would do. He tiptoed out the door and closed it quietly. He didn't belong to their family, but a strange sensation made him wish he did.

Dulcie sat on a chair beside the bed, listening to Grandpa breathe. Every now and then, she stroked his hand with her fingertips or felt his brow for fever. He didn't move. The doctor had assured her the medicine would make him sleep all night, and she should also get some rest. Somewhere in the house, a clock chimed the hour. Three AM. She'd thanked Mrs. Pryor for the basin of warm water and soap, and the loan of some clean clothes. She was grateful the woman had set up the cot, but she'd not been able to bring herself to lay down or attempt to sleep. Not yet. Not until she knew Grandpa would be all right.

In the quiet stillness, introspective thoughts arose. There was no denying she was shaken by the events of the past several hours, but more than worry for Grandpa's recovery shook her. For so many years she'd lived with anger and resentment. She'd accused God of not caring, taking her parents from a little girl who needed them. For more than eleven years, she'd questioned and blamed God, deliberately driving a wedge between her and the Lord. To protect herself, she'd claimed. But the rancor wore her down. The desire to rediscover the relationship her mama had taught her to have with God found its way to the surface of her being. Grandma's and Grandpa's persistent prayers, and God's patient whispers drew her back into a fragile relationship with Him.

So why then, after she'd finally prayed for God to forgive her, did all these bad things keep happening? He took Grandma, that awful storm swept in and lightning damaged the barn-she still was unsure to what extent. She didn't know if all the sheep had escaped the fire or if she might find the remains of some of them in the barn. Now Grandpa lay, badly injured, on the bed in front of her, his shallow breathing rattling her to her very core. Was all this God's answer to her prayer?

Her raspy whisper broke the stillness. "God, what are You trying to tell me? Did I stay angry with You too long? Did I go beyond the point that You could forgive me? Is it too late?" She laid her face on the corner of the sheet that covered Grandpa. "God, please don't leave me alone. I'm sorry I blamed You. Please forgive my bitterness." Her tears dampened the sheet. "Please don't take Grandpa."

The same whisper that filled her being when Grandma died echoed through her spirit once again. *You need Me, child. Lean on Me.*

"But, God, I don't understand all this. I don't understand why these things have happened after I prayed and asked you to forgive me. Are You telling me 'no'? Are you saying I've gone too far? I don't understand."

I didn't ask you to understand, child. I asked you to trust.

❦ THIRTY

Gavin glanced at his half-filled suitcase lying open on the bed in the plush hotel room he'd occupied for almost two months. Since he no longer had a job, he'd have to be more careful with his money. Uncle Arnold certainly wasn't going to continue to pay for his nephew's room at the Mountain Park Hotel. He'd seen his uncle that morning at breakfast, but the man had only glowered and pushed past him.

The desk clerk had informed him that his bill at the hotel was paid up through the end of the week, so there was no rush to leave—other than not wishing to run into his uncle every day. He'd seen a respectable-looking boardinghouse down the road, not far from the church. It wasn't the Mountain Park, but it would do. He planned to stop by there to inquire about a room on his way to the doctor's office to check on Mr. Chappell. Since he still wasn't sure where he was headed, he opted to remain in Hot Springs for a week or two, to make sure Mr. Chappell was recovering. He had time to decide his future later.

He had money on deposit at the little bank there in Hot Springs. Every week, his uncle had deposited Gavin's pay. He also had some funds left from his inheritance at the bank back in Philadelphia, so he wasn't destitute, but it wouldn't sustain him for more than six or eight months without employment. Cutting back was simply the prudent thing to do, especially since he wanted to pay Mr. Chappell's doctor bill.

The Mountain Park always had a stack of newspapers available in the lobby. One of them was the Asheville Weekly Citizen. Even if the copy supplied by the hotel was a few days old, he might be able to find some employment opportunities within its pages. He snagged a copy and took it back to his room, planning to scour the advertisements later.

Mr. Chappell had been groggy, but awake yesterday when Gavin looked in on him. The doctor didn't let him stay long, insisting the old gentleman needed to rest. He hoped to have a longer visit today, but only if Dulcie's mule wasn't tied up outside.

He wanted to sit by the bedside and hold the old man's hand. Gavin wanted to tell him he hoped he'd be better soon, back to normal and back home. The desire to see Mr. Chappell back in his home, back on his land, haunted Gavin. The foreign feelings he'd experienced three nights ago when he and Dulcie had carried her grandfather to the doctor still lingered. For some reason he couldn't explain, however, he made sure Dulcie wasn't there before he approached the doctor's door.

Even now, Mr. Chappell's third day at the doctor's house, Gavin paused by the corner beside the dressmaker shop to check to see if the old mule was waiting by the fence. It wasn't that he didn't want to see Dulcie. On the contrary, he missed her, missed being with her and talking to her. Maybe he missed her a little too much.

He couldn't dismiss the strange notion of wishing he was part of the family. But he wasn't. He was an interloper. Even if the goal of buying the Chappell farm had been his uncle's idea, Gavin couldn't deny he represented his uncle—at least he had for a while—and he felt responsible for much of the distress the Chappells had gone through.

No mule stood tied to the picket fence in front of the doctor's house. Gavin continued to the front gate. It squeaked on its hinges, announcing his arrival. The doctor's wife opened the door before he knocked.

"Why, I declare, Mr. DeWitt, you are surely diligent about coming to visit Mr. Chappell." She let him in. "He ate a little breakfast, and he's grumpy." She leaned a little closer and lowered her voice as she led him back to the room where Mr. Chappell convalesced. "He wants to go home, but Doc is afraid he'll try to do too much. You know what I mean?"

Gavin did indeed. A whole new set of emotions pricked him, thinking about the old man going home and trying to hobble around on his broken leg, doing things he shouldn't be doing. How would all the chores get done? How would the barn get repaired? Dulcie already had more than she could handle, working with the sheep and the wool, and goodness knew what else she did. Now she'd have to take care of her bed-ridden grandfather and do all his chores as well. She couldn't do it alone.

He entered the room and hesitated a moment. Mr. Chappell looked so old and vulnerable in the bed. "Good morning, sir."

Mr. Chappell managed a smile and held out his hand to Gavin. "Ye better quit thet callin' me 'sir' business. I'm gonna start to thinkin' I'm somebody important."

Gavin grinned. "You need to do what the doctor tells you so you can get better." He shook his finger at the old man. "Don't you go giving Dulcie a hard time, now."

"That's what I told him." Dr. Pryor stepped into the room. "The old coot wants to go home, but I know what he's going to do when he gets there. Dulcie'll have herself snatched baldheaded fussing over him."

"If I promise to follow orders, will you let me go home?" The wheedle in Mr. Chappell's voice almost made Gavin laugh out loud.

The doctor frowned. "You don't even know what the orders are yet, and I guarantee you aren't going to like them."

A scowl wobbled across Mr. Chappell's brow. "Doc, I'm gonna go plumb crazy if I set in this here bed much longer. Where's Dulcie? She comin' to take me home today?"

The doctor plopped his hands on his hips. "I expect she's coming, but she's not taking you home. Not today anyway. She might tell me to keep you here for a month."

Dulcie's grandfather protested, but the helplessness of his expression skewered Gavin.

Mrs. Pryor came in, carrying a tray with a glass of milk and a half sandwich. While Mr. Chappell was occupied, Gavin touched the doctor's elbow.

"Doctor, can I speak with you privately?" Gavin tipped his head toward the hallway.

The doctor harrumphed and proceeded Gavin out the door. "What's on your mind, other than the bill?"

"Well," Gavin rubbed his chin. "I may have an idea."

Dulcie slapped the reins on Samson's back, urging the mule to pick up the pace. Grandpa had been laid up at the doctor's office for five days, but today he sat, propped up in the back of the wagon. She was taking him home. She only hoped all her preparations were enough.

The doctor had given him a dose of pain medicine to endure the trip, and a pair of crutches with stern instructions to not use them any more than absolutely necessary. He'd given Dulcie medication and instructions as well, and assured her he'd drop by when he could to make sure her grandfather wasn't being foolish.

The pain medicine made Grandpa a little groggy, so he wasn't too chatty, but it was clear he was happy to be going home. "I know I cain't go out there to the graveyard to visit with Virginia, but knowin' I'm close to her'll be mighty fine."

Dulcie smiled, but inside, she feared. "Please do as the doctor says, Grandpa. If you try to do too much, you're libel to fall. Then what will I do?" Even she could hear the worry threading her voice.

Her biggest regret was that she hadn't had time to tear a single charred board off the barn yet. She'd been so caught up making sure everything was ready for Grandpa's homecoming, setting things up to make his care easier, she'd not had a spare minute. She hated that the first thing he would see when they approached the farm would be the ugly, partially-burned barn. The damage was bad, but not irreparable.

She halted Samson short of the yard. "Now, Grandpa, do you remember I told you about the damage to the barn? You were kind of groggy from the medicine, but do you remember?"

"I 'member. The back half o' the roof, one back corner and part of a wall."

He remembered. She'd finally had to tell him yesterday that six sheep had died. She wasn't sure if her heart mourned more for the sheep or for Grandpa. She drew a deep breath, to prepare him for what he was about to see. "I haven't been able to start yet on the barn. I'm going to talk to Dewey and Zeb, and maybe Mr. Cutler, too, and see if they can come and help."

Grandpa shook his head. "Dewey's an old man. He cain't get up on no ladder. An' Zeb's a mite put out with me. Reckon he thinks I oughta sell. Now they're all gonna think I should sell, what with the barn tore up and me laid up." He stroked his beard. "The Lord'll provide, Rosebud. He always does."

She hoped Grandpa was right. She clucked to Samson and they moved forward. But the sight that greeted them around the bend wasn't what she expected.

A stack of charred boards lay on the ground beside the barn, and a ladder leaned against the burned side of the barn. A man straddled the blackened rafters, whacking them with a hammer and loosening the burned pegs. At the sound of the wagon pulling into the yard, the man astride the rafters turned.

Gavin? What in the world was he doing here?

Grandpa shaded his eyes. "Is that who I think it is?"

Dulcie's surprise so choked her, she could barely respond. "It is." She steered Samson as close to the house as she could get, and set the brake.

"You stay put. As long as he's here, he can help us get you from the wagon to your bed."

"Bed? Why cain't I set on the porch? I've spent more'n enough time in bed."

Dulcie nailed him with her sternest look. "Because you promised Doc Pryor you'd follow orders, and that's what you're going to do."

Gavin had already climbed down the ladder and crossed the yard to greet them. His clothing and hands and face were covered in black soot. How long had he been here?

Dulcie met him halfway, her hands held out in question. "What are you doing?"

He dusted his hands the best he could, but nothing would remove the black except a good scrubbing. "I'm here to help. I don't believe I ever mentioned that one year in college, I took a semester off. I went to a place out on the barrier islands and helped build a school there. It was a service project done by an organization from the college. I learned a lot, including how to replace a roof, among other things."

Dulcie stared at him. "A service project? Sounds like charity."

Gavin looked past her in the direction of the wagon where Grandpa waited. "Look, you need help. If someone isn't here to pitch in, you know your grandfather isn't going to rest like the doctor told him to."

She hated to admit the truth of his statement. "What is your uncle going to say? Surely, he's not in favor of you spending your days out here helping us rebuild."

Gavin dragged a dirty sleeve across his equally dirty face. "It doesn't matter what he thinks. I don't work for him anymore."

She widened her eyes. The night Grandpa was hurt, he'd mentioned he was leaving but his uncle was staying. She'd not had opportunity to inquire further, but the idea of Gavin separating from his uncle wasn't at all discomfiting. A dozen questions fought for first place, but her priority still sat propped up in the back of the wagon.

Gavin must have read her mind. He held out his filthy hands and arms. "Let me go to the pump and wash up. Then I'll help you move your grandfather into the house."

Grandpa had even more questions than Dulcie did, but at Gavin's insistence and reassurance, they got him settled in bed with the promise that Gavin would answer his questions later.

Dulcie closed Grandpa's door and tiptoed out to the kitchen where Gavin was pouring two cups of coffee. He held one out to her. "Hope you don't mind me making a fresh pot."

She shook her head and accepted the cup. "We need to talk."

Gavin nodded. "I agree. Do you want to go first, or shall I?"

She couldn't be angry at him anymore, not after the way he'd helped with Grandpa. But even his announcement that he and his uncle had parted ways didn't erase the skepticism that prodded her. "All right. What do you have in mind?"

Gavin moved to the door and held it open for her. "Let's talk out here."

She leaned against one porch post and sipped.

He leaned against the other. "Well, like I told you, I have some experience with building. The man from the college, under whose tutelage I learned, was one of the best. I came out here two days ago when I knew you were in town to see your grandfather, and I took measurements and made some notes. Then I went to the sawmill and ordered lumber. It should be delivered tomorrow."

"What?" She stared at him, incredulous that he would order materials without asking.

He held up one hand. "Before you get upset, please hear me out. As I said, I'm no longer employed by my uncle. I told him I couldn't do what he demanded any longer, so it was a mutual decision. I'm free to help you out here, and my uncle has no say in the matter."

She covered her face with her fingers. If she tried to do the work alone, she'd never be able to keep Grandpa from attempting to help. If the repairs weren't finished before the autumn rains, they wouldn't have a dry place to store their winter hay. "I will have to pay you. This family doesn't—"

"Doesn't take charity. Yeah, I thought so." Gavin nodded. "The way I figure it, we'd be helping each other. Since I'm not working for my uncle, I can't afford to stay at the Mountain Park. What if I did the work on the barn and you pay me in meals and a roof over my head." He gestured toward the barn. "Or, at least half a roof. The sooner I get to work, the sooner it will be a whole roof."

She tilted her head. Could she trust him? Did she have a choice? "All right, but you won't stay in the barn. I can fix up a place out there in the wool shed, where the spinning wheels and looms are."

Gavin grinned and stuck out his hand. The lines and creases that mapped his palm still bore traces of soot, and stubborn dirt clung beneath his fingernails. "Deal." She shook his hand, and his smile faded a bit. "I have to tell you, my uncle isn't going to give up."

She lifted her shoulders. "Neither will I."

✍ THIRTY-ONE

Instead of moving to the boardinghouse at the end of the week, Gavin stuffed everything he had into his one suitcase and small trunk. Dulcie let him use the wagon and Samson, but the hotel manager wouldn't allow the battered wagon and old mule to pull up to the Mountain Park's front door. Gavin carried his things out the servants' entrance behind the hotel and loaded them onto the wagon. He didn't see his uncle, but he couldn't shake the feeling the man was watching him as he drove away.

Dulcie had asked him to pick up a few grocery items at the Emporium while he was in town. He handed Mr. Dempsey Dulcie's list. The merchant looked it over, and then peered at Gavin over the top of his spectacles.

"This here is for the Chappells? I heard James got stove up. Is that why you're fetchin' and carryin' for them folks?" He began pulling items from the shelf and depositing them in a crate, but his tongue never stopped wagging. "Seems a mite surprisin' you doin' their town-runnin'. Bet yer uncle don't take kindly to that. What'd he have to say about it? You doin' this so's yer uncle can finally get his contract on that land?"

Gavin merely gave a couple of vague answers while he waited and guarded his expression so Mr. Dempsey wouldn't speculate any more than he already was. He didn't intend to answer any of the merchant's nosy questions. By the time Gavin loaded the crate into the wagon, Dempsey stood in the doorway, scratching his head. Doubtless the man wasted no time in gossiping to the other merchants about Gavin DeWitt working for the Chappells now.

When he arrived back at the farm, Dulcie showed him to the wool shed where she had made a pallet for him. "I cleared a couple of shelves there in the corner for you to use. During the day, I will be out here working, so you'll need to roll up the pallet and put it in the corner behind the larger spinning wheel."

"Thank you. That was very kind." He ran his fingers over the smooth wood of the loom's frame. "I hope I get to watch you work sometime. This is fascinating."

"Maybe you can show me a thing or two about building." She walked to the door and propped it open.

Was she serious? She wanted to learn how to cut a piece of lumber and whittle a wooden peg to hold two beams together? With mischief in mind, he stepped over to the door and looked out over the meadow. "Maybe you can teach me how to milk a cow or shear a sheep."

He could tell by the way she jerked her head around to meet his gaze that she caught his playful tone.

"First of all, we don't shear sheep at this time of year. We shear in the late spring, and they spend all summer and fall growing their wool back. They need their heavy wool going into fall and winter. Secondly . . ." She looked at his hands, still stained from the charred wood. "I don't think the cow would appreciate your dirty hands."

He laughed out loud. "Tell the cow I promise I'll even scrub under my fingernails."

She arched one eyebrow and smirked. "You just might work out after all."

That evening and every evening for the next several days, Gavin not only joined Dulcie and her grandfather for supper, they also invited him to stay for their family Bible reading time. If he'd wondered before what it felt like to be part of a family, sitting at the table to share a meal and gathering around the hearth to listen to Mr. Chappell read the scriptures took away some of the wondering. He couldn't remember ever spending more pleasant hours, even when he was climbing up and down the ladder, and tearing out the burned sections.

What was it he had written on his list of goals? To be proud of the work he did. To build relationships with people he cared about. He actually loved what he was doing, even though he was grimy and exhausted at the end of the day. He managed to make friends with the cow, and learned how to fill the milk bucket. The dog slowly warmed up to him, especially when Gavin brought him scraps from supper. He wasn't sure about the "putting down roots" part yet, but for now, he was content.

One morning, nearly a week after he'd arrived, he carried the milk pail and egg basket into the house. Mr. Chappell hobbled with his crutches, unassisted, to his chair. Dulcie followed him with both hands extended to catch him if need be.

Mr. Chappell was as gleeful as a child at his accomplishment. "Mornin', son."

Gavin took his elbow and helped him lower himself to the chair, and then set the crutches to one side. He reached into the egg basket. "Mr. Chappell, I found this Bible out in the wool shed. I believe it belongs to your wife. I didn't want to use it without asking your permission. Would it be all right if I read it at night?"

Mr. Chappell's eyes misted. "My Virginia would love fer ye to read her Bible, son. She'd likely suggest ye start in the Gospel o' John and Psalms. They was her favorites."

"The Gospel of John and Psalms." Gavin laid his hand over top of the well-used Book. "I'll do it. And I promise I'll take good care of it. Thank you, sir."

The remainder of the day was spent tearing off the last of the burned rafters and clapboards, and cleaning up the viable ends of the beams to receive the new wood. The wagonload of lumber had already been delivered and stacked near the barn, ready for use.

Dulcie stopped by on her way from the wool shed to the house. "Looks like you're starting on the new rafters."

"I'm glad your grandfather has a good selection of tools. I hope to have all the rafters replaced by next week."

Dulcie allowed a small, but approving smile. "I know Grandpa will be happy to hear that." She glanced toward the house. "Speaking of which, I need to go check on him and then get dinner ready."

He shoved the rag he used to wipe the sweat from his face back into his pocket. "Sounds great. I'm hungry." He started back up the ladder.

"Hard work makes a man hungry, my grandma always said." The last couple of words fell away from her lips, broken. He wished he could shoulder some of her grief for her, but never having had the family relationships she did, he couldn't begin to know what she felt.

"Oh, I meant to ask you . . . That black locust wood you told me your grandfather used for the fence—can you show me where it grows? I'd like to cut pegs out of it since you told me it's such a strong wood."

Her line of focus scanned the trees. "Of course. There are a couple of trees just beyond the wool shed. I'll show you after dinner."

She scurried away, and Gavin watched her retreat. For such a young woman, she carried a huge load. Her life was hard, but she never complained. If he asked how he could help her or lighten her load, she'd only shake her head and wave away his offer. She was proud, that was for certain.

That evening, Mr. Chappell read from the book of Second Corinthians. The verses spoke of Jesus being rich, but becoming poor, so that the people who believed in Him might be rich. When Gavin asked Mr. Chappell what the scripture meant, the old man leaned back in his rocking chair, pure serenity on his face.

"My Virginia believed. She were rich. She had her a home all ready fer her in heaven 'cause Jesus gived her His riches. He done took her place on the cross and He died like a common murderer and thief. He weren't no sinner, but He died so people like my Virginia, and me, and Dulcie girl. . ." He settled his gaze on Gavin. "An' you, so we can go to heaven. He gived His very life so we could have His riches, His home in heaven." He sniffed and dabbed at his eyes. "That's how Jesus traded His riches fer our poorness, and gived us a ferever home in heaven."

The hush in the room when Mr. Chappell finished took Gavin's breath away. After a few minutes, Gavin rose quietly, said goodnight, and retired to the wool shed. He couldn't wait to read the next chapter in the Gospel of John. The story of God's Son—how He came and healed the sick, the blind, and the lame, how He walked on the water and forgave people of their wrongdoings—was more engaging than anything he'd ever read. Some nights he fought to stay awake so he could read a few more verses, but exhaustion usually pulled his eyes closed.

He unrolled his pallet and sat to pull off his boots. With Mrs. Chappell's Bible in hand, he leaned back against the wall and opened the pages to the Gospel of John, chapter eleven. *"Now a certain man was sick, named Lazarus, of Bethany . . ."*

"Are you sure you don't need the wagon?"

Gavin tightened the saddle cinch under Samson's belly. "No. What I need at the hardware store I can put in the saddle bag." He turned. "Do you need anything from town? I can take the wagon if you—"

"No." She flipped her fingers toward the work on her loom. "When I finish this rug, I'll have a stack to take to the Emporium, and that woolen yardage over in the corner is a special order for the dressmaker, Eunice Mead. But I don't want to hold you up waiting for me to finish this. You go on and get what you need for the barn."

"All right." He swung into the saddle, and Samson snorted his displeasure. Gavin laughed. "I think he'd rather stay in the meadow with the sheep."

"No doubt. He can be a lazy thing. Don't be afraid to nudge him hard with your heels."

Gavin gave the mule a pat. "I helped your grandfather to the privy, and then got him settled in his bed. But he asked if he could sit on the porch this afternoon so he can watch me work. I told him he'd have to ask you."

She smiled and he caught himself hoping she'd do it again. "We'll have to see how he's doing after dinner. I know he feels all cooped up and closed in. Maybe we can let him whittle the pegs you need for the barn."

"Good idea. I'll be back as quick as I can." He and Samson headed down the road toward town.

His errand at the hardware store didn't take long. He wrapped the roofing nails in oiled paper and tucked them in the bottom of the saddle bag, and added four dozen carriage bolts and washers on top. A spool of wire topped off his order.

He glanced at the sun. It was still early. He had time to stop by the bank. After paying the doctor bill—he'd had quite an argument with Dulcie over that—and paying for the lumber and hardware supplies, his pocket money had dwindled.

Samson seemed amenable to the detour since there was a tasty-looking patch of grass to occupy him. Gavin looped the reins over the hitching post and entered the double doors with Hot Springs Bank painted in ornate lettering on the glass door panels. The banker, Mr. Granger, greeted him.

"Well, Mr. DeWitt, the younger. I thought you'd left town." The banker flicked his gaze up and down Gavin's clothing.

"In a sense, yes. I'm no longer staying at the Mountain Park, if that's what you mean."

Granger smoothed his mustache with his fingertips. "So, how can I help you today, Mr. DeWitt?"

Gavin glanced at the blank forms lined up on the counter and selected a withdrawal. "I need to withdraw some cash from my account,
please." He began filling out the amount.

Granger cleared his throat. "Uh, uhh, I-I'm sorry, Mr. DeWitt, but
you don't have an account here any longer."

Gavin's pencil halted in the middle of signing his name. "I beg your
pardon? Yes, I have an account. Money was deposited in the account
weekly for as long I was staying at the Mountain Park. There should be
close to five hundred dollars in the account."

The banker's countenance reddened. "I'm sorry, sir, but your uncle
closed out that account a week ago. He moved the funds to his other
account."

Heat rose from Gavin's belly. His uncle had deposited Gavin's salary
in the account every week. Anger stirred, but he sucked in a deep breath
to hold it at bay. He shouldn't be surprised that his uncle would do something so underhanded, but that was Gavin's money. Money he earned
working for his uncle. Perhaps his uncle didn't feel he'd earned it since
he never delivered the contracts.

Gavin stuffed the unfinished bank form into his pocket. "Thank you,
Mr. Granger. I'm sorry to have troubled you." He exited the bank grinding
his teeth, and snatched Samson's reins from the hitching post. The mule
jerked his head up. "C'mon, mule. I need to stop at the telegraph office."

A few doors up the street, Gavin sent a quick wire to the bank in
Philadelphia, requesting a check he hoped the small bank here in Hot
Springs would honor. Uncle Arnold had no access to the funds in his
Philadelphia account. At least he didn't think he did.

Almost as an afterthought, Gavin inquired at the post office window
in the same building as the telegraph office, asking for the Chappell's
mail. The plump, gray-haired woman at the post office shook her head.
"No, nothing for the Chappells today, but I believe there is one for you."

"Me?"

The woman's flabby arm waggled as she went through the pigeonhole boxes. "Yes, here it is. Very official looking." She handed the letter to Gavin and he stared at the return address.

Official it was. From the office of the Honorable Harold DeWitt, Pennsylvania House of Representatives. Gavin could hardly believe it. Harold had answered his letter.

He thanked the woman and stepped out into the sunshine, slipping his finger under the wax seal as he went. He withdrew the single onion-skin sheet and read Harold's handwriting.

> *Dear Brother,*
>
> *Imagine how happy I was to receive your letter, but then read the news that you and Uncle Arnold have had a parting of the ways. I'm truly sorry to hear things have not gone as planned for you. I feared our uncle would coerce you into becoming involved with his less-than-honest business practices, but I must tell you, I'm proud of you for standing up for yourself. It grieved my heart to watch him and our father at each other's throats over the years, and I never wanted that for you and me.*
>
> *I'm presently in Harrisburg, but if you plan to return to Philadelphia soon, please let me know. It's been too long since we've shared a table.*
>
> *Your brother, Harold.*

Harold was proud of him? Harold didn't want the two of them to end up like Father and Uncle Arnold? He almost shouted as solace and joy tangled in his throat. He shouldn't be surprised that Uncle Arnold had lied about the reasons he claimed for taking Gavin on. The man's hatred and bitterness contaminated everything he said and did. Gavin read the letter again. The anger and betrayal he'd felt at the bank when he learned of Uncle Arnold's devious actions dissipated like dew on a hot summer's morning. His brother was proud of him, and Gavin couldn't wait to answer Harold's letter.

❦ THIRTY-TWO

"I don't know if this is a good idea." Dulcie re-pinned a lock of unco-operative hair. She turned to face two pairs of eyes—one accusing and the other amused.

Grandpa pointed at her from the rocking chair. "Dulcie girl, ye ain't been to church since I got stove up. Jus' 'cause I cain't go, don't mean ye gotta stay home." He narrowed his eyes. "Ye know what yer grandma would say."

Yes, she knew indeed. "But, Grandpa, what if you need—"

"What if I need to go to the privy?" He hooked his thumb in Gavin's direction. "Ain't that why you got me a keeper?"

A muffled sound that came across like *snarfff* pulled her attention to Gavin who sat at the table sipping a second cup of coffee.

Grandpa's mustache twitched, and she knew without a doubt the two of them were in cahoots. She planted her hands on her hips. "All right." She aimed a warning stare at Gavin. "But if anything happens, I'm never leaving here again until he is completely healed, and maybe not even then."

Gavin pressed his lips together and pulled a feigned serious look. He crossed his heart with a pointed finger. "I promise I won't leave his side for a minute. Well, except when he's in the privy."

She hitched Samson to the wagon, only because Grandpa insisted Grandma would have a conniption fit if she rode the mule astride in her Sunday dress. She climbed into the wagon seat and hesitated with a long look at the house. Why was she so sure Grandpa and Gavin couldn't manage without her?

She blew out a sigh. The sooner she left, the sooner she'd be back. "Hup, Samson."

The church bell was clanging when she reached the edge of town. She hurried Samson along, remembering how Grandma always insisted being late for church was disgraceful. With the mule safely tied in the shade of a massive oak, she hurried inside just as Otis Hogan stroked the first notes of the opening hymn on his dulcimer.

A few folks nodded a greeting to her, and one or two spoke in a loud whisper to ask after Grandpa. She acknowledged each one, and settled in, glad that she arrived too late for much socializing. It was hard to put her finger on it, but she got the feeling some of the town folk were snubbing her. Even the people directly across the aisle regarded her with coolness and uplifted chins. Probably nothing more than her imagination.

After a half dozen songs and an hour-long sermon that exhorted the congregation to help their fellow man in the manner of Christ, the service was dismissed. Dulcie slipped out as quickly as possible, but up ahead of her, Eunice Mead picked her way over the uneven ground of the church yard.

"Mrs. Mead?" Dulcie hurried to catch up to her.

The dressmaker turned, but when she saw it was Dulcie calling to her, her eyes widened and a visible grimace crossed her face. A tiny scowl tugged at the woman's mouth as she fumbled in her reticule.

Dulcie's steps brought her alongside the woman. "Mrs. Mead, I wanted to let you know the yard goods you ordered are ready. Eight yards. I can bring it later this week."

The dressmaker extracted a lacy handkerchief and dabbed her nose. "Oh, Dulcie. . . uh, well, you see . . . I, uh, I no longer have need of woolen yardage. I'm sorry." Her cheeks flushed red and she couldn't—or wouldn't?—look Dulcie in the eye.

Puzzled, Dulcie stepped closer. "Perhaps you misunderstood. This is the yardage you ordered several weeks ago."

"No, no, I didn't misunderstand. The fact is—" Mrs. Mead appeared quite uneasy, and glanced from side to side, presumably to see if anyone overheard their conversation.

Dulcie lifted her shoulders. "Go on."

The woman ducked her head and mumbled, barely loud enough for Dulcie to hear. "It's... I can't use your yard goods any longer. Excuse me, I must go."

Mrs. Mead hurried away, and if it wasn't for wanting to get home to Grandpa, Dulcie would have gone after her and demanded a reason for the cancelled order.

Dulcie gave Grandpa's pillows another pat and double-checked the position of his leg before pulling the sheet up to his chest. "How does that feel, Grandpa? Are you sure you don't need any pain medicine before you go to sleep?"

Grandpa scowled. "Iffen ye'd stop pattin' an' pokin' an' fussin' I'd be jus' fine." He gave his fingers a wave. "I'm sorry I'm such a grump. Ye take real good care o' me, Rosebud, like yer grandma woulda done." He caught her hand and squeezed her fingers. "Let me rest a while, and iffen I need any medicine, I'll thump Grandma's cane on the floor." He reached for the cane and leaned it against the bed.

Dulcie's heart constricted. After being so strong and active for all of his seventy-four years, how hard it must be for her grandpa to not be able to do anything for himself, and to have her hover over him. She leaned down and kissed his forehead. "It's getting late. I'll leave your door open a little so I can hear you. I'm going to go finish cleaning up the kitchen."

Grandpa patted her hand. "G'night, Rosebud."

She left the bedroom door ajar, and started to return to the kitchen to finish the dishes, but stopped short. Gavin stood there, dishtowel in hand wiping the last plate and stacking it on the shelf.

He picked up the dishpan and carried it to the door, tossing the wash water out beside the porch. When he stepped back through the doorway, his face reflected a sheepish grin when he realized he was caught.

"Thank you, but you needn't do my chores." She took the dishpan from him. "Your work on the barn more than pays for your meals and a place to sleep."

He lifted his shoulders. "I know, but I see how much you have to do, including caring for your grandfather. If you'll permit me, I'd like to share some of the chores with you."

The dishtowel was damp, but it absorbed most of the drips from the dishpan. "You're already milking the cow and collecting the eggs. Yesterday, when I went to muck out the stalls, it was already done."

"I want to help." He straightened the chairs at the table.

Dulcie studied him in much the same way she'd seen Grandma observe a person. If only Grandma were still with her, to teach her to be wise and discerning when it came to sizing up a person and perceiving their motives. Her scrutiny must have made him uncomfortable, because he backed up a step to the still-open door. He hooked his thumb over his shoulder. "I guess I'll go on out to the—"

"Would you like a cup of coffee?" Dulcie crossed to the stove and tentatively touched the coffeepot to make sure it was still hot. "I enjoy sitting on the porch with a cup at the end of the day."

Had she really extended that invitation? Coffee on the porch after supper and Bible reading? That had always been their family time. She bit her lip. Couldn't very well retract the invitation that left her lips only a moment before.

A hint of light played across his eyes, and a slow, easy smile tugged at his lips. "I'd like that very much. May I help?"

She lowered her voice to a whisper. "I managed to bake a batch of cookies yesterday. Grandpa thinks they're all for him, but I think we can snitch a couple to go with our coffee." She pointed to the shelf. "Get a couple of cookies out of that crock for us." *Us?* Did he hear the quiver in her voice?

For heaven's sake, what was wrong with her? She'd nailed down her feelings for anyone named DeWitt a couple of months ago—suspicion, resentment, distrust. Why were butterflies loosed in her stomach at the thought of sitting with this DeWitt on the porch? *Stop acting like one of those silly, flighty girls from the school in Asheville.* The coffee sloshed over the edge of the cup when she poured it.

Oh, great day in the morning! She grabbed the damp dishtowel and mopped up the mess. A deep breath steadied her, and she followed Gavin out to the porch. Now if she could manage not to trip or dump the coffee all over him.

She held out a cup. "Here's the coffee."

He accepted the steaming brew and handed her a cookie. "Thanks. Here are your grandfather's cookies." He grinned and lowered himself onto the top step. "Sure is a nice evening. Look at that sunset."

The colors across the mountain horizon were indeed spectacular. "Mm. I'd light the lantern, but it will draw mosquitoes."

Gavin took a bite of his cookie. "Look out there across the meadow. I think one of my favorite things since I've been here on your farm is the—what do you call them? Lightning bugs?"

She followed his line of focus. The meadow was alive with tiny, floating pinpoints of light. She'd seen lightning bugs all her life, and it seemed strange for someone to be enthralled by them. Had she become so distracted by the pressure of responsibility that she'd forgotten the things she loved about her mountain home?

Dulcie settled into Grandpa's rocker, the accompanying squeaks harmonizing with the crickets and tree frogs. She wrapped her fingers around her mug and sniffed the rich goodness of the coffee. "I found one of my rugs rolled up out in the wool shed next to your things."

"Mm-hm." Gavin took a swallow of coffee. "That's the one I bought the day we argued at the Emporium."

She rolled her lips to prevent the laugh that rose in her throat. "I seem to recall more than one time we argued in the Emporium."

A deep chuckle rumbled across the swelling twilight. "So we did. I hope you don't mind that I bought the rug. The colors and design were so unique, I had hoped to convince my uncle to contract with you for enough rugs to fill his new resort."

Dulcie set her cup on the crate that served as a table between the two rocking chairs. "It's unlikely your uncle will want to do business with the Chappells." She cocked her head. "Don't you think it's odd that we haven't heard from your uncle the entire time you've been here?"

"Honestly, I still suspect my uncle is working on hatching some kind of scheme to get you to sell. To his way of thinking, landing a successful business deal is more important than breathing. I'm beginning to wonder if there's anything he wouldn't do to win."

Even though she couldn't clearly see his face in the gathering darkness, she could hear the vexation in Gavin's voice. The memory of his silent frown the day his uncle had tried to bully Grandpa into selling nudged her. She'd intended to ask him why he'd stood there with his mouth shut, lips thinned in a frown, and his brow furrowed in disapproval. The events that followed that day had cast her intention aside. It no longer mattered.

"Can I ask you a question?" Gavin's deep voice pulled her out of her introspection.

She picked up her coffee cup. "I don't mind if you ask, but I may not have an answer."

Gavin scooted around on the step to face her. "I've been here for over two weeks, and I wanted to thank you and your grandfather for including me in your Bible-reading time. But this question has nagged at me, and I'm not quite sure how to ask it."

Dulcie waited. Doubt taunted her. She'd staunchly held God at arm's length for such a long time. Having only recently bowed her heart and her knees in surrender, asking God to forgive her resentment made her like a fledgling bird learning to fly. Maybe she should suggest he hold his questions and ask Grandpa.

"How do you learn to believe?" Darkness had fallen, but a thread of concern colored his tone. "How does one go about being good enough for God?"

Unease tightened her stomach. She'd grown up listening to God's word, but her own recently renewed faith was fragile in the midst of all the trouble and grief. She'd questioned God's mercy and forgiveness in the days since she'd prayed, especially in the wake of all the recent events. Did she have the right to answer Gavin's questions? She pulled in a deep breath and sent a quick prayer heavenward for the right words.

"It's not a matter of being good enough, because the Bible says nobody is good enough. God has promised in His word that He will forgive."

Several moments of silence followed before Gavin spoke again. "So that's it? Nobody is good enough? Your grandfather says God loves everyone. How can He do that if we aren't good enough?"

This conversation was getting uncomfortably close to her own fractious relationship with God. Heat filled her face. Even though God had welcomed her back into His embrace, telling Gavin she'd run from God for many years didn't seem like the best approach.

"There are a lot of promises in God's word. The thing is that we break promises, sometimes even if we don't intend to. But God has never broken a promise." Speaking the words to Gavin reminded her own heart of those precious promises that she'd neglected for so long. "The reason Grandpa wanted you to start reading in the Gospel of John is because you will see why Jesus came and why He died. While you are reading, remember God's promises." Her throat tightened and she had to pause.

After swallowing a couple of times, she continued. "God promised He would send His Son, and He did. God promised He would make a way for us to be forgiven, and He did. Jesus took the penalty we deserved for our sin, just like He said He would. He died on the cross, and He rose again, like He promised."

The cicadas sang and an owl *whoo-whoo*ed in accompaniment. Quiet had settled over the mountain along with the darkness, and Dulcie closed her eyes, relishing the peace that came from trusting what she'd just told Gavin.

He rose and handed her his empty cup. "Thank you for the coffee and conversation. I'll keep those promises in mind while I read." He picked up the lantern from the peg and struck the flint to light it. "I'll bring this back in the morning."

She stepped toward the door, her heart filled with the contemplative repose God had given her.

Gavin held the lantern aloft and stepped off the porch. "Good night, Dulcie."

She watched as he made his way out to the wool shed, until the lantern became a tiny floating light, like the lightning bugs.

Good night, Gavin.

❦ THIRTY-THREE

Gavin couldn't get Dulcie's words out of his head. Maybe because she'd spoken them with such conviction. He'd tossed and turned on his pallet, but nothing shut out the words. It was as if everything his father had said about him was true, and even God's word confirmed it.

The Bible says nobody is good enough.

No matter how hard he'd tried to please his father—or his uncle—he'd never been good enough. What made him think trying hard with God would be any different?

God promised He will forgive—

God promised—

God promised—

He gave up trying to sleep. He turned up the lantern wick and opened Mrs. Chappell's Bible to the book of John and reread a chapter he'd read over a week ago. The story of the woman coming to draw water from the well captivated him. She was apparently a marked woman, and had no friends, so she went to fetch water alone. But the words Jesus spoke to her gave Gavin pause. *If thou knewest the gift of God, and who it was that saith to thee, Give me to drink. . .* What exactly was living water? Was there something special about the water, or about the Man, Jesus?

He read on, only to stop again when the woman went and invited others to come to meet Jesus. *Come see a man, which told me all things that ever I did: is not this the Christ?* Gavin lowered the Bible to his lap and contemplated the woman's challenge. He'd been to chapel as a boy at boarding school, and he'd heard the name of Jesus, but now his curiosity—no, it was more than curiosity—a sense of awe, wonder, and reverence washed over him, and he had to know more. He picked up where he'd left off, and kept reading.

The eastern sky bore the first pale pink blush of daybreak when Gavin rolled up his pallet. On sluggish feet, he headed for the barn where the cow awaited. He yawned and rubbed what felt like grains of sand from his eyes to focus on splashing the milk into the pail.

Twenty minutes later, he trudged to the house with a full milk pail and egg basket. He tapped on the door first, and then opened it and stepped inside. The aroma of sizzling bacon and brewing coffee greeted him like old friends.

"Morning." Dulcie glanced his way before sliding a skillet of biscuits into the oven.

"Milk and eggs." He set the egg basket near the stove and poured the milk through the strainer that Dulcie had ready and waiting for him.

"Are you all right? Your eyes are bloodshot and you look like you didn't sleep all night."

Gavin turned his attention to her and found her frowning at him. "I didn't." He hid his mouth behind his sleeve to stifle a yawn. "You want me to help get your grandfather up?"

She tossed a skeptical look his direction. "He's up. He insisted he could finish dressing by himself."

Once Mr. Chappell hobbled out on his crutches and they were seated around the breakfast table, Mr. Chappell asked the blessing, and then announced to Gavin, "While Dulcie goes inta town t'day, I'd surely 'preciate iffen ye could help me out to the porch. I want to sit and watch ye work on the barn." Mr. Chappell slurped his coffee. "Reckon I can whittle some pegs fer ye whilst I'm settin' there. Man's gotta make hisself useful."

Amid a few narrow-eyed scowls and a bit of arguing during breakfast, Dulcie agreed to let her grandfather sit on the porch as long as Gavin promised to keep an eye on him. As soon as the table was cleared, Gavin assisted the man to the creaky rocking chair on the porch, positioned to give Mr. Chappell full view of the ongoing work.

Gavin was already climbing across the rafters when Dulcie entered the barn. He'd grown to admire the love, respect, and dedication this young woman had for her grandfather. He poked his head between two long boards and called down to her.

"Dulcie, don't worry. I'll keep an eye on him and make sure he doesn't attempt anything he shouldn't."

She craned her neck and looked up. "Thank you. I guess I'm being overly protective."

From his vantage point atop the roof, he watched as she harnessed the mule and loaded her rugs into the wagon. The colors of the rugs gave the appearance of a flower garden. Whoever purchased them would be fortunate indeed to have such works of art. His eyes drifted to Dulcie. Even though the sun hid behind the clouds this morning, the muted light against her walnut brown hair created an ethereal effect. She gathered her blue gingham skirt into one hand and pulled herself up to into the rickety seat. The old wagon creaked and groaned as she turned the mule toward town.

Gavin put in a couple of hours, climbing up and down the ladder, hauling boards and nailing them in place. Even without the sun, he guessed it to be mid-morning when he climbed down and joined Mr. Chappell on the porch. The old man had accumulated a pile of wood shavings at his feet, and in a basket were nearly a dozen stout pegs for fastening the barn beams together.

"Checking to see if you need anything."

"No, son, I'm pert near ready to climb thet ladder along with ye." He laid aside his whittling knife. "Reckon we could both use a drink o' water, though."

Gavin trotted to the pump and brought Mr. Chappell a dipper of cold water. "Mr. Chappell, I've been reading your wife's Bible—in the book of John, like you told me—and I have some questions."

The elderly gentleman gestured to the other rocking chair beside him. "Have a seat, son, and tell me what ye got on yer mind."

The two chairs squeaked in harmony as Gavin repeated the question he'd asked Dulcie the night before, and spoke how her answer perplexed him.

"So, Dulcie done told ye there ain't nobody good enough, huh? Well, she be right." Mr. Chappell nodded his gray head. "Says right there in the book o' Romans there ain't nobody righteous, not a single one."

Gavin dipped his head. Dulcie had talked about God's promises, but he still didn't see how he could possibly gain the acceptance of God if he couldn't manage to do anything right in his father's eyes. And now this gentle old man confirmed his worst fears. Gavin shook his head. "I've spent my whole life trying to please my father. He went to his grave accusing me of never having lived up to his expectations. Then I couldn't live up to my uncle's demands." He finally raised his gaze to meet Mr. Chappell's, and was taken aback by the elderly man's smile. What was there to smile about?

The lines around Mr. Chappell's eyes crinkled and deepened, but the smile softened his entire countenance. "Ye say yer readin' in the book o' John?"

Gavin simply gave a silent nod.

"Did ye read the part about Jesus meetin' that woman at the well? She had five husbands, and weren't none o' the other ladies in town that'd have anything to do with her. Ye see, ever'one in town knowed what kind o' woman she be, so there weren't no doubt but Jesus knowed, too."

Gavin cocked his head, trying to figure out the point of Mr. Chappell's Bible lesson. Perhaps the old gentleman hadn't heard him clearly. What did the story of this woman have to do with him never being able please his father?

Mr. Chappell leaned forward and tapped his fingers on Gavin's arm. "Y'see son, God knowed she were a sinner, just like He knows me an' you are sinners. Did Jesus turn her away? Did He condemn her?"

Gavin remembered the story after having read it in the wee hours of the morning. "No. If I recall, He told her to go get her husband, but then He already knew all about her." He squinted and furrowed his brow. "Is that what you're telling me—that Jesus knows all about me?"

Mr. Chappell's easy laugh wasn't in the least condescending. "Well, He does, but that weren't where I was pointin'. God knows all about us, He knows we're sinners, but He loved us anyway—so much that He sent His Son, Jesus, to die on the cross in our place."

It couldn't possibly be as simple as the old man made it sound. "But I still have so many questions."

"Well, son, I know Who's got the answers yer lookin' fer."

Dulcie halted Samson outside the Emporium. Not many folks out on the street today in the sleepy town. She hopped down and moved to the rear of the wagon. Eight new rugs, plus the wool yardage she'd woven for Mrs. Mead lay across the back of the wagon bed. Dulcie lowered the tailgate and loaded as many rugs as she could carry into her arms. Barely able to see over the top of her stack, she nudged the door to the mercantile open with her hip.

The table near the door where Mr. Dempsey usually displayed her rugs was occupied by a collection of boots and leather goods. A quick glance from side to side didn't reveal any of her goods, and her heart lifted. If all her rugs and yard goods had sold, the merchant would have a substantial amount of money to pay her. Couldn't come at a better time, what with the materials they still needed to finish the barn repairs. She'd argued with Gavin over Grandpa's doctor bill, and finally came to an agreement, albeit grudgingly on her part, that they would split it. Being beholden to anyone made her uneasy.

She heaved the load of rugs up onto the counter. "Mr. Dempsey?"

The merchant pushed his way past the faded green curtain that hung in the doorway of the storeroom. His expression went from friendly and welcoming to nervous and wary in the space of one glance. His step hesitated, and a wince flickered across his face.

"M-Miss Dulcie. Uh. . .how—how's yer grandpa keepin'?

"He's healing slowly." She'd never known the man to stumble over words before, unless he'd been caught in the act of gossiping. "It was a bad break. Doc says it'll take time until he's back on his feet."

Mr. Dempsey bobbed his head. "Sure was sorry to hear about that." He fumbled with straightening a few items on the shelves, as if he couldn't see the large pile of rugs taking up more than half of the counter.

"I noticed the rugs that were out there on the table are gone." She waited for him to tell her they'd all been sold, but he acted as if he didn't hear her statement.

He picked up his feather duster and proceeded to flick imaginary dust from the shelves.

"Mr. Dempsey, I have these five rugs here, and three more out in the wagon, along with a length of wool fabric. I'll go and—"

"No." His single word halted her in her tracks.

No? If he'd sold all her goods, why wouldn't he want more? At least she assumed he'd sold them all. Perhaps she was assuming too much.

She turned to him, her mind full of questions that no doubt showed in her expression. Before she could give voice to the questions, the merchant pushed aside the stockroom door curtain and returned moments later, his arms laden with two rugs and the roll of mauve yard goods.

He set them on the counter beside the rugs she'd carried in, his eyes downcast.

"What were these goods doing in the storeroom? Why weren't they out on the display table?" Dulcie wanted to shake him and demand he look at her, but he merely pulled out the tin box in which he kept her money.

"This here is for one rug and that blue wool fabric." His fingers trembled slightly as he counted out the money.

"Mr. Dempsey, I don't understand. Will you please tell me why—"

He stacked the two rugs and mauve wool on top of the new rugs. "Won't be needin' your goods anymore." He pushed the stack across the counter toward her. Then he closed the tin box and put it back under the counter. Still not looking her in the eye, he turned back toward the stockroom, mumbling as he went. "Sorry, Miss Dulcie."

There were no words. First Eunice Mead, and now Mr. Dempsey. At one time, she never would have imagined people who had been their friends and neighbors for so many years turning against her and Grandpa. Now, she wasn't so sure. She sent her gaze out the large front window to the street. There was no sign of Arnold DeWitt, but his presence permeated every storefront, every boardwalk. Even the low clouds that hung at the treetops, blotting out the sun mocked her as surely as if Arnold DeWitt himself had hidden the sun. She supposed if the incentive was great enough, people might do almost anything. And she'd bet her favorite hair ribbon that Arnold DeWitt was somehow behind this.

It took two trips to reload everything back into the wagon. One thing was certain—if she didn't sell these rugs and woolen materials soon, they would run out of money. She climbed aboard and steered Samson to turn the wagon around. As they headed back out of town and up the mountain, her thoughts tumbled and tangled, warring over first place of importance. Finally, she stamped her foot on the floorboard, startling the mule. Samson laid his ears back and snorted.

"Sorry, Samson. I'm just frustrated, mostly with myself. I should know better." Ignoring God for so many years had become a habit that was hard to break. "Lord, I know You aren't surprised by any of this. I don't understand how people can be friendly one minute and put a knife in your back the next. But I can't worry about that. I'll leave them up to You. But, Lord, I need to find a way to take these wool goods to some of the other towns around here and see if I can sell them."

She hated to worry Grandpa, but she might have little choice since a trip down the mountain to nearby Marshall or Weaverville would require two or three days. She rolled her lips inward and scowled. Grandpa would never let her go alone, and besides, someone needed to stay behind and care for the sheep and the chores.

Gavin's image came to mind, but she immediately dismissed the idea. She was already indebted to him for Grandpa's doctor bill, and the work he was doing on the barn was worth much more than room and board. She squirmed on the wagon seat, and another thought prodded her. If Arnold DeWitt was behind the town merchants turning her away, how could she be sure Gavin wasn't somehow involved?

✤ THIRTY-FOUR

Dulcie wiped the table after she'd finished washing the noon dishes. Grandpa had gone in to take a nap, and Gavin was already back at work, rebuilding the loft flooring, when wheels crunching the dirt and gravel outside caught her attention. She pushed back the faded curtain from the kitchen window. Arnold DeWitt climbed from a fancy carriage and dusted off his sleeves.

Vexation roiled in her gut, and her first instinct was to grab Grandma's broom. Instead, she hurried to the porch and pulled the door closed so the man wouldn't awaken Grandpa. She stepped down from the porch and strode purposefully to stand in front of the man.

She lifted her chin and nailed DeWitt with an unblinking stare. "I don't know what you want, Mr. DeWitt, but you must know that you are not welcome here."

A snarl lifted one corner of the man's lips, and he smirked at her. "Your opinion is not my concern, young lady. I'm here to speak to my nephew."

Keeping her emotions in check required every ounce of self-control she possessed. Ever since Eunice Mead and Mr. Dempsey told her they no longer wanted to do business with her, she'd suspected DeWitt was behind it. The man had an uncanny ability to unravel one's common sense.

"You wanted to see me, Uncle?"

Dulcie turned to see Gavin walking toward them, wiping his hands on a rag. Had it been up to her, she'd have insisted the elder DeWitt leave immediately, but Gavin must have seen the man arrive. She folded her arms across her chest and planted her feet.

Arnold DeWitt sent her a withering look. "If you don't mind, I'd like to speak with my nephew privately." Sarcasm dripped from his tone.

She was undeterred. "This is Chappell land. My home. I will stand wherever I wish." She glanced sideways at Gavin.

Gavin lifted his hand in a reassuring gesture along with a brief nod. "It's all right, Dulcie."

She remained in place as Gavin held out one arm toward the lane, indicating for his uncle to precede him. Wariness stirred within her. She preferred for them to speak in her presence, but for whatever reason, Gavin chose to talk privately. Needles of suspicion pricked her.

Arnold DeWitt's face turned red and he hitched his trousers with indignation, but Gavin held up a stiff hand. "Before you start to bellow and criticize, may I remind you that you are on someone else's property, and your manners—or lack thereof—will steer any business dealings."

DeWitt snorted, but turned on his heel and strode several yards away, Gavin on his heels.

Gavin followed his uncle well past where the carriage stood. Strange how in the past, every meeting, every confrontation with his uncle made him sweat. This time, no such dread shook him.

"This is far enough, Uncle." Gavin stopped under the shade of an ancient oak. "Whatever is on your mind can't take long. I have work to do."

Derision blasted from his uncle's lips. "Work?" His scornful gaze raked Gavin up and down. "You're nothing but a common laborer. You've moved up here all cozy with these hillbillies." He hooked his thumbs in his pockets and stuck out his chest. "I thought you'd left town, but my sources told me you showed up at the hardware store buying supplies for the Chappells, and then you tried to take money from my account at the bank."

Gavin spread his feet and crossed his arms. "It was my account, Uncle. My money. My salary. Seizing funds paid, in good faith, for work performed equates to malfeasance."

His uncle growled. "You didn't do the work to my satisfaction." He smoothed his bushy mustache with his finger. "I've given you enough time to change your mind. Now this is your last chance. I've already taken steps in town, maneuvering a few key people to my way of thinking. They know to whom they owe their allegiance. Chappell won't get any support from them. Now that I've laid the groundwork, maybe you can see how these things are done, and finally live up to your name."

The muscles in Gavin's neck tensed, and his thoughts raced. Nausea churned in his stomach. "What have you done?"

His uncle laughed, but no humor found its way to his menacing eyes. His brow lowered and his voice grated like a rasp. "This is your last chance. You do whatever it takes to force Chappell to sell, or I'll make sure you regret it."

Gavin curled his fingers into fists and dug his fingernails into his palms. An overwhelming urge to protect Dulcie and Mr. Chappell saturated him, and all he wanted to do was grab his uncle by the lapels and shake the truth out of him. "Uncle, what have you done?"

Uncle Arnold's face reddened. "It's none of your business, at least for now. Get the job done!"

Anger replaced dread, and Gavin refused to back down. "What job? I no longer work for you, remember? I have no desire to work for you, not if it means being a tyrant, intimidating and bullying people into knuckling under to submit to your demands. Is money really that important to you that you don't care how you treat people? Well, it's not that important to me. I've found a way of life here that I love. Hard work and sweat is a far better way to gain success and contentment. At least when I lay my head down at night, I can sleep with a clear conscience."

Purple veins bulged and throbbed on his uncle's neck. He spat, "You can't possibly have DeWitt blood running through your veins." He pointed in Gavin's face. "You will regret this. I'll make sure of that."

His uncle strode to the carriage and slapped the reins on the horse's back. Gavin turned his back on the cloud of dust raised by his uncle's departure. He could only hope it was the last time he'd have to deal with the man. A niggling fear gnawed at him, however. Perhaps he'd been too hasty. Maybe he should have tried to get his uncle to divulge this groundwork he claimed to have laid.

He walked back toward the barn, and when he glanced in the direction of the house, there stood Mr. Chappell on the porch, propped up on his crutches. Dulcie stood beside him. Gavin's heart plummeted. These people had taken him into their home, given him a roof over his head and honest work to do—work that gave him a sense of purpose and gratification. They deserved to know what had transpired between him and his uncle.

He took a deep breath and walked to the porch. Skepticism lined Dulcie's face but Mr. Chappell simply waited for him to speak.

"Could we sit down for a minute? There's something you need to know."

Silently, Dulcie helped her grandfather to one of the rockers, then pulled the other alongside.

Gavin hitched one leg on the top step and leaned against the porch post. "My uncle made a few statements that have me worried." Repeating word for word as closely as he could recall, he shared the confrontational debate that took place a few minutes earlier. "I'm not sure what he meant by making sure the town people owed allegiance to him. I can only presume he has pressured people into taking his side."

Gavin paused, expecting Mr. Chappell to question the elder De-Witt's motives, but it was Dulcie who replied first.

"I think I know."

Both men turned in unison to her. Gavin squinted at her. "You think you know what he meant?"

Dulcie nodded. "Grandpa, I didn't want to worry you, so I kept it to myself, and I was trying to figure out a way to—" She sighed. "When I was at church last Sunday, I spoke to Eunice Mead and told her the yardage she'd ordered two months ago was ready, and I could bring it to her. She told me she didn't need it and wouldn't need any more woolen yard goods from me."

The lines around Mr. Chappell's eyes deepened in puzzlement, but a small window of light allowed a minuscule sliver of understanding in Gavin's mind. Yes, he'd seen his uncle work this way in the past.

Dulcie continued. "Then yesterday, I took eight new rugs to Mr. Dempsey. I took along the yardage I'd woven for Mrs. Mead, thinking Mr. Dempsey could sell it in his store. He brought two rugs and a length of woolen fabric out of the storeroom. He'd taken it off display and put it in the back. He paid me for what he had sold, but told me he didn't need any more rugs or fabric."

While confusion and bewilderment showed in Mr. Chappell's eyes, Gavin needed no further explanation. He hung his head, guilt smiting him as sharply as a whip. Why hadn't he seen this coming?

James rubbed his chin whiskers. Somethin' sure didn't make no sense, at least to him. But by the looks of the young fella standin' across the porch from him, he knew more'n he'd said.

When Gavin finally looked up, his eyes looked as sorry as a repentant sinner at the altar. He couldn't put his finger on why, but James couldn't bring himself to believe the young fella had anything to do with his uncle's mischief—whatever it was.

Dulcie plunked her hands on her hips and glared at Gavin. "You know what it is, don't you?"

Gavin shook his head, and then gave a short nod. "I don't know for sure, but I've seen it happen before. People who are reluctant to agree to my uncle's business propositions have sometimes experienced sudden and unexpected hardships, only to have a change of heart and agree to the business deal they had originally rejected."

Dulcie's eyes narrowed into slits. "Are you saying your uncle committed acts against people to force them to do what he wanted?"

James listened as Gavin told them about how his uncle had turned folks against each other, told outright lies, and even went and done a few things the law might frown on iffen he'd been caught and anything could be proved. The puzzlement was how the man could be so evil and not have it rub off on his nephew, 'cause as sure as he had a broke leg, he were just as sure Gavin didn't hold to his uncle's doin's.

Gavin shuffled his feet. "Have you ever heard the expression, 'money talks?'" He stuffed his hands in his pockets. "My uncle uses his money to get his way, no matter who it hurts. I'm sorry that it's hurting you." He dropped his head again. "Mr. Chappell, you've taught me how a real man reacts when someone like my uncle tries to bully them. But I can't help feeling guilty, because in the beginning, I was trying to do everything I could for my uncle to get those contracts signed. Now, I can't tell you how sorry I am."

James rocked a minute, the squeaks in the old chair fillin' the quiet space. Weren't Gavin's fault what his uncle done. He lifted a prayer to heaven, askin' God what he should say to this young fella.

"Son, ever' time I git discombobulated, I turn to God's word, 'cause He's got the answers to all our questions." Did the young fella remember how they'd talked the other day? He sure was searchin', and James kept prayin' God'd use him to be the one to show Gavin how God always kept His promises. He leaned forward and propped his elbows on the arms of the chair. "Didja finish readin' the book o' John yet? Ye start readin' in Psalms like I told ye?"

Gavin nodded. "Yes, sir."

"Then ye likely already read Psalm twenty-seven. 'For in the time of trouble he shall hide me in his pavilion; in the secret of his tabernacle shall he hide me; he shall set me up upon a rock. And now shall mine head be lifted up above mine enemies round about me.'" He paused and studied Gavin's face a moment. Did the boy understand what he was gettin' at?

Dulcie's expression softened. She understood, reckon 'cause she'd growed up hearin' God's word. But he could tell by the furrows linin' Gavin's brow, worry and guilt was still eatin' a hole clean through him.

"Son, you think God didn't know any o' this was happenin'? Ain't nothin' yer uncle can do is gonna change God's plan." He waggled a crooked finger at Gavin. "God ain't never promised hard times wouldn't come, but He did promise He'd always take care o' His children."

James leaned back in the rocker and set it in motion again. "A while back, we had us a mama sheep that died. Dulcie's grandma'd named her Clara, and Clara's baby were a little girl we called Lily. When Clara died, Lily didn't have no mama to feed her or look after her." He looked out across the meadow, rememberin' how Virginia grieved over Clara's passin' and how she'd fussed over Lily.

"Then we had another mama sheep who was takin' her good ole time 'bout droppin' her lamb. Her name's Gert, and thet mama weren't in a hurry. I think she liked bein' the last mama to give birth. Anyway, when Gert finally started havin' birth pangs, Dulcie brought little Lily into the stall where Gert was. When Gert's lamb was borned, Dulcie rubbed the scent all over Lily, and then she brought both lambs over to meet Gert at the same time. Gert adopted Lily and accepted her jus' like her own." A smile born of pure joy rose up from deep within him, 'cause just speakin' the words put him in mind of how good God was. "That's jus' like God done for us. Ain't that a wonder? He covers us with Hisself—with the blood of Jesus—so we can be adopted, an' He accepts us as His own."

James studied Gavin's face for a minute. The boy were still ate up with guilt over somethin' that weren't his fault. "Son, listen to me. You don't have to prove yer worth, not to me, an' not to God. God's Son *gived* His blood an' His life for you. God don't redeem worthless things with the blood of His Son."

Nothin' but the meadowlark's song and the breeze stirrin' the trees sounded for a long while. Then James reached for his crutches, and with Dulcie's help, struggled to his feet. "I want ye to hang onto what I said, son. God ain't surprised and He ain't wringin' His hands over none o' this. I reckon we can trust Him to keep His promise to take care of us."

He moved to the door with a prayer in his heart for the young fella God had unexpectedly dropped on their doorstep. Who would o' thought DeWitt's nephew would end up stayin' with them so James could minister to the youngster's heart? God sure did work in mysterious ways.

✎ THIRTY-FIVE

ulcie helped Grandpa to the bedroom to finish his nap, and then went to the kitchen to reheat the coffee. She was painfully aware of the words Grandpa didn't speak. The rest of the psalm went on to speak of God never leaving her alone. The psalmist was so confident, so fixed on God's promise, even in the midst of obvious adversity. Regret flowed through her over the years she'd wasted being angry at God and blaming Him for her loss.

"God, all that time, You were waiting for me to trust You and lean on You, and I had such a stubborn, rebellious heart."

Yes, child, it took a while, but you came back.

"There are still so many things I don't understand. Why are all these bad things still happening? Is it because I stayed angry at You for too long? Is it too late? If that's the case, please don't punish Grandpa."

My love for you will never fail. Trust Me.

"I believe there is more You want to show me, to teach me, but I'm having trouble figuring out what it is."

Open your eyes, child.

Open her eyes? She could find her way around their farm blindfolded. She knew every fence post, blade of grass and rock. What was different?

A soft tap on the door frame pulled her attention away from the coffeepot and her conversation with God. Gavin stood in the still-open doorway.

"I'm sorry, Dulcie."

"Oh! Gavin, I didn't realize you were there. I—I was . . .uh. . ." Had he overheard her talking to God? Her neck and face heated. "I suppose you heard me talking to God, and you're probably wondering what I meant about all the bad things— Maybe I should explain."

"No, no, Dulcie." Gavin stepped into the kitchen. "I meant I'm sorry for bringing more trouble on you and your grandfather. Or at least my uncle is bringing more trouble. But I still feel at least partly responsible."

Dulcie took two cups from the shelf and poured the coffee. "You heard me telling God how I was angry at Him and how I blamed Him. I did, you know. After my parents died, I was very bitter, even as a little girl. I didn't want anything to do with God. But Grandpa and Grandma kept praying, and it took a while, but God finally showed me I'd wasted too much time being mad at Him when all He wanted me to do was trust Him."

Gavin lifted his shoulders and accepted the cup she handed him. "I did overhear you say something like that. All this time, I thought you had such strong faith. You had me fooled."

Regret sliced deeply. "I didn't intend to fool you. Well, maybe that's not entirely true. I was trying to fool my grandparents, but only because I didn't want to hurt them. I suppose you got fooled in the process. Shortly before Grandma died, I finally bowed my heart to God again."

She looked up into his eyes, the color of walnut husks, and her breath caught. Had she ever noticed before how warm and inviting his eyes were? She thought back. Yes, the day they met, that day they literally ran into each other at the Emporium, before she knew his name was DeWitt, she had fallen into the hypnotic spell of his eyes. "I apologize for giving you a false impression. In the past few weeks, hard times have poured down on us. I admit I've been fearful that maybe God's patience with me had run out. But He keeps reassuring me that's not the case, and every time I start to doubt, He strengthens my faith."

Gavin ran his finger around the rim of his cup, and a conflicted look distorted his expression. "I think I'm beginning to understand. I've spent some time talking with your grandfather and he has explained a lot of things to me." He glanced up at her. "He is an amazing man. I wish I'd been raised by someone like him." He dropped his gaze again. "After my uncle's visit today, I suspect more trouble is on the way."

Dulcie took a slow sip of her coffee and savored its richness. "Troubles are going to come, whether or not your uncle causes them. But God has promised He won't leave us."

After a long pause, Gavin touched her shoulder with his fingertips. "Neither will I."

A strange dance twirled through her insides. *Open your eyes, child.*

Dulcie muttered under her breath as she reached to get Grandpa's crutches. "I still don't think this is a good idea."

"What's that ye say, Rosebud?"

She clamped her lips tightly to hold back the words. Grandpa was so excited about his first outing since being hurt, and she couldn't rob him of his joy, even if she didn't agree with his insistence over going to church this morning.

He propped the crutches under his arms and made his way to the door just as Gavin brought Samson and the wagon as close to the porch as he could.

"Wait right there, Mr. Chappell." Gavin jumped down from the wagon seat and trotted around to the tailgate. "I fixed up something for you."

Dulcie peered around Grandpa and puzzled at the contraption Gavin pulled from the wagon. Appearing a little like a travois used by the Cherokees, the two side poles and connecting braces were lashed together with leather strips. Criss-crossing the creation were lengths of burlap sacks sewn together with twine, pieces of harness leather, and an old blanket they used to cover newborn lambs born in the early spring months.

Gavin propped the woven web of materials against the back of the wagon, and then helped Grandpa down from the porch. "Over here, sir. Stand right up against it and lean back on it. Dulcie, you get in the wagon and pull on the two long side poles, and I'll lift this end. We'll slide him right into the back of the wagon without him hurting that leg."

Dulcie hesitated, staring at the invention. When had he worked on this thing? Grandpa hadn't said anything about going to church until last night, so Gavin must have—

"Gavin, this is. . . Did you stay up all night working on this? How—?" Her mouth hung open and she snapped it closed, jerking her focus to Gavin, and then to Grandpa.

"Dulcie girl, iffen ye keep on askin' questions, we gonna be late to church, an' ye 'member what yer grandma always said." Grandpa turned tender eyes to Gavin. "Thank ye, son. That be real kind of ye."

Dulcie propelled her feet into motion, and scrambled into the back of the wagon behind Grandpa. She seized the ends of the side poles, and as Gavin lifted his end, Grandpa was laid horizontal. The two of them slid him easily into the back of the wagon.

"Grab those rolled up blankets and prop him up." Gavin pointed to the very familiar quilts.

"This is your sleeping pallet."

He sent her a breath-robbing grin. "I'm not sleeping on it right now." He closed the tailgate and secured it. "I'm going to run over to the meadow and check on Malachi and the sheep before we go. I'll be right back." His long legs ate up the ground between the wagon and the fence.

"Grandpa, I'm going to run inside and get the Bible and a jar of water." She hurried back into the house, poured several dippers full of water into a canning jar, and tightened the lid. She grabbed the Bible from beside Grandpa's chair and scurried back outside. "Here, Grandpa, can you hold these while I climb up? There comes Gavin now."

"Ever'thing right as rain over yonder, son?"

"Yes, sir. Even Malachi was laying down in the shade."

Gavin climbed up into the wagon seat, and his nearness set Dulcie's pulse to skipping. She handed him the reins and turned to check on Grandpa, only to find him smiling at her. He raised his bushy eyebrows and winked.

Not wishing to speculate what that smile and wink might imply, she simply supposed him to be happy about getting out of the house.

Dulcie stared as Gavin helped Grandpa from the wagon and steadied him with the crutches. But it wasn't the act of helpful kindness in front of the church that drew her amazement. His quiet reply to Hollis Purdue in Grandpa's defense rendered her speechless.

Hollis's remark about Grandpa being pig-headed and not caring a whit about his neighbors prompted an instant reaction on Gavin's part—one that had silenced a red-faced Hollis in the presence of a half-dozen other town folk. How was it that Gavin had only known James Chappell for less than three months but had a better understanding of Grandpa's character than a man her grandfather had called friend for nearly a lifetime?

Gavin's rebuttal to Hollis's complaint still echoed in her ears.

"I read something in Mrs. Chappell's Bible the other day. It said, 'Let the words of my mouth, and the meditation of my heart, be acceptable in thy sight, O Lord—' I question, sir, whether the words of your mouth are as acceptable to God as Mr. Chappell's."

Of even greater impact was the look in Grandpa's eyes when Gavin uttered the words. Quiet joy and unquestioned peace defined the lines age had carved into her grandfather's face. Even when a few others only mumbled short-clipped greetings or pretended to be otherwise occupied, Grandpa showed no manner of resentment. Dulcie watched the drama play out. She'd always been touched by her grandparents' character, and now evidence showed in Gavin of the influence Grandpa had on the younger DeWitt.

After settling into their seats and listening to an hour-long sermon about leaning on God when everything around you falls apart, a couple of people extended half-hearted greetings to Grandpa as the service was dismissed and they made their way back out to the wagon. Gavin's contraption drew some compliments, even from a few people who'd been critical of Grandpa. Dulcie fussed and positioned the rolled up quilts to ensure her grandfather's comfort. She accepted Gavin's help in climbing from the wagon bed to the seat, all the while hearing Grandma's voice in her heart, directing her to be respectful in spite of wanting to lash out at the people who'd spoken unkind words. She couldn't ignore the memory of Grandma's admonition any more than she could ignore God's.

She gave a brief nod to Hollis and a few others as Gavin guided Samson out of the church yard. "Y'all have a nice Lord's day afternoon." A hint of contentment settled over her. Yes, Grandma would've been satisfied with that.

Nobody spoke until they were well out of town. Then, Grandpa's voice rose from the wagon bed. "Seems t' me the preacher were a little short on advice-givin' this mornin'. Why should folks wait till things is fallin' down 'round their ears a'fore they lean on the Lord? Don't it make more sense to lean on Him even when things ain't goin' sour? Iffen they'd make a habit o' goin' to God in the good times, then goin' to Him in the bad times comes as natural-like as breathin'."

Another long, silent stretch, filled with nothing but birdsong and the mountain breeze, gave time for introspection of both the preacher's words and Grandpa's. When they were almost home, Gavin spoke.

"Mr. Chappell, I believe your sermon on the way home was better than the one we heard in church. Sure you didn't miss your calling?"

Grandpa chuckled. "Well, son, I *am* a shepherd, jus' like the preacher."

Gavin grinned from his place beside Dulcie, and the warm, easy companionship they shared perplexed her. From the day she realized Gavin was a DeWitt, companionship never crossed her mind. Perhaps the puzzlement resulted from her realization that she didn't find it disagreeable.

Gavin steered Samson to the side of the porch, but before he could set the brake and hop down, Dulcie's gaze swept across the meadow. She jerked to her feet, nearly losing her balance.

Panic seized her and stole her breath. From one corner of the meadow to the other— Empty. Not a single sheep. Even Malachi was missing and the gate stood ajar.

She caught hold of the edge of the seat and leapt to the ground. "They're gone!" Grabbing her skirts in both hands and hiking them to free her feet, she ran to the vacant meadow, the grass slapping at her legs. She stopped and turned a wide circle, but no sheep hid in the corners or shadows. An invisible fist punched her in the stomach.

"How? How did they—" She spun to look back at the gate. Gavin approached at a jog, his eyes wide and his face drained of color. His searching gaze skittered back and forth, much as hers had done.

"Wh-Where. . ."

Dulcie held both arms straight out from her sides and waved them toward the farthest ends of the meadow. "They're gone. Our sheep are gone." Her focus came to land squarely between Gavin's eyes. "After we got Grandpa in the wagon and you came over to check on the sheep before we left, did you leave the gate open?"

"No! I—I didn't . . . I don't. . ." He swallowed hard, as if trying to choke down a whole egg without chewing. "I'm sure I—" He squeezed his eyes shut and shook his head. "I could've sworn I latched it. I think I did. But. . . but I don't remember." He raked his hand through his hair.

Dulcie shifted her gaze back to the house where Grandpa still sat in the back of the wagon. "Let's get Grandpa inside. Then we'll split up and find them." Without waiting for a reply, she ran back to the wagon.

With Gavin on her heels, she faced Grandpa's lined face exuding peace despite the concern. "Any sign o' the dog?"

Dulcie shook her head. "Grandpa, you need to go in and rest, and—"

His gray hair stuck out as he shook his head. "Jus' git me to the porch. I ain't a-goin' inside no how till I see them sheep back where they b'long."

Between Gavin and Dulcie, they had Grandpa sitting in his rocker in minutes. She placed her hand on his shoulder. "Please stay put, Grandpa."

He patted her hand. "I will."

She and Gavin jogged back to the meadow. She pointed along the fence line. "You go that way, and I'll take this direction. Look at the fence. Look for a place where they broke through."

He jerked his thumb. "But the gate—"

"Wasn't open wide enough for the sheep to get through. They must have gotten out some other way."

"Wait!" Gavin held up his hand. "Listen."

In the distance, Malachi's distinctive bark echoed.

"This way! Let's go!" Dulcie led the way. Past the thick stand of oaks, she skidded to a stop.

Three rails of the fence were broken down, and beside the trampled grass in front of the breach, the outline of a boot print was sculpted into the soft dirt.

THIRTY-SIX

Gavin pushed his way through the underbrush and thorny vines, following the sound of Malachi's bark. Guilt gnawed at him. The sheep had all seemed perfectly fine when he checked them before church. Malachi lay in the grass a few feet away and thumped his tail when Gavin told him to guard the sheep. Was there something he missed?

The sight of the broken fence brought only a thread of relief. Someone had obviously kicked out the rails, but guilt lingered nonetheless. He looked guilty by association. He wouldn't blame Dulcie or her grandfather if they accused him of having something to do with the sheep's disappearance. After all, his uncle had come to visit only a couple of days ago, and the first time all three of them left the farm for a short time, this happened. Even to Gavin, it appeared as though he and his uncle had planned it.

He and Dulcie, moving from opposite directions worked their way around though the scrub brush on the hillside, funneling the sheep back toward the meadow. Low-hanging branches slapped his face and scratched his arms, and his throat was dry as sand from calling out to the sheep. Covering as much ground as possible took him to areas he'd not yet explored on the farm, including a small cemetery hidden away in the junipers. He didn't have time to examine all the headstones, but one fresh grave drew his eye. The brand-new hewn granite bore the name of Virginia Chappell.

Malachi's bark pulled him back to his task, and he kept coaxing the sheep in the direction of the dog. Malachi leapt back and forth through the brush, pushing the woolies forward, while Gavin followed the dog's lead and kept forcing the animals down the slope.

As the sheep reentered the meadow at the broken place in the fence, Dulcie stood and took a quick count. "There are still three missing."

Gavin hefted the railings. "I'll get this fence repaired, and then I'll help you search."

"No need for that. I'll go back up the hill. They probably aren't too far."

Gavin's gaze darted to her. "I don't want you to go alone."

A tiny smile lifted her lips. "Have you forgotten I grew up here?"

"But you saw that boot print." He pointed to the dirt. "What if whoever did this is still out there somewhere? It's not safe."

"If anyone was around, Malachi would let us know." She touched his sleeve and Gavin nearly dropped the rail he held. "Thank you for worrying, but I'll be fine. I'll take the dog with me."

She glanced toward the house where Mr. Chappell still sat on the porch, watching. "Just prop up the rails for now. Then would you please go check on Grandpa?" No accusation rang in her voice, but his heart stung with wondering if she suspected he'd sabotaged the fence on his uncle's behalf.

She set out, and Gavin improvised the fence. He picked up the last rail and inserted it between the uprights that held the crisscrossed horizontals. When he dusted his hands, a sticky substance grabbed bits of dirt and bark and stuck to his palm. He turned his hand up to scrape off the mess.

Blood. He bent to examine the railing he'd just put into place. Blood stains discolored the wood. Gavin spun and returned to the sheep, weaving his way through the flock. He couldn't see any obvious injuries, nor did he see any blood on the grass where sheep grazed. A sweeping glance of the hillside revealed no sign of Dulcie returning with the missing ones. He'd best go check on Mr. Chappell and let the man know what was happening.

As soon as he was close enough, Mr. Chappell called out to him. "I seen Dulcie go back up the hill."

Gavin climbed the porch steps. "Dulcie counted and three are missing. She and the dog went searching." He took the rocker across from Mr. Chappell. "We found where they got out."

"That ornery ram busted down the fence, did he?"

"No, sir." Gavin looked him straight in the eye. "Someone did this. There were three fence rails kicked out, and there's a boot print in the dirt. I also found some blood on one of the rails, but all the sheep appear to be fine. We'll have to wait and see when Dulcie brings the last three back."

A scowl deepened the lines across Mr. Chappell's brow and he stared in the direction Dulcie and Malachi had gone searching. "So twern't no four-legged animal what done this."

Nausea roiled in Gavin's gut. "No, sir, I'm afraid not."

Gavin felt Mr. Chappell's frustration at being confined to the porch while he and Dulcie had spent the afternoon searching. Relief had washed over him when she'd returned with the wayward three.

"They're all fine, Grandpa." Dulcie patted his arm and refilled his coffee cup. "Gavin and I checked them, and aside from a few scratches from the thorny vines, we couldn't find any injuries."

"The fence is fixed," Gavin added, hoping to further reassure the old gentleman. "I used leather strips soaked in water so they'll shrink when they dry. Then I'll put spikes through them."

"Grandpa, I've been thinking." Dulcie returned the coffeepot to the stove and sat in the chair across from Gavin. "We have to find somewhere to sell our woolens." She cast a glance at Gavin. "Now that neither Mrs. Mead or Mr. Dempsey will buy or sell our goods, we have to find another way. The only solution is to take them down the mountain."

Mr. Chappell shook a bony finger at Dulcie. "I ain't gonna let ye go traipsin' away from home by yerself. We jus' gotta wait till I'm fit again, an'—"

"I have another idea."

Both Chappells turned to Gavin. Dulcie's deep brown eyes held his captive, but he detected no hint of distrust.

"The barn roof will be finished in another day or two. The rest of the repairs aren't as pressing." He turned his attention to Mr. Chappell. "Would you trust me to take the goods down the mountain? I know there are a couple of towns between here and Asheville. I can stop and inquire if there are any stores that would take your rugs and yard goods. I could even try to work out a deal with them to take your woolens to sell on a regular basis." He turned back to Dulcie. "Like you did with Mr. Dempsey."

An unreadable expression spread across Dulcie's face. He couldn't decide if she was overwhelmed by the offer or by suspicion. Or something else. If she would only say something.

Finally, she looked at her grandfather. "Every day that our wool goods aren't for sale anywhere, we're losing money. What do you think, Grandpa?"

"Y'already know what I think. I don't want ye traveling down them mountain roads by yerself. A young woman shouldn't oughta travel alone. Ain't fittin', and it ain't safe." He bobbed his head to punctuate his statement.

Gavin waited. All the while they were out looking for the sheep, he'd talked to God. After listening to Mr. Chappell pray, and after the many evenings of asking questions before turning in and sitting with Mrs.

Chappell's Bible, he was beginning to understand who God was, and how much God loved him. He'd not yet told anyone that he'd been praying on his own, but he had entered into a new relationship with God— like nothing he'd ever known was possible. And so he prayed now.

Please let me do this for them, God. They've been so good to me. After what my uncle and I tried to do, I didn't deserve their friendship, but they've acted like You— You took me when I didn't deserve anything good from You, and You showed me how I could become brand new. Please, God. Let me show Dulcie she can trust me.

"Reckon you best finish up that roof, son."

Gavin jerked his eyes open to find both Chappells watching him. "I'll have it finished by tomorrow." Quite aware of Dulcie's lingering gaze on him, he turned to face her. "Do you agree with this plan, Dulcie? Because if you don't, we'll think of another way."

She tipped her head to one side, as if she were sizing up his statement. Moisture glistened in her eyes. "I agree. There is no better way."

Gavin bit the inside of his cheek and swallowed. Did that mean she felt she had no choice? The flicker of joy he'd felt a moment ago turned heavy. He'd spent his whole life trying to prove his worth to people. But he knew now his worth wasn't important, but his trustworthiness was. He cleared his throat. "I won't let you down."

Dawn barely stained the sky to the east as Gavin loaded Dulcie's rugs and yard goods into the back of the wagon and covered them with a canvas. After a long day of finishing the roof, and then examining the wagon and wheels to make sure all was in good repair, splitting extra stove wood, and weeding the garden so Dulcie wouldn't have to, he was ready to depart on his journey down the mountain.

Dulcie brought him a basket and a small jug. "There is enough food in the basket for three days. You can refill the jug whenever you come to a stream." She handed over the basket. "I put Grandma's Bible in there, too."

Gavin's throat thickened. If she suspected he might not return, she'd never give him her grandmother's cherished Bible. "Thank you."

"Thank *you*." Her eyes locked with his, sending him a look that made his pulse trip. "Please be careful." She took a step backward and huffed out a stiff breath. "Well, I'd best get back to work." She turned and headed out toward the wool shed.

He sucked in a deep breath and climbed the porch steps to where Mr. Chappell stood with his crutches. "If everything goes well and I'm able to arrange the sale of your goods, I'd like to take a couple of extra days. I have business I must tend to."

Mr. Chappell nodded and didn't ask what the business was. The man's confidence in him touched Gavin, and made him want to do whatever it might take to deserve this man's unquestioning trust. Mr. Chappell extended his hand and gripped Gavin's. "The Lord'll go with ye, son. Dulcie an' me'll be prayin' fer ye. Ye come on home as soon as ye can, y'hear?"

Home. Gavin swallowed back the lump that formed in his throat. He'd never felt such a sense of belonging before, not even in his own family. "I will, sir."

Mr. Chappell still gripped his hand. "Son, me an' the Lord been doin' a lot o' talkin' about you. Ye ain't goin' on this trip alone."

Warmth rose up from Gavin's belly, and he realized he was counting on the prayers of James Chappell. He climbed into the wagon seat and slapped the reins on Samson's rump. "Come on, mule. The sooner we get going, the sooner we can get back."

The ride to Marshall took half the morning. The town was a bit larger than Hot Springs, but not by much. His first order of business was to find the telegraph office. He didn't want to risk sending this very important telegram in Hot Springs where his uncle seemed to have people watching and reporting back to him.

He found the shabby little telegraph office and wrote out the words he wanted to send. He pushed a few coins across the counter. "I'll be in town for an hour or so, and I'll stop back before I leave."

The slight, ancient fellow with sparse wisps of gray hair bobbed his head. "Good 'nough."

At the end of an hour, he had sold four rugs to a storekeeper, and had spoken with the local dressmaker about purchasing fine wool yardage. She bought one length and told Gavin she'd be interested in more if he came back through town again. Elated by the coins for Dulcie jingling in the small leather pouch in his pocket, he returned to the telegraph office.

The wizened little man waved a piece of yellow paper when he stepped in the door. "Jus' come in, sonny. Here be yer wire."

Gavin gave him a couple more coins and unfolded the telegram from his brother. Harold had many contacts in government, even beyond the state of Pennsylvania.

The memory of the tiny, secluded cemetery on the far side of the meadow had lingered in his mind. He'd been there on the Chappell farm for over a month and never knew it was there. The sight of the generations-old stones moved him in a way few things had before. He understood now. It wasn't just the land. It was the family on the land, the generations, the heritage that was handed down from grandparent to granddaughter. He hoped the plan that formed in his mind would allow that to continue happening.

He didn't know why Dulcie and her grandfather had never mentioned the cemetery before, but that little plot of land that bore witness to the history of the Chappell family stood as a sentinel. Gavin folded the paper and tucked it into his pocket. He needed to get on down the road. He had wool to sell and a man to meet.

Dulcie walked over to Dewey Tate's place and asked to borrow Dewey's cart and horse. The animal was so old and swayback, the harness nearly dragged the ground under his belly, but it would do the job.

When she got the rig back home, Grandpa was waiting and antsy.

She helped him into the low cart—much more easily than into the wagon—and headed to town and Doc Pryor's office.

Doc pronounced Grandpa's leg healing nicely, albeit slowly, and cautioned him to continue to be careful. When they stepped out the door of the doctor's office, the sheriff hailed them.

"James Chappell, how ye keepin', ye ole buzzard?"

They traded greetings and chatted a few moments, and then the sheriff glanced to and fro.

"I heard some gossip, James, and I'd like to hear from you what's goin' on."

When Grandpa hemmed and hawed, Dulcie told the sheriff how several town folk accused them of hurting the community by refusing to sell, and even how some of the local merchants stopped buying their wool.

Sheriff Harper rubbed his whiskery chin. "That so?"

"Not only that, but someone kicked down our fence and the sheep got out last Sunday while we were in church. We found a boot print and some blood."

"Blood?"

Dulcie shrugged. "None of the sheep were hurt, but it took a while to find them all."

"But ye found blood?" The sheriff narrowed his eyes. "Ye sure it weren't an animal what busted out the fence?"

"No. There were three rails kicked out, and the boot print we found was right there where the fence was broken down."

"Hmm." Sheriff Harper shifted his weight and propped one elbow on his palm. "I'll keep my eyes an' ears open, an' that there is fer certain."

❧ THIRTY-SEVEN

Gavin counted out the money into the grimy hand of the liveryman. "You'll feed the mule until I return, and you're sure it's all right to park the wagon out back behind the barn?"

The thin man with shaggy black hair nodded. "I'll be sure an' feed the mule, and ain't nobody gonna bother about that ole rickety wagon." He stuffed the coins into his pocket. "When didja say you'se comin' back to fetch the critter?"

Gavin did some quick calculating. "It shouldn't take longer than two days."

He snatched his valise and strode off toward the train depot. Asheville wasn't as large as Philadelphia, but was nearly as noisy and crowded. Jostling his way through a wave of people heading the opposite direction made him dream of quieter, less hectic days. After spending time in the sleepy mountain town of Hot Springs, the big city grated on his nerves. How strange. Big cities were all he'd known his whole life, and here he was, anxious to return to the tiny community nestled into the hills. Maybe that wasn't completely accurate—more than going back to Hot Springs, Gavin longed to be back on the farm. The tranquil meadow, the soft wind stirring the trees, the meadowlark's concert by day and the whippoorwill's by night, the sheep *baaing* in the meadow, Mr. Chappell's kindness and wisdom.

And Dulcie.

He missed her face, her laugh, the way she went about her chores. He missed hearing her hum as she spun the wool, and watching her fingers weave the wool into cloth. He missed the way her voice crooned to the sheep, the way she doted over her grandfather, and cared for the land. He missed their evening conversations over coffee, and simply being in her presence. The day he drove away from the farm, a void as dry and hollow as a dipper gourd took up residence in his chest. He cherished the new companionship he enjoyed with the Lord, and he and God had talked along the road between towns. But being away from the farm and Dulcie prompted him to examine his feelings. What he realized startled him. He'd never paid much attention to romantic stirrings before, but this separation brought an awareness into focus. What had begun as simple attraction to the mountains and their grandeur grew and spread to include the community, the farm, even the sheep. But far more than attraction defined his connection to Dulcie and her grandfather.

The wondering accompanied him as he stepped up onto the platform at the depot and approached the ticket window. "Lord? Am I in love with Dulcie?"

"What's that ye say, young feller?" The ticket agent adjusted his visor and peered out through the window at Gavin with an inquisitive arch in his brow.

Chagrin pulled heat into Gavin's face at the realization that he'd spoken aloud. "Oh, nothing. I was talking to myself."

The agent smirked and hiked an errant suspender up onto his shoulder. "You fixin' to buy a ticket, or y' just gonna stand there talkin' to yerself?"

Gavin tugged at his lapel and pretended he didn't hear the needling in the man's voice. "When is the next train to Raleigh?"

"'Bout forty minutes. Trains run b'tween here an' Charlotte an' Raleigh twice a day."

Gavin pushed the fare across the counter and pocketed the ticket the agent handed him. "Thank you."

He settled onto a bench at the far end of the platform, and plunked down his valise beside him. The question he asked God a minute ago danced through his head once more. Was he in love? How was he to know? He'd never entertained such a notion before—he'd never had the time. Expectations always pressed him to make social contacts for the purpose of business, not romance.

He slipped his hand into his inside coat pocket and let his fingers touch the leather pouch containing the money he'd obtained for Dulcie's rugs and woolen fabric. He'd gotten more than Dulcie had told him Mr. Dempsey and the dressmaker in Hot Springs paid her. That thought tugged a smile to his lips, and a tremor of excitement trotted through him. He couldn't wait to see her face, and not only because he'd gotten a good price for her woolens.

He leaned back against the uncomfortable bench, the desire to talk to God so strong, he glanced from side to side, checking to see if anyone could read his thoughts. His eyes slid closed and he asked God to help him identify the bewildering and unsettled feelings that haunted him. He prayed God would be with Dulcie and Mr. Chappell in his absence, for their protection from whoever had damaged the fence and run off the sheep—he had a strong suspicion his uncle had hired someone to do it. And he prayed he could get a meeting with the state assemblyman in Raleigh whose name had been supplied to him by his brother, Harold.

A train whistle sounded in the distance. Gavin opened his eyes and picked up his valise. His pulse stepped up a notch and determination to accomplish this task heightened his senses. He'd never wanted to succeed at anything as much as he wanted this. *Purpose.* The reasons driving him were different now. He wasn't trying to impress anyone, achieve corporate advances, or pad anyone else's pockets. This purpose came from his heart.

The train lumbered and shuddered as it approached the depot, and then screeched and hissed to a stop. Eager to board and be on his way, Gavin tempered his impatience and stepped aside to allow arriving passengers to disembark the train. He waited for an elderly couple to board ahead of him, helped the old gentleman with his bags, and tipped his hat to the silver-haired lady, all the while trying to contain the impulse to push the train down the track.

Dulcie attempted to help Grandpa settle into the front porch rocker, and resisted the urge to fuss at his insistence to maneuver on his own. She propped his crutches where he could reach them. "Can I bring you anything before I go out to the wool shed?"

Grandpa chuckled. "Don't reckon I'll need more'n ye already brung me." He gestured with his thumb to the inverted crate beside his chair that held a cup of coffee, a jar of water, a plate of his favorite oatmeal cookies, his Bible, last week's newspaper, and a whistle she'd bought at the emporium so she could hear if he needed her.

She ignored his teasing and patted his shoulder, then moved to the top step, pausing there to look down the lane. How many times in the past two days had she looked in that direction, hoping to see Gavin driving old Samson toward the house? She'd lingered during her morning chores, taking more time than necessary to gather the eggs, feed the chickens, and milk the cow, so she could hesitate long enough to let her eyes search the road. Using the excuse that she needed to check on Grandpa, she traveled between the wool shed and the house numerous times a day, mainly so she could look down the rutted path that led to town, hope painting the image of Gavin's face in her mind. A longing ached in her chest. He'd been gone five days. What if he didn't come back?

"Stop frettin', Rosebud. He'll be back."

Now how did Grandpa know what she was thinking?

"I seen ye lookin' down that road. Ye been prayin' fer 'im, ain'tcha?"

She didn't take her eyes off the lane to turn and face him, lest he detect the unspoken emotion hidden in her heart. "Of course, I have."

"Hmmhm. I s'pect ye been prayin' fer more'n jest the sale o' yer wool. Might be some o' that anger ye aimed at him a while back be turnin' around, an' yer seein' him different." No hint of teasing flavored his tone. Instead, she heard nothing but tenderness.

Her eyes burned with unshed tears, and she drew in a tight breath. A dozen scenarios rushed through her mind. *What if—* No. She'd not allow her thoughts to imagine the worst. "I have work to do. I'd best get to it."

"Hold up there a minute, Rosebud." The huskiness in Grandpa's voice pricked her concern.

She turned and found her grandfather's eyes misty. She knelt by his chair and covered his hand with hers. The years of hard work created calluses on his palms and roughness around his fingertips, but come shearing time, his hands were always soft because of the natural oils in the sheep's wool. The contrast drew a picture in her mind of the presence of God in the midst of hard times.

"What is it, Grandpa?"

He patted her hand and sandwiched it between both of his. "Ye've heard me talk about the land bein' yer legacy all yer life. An' it's true the land be mighty precious to us." He sniffed. "But Rosebud, I'm afeared the land is all I got to give ye when the Lord calls me home. I sure ain't got no riches to give ye. Ye know as good as anybody that holdin' this land means a lot of hard work. Mayhap inheritin' all that work ain't such a good thing, 'specially iffen yer shoulderin' the work all by yer own self."

Dulcie gently extracted her hand from Grandpa's and touched the side of his face. "Grandpa, is that what you think--that the only thing you're handing down to me is the land?" She shook her head adamantly. "Grandpa, the legacy you've given to me has nothing to do with the land. You and Grandma have given me a precious gift by showing me the faithfulness of God, even when our hearts are sorrowing. I can't ever remember a time that you haven't trusted in God completely. I will fight my hardest to keep this land, but the real heritage you've given me is a heritage of faith."

She dropped her gaze for a moment. "I don't know if God will give me a husband who loves the Lord and loves the land as we do. But I know this: I can trust whatever God wills, because I know He will be with me."

Grandpa stretched out his arms and enfolded her. "Aw Rosebud ..."

She kissed his cheek. "Thank you, Grandpa."

She stepped down from the porch and made her way across the yard. Malachi greeted her at the corner of the meadow and she reached across the fence to pat his head. "If you see Gavin coming, you let me know." The dog wagged his tail and returned to his sheep.

Truth be told, she'd spent much time in prayer over the past few days, and not only for Gavin's safety and the sale of the woolens. She trusted God would work out His will in His time, but feelings she could no longer deny, feelings she'd held at bay for weeks grew and swelled and bloomed within her. Pretending otherwise was pointless. She missed Gavin more than she expected. His kindness, his willingness to do whatever was needed—no, it was more than that. His smile lingered in her thoughts by day and her dreams by night. Memories of their evening conversations, the times her fingers brushed his when she handed him a cup of coffee, or glancing up to find him watching her. His caring and consideration of Grandpa. The sound of his voice.

She missed *him*.

Gavin listened, trying to follow the detailed explanation by the North Carolina state assemblyman. Mr. Clayton Randolf leaned back in his chair behind the gleaming oak desk and rested his hands on his belly as he described how a bill was written, presented, assigned to a committee, and sent up for a vote.

Gavin fought the disappointment that taunted him. "The process sounds quite complicated." *And long.* At this rate, Uncle Arnold could force the sale of the land, build his resort, and be open for business by the time the law was passed.

Mr. Randolf shrugged. "It can be, but I've seen bills expedited through the House and Senate, and on the governor's desk in as little as a week to ten days. It depends on whether or not there is opposition to the matter. In this case, I don't anticipate any backlash." He turned in his chair and pointed to a map on the wall behind him. "Every county in the state has dozens of private family cemeteries. Many of them are tucked away on land that has been in a family's possession for well over a hundred years—like the family you described, the Chappells. So nearly every one of my colleagues represents voters in their district who have cemeteries such as these on their land."

Randolf pushed his chair away from the desk. "No, I don't anticipate much trouble in getting this passed. I'll begin working on the bill this afternoon and should be able to get it to the committee by the first part of next week." The man rose, and the chair accompanied the move with a chorus of squeaks. "In the meantime, Judge Golling of the Superior Court owes me a favor. I'll get him to write an injunction to stop any further action from taking place until the law is finalized."

Gavin stood and extended his hand across the desk. "Thank you, sir. This means a lot to me, and to the Chappell family."

The assemblyman gripped Gavin's hand. "My pleasure, sir." Randolf came around the desk and clapped Gavin on the shoulder. "I'm glad you came in. It's high time there were laws in this state to protect private family cemeteries from being overrun or disturbed. The war destroyed so many landmarks and headstones." The man tugged at his vest and *tsked.* "Yes, sir, it's way past due. My own family's land back in Caldwell County is being threatened by a timber company. Our family cemetery goes back to 1772."

Gavin detected a thread of pride in the man's voice, no doubt over the fact the Randolf family homesteaded their land before the war for freedom from Britain. Gavin was beginning to understand that pride. The Chappell family heritage, from what he saw carved on the headstones, went back five generations. Once again, he silently thanked God for allowing him to find that cemetery.

Randolf walked Gavin to the door and paused with his hand on the doorknob. "Now you understand, these things take time, but the injunction should be in place by Friday. You wire me in a couple of days and I should have more information for you."

Gavin shook the man's hand again. "Thank you for your time, Mr. Randolf."

Hope swelled in his chest. The trip to Raleigh had taken an extra three days, but worth every minute if the outcome proved as successful as he hoped.

Successful. From the time he was ten years old, he'd listened first to his father, and later his uncle, preach success no matter the cost. What one man called success another called worthless. No doubt his uncle wouldn't consider the time spent traveling to Raleigh and meeting with Mr. Randolf successful. But Gavin realized success depended on one's perspective, and his perspective had changed radically in the past couple of months. For the first time in his life, his efforts counted for something worthwhile.

The longer he was away, however, the more he worried about Dulcie and her grandfather being vulnerable should the person who vandalized their property return to do more damage. But the injunction would prevent Uncle Arnold from disturbing so much as a clover stem on the Chappell farm, effectively putting an end to his efforts to force the land into a sale. Once the bill Mr. Randolf planned to propose became law, surely Uncle Arnold would take himself and his business ambitions elsewhere.

With a lighter heart, Gavin left the capitol building and walked the eight blocks to the train depot. He could hardly wait to tell Dulcie and her grandfather he'd sold their rugs in Marshall and Weaverville. A dressmaker in Marshall was interested in Dulcie's woolen fabric, and a larger, busier store in Asheville assured Gavin they would purchase as much fine woolen material as he could bring them. The weight of the leather pouch in his pocket would surely bring a smile to her face.

He planned to wire Mr. Randolf when he arrived in Marshall the day after tomorrow, and if the assemblyman could persuade his judge friend to draw up the injunction, that would be the icing on the cake. Gavin imagined the reaction from Dulcie and Mr. Chappell, and an unusual tug of emotion and longing passed through him. Was this what homesickness felt like?

In the space of three days, he'd become acquainted with two emotions he'd never experienced before, the first being the growing affection for Dulcie. He'd prayed and asked God if what he felt for her was love. How was he to know? He'd never been in love before. Now this unexplained yearning to return to the mountains and the farm. No place he'd ever before lived or visited had left him with such a connection.

Was it because Dulcie was there, or was he falling in love with the land as well?

✒ THIRTY-EIGHT

James dropped another wood peg into the basket and sighed. He'd likely finished more'n Gavin needed for the barn, but pegs always come in handy around the place. The mornin' air was still and cool, and wispy clouds hung low, wanderin' around the top o' the mountain like a man tryin' to find his way to the privy in the dark. James sucked in a deep breath. Settin' on the porch was gettin' mighty wearisome. He itched to get out to the barn and help Gavin with the work *he* should be doin'. Not that he weren't grateful for Gavin and all the hard work the young feller put in every day. Even if he didn't have a busted leg, he'd have a hard time climbin' up and down that ladder and carryin' beams on his shoulder. Appeared like God sent the boy for more'n James speakin' truth to him. James needed Gavin as much as Gavin needed a family. Once again, God knew 'xactly what he needed.

He picked up another piece of black locust and started settin' his blade against the hard grain when a rider come up the road. He squinted through the mottled shadows and sunlight tryin' to break through the clouds. Didn't appear to be Gavin. A few moments later, Sheriff Harper loomed from the tree-lined path and nudged his horse on up to the house.

James raised his hand in greetin'. "Mornin' Sheriff. What brings ye all the way up here?"

The man dismounted and wrapped the reins around a porch post. He clomped up onto the porch and picked up a few of the pegs from the basket. "Keepin' busy?"

James held back a grumble. Bein' stove up sure made a man feel irritable. "Tryin'. Have a seat."

The sheriff set his backside into the other rocker and set it into motion. "Sure is a purty day."

"Yep." It likely would be iffen the fog ever burned off. They needed more rain, but James didn't reckon the sheriff come to debate about the weather.

"How's your garden doin' this year?"

James poked a toothpick in his mouth. "Mighty good. We'll have some 'maters and squash in another couple weeks." Was the sheriff hintin' he wanted some fresh garden produce?

They rocked in silence for a minute before Harper spoke again. "Yesterday, I was over at Doc's place. We was havin' our game o' checkers like we do most every Tuesday. Whilst I was fixin' to beat him for the third straight game, that DeWitt feller—the older one—come a-hobblin' into the doc's office." Harper gave a huff. "Iffen ye ask me, I think Doc was happy to see a patient comin' in, so's he wouldn't get beat again."

James knew the sheriff would get to the point eventually. The man weren't in the habit of ridin' all the way up to the farm just to have a set-down visit. But when Arnold DeWitt's name were mentioned, James wished Harper would quit wastin' time an' speak what was on his mind.

"Ye fixin' to tell me what ailed DeWitt or how ye beat Doc three games straight?"

The sheriff picked up another wood peg and examined it. "DeWitt said he cut his leg gettin' into the buggy a few days back, and it were beginnin' to fester. Nobody told me to git, so I hung around and had me a chat with DeWitt whilst the doc was workin' on him. When Doc started to pull back the trousers, DeWitt hollered like a coyote." Harper chuckled. "So Doc took him a pair o' scissors and cut off the pant leg. Ye shoulda heard DeWitt cuss and git his dander up 'cause them britches was so costly. A more cantankerous feller I ain't never seen."

Sheriff Harper liked tellin' stories, that was for certain, 'cause he were draggin' this one out as long as he could. "Sheriff, I ain't gittin' no younger. Wouldja mind tellin' me what ye come to say?"

Harper smirked. "Impatient, are ye?" He cackled. "Well, DeWitt's leg was swoll up and festerin' alrighty, just like he said. Was all red an' oozy, and the skin were stretched tighter'n a pig's hide nailed to the side o' the barn. Looked to be mighty painful. Doc told him he was gonna hafta drain out the infection. Then Doc says to DeWitt, 'Ye didn't get this climbin' in and out of no buggy.'"

The sheriff dropped the peg back into the basket and leaned one elbow against the arm rest. "Doc said it were a bite. A dog bite. Pointed to the teeth marks whilst I were standin' right there. He told DeWitt he shoulda come in sooner, when it first happened, 'cause dog bites can be serious. 'Specially iffen the dog has the hydrophoby."

Harper's story were finally gettin' to the interestin' part. James leaned forward. "A dog bite, ye say?"

The sheriff nodded and scratched his head. "Ye shoulda heard that DeWitt feller yowl when Doc commenced to cuttin' into him. Cut weren't no bigger than a peanut, but DeWitt hollered like Doc was amputatin' his whole leg." Harper's belly shook. "An' then . . ." He laughed harder. "DeWitt screamed like a little girl when Doc poured whiskey over it."

The sheriff wiped his eyes, and James leaned back and commenced to rockin' again. It weren't hard to picture what happened that Sunday when they come home from church and found the meadow empty and the sheep missin'.

The sheriff rubbed the back of his neck. "Reckon that dog o' yours would bite a feller what tried to break down a fence and hurt the sheep?"

James grinned. "He might."

The rockin' chair Harper occupied creaked when the man rose. "That's what I figgered." He stepped off the porch and pulled the reins from the post. He paused with one foot in the stirrup. "That dog o' yours ain't got the hydrophoby, does he?"

James ran his fingers through his whiskers. "Not that I know of. Iffen he commences to gettin' foamy-mouthed and wild-eyed, I'll be sure'n let ye know."

A smile stretched across the sheriff's face. "You do that." He mounted and reined the horse around. "Soon as you git back on yer feet, let's me 'n' you go coon huntin'."

"Lookin' forward to it." James waved as the man rode off. As he picked up the peg he'd started to whittle, a chuckle rumbled up from his middle. Reckoned he might have to take that ham bone Dulcie was savin' to make a pot of beans and give it to Malachi, seein' as how he was such a good watch dog and all.

Dulcie threw her head back and laughed out loud. "I'll gladly give Malachi that ham bone." A sliver of guilt poked her. She really should feel sorry for poor Mr. DeWitt, and at some point, she would. But not right now. The revelation that Arnold DeWitt had tangled with the dog while committing an act of vandalism cleared Gavin of all suspicion. Now the town folk would see for themselves what kind of man Arnold DeWitt really was, and would be sorry they ever accused Grandpa.

It felt good to laugh. All the hardship and sorrow of the past few months had robbed her of joy. She'd found it hard to even smile since Gavin had been gone, but this bit of news was the breath of fresh air she needed. She rose and began clearing the table of the lunch dishes. "There's a patch of blackberries up the slope from the meadow. I saw it last week while we were hunting for the sheep. They ought to be ready to pick now. How does a blackberry cobbler sound for supper?"

Grandpa's eyes brightened and his brows arched. "Sounds mighty fine, but why don't we wait and have it when Gavin comes home."

Gavin comes home. Those words sounded like music to her, but she couldn't presume Gavin would ever think of this place as home, and she was afraid to let her thoughts linger there. "I'll go and pick them and put them in the root cellar. They'll keep for a week or so." She turned so Grandpa couldn't see the worry that pulled her face into a frown, and busied herself washing the dishes.

She hastened through her tasks cleaning up the kitchen and set a pot of beans to soak, minus the hambone. She'd gladly sacrifice her share of morning bacon to add to the beans.

Grandpa offered to churn the butter for her, since, as he said, it was something he could do sitting down. She set the butter churn on the porch beside Grandpa's chair. "Can I bring you anything else before I go back out to the wool shed, Grandpa?"

"Not right now. But I'm hankerin' to take some wildflowers out to yer grandma's grave." Sadness threaded his voice. Dulcie knew it was more than just missing Grandma. He couldn't walk that far, not even with crutches, over the uneven terrain, and delivering the flowers was something he wished he could do himself.

She squeezed his hand. "I know where there are some daisies and black-eyed Susans growing. I'll pick them and take them out there this afternoon." He responded with a tiny smile, but didn't need to tell her his desire was to sit beside his beloved and 'be with her.'

After glancing at the position of the sun, Dulcie calculated how long she could work and still have time to pick the berries and the flowers. She hurried toward the wool shed, but slowed momentarily to look down the road. "God, please be with Gavin and bring him. . . home." Perhaps she understood a bit of what Grandpa felt. More than only missing Gavin, she wanted to be with him.

James lifted the lid of the butter churn and peeked inside at the thick, pale yellow butter. 'Peared to be ready for rinsin', but iffen he couldn't get the churn down into the root cellar, it'd spoil settin' here in the afternoon sun. He looked out across the yard toward the wool shed. He reckoned he should call Dulcie to come fetch the butter, but he hated disturbin' her.

"Halloo."

No mistaking Dewey Tate's customary greeting. "Howdy, ye ole coot. What ye doin' up this way?"

Dewey held up a small paper poke. "I brung ye somethin'." His friend hobbled up the steps and held the package out to James. "I was in town, an' I picked up some peppermints fer ye. Know they's yer favorite."

James picked a peppermint out of the package and offered some to Dewey. "'Preciate it. Say, since yer here, can ye carry this here churn down to the root cellar? Dulcie'll be peeved iffen the butter spoils."

Dewey grinned. "Cain't have no peeved womenfolk." He *oofed* as he picked up the churn and toted it around the side of the house to the cellar. When he returned, he plopped down into the rocker next to James and helped himself to another peppermint. "Ain't seen Arnold DeWitt around too much in the past few days. I figgered he'd be raisin' cain around here, tryin' to get ye to sell yer land. Reckon what he's waitin' fer?"

James had a pretty good idea why DeWitt was stayin' put in his hotel room, but it weren't fer him to go spreadin' gossip. He lifted his shoulders in a mute shrug.

Dewey rubbed his chin. "Let's see, what news be goin' on around the county? Um, Thatch Davis's wife is expectin'. I think this makes her fifth. . . or sixth. The school teacher, Fern Busby, turned in her resignation. Says she's gonna teach down Asheville way, prob'ly fer more money than our little school in Hot Springs can pay. Ye remember young Lester

Marlow fallin' and hurtin' hisself, an' they took him down to Asheville after he soaked in the springs? He's up an' walkin'. Ain't runnin' 'r climbin'
yet, but he's doin' a sight better."

James grunted his approval.

Dewey squinted at the clouds like he were tryin' to remember somethin' he left off the list. "Oh! All that big talk Luther Dempsey and Otis
Hogan was doin' about buildin' on to their places and expandin' their
businesses, ain't heard no more about that. It's all over town that DeWitt
and his nephew parted ways, and the nephew is workin' fer you." He
glanced sideways at James. Was he waitin' for James to deny it?

"He's been here helpin' to rebuild the barn."

Dewey leaned to peer across the way at the barn. "Heard yer barn got
hit with lightnin'. Looks like the young feller's doin' a respectable job."

It plumb warmed James's heart to hear praise for the work Gavin
were doin'. "Yep, he's doin' a right good job."

Dewey kept rockin'. "Reckon why him and his uncle ain't workin' together no more? Some folks say the young feller were lazy, and some others're sayin' he didn't have no head fer the business. Hollis Purdue said
the nephew were tryin' to go into business fer hisself. Then, I heard—"

"Dewey, I can tell ye the boy ain't lazy." James held up both hands,
fendin' off any more o' Dewey's gossip. "But if I didn't know nothin' fer
fact about what happened 'tween them two, I don't b'lieve I'd be goin'
around spoutin' what other folks is sayin', not iffen ye ain't sure if it's
truth. Whatever them folks is sayin', ye ought not repeat it." James twisted around as far as the splint on his leg allowed, and tried to face Dewey.
"Some o' them same folks is sayin' untruths about me, too. I sure hope
my real friends ain't goin' around spreadin' such lies."

Dewey ducked his head. "Yer right. Reckon I didn't think it clear
through. Ain't none o' my business, anyway. I'm curious, I reckon, like
ever'one else. The young feller seemed to be a nice, friendly sort."

"He is." James picked up the sack of peppermints and held it out to
Dewey. "Want another one?"

The tiny smile that worked its way over Dewey's face made 'im look like a young'un caught snitchin' cookies. "Nah. I brung 'em fer you." Dewey pushed himself up from the chair. "I promise ye, James, iffen I hear anyone speakin' ill of ye, I'll put a stop to it."

James extended his hand and shook Dewey's. "Thank ye, friend. And thank ye fer the peppermints, too."

✤ THIRTY-NINE

The first glimpse of Hot Springs up ahead stirred Gavin's senses. He was home—or nearly so. As anxious as he was to reach the farm and Dulcie, he needed to speak to the sheriff first. The sun lingered above the mountain range, giving him about two hours before dark. He hurried Samson along as they reached the edge of town.

Shifting his gaze right and left, Gavin didn't see his uncle anywhere in town. Not that he would run from a confrontation, but he didn't relish the idea, either. With so many in town having been hoodwinked by the elder DeWitt, there was little doubt he already knew Gavin had left Hot Springs for several days. Gavin had prayed almost non-stop for a week for God's protection over Dulcie and Mr. Chappell and the farm. He wasn't going to give in to fear now.

He halted Samson beside the unpainted building with the faded shingle marking the location of Sheriff Grant Harper's office. The door stood propped open by a rickety chair with chipped green paint. Gavin rapped on the doorframe. "Sheriff?"

"Mr. DeWitt. Come on in." The sheriff beckoned from his desk, the top of which was littered with a disarray of papers. "Wondered when you'd be back." He tilted his head toward a chair every bit as dilapidated as its partner standing guard by the door. "Have a seat."

Gavin grimaced. "If it's all the same to you, Sheriff, I'd rather stand. That wagon seat got a little harder and more uncomfortable every mile."

The sheriff snorted. "Suit yerself. What can I do fer ye?"

Gavin reached into his pocket and pulled out two folded pieces of paper. He smoothed out the creases the best he could as he laid them on the sheriff's desk. "After I took Miss Chappell's woolen goods down the mountain to sell, I went—"

"Wait a minute." The sheriff's head jerked up. "Why'd you take her goods down the mountain? Miss Dulcie's always sold her rugs and wool material right here in Hot Springs."

"Not anymore." Gavin bit his lip to stop the anger over what his uncle had done from spilling out. "Mr. Dempsey told her he won't be selling her rugs any longer, and the dressmaker lady told her she can't use any more of her woolen fabric." He huffed out a stiff breath. "I'm pretty sure my uncle had something to do with their decisions."

The man's brow dipped and he screwed up his lips into a perturbed frown. "I see." He fixed his gaze in the direction of the open door and narrowed his eyes. "So, you had to leave here with Miss Dulcie's goods to find someplace to sell them?"

"Yes, sir."

"Hmm." The man rose from his desk and walked to the door. "Didja sell 'em?"

A thread of joy rose within Gavin's chest, and he was impatient to share his answer with Dulcie. "Yes, sir, and at a higher price than what she told me she got from Mr. Dempsey or the dressmaker here."

Harper lingered by the door, as if watching for someone, but he glanced back at Gavin. "Good. So why ain'tcha on yer way up there to the Chappell place?"

Gavin picked up the two papers from the desk and held them out. "Because you need to know what happened after I sold everything. I boarded the eastbound train in Asheville and went to Raleigh to see Mr.

Clayton Randolf, a state assemblyman. These two documents will explain everything."

Sheriff Harper turned from the doorway and took the papers. His lips moved silently for a whole minute as he read the first. "Representative Randolf is sponsorin' a bill through the House and Senate that'll protect private cemeteries from bein' disturbed?" He looked up at Gavin, a mixture of surprise and pleasure brightening his features.

"Yes, sir. Mr. Randolf assured me he could push the bill through in as little as a week or ten days. The injunction mentioned there is in place until which time the bill is voted on and becomes law." Gavin pointed to the second piece of paper in Harper's hand. "That telegram is the confirmation that the judge signed the injunction. What this means is my uncle can't touch James Chappell's land because there is a cemetery on it."

A wide grin split the sheriff's face. "An' to think yer uncle said you was no account. Yer smarter'n he is." He held up the two papers. "This is . . . brilliant." He slapped Gavin's shoulder.

"Now that you are aware of the pending legislation, is there anything else we need to do to stop my uncle from doing any more damage?"

Harper swallowed back a muted guffaw. "Yer uncle already done hisself some damage." The sheriff explained about Arnold DeWitt showing up at the doctor's office, and the doctor stating the infected wound was from a dog bite. "Yer uncle an' me already had us a toe-to-toe, eyeball-to-eyeball meetin' this mornin'. I made it real clear that the news is spreadin' around town that he went up there to James Chappell's place a couple Sundays ago, tore up the fence, run off the sheep, and got dog-bit fer his trouble. He tried to deny it, o' course. Said he weren't up there. But the more he argued, he slipped up an' said he's gonna sue James Chappell fer havin' a dangerous dog on his property."

Gavin wanted to see the humor, but sorrow pricked him. Even in the commission of a crime, his uncle was trying to blame someone else. "And to think at one time, I was trying to do everything I could to please him."

"What's that ye say?" Harper looked up from the papers in his hands.

"Nothing." Gavin waved his muttered remark away.

Harper folded the papers and tucked them in his pocket. "I'd like fer ye to come with me on down to the courthouse. The county judge ain't there today, but he will be by week's end. Meanwhile, I want the clerk to file these and you'll need to sign a statement." He patted his pocket. "B'sides, there's more ye oughta know." He motioned for Gavin to follow him out the door.

As they walked down the street, Harper told him about a visit he'd had from the banker yesterday. "Seems Zeb Huxley and Reuben Ludlow took their contracts to the bank and had Waldo Granger read 'em over. There was some wordin' in there that gived Arnold DeWitt much more than just the land."

By the time they reached the courthouse, Harper had explained how Huxley wouldn't have access to or from his property unless he wanted to climb Devil's Backbone—a dangerous rocky ridge to the south. Ludlow would lose his rights to the water he always used in the summer if there was a drought and his well ran dry.

Harper held the door open for Gavin. "Waldo Granger advised both of 'em not to sign those contracts."

Gavin sighed in relief. "So my uncle—"

"...was advised to move on an' do business somewheres else. C'mon. Let's get the clerk to file these documents."

Dulcie peered out the single window of the wool shed at the position of the sun. The afternoon was almost gone, and Grandpa would surely ask her if she'd put flowers on Grandma's grave yet.

She hurried through the tasks of wrapping up her work, and headed for the southeast fence line where the last few daisies and black-eyed Susans of the season still bloomed. Malachi welcomed her with his cold nose and a whine. She took a moment to scratch his ears before plucking up every flower she could find. With a respectable bouquet of wildflowers, she hiked up the slope past the junipers, and laid the flowers on her grandmother's grave. Grief still twisted a sharp blade in her chest, and she sank to her knees and ran loving fingers over the carved name on Grandma's headstone.

"God, I don't have to tell You how much I miss Grandma, but I know You're taking good care of her. I'll be all right without her because she taught me so much. Mainly she taught me about You. My memories are filled with her humming 'Guide Me, O Thou Great Jehovah,' or telling me how spinning the wool threads together is a picture of You and Jesus and the Holy Spirit wrapping Your arms around us. I remember Grandma with her Bible, I remember watching her pray. It was the only time she was still."

A tear slipped down her cheek, but she didn't bother to wipe it away. "God, I'll be all right because You gave me a grandma who made sure I knew how good You are, even when I didn't want to speak to You. But I'm not sure Grandpa will be all right. Please comfort him and give him Your peace. I pray You will work everything out so this place, this land will remain in our family always. All Grandpa wants is to know I'm safe and the land is safe before You call him home."

She fingered the wildflowers adorning Grandma's resting place. Oh, how Grandpa wished to place them there himself. She smoothed the dirt mound, pulled a few weeds, and brushed some twigs and leaves off Grandma's headstone as she rose. "Thank You, God, for loving us, and never leaving us. Amen."

"Amen."

Startled, she whirled about, her hand over her middle. Gavin stood a few feet behind her, his hat in his hands. Her heart leapt, and joy snagged her breath. She teetered as the sight of him weakened her knees, and he reached out and caught her hand.

"When did . . . I didn't hear . . ." She covered her mouth with her fingertips. She'd missed him so, and here he was, holding her hand. His touch was firm and steady, but gentle, like Grandpa's touch when he tended the sheep.

His brown eyes warmed. "I just got back. I had a feeling you might be here."

She couldn't tear her eyes away from his. "How did you know"—she gestured around them—"the cemetery was here?"

He increased the pressure on her hand for a moment before he let go. "The day we were looking for the sheep, I came across it." He stepped from one headstone to the next, touching each one. He came to her parents' and her brother's graves and paused before finally returning to Grandma's. His steps were quietly respectful, the movements of his hands almost reverent, the expression on his face full of empathy and insight. "I think I'm beginning to understand what you mean about your heritage. I say 'beginning to' because it will take a lifetime to grasp how deep your roots go in this place. These people, these generations—you're connected to them by far more than blood and a name. You all share a kinship with this land."

He stepped closer and reclaimed her hand. "I have two things for you." He reached into his pocket and pulled out a leather pouch, placing it in her hand. "Every rug and every yard of fabric sold."

She hefted the pouch and blinked in surprise. "This is more than you were supposed to get for the woolen goods."

He nodded. "When we get back to the house, we'll sit down with your grandfather and I'll tell you about the places that bought your goods and want to buy more."

She tipped her head and regarded him with curiosity. "You said two things. What's the other?"

He took a deep breath, not as one filled with dread, but rather with relief. A smile tugged at his lips. "The reason I was gone so long is because I took the train to Raleigh and met with a North Carolina State Representative about passing a law that will protect private family cemeteries. There is an injunction in place right now, and by the end of next week, the law should be on the books. Your land is safe from my uncle and others like him who would try to force it away from you out of greed."

Tears filled her eyes and joy surged through her with such a rush, it robbed her breath. God had already answered her prayer before she even prayed it. She raised her eyes toward heaven. "Thank You, Lord. Thank You for using Gavin to answer my prayer." It was all she could do to hold herself back from throwing her arms around his neck.

"Thank you, Gavin. You have no idea what this means to us." She paused. "Well, maybe you do have some idea."

She handed him the pouch to carry for her, and he tucked it away. With her hands free, Gavin clasped them both in his. "Dulcie, you and your grandfather have shown me a way of life I've never known, centered around lasting things that matter—things like family, the value of heritage, and faith in God."

She loved the way his hands felt enfolded around hers like the warp and weft threads on her loom, creating a seamless connection. Her pulse tripped as if she'd run a foot race. Words failed to form a reply, so she simply stared at him, afraid to blink for fear it was nothing but a dream.

His voice grew husky and thick. "I've found a new faith, thanks to you and your grandfather." He smiled. "And your grandma's Bible. I learned that God cares about me. My life is re-shaped, changed in a way I never knew was possible. You and your grandfather have helped me realize my hope doesn't lie in temporal things, or in man's approval." His lips pressed together and he swallowed hard. "The entire time I was gone, I longed to be back here, on this land, with the sheep and Malachi, and Samson. Your grandfather. And you, Dulcie. I've never known what family truly means before. Until now." He reached over and thumbed away moisture from her cheeks, tears she hadn't realized had fallen.

She offered a shy smile. "The entire time you were gone, I longed for you to be back—to come. . . home."

His hand cupped the side of her face and she leaned her head against it. "I've fallen in love with you, Dulcie Chappell. With this place, this land, this farm, the pure water, the mountain air, every one of those wooly critters, the mockingbirds that serenade us during the day and the whippoorwills at night. I love your incredible grandfather, and. . . you. I love you, Dulcie." He lifted her hands to his lips and placed a soft kiss on her fingertips. "Do you think a city boy like me can love the land as much as you do?"

A smile filled her whole being. "If a mountain girl like me can learn to love a city boy, then I reckon there's hope for you, too." She leaned into him as he lowered his head. As his lips brushed hers, she realized her legacy was safe, her future bright.

God had known all along.

The End

ABOUT THE AUTHOR

Connie Stevens lives with her husband of forty-plus years in north Georgia, within sight of her beloved mountains. A lifelong reader and lover of history, Connie began creating stories by the time she was ten. Her office manager and writing muse is a cat, but she's never more than a phone call or email away from her critique partners. She enjoys gardening and quilting, but one of her favorite pastimes is browsing antique shops where story ideas often take root in her imagination. Recently, Connie has recently stepped out by faith and launched her speaking and teaching ministry. Her published works include two Carol Award finalists and an Inspirational Readers Choice Award winner. Connie has been a member of American Christian Fiction Writers since 2000.

Est. 2013

Wings of Hope Publishing is committed to providing quality Christian reading material in both the fiction and non-fiction markets.

Made in United States
North Haven, CT
17 November 2022

26862010R00180